PIMLICO PEOPLE

PIMLICO PEOPLE

Rupert Stanbury

Copyright © 2024 Rupert Stanbury

All rights reserved.

The characters and events portrayed in this book are fictitious. Any similarity to real persons, living or dead, is coincidental and not intended by the author.

No part of this book may be reproduced, or stored in a retrieval system, or transmitted in any form or by any means, electronic, mechanical, photocopying, recording, or otherwise, without express written permission of the publisher.

This book is self-published by the author through Amazon KDP.

ISBN 9798338117200

Cover design by Tim Stringer

This book is dedicated to the staff and volunteers of The Passage, a charity for the homeless located in London's Westminster area.

Contents

Principal Characters

Introduction   *Page*

1	The Bard on Mount Olympus	1
2	A Visit to The Gardens	12
3	One Person, Many Names	23
4	The Gallery	36
5	The First Day in London	51
6	Getting to Know You	65
7	A Long Night	79
8	Pongo	94
9	Welcome to Pimlico	108
10	Holbein	120
11	A Difficult Client	133
12	Old Friends	145
13	Escape Plan	159
14	The Park	170
15	Mysterious Visitors	184
16	The Plan in Action	199
17	Surveillance, Lilliput Style	213
18	Mutual Disclosures	226
19	Alarming Information	237
20	The Battle for Duck Island	250
21	Romantic Interlude	265
22	An Overseas Trip	279
23	The Long Walk Home	292
24	Breakfast at The Gardens	304

Epilogue   316

Principal Characters

Mount Olympus

Artemis* - Goddess of the Hunt; recently developed an interest in feminism and equality matters
Athene - Goddess of Wisdom
Bacchus - God of Wine; also proprietor of the Dog and Duck public house
Fearless Frupert – A 6-year-old boy
Hebe* - 'Servant' Goddess
Hera - Goddess; Zeus's wife
Iris - Messenger Goddess; also Goddess of the Rainbow
Mrs Bumble - Housekeeper to Zeus and Hera
Totty – An 18-year-old girl; formerly from Romford, Essex
Zeus - King of the Olympian Gods

Both Artemis and Hebe are also called by other names in the book, depending on the people they are with and the situations they find themselves in. (Artemis: Bow and MacArtemis; Hebe: HalfPint and MacHebe).

The Underworld

Aggy - Head Cook in charge of the Kitchens
Attila - Former King of the Huns
Bill Sikes - A former villain
Budiwati – Deputy Head Builder
Cerberus - A three-headed dog
Charon – A ferryman
Death - A 'being' who transports people to the Underworld
Fairy - A former Pharoah of Egypt
Genghis - Former Mongol King
Gigliola - Works in the Kitchens
Greenbeard - A former pirate

Hades - God; King of the Underworld
Ming - Vesta's friend; works in the Kitchens
Mrs Carver – A woman who likes throwing eggs
Persephone – Goddess; Hades' wife
Popsy, also known as 'Billie' - a small dog
Satan - Director of the Torturing Department
Sisyphus - A former king who used to push a boulder up a hill; now works in the Quarry
The Marchioness (+ many other names) - A new arrival in The Underworld
Vesta – A nearly 14 years old girl; works in the Kitchens

London (excluding the Parks)

Betty Bungalow – Runs a cleaning business; former Housekeeper to the Brassington-Bears
Cesare Shiftyopolous – Director of The Gallery
Chloe – Works for Betty Bungalow
Constable Cherry Cake – A police constable
Dame Pauline – A trustee of The Gallery
Emily – Sir Cedric's and Lady Felicity's granddaughter
George – Senior Porter at the Hotel Savoire
Jako, Matt, Ricky and Vince – Young men in a pub
Karate Chops, Muscles and Scampi – Work for Betty Bungalow
Lady Felicity Brassington-Bear – Lives in The Gardens; married to Sir Cedric
Miss Jones – Personal assistant to Mr Smith
Miss Mulverhill – Head Receptionist at the Hotel Savoire
Mr Smith – An American lawyer visiting London
Mopp ('Jade') – Works for Betty Bungalow
Mrs Moncrief – A friend of Lady Felicity's
Octavian Stegosauras – Drives a taxi; Betty Bungalow's uncle
Panos Pantaloonos – A resident of Knightsbridge
Sergeant Dufflecoat – A police sergeant
Sir Cedric Brassington-Bear – Chairman of The Gallery's Board of Trustees

Terry – Drives a white van; lives on The Estate

The Parks

Acting Captain MacGobo – Military Attache at Lilliput's Embassy in London; former Sergeant in the Argyll & Sutherland Highlanders Regiment
Adjutant, Capitaine and Colonel – Members of the Blefuscu military
Blefuscu Ambassador
Elvis – A young pelican; a friend of Emily's
Lilliput Ambassador
Rach – Head of Special Projects at the Lilliput Institute of Science
Sir Peregrine – Senior Pelican
Sir Sigmund – Senior Swan
The Marshal – Marshal in the Blefuscu military

Introduction

I've only really lived in two places in my life. Yes, I've resided in other locations for periods, but I've had no great attachment to them. They've not felt as if I could say: "This is where I belong. This is my place!" Perhaps I'm old-fashioned, but I believe everyone needs a PLACE – somewhere they feel comfortable, somewhere they fit. Call it a sense of belonging; it's important to people.

I was born in Manchester, my parents living in Cheshire at the time. It's where I first started school. The little I remember of my early education was of changing schools practically every year. This wasn't because I was being expelled all the time; instead, my mother and father were perhaps a little over-critical about the lessons I was being given, so we had this annual movement from one seat of learning to another. This meant that I was always having to make new school friends, so with time I'd probably got to know every other boy of my age in the area.

My mother was a great believer in the community. She was friends with our local vicar, Canon R who lived with his wife in a great big old rectory a few minutes' walk from our house. Mother had a great talent for getting money out of people, so she and Canon R were always involved in charitable events together. She would often call in at the rectory for tea, sometimes taking me along during the school holidays. During this time, which must have been when I was somewhere between seven and nine years old, the subject of my future was much spoken about. I recall my mother was determined I should become a 'bishop' in later life, a proposal which my father, a businessman, completely ignored.

There was one occasion when I was taken off for tea with the Canon and Mrs R. We were all sitting there when Mother raised the idea of my future prospects. The Canon explained that before I became a bishop, I would have to start off as a curate, then in due course I'd become a vicar, possibly afterwards a canon and only then might I become a bishop. Mother was less interested in these early and intermediate steps; what she wanted was Canon R's confirmation that I would definitely end up as a bishop. Eventually he gave her what she wanted by saying something like "he was sure any son of hers would achieve that elevated status." He then asked me what I thought about becoming a bishop. I probably had a cream bun in my mouth at the time, but I'll always remember my answer which was: "I want to be a spaceman!" I've honestly forgotten how the conversation progressed from that point, but for those who are interested, I didn't become either a bishop or a spaceman in later life.

One part of living in the North has always remained with me and that was my support for Manchester United. This was the time of the Busby Babes and the Munich Air Crash in 1958 which ripped the heart out of the team. Then there was the rebuilding over many years, with the Holy Trinity of Bobby Charlton, Denis Law and George Best becoming one of the greatest forward line-ups of all time. The 'Reds' were the team I supported as a boy, and I've continued to do so ever since – despite now living 200 miles away.

So, the North was the first place I really lived. The second was Central London, particularly one small area just north of the Thames. It all started in my teens when the family moved south to the capital. Our home was a flat in Marsham Street, a ten-minute walk from Parliament. This area has been 'my place' ever since, despite a few years at university and then living for a while in Surrey after my parents died.

Let me describe this particular part of London since it's where a lot of the action in *Pimlico People* takes place.

Geographically, start on the North side of Parliament Square by the Treasury building. Walk westwards towards Buckingham Palace along Birdcage Walk with St James's Park on the right. Eventually, you'll come to the Palace where you bear left down Buckingham Palace Road which leads to Victoria Station. Follow the railway line until it's about to cross the River Thames. Don't go over the river, but instead turn left and travel along its north bank; firstly, go down Grosvenor Road and then Millbank until you reach Parliament Square again.

This area is bisected by Vauxhall Bridge Road which is a major thoroughfare between Victoria Station and Vauxhall Bridge. It crosses the Thames just at the point where Grosvenor Road becomes Millbank. I have always viewed Vauxhall Bridge Road as being the dividing line between Pimlico on the west and Westminster on the east. Sometimes, people will refer to the Victoria area which encompasses those parts of Pimlico and Westminster which are close to Victoria Station. However, there is no clear boundary for Victoria, so it's best to keep the simple distinction between Pimlico and Westminster.

Despite drawing this distinction, it's important to emphasise that Pimlico and Westminster are in many respects the same community. I currently live in Westminster, but every day I make a five-minute walk from my flat to cross Vauxhall Bridge Road and then I'm in Pimlico. It's where my gym is, where I do much of my shopping, especially at the large Sainsbury's store, and where there are a host of pubs, cafes and restaurants for eating and drinking.

This is the area I view as 'my place'. In some ways it's changed a lot over the decades, but in many more it's stayed the same. So, what's there? Well, it has a number of distinctive national landmarks - obviously, Parliament, but also Westminster Abbey where English kings and queens have been crowned for centuries, the Roman Catholic Westminster Cathedral and the Tate Britain Art Gallery. We also have Buckingham Palace next door! The area has a main line railway station as well as Victoria Coach Station, two highly regarded West End theatres and a smaller local theatre. We've recently lost the Army and Navy department store, but Victoria Street, which runs from Parliament Square to Victoria Station, has a mass of retail, including hospitality venues. This street has been extensively re-developed in recent years and, as well as new retail, also now includes a number of large, modern office blocks.

Along the area's northern boundary is St James's Park. This is my favourite park in London with its lake and mass of birdlife. I describe it in greater detail in one of the book's chapters, but it's important to recognise that many of us in the Westminster / Pimlico community view it as 'our local park', despite it usually being full of tourists.

There is a lot of residential in the area since it is home to a significant population. It's very mixed – on the private side, there are expensive new flat developments, many of them near Victoria Street; in addition, there are the large mansion blocks dating back to Victorian times, art deco buildings and large terraced houses down individual streets as well as being integral to the design of Pimlico's principal squares. All this exists next to the area's large council and social housing complexes. Pimlico itself has the award-winning Churchill Gardens Estate, then there are other council blocks and several Peabody Estate properties in a variety of locations, especially on the Westminster side of Vauxhall Bridge Road.

This diversified community has always managed to coexist, sometimes making up its own rules. I first became aware of this as a teenager when I and my parents lived in one of the art deco blocks down Marsham Street. In those days we had the Westminster Hospital almost next door before it merged to become the Chelsea and Westminster and relocated to the Fulham Road. There was a nurses' home nearby and everyone in the locality shopped at the small family run stores in the neighbourhood. There was one owned and run by a tough South London lady called Mrs B, who knew how the world worked. For example, if a nurse went in to buy a banana, she would be charged, say, 1p. If someone from an art deco block followed, also wanting a banana, the charge would be 2p. After all, we were viewed as being the 'nobs' so could afford to subsidise the nurse's banana. We all knew what was happening, but no one dared challenge this localised redistribution regime. Why? Because there was a sense it was fair; it just seemed right.

There's a lot less scope for that sort of thing these days; and clearly, we'll never go back to what happened fifty or sixty years ago. However, it did actually work!

There has always been a degree of homelessness in the Westminster – Pimlico area with people sleeping rough on the streets. It used to be minor but has got a lot worse in recent years due to social and economic issues as well as geo-political events triggering increased migration. The community is, however, responsive. There are a number of charities actively working in the area, especially The Passage near Westminster Cathedral; these charities not only assist in providing temporary accommodation, but also help people in the long-term to rebuild their lives. The local council is also particularly responsive and works hand in hand with the charities.

I spoke earlier about what it means to 'have a place'. I've been fortunate in my life because I've always had a place. However, the homeless don't have a place – most feel abandoned, often to the point of despair. Because of this, I'm committing for the next five years to give all the royalties I earn from the sale of *Pimlico People* to charities for the homeless, particularly The Passage, to support their very valuable work. This book, by the way, is not about homelessness – it's just that I feel donating the royalties to such charities is the right thing to do.

Pimlico People is the third book in the Gods Galore series about the Olympian Gods in the 21st Century. All these books are a mixture of fantasy and comedy but often in a real-world context. In this Introduction, I've attempted to describe the area which has been my home for much of my life and is still 'my place'. I've done this because some of the gods recently spent a few months living in this combined community of Westminster and Pimlico. *Pimlico People* tells the story of what they got up to while they were here.

Rupert Stanbury

1
The Bard on Mount Olympus

Three figures sat on stones, each holding a book. It was late afternoon, and they were in a clearing surrounded by trees. They were all female and wearing black dresses with round, pointy hats on their heads. The only difference between them from a distance was their respective heights. Despite being seated, it was clear that one was tall, one medium height and the third was small or, as a certain spectrum of society would say, 'vertically challenged'.

Suddenly the small female, whom we will refer to as the *First Witch*, began reading from her book:

"When shall we three meet again in thunder, lightning or in rain?"

Her two companions then joined in.

Medium height female or *Second Witch*: "When the hurly-burly's done; when the battle's lost and won."

Third Witch, being the tall one: "That will be ere the set of sun."

First Witch: "Where the place?"

Second Witch: "Upon the heath."

Third Witch: "There to meet with Macbeth."

First Witch: "I come Graymalkin!"

Second Witch: "Paddock calls."

Third Witch: "Anon."

All Three Witches: "Fair is foul, and foul is fair; hover through the fog and filthy air."

The *Third Witch*, otherwise known as the goddess Artemis, yawned: "I still don't get why we're having to read all this stuff, Hebe."

"Because it's about time we all got properly educated," Hebe, the *First Witch*, replied. "I'm tired of Athene viewing us all as a bunch of thickos."

"Well, we are," said Iris, who was the one in the middle. "At least compared to Athene. After all, she is the Goddess of Wisdom."

"There are different levels of thickness, and I intend to move up a level or two," Hebe responded. "I thought you two would as well."

"My problem is I don't understand what all this Shakespeare stuff means. Do you, Iris?"

"Which bits?"

"This hurly-burly thing that you said for a start. What's that all about?"

Iris frowned and then looked at Hebe. "Do you know?" she asked.

Hebe shook her head. "Not really. Maybe it's a person."

"I've never heard of anyone called hurly-burly," Artemis responded.

"Well, it could be a description of a person," Hebe volunteered hopefully.

The three of them sat in deep thought for a while until Iris suddenly exclaimed: "I bet it's Bacchus! He's burly with all that beer he drinks."

"But what about the hurly bit?" Artemis asked.

"Hurly suggests action such as hurling," Hebe replied. "The obvious person is you, Arty. You're the sporty one amongst us."

"I agree," Iris said. "But the words say 'when the hurly-burly's done', but they don't say what you've done."

"That can't be right." Artemis replied. "What could Bacchus and I possibly do?"

"Well, you know," Hebe managed to say, while beginning to giggle.

"The mind boggles!" Iris added, also starting to giggle.

"Don't be stupid!" Artemis exclaimed. "We just don't know what this hurly-burly is. We should ask Athene; she's bound to know."

"You're probably right," Iris agreed. "Let's create a list of what we don't understand for Athene."

"I suppose we should," Hebe muttered, having now stopped giggling. "What have you two got next?"

"All these names," Artemis said. "Who's this Macbeth bloke?"

"I know that one," Hebe replied. "He's a big, important Scottish lord who becomes King of Scotland. It's what the play's all about."

"And Graymalkin, Paddock and Anon?"

"Dunno. I suppose they're friends."

"Possibly our boyfriends," Iris helpfully added.

"Could be."

"I think we should ask Athene," Artemis said. "Just to be sure."

"Okay," Hebe said. "What's next?"

Both Iris and Artemis shook their heads, suggesting nothing more.

"Do we carry on?" Artemis asked.

"No; Iris and I have got to go and see Zeus now," Hebe said.

"We've not got very far. Are we really going to finish it before we set off for London?"

"We'll make faster progress tomorrow," Hebe replied.

"And you're sure we have to read all this stuff?"

"Yes. It's not only for our education, Arty, but also for when we're in London. Macbeth's on at the Globe Theatre in a few weeks' time and I've got us tickets to go. After all this studying, we might be able to understand some of what it's about."

"If you say so," Artemis muttered sceptically. "I just can't see how it's going to help us on the Equalities Committee."

The three goddesses then got into a long discussion about the trip to London that Hebe and Artemis were soon to make. It had been organised because Artemis was Chairperson of the Equalities Committee which had been set up to look at a wide range of equality issues amongst humankind. Unfortunately, Artemis was probably not best equipped for this role because she was the Goddess of the Hunt. This meant that when she visited the world, she spent her time hunting in the forests and the countryside and knew little about towns and cities where large numbers of people lived. She was well aware of this deficiency of hers, so she had agreed with Hebe, who was also on the Committee, that they would spend a number of weeks together in London. This would allow Artemis to get an understanding of the lives of city people and also to see the many inequalities they experienced firsthand. Hebe was the ideal goddess to accompany her since she spent as much time with humans as with her fellow gods and goddesses.

"Come on, Hebe." Iris said after they'd run out of things to say about the London trip. "We've got to go to Zeus."

"What are you going to see him about?" Artemis inquired as she stood up.

"That household issue I told you about a few days ago," Hebe answered.

"Oh that. I do wish Father would grow up."

"He'll never change," Iris said as she got onto her broomstick.

Both Hebe and Artemis also had broomsticks which they mounted.

"Riding these things is the best part of being a witch," Hebe called as she set off. "See you at the Dog and Duck this evening, Arty. You and Bacchus could start doing your hurly-burly thing together."

"Good idea," agreed Iris as she set off after Hebe.

Artemis was the last to leave, but not before she'd made a rude gesture towards her two fellow goddesses as they sped off towards Zeus's palace.

•

Mrs Bumble was in the far corner of the back garden. She was watering her small rose bed which Lady Hera, Zeus's wife, had agreed she could cultivate after many years of loyal service as Head Housekeeper. Before finishing, she became aware of voices from the sky. She heard strange phrases like "if music be the food of love, play on" and "alas poor Yorrick, I knew him well."

Looking up, she saw two black figures with pointy hats on broomsticks swooping backwards and forwards over the garden, each calling out these strange words. One of them swooped in front of her and then over her head shouting out: "Mrs Bumble, Mrs Bumble, wherefore art thou, Mrs Bumble?" As Mrs Bumble turned round and began to call out where she was, she suddenly heard these ominous words behind her: "Double, double, toil and trouble; fire burn and cauldron bubble." She spun back again to see the second black figure zoom off to her left. Then even more ominous words came from behind her which sounded like: "I will have my pound of flesh." At that point Mrs Bumble lifted up the hem of her dress and, despite being somewhat portly in stature, began to run towards the safety of the palace.

"Wherefore goes thou, Mrs Bumble?" asked Hebe who landed her broomstick ten yards in front of her and took off her pointy black hat so the Head Housekeeper could see who it was. The next second Iris landed beside her and also removed her head gear.

Mrs Bumble came to an abrupt halt in front of the two goddesses. She hadn't run far but was already out of breath.

"Heavens above, it's you Hebe and Lady Iris," she said, panting away. "You gave me such a fright with those words, especially the ones about a pound of flesh and double trouble. What were you talking about?"

"We were quoting Shakespeare," Hebe replied laughing.

"Well, he should learn to write about more pleasant things."

"Do you want to hear about the eye of newt and toe of frog?"

"No!" Mrs Bumble exclaimed. "I certainly do not."

"It's a new recipe," Iris added mischievously. "You could serve it up to Lord Zeus and Lady Hera."

"No, thank you!" Mrs Bumble said emphatically. She then looked at the two goddesses and asked: "Why are the two of you dressed up as witches and flying around on broomsticks?"

"To be or not to be that is the question," Hebe said, looking quizzically at the Head Housekeeper.

"To be what?"

"Dressed as we are; that is the question," Hebe said.

"So, what's the answer?"

"It doesn't matter. We're having a Shakespeare day," Hebe replied before adding: "Friends, Romans, Countrymen, and Mrs Bumble, lend me your ears."

Mrs Bumble's immediate reaction was to put her hands over her ears. "You leave my ears alone, Hebe," she replied anxiously. "You've got your own ears."

"She's only joking, Mrs Bumble," Iris said with a laugh. "We've come to see Zeus. Is he in?"

"He's in his study," the Head Housekeeper replied, bringing her hands down from her ears.

"Thank you; then we'll leave you to your rose garden."

"See you later, Mrs Bumble," Hebe said as she followed Iris towards one of the back entrances to the palace. "Didn't mean to frighten you." She then called out to her fellow goddess: "Once more unto the breach, dear friends. Once more."

Zeus was sitting on a comfortable armchair in his study staring at the large sign on the wall behind his desk. It had the following letters all in gold: TOP GOD, being positioned in such a way that anyone coming into the room would immediately see the words. Zeus was rather proud of the sign. He'd got his son, Hephaestus to put it up a couple of weeks ago because he decided it was time to emphasise to his fellow gods who was boss around the place. He also had a similar sign placed on the palace's front door, being TOP GOD'S PALACE. His wife, Hera, had reminded him that she also lived there, so he'd reluctantly offered to change the words to TOP GOD'S AND TOP GODDESS'S PALACE. Her reaction was to decline his offer, saying that she thought it was all a bit common, nouveau riche, naff and that sort of thing. Zeus disagreed with his wife but was relieved to be able to keep the sign as the short and simple TOP GOD'S PALACE, since the inclusion of Top Goddess made the whole thing unwieldy.

As well as looking at his sign, Zeus was also contemplating what to do over the next fortnight. A couple of days ago, Hera had left with her sister Hestia for a two-week break on Crete, leaving Zeus to his own devices. This was an opportunity to have some fun, otherwise known as chasing after attractive females; a pleasure generally denied him when his wife was around. At the top of his list were a few days in Paris where he hadn't been for many years. He was trying to decide whether he would stay in a hotel or zoom back to Olympus each evening after having had a day of hanky panky. Whatever he did, he'd have to make sure he took some money with him; last time he'd gone off on one of his fun ventures it had come to a grinding halt due to a complete lack of funds. He would speak to his daughter, Hebe on the matter; she was always able to get money from somewhere.

Coincidentally, just at that moment the study door opened, and Hebe walked in with Iris.

"Hail Zeus!" Iris said, raising her right arm once she saw the Top God.

"Hail Father!" Hebe followed.

"You do know that looks incredibly gauche," Iris continued pointing at the TOP GOD sign behind Zeus's desk.

"Not at all. I think it's entirely appropriate. It reminds you lot who's in charge around here. There's been a lack of respect developing recently."

"Respect is earned, Zeus," Iris replied tartly as she sat on a sofa.

"What does that mean?" Zeus swiftly demanded.

"Precisely what we've come to talk to you about," Hebe said, sitting next to her fellow goddess. "Beware the Ides of March, Father. Beware the Ides of March."

Zeus blinked. "No doubt you'll explain what you mean by that in due course, but since you're here, Hebe, could you please let me have some French francs. I'm planning on going on a short trip to Paris while your mother's away sunning herself."

"They use Euros these days; you're more than twenty years behind the times. How many do you want?"

Zeus blinked. "I'm not sure. I'm planning on being away three or four days; I'll leave the day after tomorrow."

"Okay. I'll go and print some off tomorrow morning and bring them round." Hebe said. She was always doing this for her fellow gods and goddesses, since she had her own multi-currency printing machine which none of the monetary authorities knew anything about.

"Now to business, Zeus," Iris said, giving him a rather stern look.

Over the next twenty minutes, Iris and Hebe tackled Zeus on his behaviour. The two goddesses lived together in a modern 4-bedroom bungalow, deciding not to have their own spacious palaces to which they were entitled. Their household also consisted of Fearless Frupert, a 6-year-old boy who had been living with them for over 50 years and Totty, an attractive 18-year-old girl from Romford. Totty spent half her time on Mount Olympus where she acted as Personal Assistant to both Iris and Hebe, and the rest of her time in the Sea Cavern since she was close to the Sea God, Poseidon and his wife, Amphitrite. One of Totty's many duties when on Olympus was to run a morning fitness class on the lawn of the Top God's palace, which was well attended by many members of the deity, together with their servants. Even Mrs Bumble and her husband sometimes participated. Zeus made a point of never attending, although he watched the proceedings from the privacy of his own dressing room where he sometimes tried some of the easier exercises.

"So, that's it, Father," Hebe said after the discussion had begun to go round in circles as everybody began repeating themselves. "No more attempts at trying to have a bit of hanky panky with Totty. She doesn't fancy you."

Zeus had been blustering for some time and by now had a very red face. "I strongly resent these allegations the two of you are making!" he said in a loud voice. "All my dealings with Totty have been entirely consensual."

"That's bollocks," Iris replied. "Every time you go near her you try to pat her on the bum. She says you're always doing it or trying to grope her. We've lots of witnesses."

"Who are these witnesses?" Zeus demanded.

"Never you mind, Father!" Hebe said forcibly. "It's got to stop."

Zeus remained silent for a few seconds before deciding that attack was the best form of defence. "You do know I'm Top God!" he said in a loud, belligerent tone. "I'm the most powerful figure in the Universe which means I can do whatever I like and none of you can stop me. I could squash the two of you like flies!" As he said this, he slapped both hands down on the sides of his armchair, mimicking the squashing movement.

Iris and Hebe looked at each other before Iris said in a very deliberate tone: "Individually, yes, you can take us on. But if the gods rose up in unison against you, it would be a different matter."

"Don't be ridiculous! They wouldn't do that!"

"Don't be so sure, Father," Hebe replied. "This could be the winter of your discontent."

Zeus blinked. "What's that meant to mean?" he asked, looking at his daughter.

"Shakespeare. Richard The Third. Look at what happened to him."

"Psssh! Don't you think you're exaggerating matters."

"No," Iris replied. "After all, you're the one who's talking about squashing us like flies."

"Only because you're trying to put restraints on me. All I'm doing is what men and women have been doing ever since we created them."

"But the rules have changed now, Father. You need to move with the times. You just can't go around groping any attractive female you fancy."

"Who says so?"

"Society!" Iris exclaimed. "There are different movements like Me-Too, who are standing up to dominant males like you."

"And are you both members of this so-called Me-Too movement, which I've never heard of?"

"We support them and so do lots of gods, especially the younger ones."

"So, what are you going to do to stop me?"

"In Totty's case, we'll tell Mother," Hebe replied.

Zeus laughed. "You wouldn't dare," he said. "You know how she handles these situations. She'll just demand that Totty is returned to the Sea Cavern and then she'll be lost to you altogether."

"Do you want to risk it?"

Zeus thought for a while. He knew full well that despite what he'd said about his wife adopting a policy of banishment for any female she caught Zeus with, his life would also be made hell by Hera for several weeks. Before he'd worked out how to respond to this threat, Iris added more fuel to the fire.

"Actually, Zeus, we'll tell Athene first," she said, which caused the Top God to swallow hard at the prospect of relentless lecturing by the Goddess of Wisdom. "Also, your brother, Poseidon. He takes a very fatherly approach to Totty; if he heard you were trying to have some unwanted hanky panky with her, he'd probably descend on Olympus once more and lay one on you."

"Just as he did to Mars last time he was here," Hebe added, reminding her father how the Sea God had knocked the God of War unconscious, as well as breaking his nose and knocking out a number of teeth, all with one blow.

"So, they're some of the things we're going to do Zeus, if you carry on as you have been with Totty," Iris said. "As for the here and now, we've already appointed Fearless as her bodyguard and he's under strict instructions to jab you really hard with his sword if there's any evidence of you misbehaving. Remember, he's already defeated both Mars and Pestilence in battle, so an old chap like you shouldn't be any problem."

Zeus by now had stopped arguing as he looked resentfully at the two goddesses.

"Time for us to go," Hebe said before Zeus was able to work out how to reply to this barrage of threats. "Beware the Ides of March, Father," she said as she walked to the door.

"Yes. Beware the Ides of March, Zeus," Iris repeated as she followed Hebe out of the room. After a couple of seconds, she put her head back round the door. "Oh, and Zeus. Please get rid of that terrible sign. You know what you're being called?"

"What?" he growled.

"POT DOG!" Iris called out before disappearing again as she and Hebe started walking down the corridor.

2
A Visit to The Gardens

Betty Bungalow came out of her flat on the fourth floor of the 9-storey tower block; she took the lift to the ground floor and was soon walking through The Estate to reach Lupus Street. Crossing the road, she continued down Gloucester Street and then made her way through the labyrinth of streets designed by Thomas Cubitt in the first half of the 19th Century. These followed a standard formula consisting of large white, stucco-fronted terraced houses, normally with four or five floors. Many were still occupied in their entirety as family homes, although a fair number had been converted into one- and two-bedroom flats with a few larger apartments over two floors.

On reaching Tachbrook St market Betty bought a few bananas which she put into her bag, then crossed Warwick Way and continued until she reached the busy Vauxhall Bridge Road. Crossing at the traffic lights, she walked down Francis Street before turning left into The Gardens, a series of mansion blocks leading to the ever-busy Victoria St, the key artery between Parliament and Victoria Station with Buckingham Palace nearby. The Gardens had been built towards the end of Queen Victoria's reign, and still retained two characteristics from over a century ago – porterage, and therefore a sense of security; as well as a community spirit as many families had lived there for several decades, with flats sometimes passing from one generation to another.

Reaching one of the blocks overlooking Westminster Cathedral, Betty climbed the stone steps and pressed the top-floor bell on the left. Within a matter of seconds, there was a click, and she pushed the front door open, walked across the hallway and was soon in the small lift only capable of taking three medium-sized people. When it reached the fifth floor, she came out and turning left saw a small girl with blonde wavy hair holding the flat door open.

"Hello, Emily," she said walking through the door. "I heard you were staying with Grandma for a few days."

"Hi, Mrs Bungalow," Emily replied. "I'm here until Saturday. Mummy and Daddy are in Paris, both working, so they couldn't take me with them. Anyway, I like staying with Grandma and Grandpa – they give me things."

"I should think you're being spoilt rotten, aren't you?"

"Well, sort of. But I give them things too! Do you want to see what I've just brought them from my walk with Maisie this afternoon? You'll be really interested because you're old like them."

At that moment a tall, elegant lady in a white dress appeared in the hallway. "Hello, Betty," she said going up to her and giving her a kiss on the cheek.

"Lady F," Betty replied. "Emily's just been telling me she's brought you something from her walk. Is it a present?"

"Let me get it and show you," Emily said, racing past the two adults and into the living room.

Lady F, whose full name was Lady Felicity, raised her eyebrows. "Come this way and see what my 10-year-old granddaughter has brought home."

"Here it is! Have a look," Emily said excitedly as she held up a brochure before thrusting it into Betty's hands.

"Let me take it," her grandmother said as she looked at her visitor's confused expression before continuing: "Emily went out for a short walk with Maisie, who lives on the second floor. There's a new funeral director who's just opened round the corner, and she called in for a brochure for me and grandpa. Isn't that kind?" Lady F finished with a touch of sarcasm as she raised her eyebrows.

Betty tried to stifle a laugh.

"I like their name. They're called Eternity because you go there forever when you die." Emily chirped out merrily before looking at her grandmother. "Grandma, am I in your will?" she asked.

"Emily, that's not a polite question," was the reply.

"Why?"

"It just isn't."

"Well, am I? Also, what about Grandpa? Am I in his?"

Lady Felicity sighed. "Enough about wills, young lady. I think it's time you went to your room and got back on your computer. Betty and I need to have a good chat over a cup of tea."

"Can't I stay and listen?"

"No, you can't."

"Why not? Is it about what's in that locked case on the big table."

"Never you mind," her grandmother replied. "And how do you know it's locked?"

"I tried to open it."

"Emily, that's very naughty! Come on – to your room," Lady F said in a mock angry voice as she took hold of her granddaughter by the shoulders and began to propel her out of the living room into the hall.

"Can't I use your computer instead, Grandma?" she asked, breaking free.

"No; you've got a perfectly good computer of your own."

"But it's got all these restrictions which Mummy put on it."

"Quite right too," Grandma replied as she walked behind Emily down the corridor.

"Are they to stop me seeing these things called adult sites?"

"Amongst other things."

"What are adult sites, Grandma? I don't understand why I can't look at them."

"None of your business at your age. They're only for people over 18; they're not for children."

"Do you look at them then?"

"I most certainly do not!" Lady Felicity replied emphatically.

"Does Grandpa?"

"No!"

"How do you know?"

"Because he doesn't want to."

"If he did, would you let him?"

"No, I wouldn't!"

By now the two had gone into Emily's bedroom at the end of the corridor.

"You're like Mummy," Emily said, turning round. "She always tells Daddy what he can and can't do."

"That's because she's my daughter. The women in our family have a long tradition of being the boss. We rule."

"Will I rule when I get married?"

"I'm sure you will, Emily."

"How do you know, Grandma?"

"Believe me, my darling, you will definitely rule."

"But what if my husband won't let me?"

"Have no fear, you'll find a way. I'm a hundred percent certain."

Emily smiled. "That's good," she replied. "I want to rule. Being honest, Grandma, I don't think I could love anyone who didn't do everything I told him. And he'll have to have lots of money as well."

"That's my girl," Lady F said, deciding not to get into a discussion with her granddaughter about how she might react differently when she first experienced true love. "Now, get on your computer and I'll bring you a cup of tea and a piece of fruit cake. Betty and I are going to have a long chat."

"About the case?"

"Never you mind."

While Emily and Grandma were having their chat about family matters, Betty had gone into the kitchen and started to make tea for the three of them. She knew the flat intimately, having begun working as Lady F's housekeeper forty-two years ago. Betty was thirty at the time and Lady F was five years younger, being the newly married Felicity Brassington-Bear who had moved into a one-bedroom flat in The Gardens with her husband. With time, they had progressed to a large two-bedroom flat and then their current four-bedroom apartment where they had lived for the last twenty-five years. During all these years Betty had remained with Lady F, as she later became, until she retired when her state pension came through. Since that time, her youngest daughter Amelia had looked after the Brassington-Bears with occasional breaks for childbirth when another member of Betty's family would temporarily take over. All of this was supervised by Betty, now a widow, who was such an integral part of Lady F's life that she came round for tea every Thursday afternoon.

When Lady F returned from Emily's room, she and Betty quickly finished preparing the tea, Grandma taking a cup and a piece of cake to her granddaughter while Betty carried the tray into the living room.

"That's one precocious young monkey settled down for a while," Lady F said as she closed the door on her return and sat down on the sofa opposite Betty who was already ensconced in her usual armchair.

"We were probably like that at her age."

"Maybe so; and we needed a firm hand to make sure we didn't stay that way. Anyway, enough about Emily; let's talk about Amelia. I was really delighted to hear from you on Tuesday that she'd given birth to a son. Are they both well and back home?"

The two ladies spent some time talking about Betty's new grandson who'd been born a couple of days earlier.

"And are you really sure about the name?" Lady F asked after a while.

"We are, but only if you're happy for us to use it. You and -----"

"We're both very happy," Lady F interrupted. "And my beloved husband is deeply honoured that you want to give your new grandson his name. But isn't Cedric a bit old-fashioned? Won't he be ribbed at school as he's growing up?"

"Oh, the old names are coming back," Betty replied. "The days of Wayne and Kevin have long passed."

"Isn't Arlo the in-name for boys at the moment?"

"It's quite popular, yes, but Amelia and Roddy, her partner, are really keen on naming their second son after Sir Cedric."

"Well, I won't debate it with you anymore, Betty. May we come to the christening, please? There'll be two Cedric's in the church on that occasion."

"Of course," Betty replied with a smile, then after a short pause continued. "Can I just ask about how Chloe's getting on?"

"Absolutely fine. Your niece's daughter has been brought up just like your children. Anyway, she's a recent addition to your team, so I knew it would work."

"She's only eighteen and I-----"

"No problems at all, Betty. I spend a bit more time with her than with Amelia, but we've already become a good team. She's a bit timid around Sir Cedric, but she'll get used to him in time. Anyway, he's rarely here."

"Well, I'm glad it's working. You'll tell me if you've got any concerns, will you?"

"We're fine."

Betty nodded. "Amelia hopes to be back with you in about six months."

"Please tell her not to rush. Young Cedric has to be her number one priority." Lady F paused before saying: "Now, to other matters….."

At this point, Lady F quietly got off the sofa while mouthing "keep talking" to Betty as she silently moved towards the living room door. When she got there, she yanked it open, causing Emily to screech out aloud in surprise.

"What are you doing, you naughty girl? You were listening, weren't you?"

"No, Grandma," Emily blubbered, backing away from her grandmother. "I was just returning my tea things to the kitchen."

Lady F walked into the kitchen, saw no sign of them and then returned to Emily. "Fibber!" she said very loudly. "They're not in the kitchen and they're not in your hands."

Emily, who was now blushing, looked at the floor. "I must have forgotten them," was all she could think of saying.

"Don't treat me like a fool, Emily. You were listening."

"Well, only a bit," Emily sniffled.

"Back to your room," Lady F pointed down the corridor.

Emily hurried away with Grandma after her. "You're not going to lock me in, are you?" she asked when she reached the relative safety of her bedroom.

"No; I don't do things like that, Emily. But this door is to remain firmly shut until Betty leaves. I'm going to leave the living room door just slightly ajar, so I'll hear you if you come out of your room. Do I make myself clear, young lady?"

"But what if I want to go and have a pee?"

"Then hold it in!" Grandma responded firmly as she shut the door.

Back in the living room, Lady F smiled at Betty. "I'm leaving the door very slightly open, so we'll hear if the little monkey tries to come out. She won't be able to hear us talking."

"I think she'll now do what she's told."

"I agree, but given what we've got to go through, best not to take any risks."

Lady F went over to the large table and carried the aluminium case back to her sofa, which she unlocked with a key that she kept in her handbag.

"Here it is," she said looking at Betty. "£90,000 in twenty- and fifty-pound notes. I've taken my £10,000 share. Come and check it."

"I don't need to. I trust you, Lady F."

"You and I always have this conversation, Betty. I know you trust me, but I do feel more comfortable if you do some checking. Come and sit on the sofa and at least count the bundles and sample check one or two of them."

The two swapped places for a few minutes and Betty did some random checking as suggested. Meanwhile, Lady

Felicity got up and went over to her desk and took out a letter from one of the drawers.

"That all seems correct," Betty said after a short while as she closed and locked the case with the key that Lady F had handed her. "Will they get the reward back on the insurance?"

"No. Lady P is just delighted to have her jewels returned to her. She even suggested paying an additional bonus, but I said that we worked to a flat ten percent of the value, and we didn't want to deviate from that. As I stressed to her when we took on the assignment, she was to ask no questions if we were successful, and we had to be paid in cash."

"But what about the insurance?"

"Oh that. She doesn't want to tell the insurers. There'd be no use trying to claim the £100,000 back because they'd just jack up her premiums in the next few years. You can't win with these insurance companies these days."

"I see," Betty replied before a brief pause. "Can I just say again that none of us girls pay any tax on our share. That is alright, isn't it?"

"Betty, you ask me that question every time," Lady F said with a smile. "No, it probably isn't alright as far as the tax authorities are concerned. However, everyone does it and given what we do, it's best to keep it all under the radar."

"You mean we rob the robbers?"

"Precisely! We recover stolen goods from the villains and return them to their rightful owners, taking our ten percent commission. We're a bit like modern day Robin Hoods. Imagine describing that to the taxman."

"I suppose so," Betty said. "But you disclose it on your tax form, don't you, Lady F?"

"Yes, but as income for consultancy services. I get tax relief because I give it all to the homeless charities I support in the area. We've far too many very needy people on the streets. I blame the government!"

"But Sir Cedric was-----"

"I know, Betty," Lady F interrupted. "He was in the government and must take his share of the blame. He even agrees with me on that. However, we are where we are and in the absence of any effective action by the state, we have to rely on the charities to do what they can."

"I always think, listening to you Lady F, that you should take a greater share of what we get. After all, we'd get nothing without you providing us with the opportunities, you having all your contacts and the like."

"No, Betty. I take ten percent of ten percent. That is ample reward for my role. I also obtain a wide circle of friends and acquaintances who are eternally grateful to me. They regularly give me tickets to the best shows and concerts in town; invariably the most expensive seats, I should add."

"Well, if you're sure."

"Quite sure."

Betty thought for a few seconds before continuing. "Just going back to what we do and the taxman and all that – does Sir Cedric know about what we're up to?"

Lady F swallowed. "Sort of," she replied. "He has the most general of ideas, but he's a bright fellow despite marrying me. He knows it's probably better if he doesn't know too much – if you follow what I mean."

Betty nodded. "Do you want to know the details of the operation, Lady F?" she went on to ask.

"Not really. Just as we insist on a no questions policy from our clients, I tend to apply that same policy to myself as far as how you and your team go about your business. However, I know enough from you about who the villains were in this matter. The usual suspects?"

"Yes," Betty replied. "The usual suspects."

"They're not very good, are they?"

"Not good at all. They drink too much in the pub and always let slip something about what they're up to."

"That's men for you. And they have no idea that you and your girls have anything to do with relieving them of their stolen goods?"

"Not as yet."

"Even though you all live on The Estate, and you're related in some cases?"

"Distant relations. Second cousins, I think we're called."

"Have you ever thought what would happen if they found out about your involvement?"

"Frequently, and the honest answer is 'not a lot'. If it got widely known on The Estate, they'd just be laughed at everywhere and viewed as even bigger prats than they are now."

Lady F smiled. "Well, take care, all the same." She paused before opening the letter she had taken from her desk and continuing: "Now, I've a couple more matters to ask your help with. The first one relates to a letter I've received from a very old friend of mine. As you know, I have contacts in all sorts of exotic places. Anyway, this friend of mine has two sisters who are coming to London for a few weeks, probably months, in the very near future. One of them knows the capital well, but the other is more of a country girl and doesn't know much about big cities. This friend of mine has asked if I can arrange for someone to keep an eye on them and make sure they don't get into too much trouble."

"I thought you said one of them knows London well," said Betty.

"She does but she's rather inclined to go looking for trouble and that's what my friend is concerned about. Hence the request. Also, my friend and I think it's probably best if I don't meet the two sisters for a while but ask someone else to take on the main responsibility for keeping them in check. Here, have a read of this letter which gives all the details about them."

Betty spent the next few minutes reading the letter which Lady F had handed her before returning it. "I see they're going to live in the area. They've also got certain skills which might be useful to our team."

"Precisely what I thought," was the reply. "I don't think the bad boys on The Estate would want to get into a pub brawl with them."

"No," agreed Betty. "Leave it to me. What's your other matter, Lady F?"

"Sir Cedric's got a problem. In fact, I think it's a big, big problem and it's going to get a lot bigger, although he doesn't realise it yet. Sorting it out could be the next project for you, me and the girls. We're talking mega-bucks, but far more importantly, my husband's sanity. Let me tell you all about it….."

3
One Person, Many Names

"You stupid man!" the woman said angrily. "Now look what you've done!"

The boat had knocked against the jetty and a small amount of water had splashed over the side onto the woman's dress.

The ferryman gave a few grunts by way of apology and looked at the other figure in the boat who was beginning to climb ashore.

"Take my hand," he said to the woman when he was on the jetty.

"Keep that nasty thing away from me," she replied with a shudder. "You need to start wearing gloves. No one wants to touch those horrible cold bones of yours."

Death stood back and let the woman climb out by herself. When she was ashore, she straightened her salmon pink dress. The woman herself was a striking platinum blonde of indeterminate age. She wore crimson lipstick and was heavily perfumed with Chanel No 5. She carried a small golden coloured handbag which she'd bought from one of the major fashion houses.

The ferryman continued to look at Death and then mumbled a few incomprehensible words.

"It's usual to give the man some coin," Death said to the woman.

"What for?" she haughtily demanded. "I didn't ask to come here. You turned up and took me away against my will."

The ferryman now made a more aggressive set of grunts. On occasions, Death would throw him a coin instead of his passenger, but not this time. He didn't like the woman.

"You must pay!" he said firmly. "Or there will be trouble."

"Don't threaten me, you horrible whatever you are."

Death's dislike was increasing with every word she spoke. "Just pay," he replied firmly.

The woman looked at him, scornfully. "What if I don't?" she finally asked.

"The river's got piranha fish in it. They bite."

"You wouldn't dare!"

Death didn't reply because he'd never pushed anyone into the river beforehand. Despite his dislike of the woman, he wasn't sure if he would do so now. Instead, he merely stared impassively at her; he knew most people found it disconcerting to be eye-balled silently by a skeleton wearing a black cloak and carrying a scythe.

The woman didn't know if Death was bluffing or not, but she decided after a while not to take the risk.

"Alright," she eventually said as she petulantly opened her bag. "I don't carry coins. Does he take American Express?"

Death knew he was on a loser here and decided to give up. The prospect of describing how American Express worked to Charon, the ferryman, was far too much to contemplate. Instead, he just said "forget it," before putting his hand in his pocket, pulling out a coin and throwing it at the man in the boat who caught it easily. Charon normally grumbled that it should be the passenger paying but didn't bother this time. Like Death, he didn't like the woman, and he just wanted to get away as soon as possible.

"Follow me," Death said to the woman and began to walk away from the ferry.

"Don't walk so fast, you idiot," she replied as she tried to catch up. "Can't you see I've got high heels."

Death turned round and was about to give an angry response, but his attention suddenly shifted to the jetty. A very small brown figure had just jumped onto it from the boat as it started moving away.

"Damn," he muttered to himself, as he realised he hadn't got rid of the figure as it scampered after him and the woman.

"Woofy, woofy!" it went.

"Popsy!" the woman called out as she turned round and bent down to pick up the small chihuahua once it had caught up with her. "Come to Mumsy," she said, cuddling it to her bosom.

"It's not allowed to be here!" Death shouted angrily. "I told you; you couldn't bring it."

"Woofy, woofy," the small dog whimpered as it heard Death's words.

"Don't listen to the horrible thing, Popsy. You're here with Mumsy now. Mumsy loves you and you love Mummy, don't you? Did you hide in that dirty old boat?"

"Woofy, woofy," was barely audible as Mumsy and Popsy rubbed each other's noses.

Death moved over towards the woman and was about to snatch the small dog away and put it back in Charon's boat, but he realised it was too late. The ferry had already gone round the bend and was out of sight. There was no use calling out as Charon's hearing was poor, especially when he didn't want to listen to what you had to say.

Death sighed. He didn't know how Hades would react to a small dog in the Underworld. He suspected he would get the blame, so he'd try and keep it out of sight until he had left.

"Put the dog down and let it walk," he said irritably to the woman after she and Popsy had finished rubbing noses.

"Popsy's very delicate," the woman said. "She can't walk far."

"It's not far," Death snapped.

The woman looked at the small dog in her arms. "The nasty thing wants you to walk on the ground, Popsy. Are you happy to do what it wants for a few minutes?"

Popsy was an intelligent dog and had heard the tone of Death's voice. She thought it would cause a lot less trouble if she had a little walk instead of being carried by Mumsy, so she went "woofy, woofy," and nodded her head.

Just as the woman was putting Popsy on the ground, Cerberus came bounding up from behind a boulder.

"Woof; woof!" he went; his voice being far louder than Popsy's. "What's going on here?"

"Aaaah!" the woman shrieked, seeing the large black dog about five feet high with three snarling mouths coming towards her. She quickly ran behind Death. "What's that horrible monster?" she screamed, as she manoeuvred to keep Death between herself and Cerberus. Meanwhile, Popsy had done the sensible thing of running back towards the jetty from where she could observe proceedings.

Cerberus had come to a halt about six feet from Death and the woman. He decided to growl menacingly with all his mouths since he didn't like being called a horrible monster.

"You need to meet Cerberus," Death said as he turned round to the woman. "He's the Underworld's Head of Internal Security."

"But what sort of creature is it?" demanded the woman as she peered over Death's shoulder.

"It is a he and he's a dog," Death replied.

On hearing this, Cerberus gave an extra-large growl with two of his mouths, while at the same time barking with his third.

"But...but... he's got three heads and he's massive," the woman said and then suddenly jumped back and screamed "Aaaah!" again. This was due to Cerberus's long tail stretching forward and giving a loud hiss.

"That's right," Death said. "And he's got a snake's tail called Audrey." There was another hiss as the tail made its presence felt.

"But why?" the woman asked.

"That's for you to answer, Cerberus?" Death said looking at the large dog.

"Answer what?"

"Why you've got three heads and a snake's tail."

"Woof, woof! Because I have!" was the reply.

"So, now you know," Death said to the woman. "Come on; we've got to go to Hades."

Before the two of them could move far, Cerberus had bounded round Death, so he was next to the woman. "Aaaah!" she screamed and tried to back away, but Death wouldn't let her, having now taken hold of her shoulders. "Aaaah!" she went again at the touch of the skeleton's bony fingers on the top of her dress. Death released his grip but barred the woman's way, so she had Death directly behind her and Cerberus's three snarling faces two feet in front of her.

"Give us a Mars bar or I'll bite yer bum," the middle mouth growled.

"What?" the woman said, backing into Death. "What's he saying?"

"Give us a Mars bar or I'll bite yer bum," Cerberus repeated, still growling and snarling.

"What?" the woman again asked, looking genuinely perplexed.

"He wants you to give him a Mars bar to eat," Death said helpfully.

"What's a Mars bar?" she asked.

"You really don't know?" Death responded, genuinely surprised.

"Of course not!"

Cerberus was also amazed that there could be a person who didn't know what a Mars bar was. He took this to mean that she hadn't got one, so he decided to say: "Woof! I'd better bite yer bum then."

"Aaaah!" the woman screamed, rapidly managing to dart behind Death once more for protection as Cerberus moved towards her.

Death sighed. He wanted to hand this woman over to Hades as soon as possible and get back above ground. There was a war going on between competing militias in Central Africa and he had a lot of work to do.

"Here's a Mars bar," he said to Cerberus, pulling one out of his cloak pocket and throwing it into his open mouth on the left. "You can bite her after she's seen Hades."

"What!" the woman exclaimed.

Death's only response was "follow me," as he trudged off towards Hades' palace with the woman following, marshalled by Cerberus growling continuously from a few feet away.

Suddenly the woman stopped and said in a loud voice: "Where's Popsy?" At that moment the small dog raced up to the group, barking "woofy, woofy!" and jumped into Mumsy's arms again. The two repeated their previous love-in, including rubbing noses, while Death and Cerberus watched.

"What's that thing?" Cerberus asked Death in a quiet voice as he moved towards the skeleton.

"It's a dog," Death replied.

"But it's only got one head."

"That's normal up above. It's only down in the Underworld that dogs have three heads."

"I never knew that," Cerberus replied thoughtfully. "Will it grow two extra heads now it's here?"

"I doubt it."

"What's it doing in the Underworld anyway?"

"It jumped onto Charon's ferryboat unnoticed."

"It shouldn't have done that. It's not meant to be here, you know."

"I know."

"What's Hades going to say?"

Death shrugged his shoulders. "Can't you get rid of it somehow before we get to Hades?"

"What do you mean?"

"Wouldn't it like a swim with the piranha fish?"

"Woof! Woof!" Cerberus barked angrily before saying in a loud voice: "No! That's not very nice, Mr Death. No!"

Death shrugged his shoulders and said: "You're probably right."

Cerberus's bark had drawn the attention of the woman and Popsy. "What's that you're saying?" she asked looking at the other two.

"Nothing," said Death. "Just put your little dog down and tell it to keep at the back."

"I don't know," the woman said. "That horrible monster thing might eat my beautiful Popsy. You don't want---"

Cerberus decided to interrupt the woman as he'd had enough of her insults.

"Woof! Woof!" he barked very loudly as he moved over to her before continuing in a very assertive tone: "Let me tell you, Madam, I am not a horrible monster! I have a responsible job in the Underworld, being Head of Internal Security. I eat Mars bars; I do not eat new arrivals when they disembark from the ferry."

"But you bite people on the bum!" he woman responded.

"Well, yes, but not very often," Cerberus was forced to admit. "But forget that for today. Just do as Mr Death said and put your little dog on the ground and let it walk behind all of us. I'll look after it."

Before the woman could respond, Popsy had gone "woofy, woofy" again and nodded at her, realising it was best to do what had been suggested.

"Are you really, really sure, my lovely?"

"Woofy, woofy," followed by further vigorous nods.

This went on for a couple of minutes before the woman reluctantly put Popsy's feet onto the ground and the small group trooped off towards the palace.

•

Hades was sitting on one of the two thrones in the throne room. He was by himself since Persephone, his wife, was currently on Olympus where she spent much of her time. Hades was wearing a dark red velvet robe, and he had a golden crown on his head. He had a number of parchments on a side table, and was busy perusing one of them when Death walked in.

The woman had been complaining during the walk from the jetty to the palace about a whole range of matters, in particular about how dismal the Underworld looked. However, when she saw the immense size of Hades' palace and the fact that it was made of solid gold, she became somewhat overawed and quieter.

"Will I be living here?" she enquired as they walked up the palace steps and through the archway into the interior.

"No," Death replied.

"Then where will I be living?"

"That's for Hades to decide." After saying this, Death quickened his pace, so the woman had no further opportunity to ask any more questions.

The group walked into the middle of the throne room and came to a halt about fifteen feet from Hades; Popsy remaining well behind everyone else.

"Lord Hades," Death said in a loud voice. "I've brought you the woman who has many names."

"Ah, yes," the god replied, looking up from his parchment. "I've been expecting her." He then stared at the woman who was standing beside Death. "Please sit on the stool," he continued, addressing the woman while at the same time motioning to a small stool a few feet in front of his throne.

"What!" she exclaimed. "I can't sit on that tiny little thing. It's only got three legs and is nearly on the ground."

Hades just stared at the woman without saying anything. Death by now was quietly leaving the room as was his normal practice, while Cerberus went and lay on the floor near the woman. He also just stared at her, while emitting a low growl.

The woman continued to babble away, with Hades and Cerberus continuing to stare at her. Eventually she ran out of things to say and at that point, Hades stood up, pointed his arm at the stool and shouted in a very loud voice: "Sit!"

The woman was so stunned that she promptly sat on the stool and looked at the god, her face trembling with the shock of being shouted at.

Hades retook his seat on the throne and then said fiercely: "Don't you ever try to defy me again! Do I make myself clear?"

The woman just nodded.

"Good, then we will proceed." At this point, Hades took all the parchments from the table and rested them on his knees. "You have an interesting history and have had many names," he continued before being interrupted.

"I am the Marchioness de----"

Hades now interrupted the woman by saying in a loud voice: "Stop! I will decide what your name is."

"But…"

"No buts. It is necessary first of all to examine your history which we will do in some detail. Only then will I decide what your name is in the Underworld, what role you will play here and what punishment you will endure for all your past misdemeanours."

"Punishment!" screeched the woman standing up. "What do----"

At this stage Hades had had enough. He stood up, marched towards the woman, grabbed hold of her by the shoulders and pushed her down on the stool. "Sit down and shut up!!!" he screamed so loudly her ear drums nearly burst. He then returned to his throne leaving the woman trembling with fear.

"Now, let us make a start" the god said in a calmer voice as he looked at his first parchment. "It says here you were born in Wigan where your name was Tracey Carbuncle. Your father was either in prison for petty crimes or unemployed most of his life and your mother was a cleaner. Is that right?"

Tracey nodded.

"You, however, decided that you wanted a different life to your parents; you also wanted to see the world." At this point, Hades replaced the first parchment with another one before continuing. "So, you decided to get a job as a stewardess on a luxury cruise ship. You'd been doing this for three years before meeting Baron OldBanger. He was an elderly widower in his mid-80's who was on a Mediterranean cruise with his even older spinster sister. Despite his age, he was still partial to the attractions of the female sex. You happened to be his stewardess, and you were soon providing him with additional services. The result was that by the end of the cruise, the two of you were engaged to be married, which you duly were a few weeks later, so becoming Lady OldBanger. This was despite the protestations of the elderly spinster sister, who was speedily packed off to a nursing home, having previously been living in her brother's house. Right so far?"

Lady OldBanger again nodded.

Hades continued. "A few months after your marriage, for totally inexplicable reasons, you and your husband took up parachuting. On the first jump, his parachute failed to open, and you became the widowed Lady OldBanger with an inheritance of £10m. This unfortunate occurrence for his Lordship arose because you tampered with his parachute without being spotted by the jump instructors."

Hades looked at Lady OldBanger, who avoided his gaze by staring at the floor.

"Your second husband was equally unfortunate. You met Le Comte de Grossmenthe in the cocktail bar of the Ritz in Paris. You were now able to stay in such places due to the OldBanger inheritance. The Comte was an unattached international businessman involved in various shady deals to do with the arms trade. You and he became enamoured with each other and, after a rather long courtship due to your fiancé's many business trips, you became La Comtesse de Grossmenthe. As I'm sure you were aware at the time, a Comtesse or Countess was a step up from a mere Lady in the nobility rankings." Hades paused before continuing: "For a number of years, you accompanied Le Comte whenever he went abroad. This allowed you to meet a number of his business associates, most of whom were as shady as your husband. In particular, you cultivated one of them in a certain Central Asian republic and, pretending to be drunk at a reception, just happened to let slip when Le Comte was not around that your husband was about to swindle him out of a lot of money. This was perfectly believable but wasn't in fact true in this instance." Hades paused before continuing: "Do you want to finish the tale?"

"You know full well what happened," the countess murmured.

The god nodded before carrying on. "Early the following evening, while you were downstairs in your hotel's hairdressing salon, two masked men managed to get into your suite. Finding Le Comte alone, they bundled him out of the window on the eighth floor, ransacked the place and took your jewellery making it appear that burglary was the motive. You naturally were overcome with grief but as compensation inherited over 100 million euros."

Hades sat silently for a good ten seconds, the countess still looking at the ground. "We now come to the Marquis de Muddlepuddle. It took some years before you found your next husband, or perhaps I should refer to him as your next victim. The two seem to go together in your case. I think I'll skip the preliminaries about how you both met. It's enough to say that he didn't last long due to you encouraging him to swim in the Florida Everglades towards the end of your honeymoon. He'd just finished consuming significant quantities of wine and cognac with his dinner, so the alligators he came across must have had a particularly intoxicating meal that evening. Needless to say, his new will left everything to you, so you became the owner of a number of landed estates in England and Scotland. Also, being a Marchioness was one step higher than a Countess, so you were continuing to make progress in the nobility pecking order. Any comments?"

The Marchioness remained silent, still looking down on the floor.

Hades now took another parchment to read. "We now come to husband number four. Being unable to find a spare duke, you decided to focus on the American billionaire sector. After a while you came across an appropriate candidate, Mr

Alabama PorkyPie the Third, the Chairman and CEO of one the largest sausage, pie and meat producers in the Americas. His estimated fortune was more than $10 billion and you were keen to get your hands on it at the earliest opportunity. Unfortunately, you weren't able to convince him to go parachuting or swimming with alligators and you couldn't find any business associates willing to push him out of top floor windows. So, what you did instead was to resort to the old-fashioned method of poison. How you expected to get away with it in today's scientific age is beyond me. Anyway, the matter never arose because Alabama saw you slip something into his wine glass one evening. Instead of challenging you, he thought it would be fun merely to swap glasses when you weren't looking just to see what would happen. Unfortunately, you poisoned yourself and poor Alabama's up on a murder charge in a state which still has capital punishment."

Hades stopped talking and the woman continued to remain silent. Eventually Cerberus decided to participate in the proceedings. "Woof, woof! What happens now, Boss?" he asked.

"What happens now is that you should take Mrs PorkyPie to the Women's Quarters where she's expected. Tomorrow, she'll join the Laundry Department but first she needs to meet Satan----"

"Who?" the woman interrupted, suddenly coming to life. "Who's Satan?"

"You must have heard of him," Hades replied. "He now works for me in the Underworld, being the Director in charge of our Torturing Department."

"Torturing Department!" the woman screamed, standing up again. "What's that?"

The woman became hysterical and started to babble as well as scream. Hades ignored her; he just got up, gathered all the parchments under his arm and began to walk out of the Throne Room. Suddenly he stopped, turned round and said: "Oh, and Cerberus, please return that small dog to where it came from. It shouldn't be here."

As Hades left, Popsy began going "woofy, woofy!" in alarm and started to run around the throne room. The woman ran around after her, while continuing to babble and scream; this caused Cerberus himself to start barking "woof! woof!" very loudly as he tried to deal with the mayhem that Hades had bequeathed him.

4
The Gallery

Sir Cedric was pacing up and down in his spacious top floor office. He was a tall, thin, muscular man in his late 60's. He was very fit for his age, reflecting his weekly exercise routine which he'd maintained ever since his days in the Coldstream Guards. He had a full mop of hair, being a mixture of grey and white, with the grey fighting a losing battle for relevance as each year went by. Whenever he was on duty – and work was duty as far as he was concerned – he was always dressed in one of his three-piece Savile Row suits.

As he paced up and down, he was reflecting on the past six years. Before then, he'd enjoyed life. Yes, he'd been busy as he built a complex engineering concern into a major FTSE100 group. However, despite all the challenges, things in the main had worked out well. He'd made a fair amount of money and received a knighthood, but they were really secondary to the sense of satisfaction he'd got from seeing the business grow. It wasn't just his own contribution he was proud of - he attributed much of the company's success to his team. They were a joy to work with – people who addressed problems in a mature way, worked out solutions and then did what they agreed to do. Naively, over the years he let himself be lulled into thinking that's how much of the country worked. Then he retired!

Retired! What a stupid word. Every day since he'd stood down as Chairman of the FTSE100 group, Cedric thought about what a fool he'd been. For the first time in his life, he'd been 'seduced'. Somehow, and he still couldn't work out exactly how, he'd let himself be talked into standing for Parliament at the upcoming General Election. It all seemed so neat and tidy – the MP in their Central London constituency had made a last-minute decision to stand down in the election which was about to take place; Sir Cedric had just retired and was available, so him standing was perceived by all and sundry as a 'no brainer'. Not quite all and sundry – Lady Felicity had her reservations, but Cedric was determined to be seduced! He had to admit that an important influence was the promise of an immediate seat at the Cabinet table, assuming his party won – which was a reasonable bet given its strong lead in the opinion polls.

So, Cedic became a politician and found out that the country didn't work quite as he'd believed. His first problem was that it was absolutely forbidden to admit that anything was a problem, unless of course it had been caused by the other side. Then it was escalated into the biggest problem imaginable with blame being attributed in bucketloads! Next, he learned that you were simply not allowed to admit publicly that you didn't know the answer to matters – even if you didn't! Instead, you had to waffle away and bore the audience senseless, by which time they were hopefully fast asleep, and you could move on to some other matter. Finally, if you were asked a direct question, to which the honest answer would be embarrassing to the government, you simply had to lie. It was as straightforward as that – only tell the truth if it suited you.

Unsurprisingly, Cedric came a cropper on all these matters. His first television interview as a cabinet minister involved him being quizzed by a rather charming lady, who clearly intended to give him an easy ride because of his 'beginner status'. However, he still managed to commit every cardinal sin in the politician's handbook. In particular, his interviewer was often lost for words when he admitted that he didn't know the answer to many of her questions. This surprise was only exceeded when he admitted that the opposition's policy on a particular matter was much better than the government's. When pressed as to why he didn't adopt this alternative policy, he told the truth which was that he wasn't allowed to because the PM hadn't thought of it. This led to him being asked if such an approach wasn't rather stupid, to which he replied: "Yes!" At that point, the charming lady took pity on him and brought the interview to a swift and premature conclusion.

Over the next few days, Cedric was lambasted by many of his fellow cabinet members who wanted him sacked. His only supporter turned out to be the Prime Minister who was determined to keep him on and rejected Cedric's resignation letter. This continued for the next few years – every minister wanted rid of him, he wanted to go, but the PM wouldn't have any of it. It was only near the time of the next election that he found out why – over eighty percent of the party's major donors had indicated they would stop all financial support if Cedric left the Cabinet. They were determined there should be a 'vaguely competent businessperson' at the top of government and he was considered to be that person.

So, Cedric persevered. The PM himself tried to tutor him as to how to handle interviews in a political sense, and eventually an uneasy compromise was reached between the two of them. Cedric was adamant about not telling lies and trying to be as honest as possible, so he was given a series of stock responses to pull out whenever the questions were becoming uncomfortable, which was most of the time! The result was that he was continuously saying: "I've got nothing further to add on that matter"; "What's your next question, please?"; "I've already dealt with that" (even if he hadn't); "No further comment", and the like. The result was that most of the time he managed to avoid any more complete shipwrecks like his first interview, although the whole process was completely useless. No one learned anything because the name of the game was to say nothing. That was the whole point of being a cabinet minister – say nothing and then do nothing which could be of any use to anyone!

While the PM may have been outwardly forgiving to Cedric, the media certainly wasn't. He was attacked from both the right and the left. One leading newspaper spent his entire time in office questioning his mental abilities with headlines such as:

Is Ced Dead?
Ced's Head is Made of Lead

PIMLICO PEOPLE

Ced The Red - after he'd once rejected the idea of abolishing all trade unions.
Ced's Head's Still in Bed

The paper's editorial staff clearly had so much fun with these headlines that they started creating cartoons of his head every time he was on the front page. After two years in the Cabinet, Cedric's head became the subject of their annual Christmas quiz. The front page was dominated by a gormless looking cartoon drawing of his head. It was divided into four sections - A, B, C and D - and readers were asked to decide which section was: 1) Dead; 2) Full of Lead; 3) Red; 4) Still in Bed. There was also a link to the paper's website where they could submit their entries to the editor with the winner being chosen at random from all the correct entries the following day.

This quiz seemed to take the country by storm with over two million responses. The winner was officially announced on the 6pm news, as being a Mrs Megan Pontyplod of Bridgend. She had correctly submitted that all four sections of Ced's Head were at the same time Dead, Full of Lead, Red and Still in Bed. This was an option which had been hidden away on the website, so only computer literate readers who were particularly persistent could find it. Apparently, one such reader was Ced's granddaughter, Emily, who within five minutes of the result being announced was on the telephone to Grandma Felicity to tell her that she'd got the right answer as well. Grandma had naturally told her she was a very clever young lady and agreed to give her a nice, crisp £10 note as a prize when she next saw her; the £10 having been aggressively negotiated upwards from an initial offer of £5!

Eventually, it was time for another general election. Cedric wanted to retire from politics, but everyone was insistent that he should contest his seat once more as it was now looking like a marginal since the governing party was well behind in the national polls. Even Lady Felicity supported this view, but principally because she thought her husband would lose and it would be better 'to go down fighting' as opposed to 'quitting a sinking ship'. So, the campaign took place and Cedric tried his best, while hoping to lose. The problem was that he was just too popular in the constituency which was reflected in a telephone call from his agent at 9 o'clock the evening before polling day. The agent was buoyant – the canvassing returns indicated Cedric would likely just win since the swing against him was far less than the party was experiencing nationally. Cedric thanked him for the information and went and told his wife. The couple sat in silence for about five minutes until Lady Felicity sprung out of her chair with a determined look on her face.

"I'm going to see Betty," she said.

"Why?" Cedric asked.

"Leave it to me," was the reply before she walked out of the living room, phoned for a cab and promptly left the flat.

The next day was spent smiling and shaking hands at the different polling booths in the constituency, before the count in the evening. After a recount, at 11am the following morning Sir Cedric ceased to be an MP, having lost by five votes. This result had been assisted by both Cedric and his wife voting for the main opposition candidate who ultimately won. In subsequent days, it emerged that Betty and her family had managed to ensure that seventy-one voters on The Estate suddenly changed their minds and decided not to support Cedric. This was in part offset by a number of other candidates in the election admitting privately to Sir Cedric that they'd voted for him because "he was a good bloke!" Anyway, the result was that he'd lost, much to his and his wife's great relief.

"What did you say to Betty?" Cedric asked Lady Felicity once Betty's contribution became known.

"That I'd divorce you if you'd won."

Being a bit perplexed by this reply, the next day Cedric walked round to The Estate and called in on Betty for a cup of tea and a chat.

"What did Lady F say to you when she visited you that evening, Betty?" he asked.

"She told me the truth, Sir Cedic. She said neither of you wanted to win, and she needed help to stop it from happening. To be honest, I'd suspected it for a long time but supported you out of loyalty until Lady F came clean."

"Then?"

"Then I and the girls we went into action, didn't we? Had a late-night chat with a few people."

"A few being seventy-one."

"Something like that."

"You didn't ----?"

"No, don't worry. No one knows what Lady F and I spoke about. I just told people you were a suspected Russian spy!"

"You what!" exclaimed Cedric.

Betty didn't reply but instead burst out laughing and offered her guest a piece of fruit cake. He started laughing himself and the two said no more about the matter, with Cedric never really finding out precisely how his wife and Betty had engineered this last-minute change in his fortunes.

Although he'd lost the election, leaving the public eye took Sir Cedric some time. All the national newspapers spent weeks analysing the heavy defeat of the governing party. A number of them contained lengthy editorials about the highly regrettable loss of Sir Cedric. One of them in particular claimed he was by far the most talented member of the outgoing government, expressing a wish that he would soon return in a bye election – after all, the party needed his leadership, as he would obviously go on to be one of the most outstanding Prime Ministers of the last 100 years. Cedric read the piece a number of times while checking that it wasn't April Fool's Day. He was also clear that he hadn't touched any alcohol that day.

"How sweet of them," Lady F commented when she'd read the editorial. "Isn't this the paper that ran that quiz about your head?"

"Yes," Cedric grunted, before getting up and pouring the two of them a glass of sherry.

In the following weeks, all sorts of offers came Cedric's way. Eventually he agreed to take on the Chairmanship of The Gallery. All that was required was two days a week of his time, so semi-retirement could now begin. At least that was the plan until he met Cesare Hamid Maximillian Shiftyopolous, The Gallery's Director. Then two days a week rapidly grew into eight days a week as Cedric began to bitterly regret leaving parliament.

At that moment, there was a knock on the door and, without waiting for an answer, Cesare Hamid Maximillian Shiftyopolous walked into Cedric's office for their 10am meeting.

Cesare Shiftyopolous had been The Gallery's Director for the last eight years. He was eminently qualified, having spent many years in senior positions at Madrid's Prado, the Uffizi in Florence and the Louvre in Paris. He had degrees or doctorates from a range of European and American universities and was viewed as one of the leading authorities in the world on both Renaissance art and the 17th Century Dutch masters.

Cesare's background was worldwide. He was part South American, part Italian, part German as well as having blood from what he insisted on referring to as Mesopotamia, which was pretty vague until you learned that he'd been born in Beirut before his parents moved to Italy when he was five. All these heritages had resulted in the creation of a short, thin man who was now in his early 50's. The top of his head was bald, but he still had hair at the sides and back of his head as well as a tidy moustache. This hair was jet black reflecting the regular application of various cosmetics because Cesare was vain. This was only rivalled by another of his personality traits which was that he was 'shifty' – a matter well-advertised by his name, suggesting his family had large quantities of genes linked to shiftiness in their body cells.

Naturally, with a name like Shiftyopolous, together with his particular personality, the Gallery's Director was referred to as 'Shifty' behind his back. Cedric's great fear in his dealings with Cesare was that he would accidentally call him Shifty to his face. He'd avoided it so far but was continuously on his guard since it would immediately result in a complaint by the Director to the other trustees on the Board. If there was one thing which Cesare was determined to do, it was to get rid of Sir Cedric as his Chairman; this determination was only equalled, if not surpassed, by Cedric wanting to replace the Director with a more responsive individual.

•

An hour later, the Chairman was still getting nowhere with the Director.

"So, the Cezanne has still not been found," Cedric said, half stating a fact and half asking a question.

"I am confused by your note, Sir Cedric."

"Why? It was perfectly clear. You sent a curator with what was supposed to be the painting, but it was the wrong one. Didn't I say that in the note?"

"In a manner of speaking, possibly yes," Cesare replied. "But I also spoke to Dr Verkingetoblob and he was perplexed by his meeting with you."

"That's because he couldn't either understand or speak English. What you're doing employing a curator like that in a major British institution, I really don't know."

"He is a world-renowned expert in his field. He brings The Gallery great prestige."

"But can anyone communicate with him?"

"I can."

"How?"

"We speak Uzbek together." Cesare paused before continuing: "I take it you don't speak Uzbek, Sir Cedric?"

"No, I bloody don't! Anyway, that's not the point. Your curator got the paintings mixed up."

"This is what I'm confused about. In what sense do you mean 'mixed up'?"

"I've just told you, Cesare. He brought me the wrong painting; I also spelt it out clearly in my note."

"So, he didn't bring you a Cezanne?"

Cedric was trying his best to keep his cool, having learned from past experience that 'blowing his top' never had any effect on Cesare. Instead, he just had to keep relentlessly plugging away, even if it meant repeating himself a hundred times.

"Cesare," Cedric replied wearily. "Mr Verkingetoblob - ----"

"It is Dr Verkingetoblob, Sir Cedric," the Director interrupted.

"Well, whatever his name is -----"

"Titles are very important," Cesare interrupted again. "I myself am a Doctor as well as a Professor; you yourself are a Sir, a Knight of the Realm. These are important matters."

"Agreed," Cedric said wearily. "But it's beside the point ----"

"With great respect, it is not beside the point, Sir Cedric," Cesare interrupted again. "If an institution like The Gallery fails to give appropriate recognition to its human assets as well as its artistic treasures, then it is nothing. Its prestige on the worldwide stage will plummet from being near the top, if not at the top, to absolutely nothing. Zero, just like that," and Cesare clicked his fingers to emphasise his point.

Cedric glared at him for a full ten seconds as he worked out how to reply. He decided not to pick a fight this time; he wanted to find that Cezanne.

"I understand what you're saying, Cesare," he eventually replied. "Let us, however, get back to the missing Cezanne ----"

"It is not missing, Sir Cedric! I keep telling you that. I must ask you not to use the word 'missing' anymore. It is factually incorrect!"

"Very well. All I have been trying to say in the last few minutes is that Dr Verkingetobook ----"

"Verkingetoblob," Cesare corrected him.

"Thank you. Verkingetoblob then, brought me one of Cezanne's paintings of bathers, not Les Trois Filles, as I requested."

"Were the bathers not girls?"

"No. Les Trois Filles consists of the girls in a woodland setting, not ……" Cedric paused before continuing. "Why am I telling you this, Cesare? It's your Gallery; you must know the painting better than I do."

Cesare looked at Cedric and realised he wasn't going to get very far by pleading ignorance of Les Trois Filles.

"You are quite right, Sir Cedric. It was my intellectual curiosity getting the better of me. I was just interested in which of Cezanne's paintings of bathers Dr Verkingetoblob brought you."

"Well, let's focus on Les Trois Filles. My question is very simple, as it's been for the last two months – where is it?"

Cesare remained silent for a while, looking out of the window behind Cedric's desk, deep in thought.

"Well?" Cedric asked after a while.

"It would help me tremendously," Cesare responded now coming back to life. "If you could tell me who your source is, and where he claimed to have seen, what he alleges to be the original Les Trois Filles."

"I've already told you all I'm prepared to say on the matter, Cesare. A long-standing banker friend of mine, who has always taken an interest in the Arts, saw the painting hanging on the wall of one of his billionaire Far Eastern clients."

"But who is this banker? Who is the billionaire client? Which country? Why won't you tell me, Sir Cedric?"

"I was told the matter in confidence and I'm respecting that confidence."

"But it would help to know these ‐‐‐‐‐"

"No, it wouldn't, Cesare!" Cedric interrupted loudly. "If you bring me Les Trois Filles, then the whole matter falls by the wayside. Until then, it's an outstanding issue as far as I'm concerned."

"This thing on the billionaire's wall is probably a fake," Cesare grumbled in reply.

"That may be so, but the best way of establishing that matter is to bring me the original of Les Trois Filles."

"With great respect, Sir Cedric, could you tell the difference between an original and a fake?"

Cedric gave the Director an angry look. "I like to think that The Gallery's Director would not try and pull the wool over his Chairman's eyes. Am I right or wrong on that matter, Professor Shiftyopolous?"

Cesare shrugged his shoulders and again looked out of the window without replying.

"Well, what's your answer?" Cedric demanded after a lengthy interval.

"I am offended at being asked such a question."

"Tough, Cesare. But let's move on. Can you please answer my original, long-standing question - Where is Les Trois Filles?"

Cesare frowned. "It could be in a number of places," he replied. "For example, it could be out for restoration. Another alternative is that it might be part of a swap arrangement for a few weeks with another gallery, possibly in the provinces. Then, of course, it could have been moved within our storage system. As I'm sure you're aware, Sir Cedric, we have many more paintings in store than are actually exhibited on our gallery walls. Items often get moved around and can remain hidden or unseen for years before they resurface. It's the case with many other art galleries."

"All that you say sounds very plausible, Cesare," Sir Cedric said with a sigh. "But I'm not interested in debating possibilities and alternatives. All I want to know is where Les Trois Filles is. You or someone in The Gallery must know! What do your records show you?"

"Records?" Cesare replied, looking perplexed.

Cedric sighed again. "Silly question," he said. "I shouldn't have asked. I'd forgotten that you don't keep records. Have you held a meeting yet with those computer people I put you in touch with?"

"I do not like computers," was Cesare's response.

"Well, we're going to have them throughout The Gallery over the next twelve months, whatever you say, Cesare. That decision's been made by the Board of Trustees."

Cesare merely sniffed in response.

"I don't know what your problem is. Once we have a stock control system, we can record exactly where each painting is. If it goes to a restorer or is lent to another gallery, it will all be there to see at the press of a button."

"I do not like this term 'stock'. These are magnificent works of art we have in The Gallery; they are not tins of sardines or cans of baked beans."

"Then we'll find a different term to describe the system when it's introduced. It's what it does, that's important. Don't you see the benefits of it?"

Cesare sniffed again.

"Well, what do you do now?" Cedric asked after a while, realising that the only response he was going to get was a sniff.

"Each curator has an intimate knowledge of all the works of art for which he is responsible. He knows far more than anything you can put on a computer system."

"Well; Mr What's-his-name doesn't -----"

"Dr Verkingetoblob!" Cesare interrupted forcibly.

"Very well. Dr Verkingetoblob can't tell us where Les Trois Filles is, can he?" Cedric replied equally forcibly.

Once more Cesare's response was to sniff and stare out of the window.

"Tell me, Cesare," Cedric continued, not bothering to wait so long this time for a response which he was unlikely to get anyway. "If your curators are the people who have all this knowledge, what happens if one of them gets run over by a bus? All that knowledge is lost with no back up."

"It is entirely hypothetical, Sir Cedric. I can assure you that in The Gallery's long history, no curator has ever been knocked over by a bus."

"You know exactly what I mean, Cesare. It doesn't have to be a bus. A curator could just drop dead because of a heart attack, or he might just walk out at short notice. What would you do then?"

"Our curators do not 'just drop dead' as you say; they also do not 'walk out at short notice'."

"But what would you do if it happened? What's your contingency plan?"

"We would address it at the time."

"Which means you don't have a contingency plan!"

Cesare didn't reply. Instead, he sniffed once more and stared out of the window.

"Let me ask you another question," Cedric said. "If you have no records except those in each curator's head, what's to stop a curator secretly selling one of his works of art on the black market? How would you ever know?"

The Director gave the Chairman a look of complete astonishment. "Mein Gott!" he exclaimed. "I cannot believe you can ask such a question, Sir Cedric. Are you seriously suggesting that our curators are thieves?"

"No! I'm merely asking how you would identify the fact if it ever happened?"

"It is a ridiculous question. It has never happened and never will happen. End of debate!"

"Oh, get real, Cesare! Everyone's got a price in this world, and you know it. Also, don't pretend that the art world is full of saints. There are lots of dodgy things going on all the time."

"Not by The Gallery."

"Look Cesare, we all know curators aren't the highest paid people in the world. What if one has a very expensive wife, or a son who's built up lots of gambling debts, or a daughter who needs expensive medical treatment only available in the States? It could be anything which involves the need for a large sum of money which he doesn't have. Don't you think he might be tempted to do something irregular? As I've said before, everyone's got a price."

"I do not have a price! My curators do not have a price!" Cesare replied emphatically.

"Then it's a strange old world you seem to live in. Let me tell you the tale of my father. He was a successful merchant operating in Africa. All the time he was coming up against other traders from the Middle and Far East. They had different business ethics, very often offering my father a bung to do a deal. Because he was old school British, he kept declining these bribes, but they kept being offered to him. One day he got so fed up with it that he calculated what he would lose financially if he took a bung, was then found out and lost his job and never worked again. He calculated the sum at £500,000. Bear in mind, that was nearly eighty years ago, so it would probably be worth about £10 million today. Anyway, the next time a trader offered him a bribe, he was delighted to hear that my father was for once open to discussing the matter.

> *"However, I don't think you can afford me," my father said.*
> *"I'm sure we can," the trader replied.*
> *"Very well. My price is half a million pounds."*

Apparently, the trader's jaw dropped as the deal they were discussing was only for about £20,000. So, no deal, no bung and Father never got pestered again to take a backhander, which was what he was hoping the outcome would be all along."

Cesare looked perplexed at the end of this tale. "So, are you saying, Sir Cedric, that your father would have taken the half a million if he'd been offered it?"

Cedric smiled. "I asked my father that very question and he just laughed. In a sense it doesn't matter – the point of the story is that eventually everyone has a price. Everyone!"

"And what is your price, Sir Cedric?"

"I don't have one. I'm the exception to the rule."

"Aha! So not everyone!" Cesare replied with a big smile as he pointed a finger at The Gallery's Chairman. Before he could respond, the fire alarm went off and Cesare jumped off his chair and hurried out of the room, muttering about needing to find out what was going on. Cedric followed him at a more leisurely pace.

"Damn!" he said to himself. "I fell for that one. And I didn't even get the chance to ask about the missing Modigliani."

5
The First Day in London

As Hebe's chariot slowly descended over Central London, she phoned the hotel on her mobile to let them know that she and her sister would be arriving in the next few minutes. They had a large number of suitcases, so would need the porterage team to help carry them in.

Iris was travelling with Hebe and Artemis to take the chariot back to Olympus. Although Hebe usually left her four stallions at the stables near Hyde Park for short visits, she and Artemis would be staying in London for a few months. In view of this it seemed unfair to keep the horses cooped up in such narrow confines for a long period with only the occasional nightly run in the park. Also, Iris needed the chariot since she was going to carry out a lot of Hebe's tasks while she was away.

Much of the luggage consisted of clothes for the two goddesses during their stay. Artemis had no suitable fashion wear for city living, so Hebe had decided to kit her out beforehand. At present the two of them were wearing identical, sleeveless, light blue dresses, each with a wide golden belt. Artemis refused to wear a bra, despite Hebe pestering her to do so. She was sure this was asking for trouble in a busy London environment, so would suggest they changed into jeans and T shirts once they were unpacked.

There were few cars outside the Hotel Savoire, so Hebe brought the chariot to a halt directly in front of the main entrance. A tall, thin, nearly bald man in his late 50's was waiting for them. He was wearing silver tails over a dark waistcoat; behind him were two young bell boys similarly attired, each with rosy cheeks and looking distinctly nervous.

"Hiya, George," Hebe called as she climbed out of the chariot.

"Good morning, Lady Hebe," George, who was the Senior Porter at the hotel, replied. "I trust you had a pleasant journey?"

"All fine." Hebe replied. She saw her companions had also alighted from the chariot, so she continued: "You know Lady Iris, don't you? Also, this is my sister, Lady Artemis."

"Morning George," Iris said in a businesslike manner as she started to pull the cases out of the chariot.

"Lady Iris."

Artemis knew it was now her turn, so she looked at the Senior Porter and said: "Ey up, George," before giving him a smile.

George blinked; he was a bit non-plussed by this greeting, so all he could say was: "Excuse me?"

"Ey up, I said," Artemis repeated before moving over to assist Iris who had now been joined by the two bell boys.

"Delighted to meet you, Lady Artemis," George replied, still uncertain what this 'ey up' term was about.

Artemis was rather pleased with herself for using what she thought was the local lingo. For the past few days, she'd been tutored by Hebe on various phrases which people used in England. She'd recorded them in a notebook which she re-read during the journey from Olympus. The one she liked best was 'ey up', if only because she'd heard Hebe use it from time to time over the years. Thinking it had gone rather well with George, she decided she would use it again in the hotel.

Hebe had heard Artemis's 'ey up' and realised that she hadn't told her sister that it should only be used in the North of the country. It certainly wasn't a phrase commonly spoken in Central London, especially not in the Hotel Savoire. She'd have to mention it to Artemis when they got to their suite. In fact, she'd only included it on the list for her fellow goddess in case they visited Yorkshire for a long weekend over the next few weeks.

More bell boys appeared from a side entrance with buckets of water and plenty of straw for the horses. When all the cases had been offloaded and George and the first two bell boys had carried them into the hotel, Iris said goodbye to Hebe and Artemis, before climbing back into the chariot ready to return to Mount Olympus.

Once in the main hall, Hebe turned right towards the large Reception desk, with Artemis following. She was greeted by Miss Mulverhill, the Head Receptionist, whom she'd known for many years and then the hotel's General Manager came out from a back office to also welcome the new arrivals. In both instances, Artemis said "ey up" once introduced, resulting in further strange looks from the hotel's management. For the next few minutes, Hebe completed all the paperwork as she signed in for both herself and her sister before the two of them were escorted by Miss Mulverhill to their suite on the fourth floor. They were followed by George and the two bell boys who were carrying the suitcases.

When the hotel staff had left, Hebe took charge of the unpacking. Before leaving she had put everything they would need for their short stay at the hotel in one case. The other cases could be unpacked in a couple of days when they moved into the flat which she had rented for the rest of their London stay. Meanwhile, Artemis went exploring around the suite. On Olympus, there was only electricity in Hebe's and Iris's bungalow with the rest of the gods and goddesses relying on candles to light their magnificent palaces. Artemis had been shown how light switches worked by Iris in the last few days, so she went around the entire suite turning on every switch and pressing all the buttons. Unfortunately, this resulted in her inadvertently calling maid service on three occasions with regular rings on the front door by the same young Filipino. She also managed to press the 'Emergency Red Button' in the bathroom which led to the Head Housekeeper and George both arriving to provide unnecessary assistance at the same time.

"Have you pressed everything you want to press now?" an exasperated Hebe asked Artemis, after apologising for the emergency call out which was her fourth apology in the last hour.

"Well, I didn't know some of the buttons were for calling people," her sister replied. "You don't have one of those red buttons in your bungalow."

"Alright but be careful. If you don't know what it's for, just ask me."

"But that's why I've been pressing all the buttons, so I can see what they do."

Hebe sighed. "Okay, but are you finished now?"

"Yes, I think so. I've just got all those things to press on the big box in the sitting room and the smaller box in our bedroom."

"Don't worry about them for the time being. They're televisions. I'll show you how they work later."

"They're those picture things, aren't they? You've got one on Olympus, but it doesn't look like either of these two."

"Don't worry; all will become clear later. Come on, put these on; we're going to go out exploring and we'll get some lunch as well."

"I'm not wearing a bra!" Artemis said firmly.

"You should. I've explained why on more than one occasion."

"No way. I'll put the tight trousers and the T shirt on, but not the bra."

"You'll learn," Hebe muttered as she also began to change.

A short while later the two sisters walked out of the Savoire's back entrance to look at the Thames. Reaching Blackfriars, they soon double-backed up Fleet Street, before arriving at the Aldwych. They then made their way to Covent Garden where they found a table in an outside restaurant, and both ordered pasta and a glass of wine.

"Why's it called Covent Garden?" Artemis asked as she began eating. "I can't see any trees and plants around."

"It used to be a market for fruit and vegetables, until it got moved south of the river. The whole area's now been turned over to tourism with all these restaurants and boutique shops."

"Umm...." muttered Artemis looking around. "Seems very popular; all the tables are teeming with people. Are they tourists?"

"Most are; just like us," Hebe replied.

"Picking up what we were talking about earlier, I take it I'm not meant to say 'ey up' to tourists as well as Londoners?"

"Only to be spoken if and when we visit Yorkshire."

"Pity that. I like 'ey up'."

"Isn't there another phrase you can use?"

"I suppose so. What's that one which you chant about ugly? I quite like that one as well."

"It's '*Oggy*'," Hebe corrected her. *"Oggy Oggy Oggy!"*

"That's it, and then someone else says what?"

"Oi Oi Oi!"

"Can I say that while in London?"

"Yea. I suppose so."

"What about to tourists?"

Hebe shrugged her shoulders, then laughed. "We could try it now."

"What! Here?"

"Come on. Let's try." She then called out *"Oggy Oggy Oggy!"*

A few people in the restaurant gave her funny looks, but a couple of young lads sitting at a nearby table went *"Oi Oi Oi!"*

Hebe again chanted more loudly: *"Oggy Oggy Oggy!"* This time Artemis and a few more people, including one of the waiters, went *"Oi Oi Oi!"*

Hebe now felt she was on a roll, so she stood up, walked over to a group of three pot-bellied Germans and gave them an *"Oggy Oggy Oggy!"* in an even louder voice.

"Das ist gut!" one of the Germans said to his two companions, so they all responded with an *"Oi Oi Oi!"*

Artemis now felt like entering into the spirit of matters, so she also got up and looked round at the table behind her. A middle-aged couple with a young teenage son and an even younger daughter were all eating pizzas. Artemis moved towards their table, eye-balled the parents and joined Hebe in the next *"Oggy Oggy Oggy!"*

"Elle est folle," the mother said disapprovingly while looking at her husband. Suddenly her son joined in the *"Oi Oi Oi!"* response to which he received a sharp "tais toi." When it came to the next *"Oggy Oggy Oggy,"* he muttered the words loud enough for his mother to hear, so she shouted "arret!" and gave him such an angry glare that he decided not to risk any future participation in the *Oggy* chant.

By now most of the guests in the restaurant had joined in. The Germans had ordered more beers, and the few empty tables had quickly filled up as other tourists felt this was a fun place to be. Hebe was in her element walking around and leading the chant. She moved across to a neighbouring bistro and soon enlisted support from its customers. Many of the waiters were also chanting the *"Oi Oi Oi!"* reply — after all, everyone was happy, and all the tables were now occupied. Artemis, who was less precocious that her sister, was also drumming up support, although she remained in the original restaurant while Hebe had by now disappeared out of sight.

With time, the whole of Covent Garden was creating a tremendous sound of *"Oggy Oggy Oggy!"* followed by *"Oi Oi Oi!"* Eventually a number of police vans with their sirens blazing arrived. Approximately thirty officers ran into the market area, some with firearms but most wielding their truncheons. At this point the chanting died down and all the tourists stared at the sudden arrival of such a large number of police who were now standing around unsure what to do next. The manager of Hebe's and Artemis's restaurant walked over to the inspector in charge, who was a bit non-plussed at what he was seeing.

"What's going on here?" he asked the manager. "We've been informed there's a riot taking place."

"Who said so?" the manager answered with his own question.

The inspector shrugged. "An anonymous call is all I know."

"I think there's been a big misunderstanding," the manager said.

"But what was all that noise when we arrived?"

"Only everyone having a big sing song, both in this restaurant and adjoining ones. People enjoying themselves before, with great respect, being frightened by the arrival of armed police."

"Yes," the inspector conceded. "It certainly doesn't look like a riot."

"That's because it's not," was the tart reply.

"So, what was being sung? Any revolutionary songs, anything likely to incite hatred or violence?"

"Have you ever heard of the chant *"Oggy Oggy Oggy!"*?"

The inspector nodded. "Nothing else?" he asked.

"Nothing else. In fact, it was actually started by the two ladies sitting at that table there, especially the small blonde one." The manager pointed at where Hebe, who had now returned to her table, and Artemis were sitting. Both were looking in their direction and Hebe gave the police inspector a friendly wave.

"What, that sweet little thing?" the politically incorrect inspector asked.

"Would you like to go and talk to them?"

By now the inspector realised he and his officers had been called out on a wild goose chase. He declined the invitation to speak to the 'sweet little thing' and her companion since enough time had been spent on this matter. He encouraged his officers to put away their firearms and truncheons and to return to the police vans. He thanked the restaurant manager for his time, apologised for the interruption, then walked around the area for five minutes purely for form's sake before leaving for the station.

"What was all that about?" Artemis asked after the police had left.

"Dunno," Hebe replied. "Nothing to do with us. Come on; let's eat up and go back to the hotel."

After an early supper in their suite, Hebe and Artemis walked out of the Hotel Savoire and turned left towards Charing Cross. They were followed from a distance by a tall young woman with an Afro hairstyle. She was wearing a blue jacket, had a large brown bag over her shoulder, and was talking on her mobile.

"So, we're not to use our goddess powers while in London then?" Artemis enquired as they walked down the stairs into the Underground station.

"Only if there's a real emergency."

"Can I ask why?"

"We're going to act like normal people. It's the only way to experience the real London."

The two took the Bakerloo line to the Elephant and Castle. Coming out of the tube station, they had a ten-minute walk to a pub that Hebe had read about. She'd never been there before, but it had an interesting name, and she thought it would be a good idea to spend their first evening there.

When they arrived at the pub, the two stopped outside with very different reactions.

"You must be joking!" Artemis exclaimed, while Hebe burst out laughing. "Who on earth is that?"

They were both looking at a large picture on the wall of a voluptuous, dark-haired woman wearing a crown who was drinking a pint of beer. Above her were the words The Greek Goddess, being the name of the pub. The same picture was on a large sign hanging over the doorway, the only difference being that someone had drawn a moustache on the one on the wall.

"Let's go in. One of the attractions is they have Hanseatic Headbanger," Hebe said still laughing.

Hanseatic Headbanger was the favourite beer at The Dog and Duck tavern on Mount Olympus. When they got inside, Hebe ordered a pint for Artemis and a half pint for herself.

"Who's the Greek Goddess?" Hebe asked the landlord when she was paying, pointing to a third near identical picture on the wall behind the bar.

"Aphrodite. She's the Goddess of Love," was the reply.

"No way!" Artemis, who was standing next to her sister, exclaimed. "We know Aphrodite. She doesn't look like that at all."

"Oh, you know her, do you?" the landlord said sarcastically. "Have you been somewhere else before coming here?"

"What do you mean?" Artemis demanded.

"She's just joking," Hebe intervened, while giving her sister a 'shut up' look.

"I agree with you," the landlord's wife said, walking over from the far end of the bar where she'd been serving another customer. "I think it's the Goddess Athene!"

"Athene!" exclaimed Artemis, who didn't continue because she'd just received a sharp kick from Hebe.

"Don't tell me you know Athene as well," the landlord said provocatively.

"I'm not sure about Athene," Hebe said reflectively, while now standing on her sister's left foot to indicate she shouldn't get involved in any further discussions on goddesses.

"Of course, our daughter Hollie - she's read a book on Greek mythology and says it's the Goddess Artemis. She's the one who------"

"This is absurd!" Artemis reacted, refusing to keep quiet at the suggestion she looked like the picture on the wall. "Seriously! Do I look like that? Come on – do I?"

Both the landlord and his wife looked at Hebe in the hope of at least receiving a modicum of common sense from her. They were unsure about her companion and thought she'd been drinking heavily beforehand.

"My friend is an archer as you can see from the bow she's carrying." Hebe replied. "She views the Goddess Artemis as her role model so compares herself to her."

"What rubbish! You know….. Ow!" Artemis had just received a painful kick on the ankle which stopped her in full flow.

"Well, who do you think it is?" the landlord's wife asked Hebe.

"Have you ever heard of the Goddess Hebe?" Artemis stepped in to reply, refusing to keep being silenced.

"No. Have you, Sam?"

The landlord shook his head. "She can't be important; some sort of minor goddess."

Hebe coughed and now felt the need to stand up for herself in some small way. "She's actually the daughter of Zeus and his wife, Hera. Top pedigree."

"But what does she do?" the landlady enquired.

"Not a lot," replied Artemis, feeling the need for a bit of retaliation for her sore toes and ankle.

Hebe sighed, deciding it was pointless continuing this conversation. "Thank you," she said to the landlord and his wife as she took up her half pint glass. She then turned to Artemis and suggested they should go and sit at one of the empty tables.

The Greek Goddess slowly filled up over the next half hour. Most of the customers were in their 20's and 30's but soon a couple of elderly ladies came in, ordered two Pinot Grigios and went and sat in a quiet corner, occasionally chatting but also observing proceedings.

As the evening progressed, the pub was increasingly lively. There was a darts board near where Hebe and Artemis were sitting and when it became free the two of them decided to have a game. Artemis had played a lot of darts in the last year since Bacchus had installed a board in the Dog and Duck; Hebe was an occasional player, and it tended to show in her play.

After a few minutes, a group of young men gathered round to watch the game. Hebe, despite being naturally confident and outgoing, was aware of the audience and this was a factor in her frequently missing the board. Artemis meanwhile hit every number she aimed at. When it next came to Hebe's turn, she again missed the board with her first dart.

"You play this game a lot, do you love?" one of the young men asked with sniggers from his friends.

Hebe turned round to him and smiled. "You can tell I don't," she replied. "Unlike my sister here."

"Yea, why don't you two play a game against us?"

"There are four of you and only two of us. How's that going to work?"

"Me and Vince here, we'll play the first game against the two of you, and then Matt and Ricky will take over for the next. I'm Jako by the way. How about it?"

Hebe looked at Artemis who said "yes, alright."

Jako made the introductions. "And what's your names, my lovelies?" he then asked.

"I'm Hebe and this is Arty."

"Hi," said Artemis.

"Hebe!" Jako exclaimed. "Never heard that name before. You're not kidding, are you?"

"No. It's Greek."

"Oh, I like Greek girls," Ricky said with a grin as he came up to Hebe and gave her a little nudge on the shoulder. "You Greek as well, Tarty?" he then asked, looking at Artemis.

"It's Arty, not Tarty. And yes, I also have Greek blood in me."

Ricky turned round to his friends. "We're going to have some fun tonight, lads," he said as he nudged Hebe again.

"Yea, specially if we've got a tart!" Matt responded laughing.

Artemis glared angrily at Hebe who put a finger to her lips to suggest she shouldn't say anything.

"Let's start then. What game are we playing?" Hebe asked.

"I suggest we keep it simple to begin," Jako answered. "Do you know 'Around the Clock'?"

"Yes," Artemis replied.

"Do I?" Hebe asked looking at her sister.

Artemis briefly explained that it consisted of going round the board from 1 to 20 in order, then hitting the bulls-eye. She would throw three darts to begin with, then Jako or Vince. After that Hebe would continue where Artemis had left off and so on. The first team to hit the bulls-eye would be the winner.

"Okay," Hebe said. "And the losing team buys the next round."

"Agreed," said Jako.

The six of them played two games, both of which the goddesses won. Artemis hit every number she was aiming at first time while Hebe only occasionally contributed. However, it was enough to beat the men. Jako and Vince were okay players, but both Ricky and Matt had little if any success. They were also pretty drunk and spent most of the time making sexist remarks, principally directed at Artemis.

After the two games, Jako went off to the bar to get the drinks in. He asked Hebe to accompany him to help carry them back. She agreed but was continuously looking over her shoulder because she didn't like the idea of Artemis being left too long by herself.

"So, where are you staying tonight, Tarty?" Ricky asked.

"In our hotel. And I keep telling you, it's Arty."

"Yea, well, whatever. Anyway, you're going to come back with Matt and me first, eh? We only live five minutes away."

Artemis didn't reply but gave Ricky a disapproving look.

"Don't look at him like that," Matt said laughing. "A girl like you with all that equipment needs to put it to good use. We're offering you a good time with two handsome young men. Come on, Tarty; be a tart with us for an hour or two."

Ricky laughed. "Yea," he said, putting a hand on Artemis's bum and giving it a squeeze.

"Get off!" Artemis shouted and elbowed Ricky in the chest.

"Oh, you want to play it rough, do you?" Matt said as he stood in front of Artemis. He grabbed hold of one of her boobs with one hand while starting to put his other up her T shirt. "Nice big ones like------"

Matt never finished his sentence because Artemis's fist went into his mouth, knocking out lots of teeth with blood pouring everywhere. She then hurled him backwards, so he banged against an adjoining table, pushing a middle-aged couple onto the floor. The man got up, swore at Matt, who was trying to raise himself while holding one hand over his mouth, and punched him on the nose, sending him flying against another table.

By now Ricky had one arm round Artemis's throat and with the other he thumped her in the kidneys. She grimaced with pain but didn't go down. Instead, she elbowed him again but this time so hard that he was forced to double up. She then turned round, grabbed him by an arm and swung him around before letting go and sent him flying against another group of drinkers, knocking one of them over. One of his friends cracked a beer glass on Ricky's head, knocking him out completely.

Meanwhile, Vince who had been quiet most of the evening got involved. He tried to kick away Artemis's legs but wasn't strong enough. She turned round and thumped him in the face as well. By now Hebe had raced over and gave Vince a firm kick in the groin before he'd had time to respond to the punch he'd just received. Jako was also racing over but tripped against a table sending more people flying. Someone got up and threw a beer glass at him but missed. Instead, it hit a woman on the back of the head. Her husband went over to the person who threw the glass and started beating him up. More people got involved, more beer glasses were thrown, and more of the pub's customers got hurt.

At an early stage of the brawl, the landlord called 999 for the police. He'd experienced one of these incidents some years ago and knew it was best not to intervene, but to wait for the authorities to arrive. Instead, he and his wife hid behind the bar where they were safe until a couple of beer glasses shattered the mirrors behind them, although they escaped any injury.

Eventually, there was the sound of sirens and a number of police vans arrived. The pub was soon full of officers wielding their truncheons, although the mere fact of their arrival quickly caused the fighting to come to an end.

"Let's get out of here," Hebe said to Artemis as she pulled her to a side door. As they opened it, they were confronted by two large male officers.

"And where do you think you're going?" one of them asked in an officious tone.

"We're just trying to leave this appalling place," Hebe replied. "We're tourists here."

The same officer shook his head. "I don't think so," he said and pointed back inside.

In a split second, Hebe decided it was better to do as they'd been told. While she was sure Artemis and she could overpower the two police officers, they'd no doubt be subject to a manhunt over the next few days and weeks, which would mean they would have to abort their visit to London.

"Of course, Officer," Hebe replied with a smile. "If you think it will help."

The two elderly ladies sitting in the quiet corner had not been affected by the brawl. Instead, they carried on sipping their Pinot Grigios, as they continued to watch.

6
Getting to Know You

It took Cerberus nearly two hours to get the PorkyPie woman to the Women's Quarters. She spent much of the time screaming and running around in circles which got the two of them precisely nowhere. She was definitely Cerberus's most difficult new arrival in decades, so after a while he decided that special measures were called for. His three heads snapped at her continuously as he attempted to drive her in the right direction. He tore her dress in a few places, but only once gave her a little bite on the skin and that was Audrey who was keen to play a role in the proceedings. Eventually, the two of them reached the Women's Quarters where Mrs No-Messing, the Chief Warden, was waiting for them. She quickly assessed the situation and, being a large lady with plenty of muscle power, took firm hold of the new arrival and propelled her into one of the dormitories that had a free camp bed.

During all this time, Popsy had been following Cerberus and her mistress. When they arrived at the Women's Quarters, the PorkyPie woman called over to Popsy to come to her, but the small dog didn't move. She just stood there looking at the little group before Mrs No-Messing and her new charge had disappeared into the building. Then Popsy was alone with Cerberus who was taking a series of deep breaths as he tried to lower his blood pressure after the last two hours ordeal.

"Woofy, woofy," Popsy went after a few minutes since Cerberus appeared a lot calmer but was doing nothing but mooch around. Her voice was quite soft, and Cerberus gave no indication of having heard her, so she went "woofy, woofy" again, this time more loudly.

Cerberus looked up. "Oh hello," he replied. "Don't worry; I haven't forgotten you. Is the PorkyPie woman always like that – a complete nightmare?"

"When things don't go her way – yes."

"You're not like that as well, are you?"

Popsy shook her head. "I'm really a bit on the shy side," she murmured.

Cerberus nodded, then gave Popsy a good hard look. "You look absolutely shattered," he said. "Come on; we both need a rest. We'll go back to my place."

"Is it far?"

"Ten or fifteen minutes. Would you like to ride on my back?"

Popsy looked bemused. "How would I get up there?" she asked.

Suddenly Cerberus's tail shot round from his back. "I'll lift you up," Audrey said with a smile.

Popsy jumped back in fright.

"Don't be like that. I'm a nice friendly snake. I wouldn't harm anyone."

"I'm sorry," Popsy replied. "It's just that the only snakes I've come across were in America and they were very dangerous. Also, I saw you bite the Marchioness earlier, so it's not true that you wouldn't harm anyone."

Audrey was a bit stumped by Popsy's allegation since it was actually true. However, Cerberus's left head called Lefty came to the rescue.

"That was an exceptional case," Lefty said. "And anyway, she deserved it. I can personally vouch for Audrey being an okay sort of tail. We've never tried to replace Audrey with another one, so that must prove something!"

There was a dead silence for a while after Lefty's statement. Audrey thought it was best to keep quiet while the other two front heads looked at each other, neither entirely convinced by the force of this argument. They were also wondering why Lefty had decided to speak. Normally, it was Middly's job to do the talking, while Righty was the best barker and biter, leaving Lefty to be the principal consumer of Mars bars. Talking was definitely not Lefty's specialty, and he'd have to be reminded of that when they were not in company.

Popsy thought about matters, but finally declined the offer, saying she'd be able to walk for another ten or fifteen minutes.

The two dogs walked along side by side, with Cerberus going slowly so Popsy wouldn't have to run to keep up. Neither of them spoke for a while because they were both deep in thought.

Cerberus was trying to work out what to do with the small dog. He kept mulling over Hades' words about returning Popsy to "where it came from." Then he'd also said, "it shouldn't be here." The last bit was easy to deal with if you viewed 'here' as being Hades' palace. Well, Popsy wasn't in the palace anymore, so Cerberus could give a tick to that part of the instruction. The difficulty arose with the words about where the small dog had come from. Cerberus had a hunch this meant out of the Underworld altogether, but then decided that Hades would never have asked him to take responsibility for that. After all, he'd only ever been out of the Underworld once when he was kidnapped by that 'so-called hero' Hercules, whom Cerberus viewed as nothing but a 'thug'. No, he couldn't be expected to take Popsy there. Also, Death and the ferryman only ever brought people into the Underworld; it simply wasn't part of their job description to take people, let alone little dogs, in the other direction. The more Cerberus thought about it, the more he managed to convince himself that he'd be complying with the god's order if he took Popsy to some place near the river. Since he lived in that direction, he decided he was doing what Hades wanted him to do – at least he'd say that if the god ever told him off!

Popsy's challenge was far greater than Cerberus's. Her life had been turned upside down in the last 24 hours and she had to work out how to handle this new environment she'd been thrust into. She was small and had always been looked after by the Marchioness, as she still called her. It would take her some time to adapt to the Mrs PorkyPie name. She had never been sure if she liked her old mistress; she'd just never known anyone different. However, one thing Popsy had learned from the Marchioness was that it was important to have rich and powerful friends. She didn't need any 'A' levels to realise that her former protector no longer fitted into that category in the Underworld – in fact, it looked as if she'd be at the bottom of the pile for a very long time. So, Popsy had to look elsewhere. From what she'd seen, Hades would fit the bill, but he didn't come over as in the least bit friendly towards her; quite the opposite – he wanted to get rid of Popsy. So, that left Cerberus. She didn't know what to make of a three-headed dog with a snake's tail, but he did seem to be quite important. After all, he was Head of Internal Security; he was also big and strong and was taking her off for a nice rest. In the absence of any other candidates, Popsy decided he was her only option for protection at the present time.

After Cerberus had done his thinking about how to interpret Hades' instructions, he started to feel uncomfortable with Popsy walking at his side. Since Vesta had arrived in the Underworld, his social skills had improved markedly, and he could talk on a range of subjects to lots of people. However, he had never spoken to another dog before and was feeling awkward about what to say. Eventually, he decided he ought to make an effort.

"So, your name's Popsy, is it?" he asked nervously, knowing full well it was.

"Actually, my full name's PopsyFlopsyTopsyWopsy-FluffyTail, but most people call me Popsy for short," the small dog replied.

"I see," Cerberus said pensively. "So, if you don't mind, I'll join the crowd and also call you Popsy."

"I'd rather you didn't."

"Woof! You don't want me to call you PopsyFlopsy and all the rest, do you?"

"No," Popsy replied. "I'd like you to call me Bill."

"Bill!" exclaimed Cerberus. "Where did that name come from – your father?"

"No. I just happen to like the name Bill. Since being in the Underworld is a new start for me, I thought it would be a good time to change my name. I've always wanted to be called Bill, so now's my opportunity."

"But isn't Bill a gentleman dog's name and aren't you a lady dog?"

"Yes, but sometimes it's good to defy convention, don't you think?"

"Umm," was all Cerberus's reply, somewhat perplexed by this short conversation with Popsy, now called Bill. He thought there must be something very strange about the dog population in the world above if lady dogs wanted to be called by gentlemen dogs' names. He wondered if it worked the other way round - if gentlemen dogs with names like Rover and Boxer were keen to be called Annie and Princess instead. It was a mystery, and he'd have to talk to his friend Vesta on the matter.

The two dogs soon arrived at Cerberus's new home which was behind a number of boulders near the river and the jetty. This new home, variously described as a kennel, a hut, a house and a palace, had recently been built for the Head of Internal Security by Budi, the Deputy Head Builder. Although the original specification of twelve ensuite bedrooms and innumerable reception rooms and staff quarters had been pared back to one large room, Cerberus was very pleased with the end product since it was extremely spacious and could easily house three dogs of Cerberus's size.

"You go and have a sleep in that corner, Bill," Cerberus said, nodding with his middle head once the two of them were inside. "I'll have a nap in this one."

"Woofy, woofy," Bill replied followed by a big yawn as she went and lay down where Cerberus had indicated. He also yawned, rolled on his side and was soon dreaming about whether he should change his name to Daisy in the future.

After less than half an hour, Cerberus woke from his power nap. His small companion was already awake and was staring at him.

"Did you sleep?" Cerberus asked.

"Yes; I only woke up a few minutes ago. What happens now?"

Cerberus wasn't sure, so he asked Bill what she'd like to do.

"I'm hungry and thirsty," was the reply.

"Come along then. We'll go to the Kitchens and drink some water, and each have a Mars bar."

"I've never had a Mars bar. Are they made of meat?"

"I don't think so. They're all gooey inside and covered in chocolate."

Bill pulled a face but didn't say anything.

When the two got outside, the small dog yawned again.

"Are you sure you don't want to ride on my back?" Cerberus asked again. "It's another fifteen minutes' walk."

Bill thought about the offer. She was very tired after the day's exertions and didn't really fancy another long walk – fifteen minutes was long for her. However, she was still wary of Audrey and was also concerned that she might fall off Cerberus's back if he made a sudden movement.

Audrey must have been mind-reading because the tail moved over towards Bill and gave her a nice friendly smile. "I promise to be very gentle," the snake's head said and then gave another smile.

The small dog looked at Audrey and then gave a reluctant "woofy, woofy," followed by a slight nod of the head.

"I'll just wrap my body around you," Audrey said getting closer to Bill, "and I'll keep my head away from you."

Bill shuddered as Audrey touched her, but within seconds found herself on Cerberus's back looking straight ahead.

"That wasn't too bad, was it?" Audrey said as the tail unwrapped itself from the small dog.

Bill looked at the smiling snake's head and gave a more enthusiastic "woofy, woofy" this time, as well as a smile back.

"Let's go," Cerberus said as he began to move off.

"Can you walk slowly please," the small dog called out from his back. "I don't want to fall off. It's high for me up here."

"Woof! Wilco!" Cerberus called back.

"Wilco. What does that mean?"

"It's a military term. We use phrases like that in Internal Security."

"I see," Bill said pensively. "But what does it mean?"

"It means will do as requested."

"Well, shouldn't you say wildo instead of wilco?"

"Umm," Cerberus replied. "I'll have to consult my military advisers on that."

"Who are your military advisers?"

"I've got a whole load of them – Julius Caesar, Napoleon, William the Conker."

"Do they all say wilco?"

"I'll tell you when you're formally employed in Internal Security. At the moment, such matters are classified information - subject to the Official Secrets Act."

"What's the Official Secrets Act?"

"That's an Official Secret."

"It all seems very mysterious," Bill replied. "But tell me, Cerberus – is that what's going to happen to me? I'm to stay in the Underworld and be a member of the Internal Security team?"

"Woof! Provided you pass the interview."

"Is it difficult?"

"I don't know. You'll be the first person to take it."

"But what about all these people like William the Conker?"

"They're merely advisers. Not actually formal members of Internal Security."

By now Bill had a hunch Cerberus was the only current member of Internal Security, so she asked him directly. The only answer she got was that membership was an Official Secret which left her none the wiser.

"So, what if I fail the interview - will I be returned to the world upstairs?"

"I think you'll pass. You need to think positively, Bill. Failure shouldn't be an option."

"Then if I do pass, where will I live?"

"Here, with me, I suppose."

"In your hut?"

"Palace," Cerberus corrected her.

"What? Forever?"

"Woof!" was all Cerberus replied.

"That's a long time," Bill murmured.

Cerberus spent the rest of the walk telling Bill about some of the people she would probably meet. The Head Chef who ran the Kitchens was called Aggy, who came from Eskimoland. Aggy was generally viewed as 'a good egg' by people in the Underworld. Cerberus couldn't explain why she was called 'a good egg', but that's how lots of people described her, especially the builders when she dished them out an extra sausage at breakfast-time. Perhaps she should be called 'a good sausage' instead – he would get Vesta's view on the matter.

Vesta was Cerberus's best friend. She worked for Aggy in the Kitchens; was nearly fourteen years' old and in his view was the most intelligent person in the Underworld. She was even more intelligent than Lord Hades, although it was best not to mention that in his presence. Vesta spent a lot of time with Ming who had been in the Underworld for ages. At first, Ming and Cerberus hadn't hit it off, but they were okay now and had recently formalised becoming friends. Vesta had been very helpful in bringing about this reconciliation, having advised Cerberus not to keep threatening to bite her bum if she didn't give him a Mars bar. He'd been a bit sceptical about this advice at first but had to admit that dropping those words from his general conversation had made him more socially acceptable in the Underworld.

Cerberus spent a lot of time talking about all the friends he now had. He explained that only in a few rare instances would he become immediate friends with somebody.

Normally, there was an initial status referred to as 'temporary, associate friends on probation' and then over time the words 'temporary', 'associate' and 'on probation' would be dropped one by one until full friendship was reached. Aggy had been responsible for this approach which she and Cerberus had at first adopted before finally becoming full friends.

Bill listened to all this and became totally confused. However, she decided not to ask any questions since she expected to eventually understand what Cerberus was on about if she was going to live in the Underworld forever.

When they got close to the Kitchens, Cerberus could see through one of the windows that Aggy was in her back room, sorting out various cupboards. He pushed open the door and went "woof, woof."

Aggy turned round and stared at the large black, three-headed dog with a small chihuahua on his back.

"Before you say anything, Cerberus," the Head Chef said, "please wait a minute." She opened one of the doors to the main kitchen area, saw Ming and called to her to find Vesta and Gigliola and then join her in the back room.

"So, what have we here?" she asked, turning round to Cerberus. "A small dog."

"Woof. This is Bill," Cerberus replied. "She's just arrived."

Aggy bent down to look at Bill whom Audrey had now taken off Cerberus's back.

"Woofy, woofy," Bill whimpered nervously.

Aggy smiled. "Hello, Bill," she said. "My name's Aggy. May I lift you up, my dear?"

Bill looked in Aggy's eyes, decided she liked her smiling face, so went "woofy, woofy," again and nodded her head.

Aggy gently raised Bill from the ground and held her to her chest, having had a quick look underneath.

"Bill's an unusual name for a girl dog," she said. "It's more of a boy dog's name."

"I'm actually a lady dog," replied Bill.

"Of course you are. I should have realised. So, you've always been called Bill, have you?"

"No. I used to be called PopsyFlopsyTopsyWopsyFluffyTail or Popsy for short. But now I've arrived in the Underworld, I've decided to be called Bill instead. I've always wanted to be called Bill."

"Have you ever thought of being called Billie?" Aggy asked. "It's a bit more ladylike than Bill."

Bill looked at Aggy, thought very hard for a few seconds and then gave another "woofy, woofy" and said she liked that idea.

"So, we'll call you Billie from now on – that's alright, is it?"

Just as Billie was giving a nod of her head, Cerberus decided to get involved in the discussion. "Woof, woof!" he barked. "Aggy, can we each have a Mars bar, please. Bill's very hungry."

"She's called Billie now, Cerberus," Aggy replied.

"Woofy, woofy. I'm also very thirsty."

"Then let's get a nice bowl of water for you. I'll just put you on the table and bring it over to you."

"And a couple of Mars bars," Cerberus added.

"Have you ever had a Mars bar, Billie?" Aggy asked.

"No."

"Wouldn't you like a nice plate of chopped meat or even mince instead? You can always try a Mars bar later."

"Woofy, woofy!" was the enthusiastic response.

A few minutes later Cerberus was eating his Mars bar while Billie was drinking from a large bowl of water before starting on a plate of mince. There was a quick tap at the door and Vesta and Ming walked in without waiting for a reply.

"I couldn't find Gigliola," said Ming before stopping dead in her tracks as she stared at the table.

"What a lovely little dog!" Vesta exclaimed, moving over to Billie, picking her up and cuddling her while giving her a big smile. "Hello," she said. "I'm Vesta. Who are you?"

Before Billie had a chance to reply, Ming also came over and started stroking her. "And I'm Ming," she said.

"Woofy, woofy," went the small dog, enjoying all this attention.

"This is Billie," Aggy interrupted. "And she's a very thirsty and hungry little dog, so I suggest you girls put her down and let her finish her meal. We can have a good chat afterwards."

"Woof, woof!" Cerberus barked. "Billie's a friend of mine."

Aggy moved over to the girls, took the small dog from them and put her back on the table. "Now you just eat away, Billie," she said. "You can get to know the two girls later."

"But---" said Vesta.

"No buts," Aggy interrupted her. "In fact, Vesta, what I want you to do is go off with Cerberus to show him that security matter in the Potatoes section, while Ming and I stay here with Billie and make sure she's properly fed."

"What security issue?"

Aggy stared at her very hard without blinking. "You've forgotten," the Head Chef eventually said. "It's the one by the window. Go and show Cerberus and the two of you can also chat about how he's got to know Billie."

"What's all this security issue about?" Cerberus asked. "As Head of Internal Security, I should have been told about this immediately."

By now Ming was gesturing to Vesta to take Cerberus away. All of a sudden, the penny dropped with the most intelligent person in the Underworld. This was all an excuse to go and get Cerberus's version of how Billie had got into the Underworld.

"Oh, that security issue!" she exclaimed. "Of course, I now remember. Come on, Cerberus; it's important."

"But why wasn't I told about it before? And what about you, Billie? Will you be alright?"

"You're being told about it now, and Billie will be fine," Aggy replied forcibly. "Here's another Mars bar and when you come back, you can collect Billie."

"And another Mars bar?"

"Possibly," the Head Chef conceded as she proceeded to shoo Cerberus and Vesta out of the room.

•

Gigliola returned with Vesta and Cerberus. She was Aggy's number two, being a small blonde Sicilian lady who used to run a restaurant in Palermo. She'd heard enough of the conversation between her two companions to understand what was going on, but once she was in the back room, like the other girls, she spent a few minutes cuddling Billie and getting to know her.

By now the small dog was no longer hungry, so Aggy suggested that she and Cerberus should go off and come back and see them all tomorrow.

"Has Billie tried a Mars bar yet?" Cerberus asked as they were leaving.

"That's for tomorrow," Aggy replied as she closed the door after the two dogs. She then walked over to the table, sat down and motioned to the others to follow suit. "So, where do we begin?" she asked.

The Kitchens team looked at each other, but none of them replied.

"Well, I suppose we all know how Billie got here with the Marchioness," the Head Chef said, answering her own question.

"I think we're meant to call her Mrs PorkyPie," Vesta replied. "At least that's what Hades said."

"But should she be in the Underworld?" Gigliola asked. "And is she dead or alive?"

"I think she's alive; at least that's the impression I got," said Aggy.

"I agree," Ming added.

"As for what she's doing here, well it's pretty obvious it's all a big mistake. She shouldn't be here," Aggy continued.

"But now she is here, presumably she can stay? She's so cute," Vesta said.

"I think it would be good to have a little dog around the place," agreed Ming.

"So do I. Perhaps she could become Cerberus's girlfriend," Gigliola joked.

"That would be nice," Ming said.

"Perhaps they could get married, and we could have a big wedding?"

"I think you're being mischievous," was all Aggy could say.

"If they got married, could they have children?" asked Ming.

"Why not? I wonder if mating a three-headed dog and a one-headed dog would result in a baby dog with two-heads," Gigliola said with a laugh.

"Or perhaps a dog with one very large head," Ming speculated.

"Or maybe just three small heads," Vesta added as she and Ming also laughed.

"I think Billie would have a size problem, carrying Cerberus's child. It's likely to be about twenty times bigger than her," Aggy said, unable to resist participating in the conversation about a possible love match between the Head of Internal Security and Billie.

"That would be a big problem," Gigliola agreed with a slight snigger. "Perhaps we should ask Lady Aphrodite to come and advise on how to deal with it."

"Maybe so," Aggy replied. "But there's a more serious problem we have to address first and that's Lord Hades. I just don't think he will agree to Billie staying here, especially if she's still alive. He'll want her returned to the outside world."

"But she's not doing any harm," Ming said. "And now she's here, why won't he let her stay?"

"I don't think he will. Our only hope is Persephone. If she takes to Billie, then she might be able to persuade Hades to let her remain."

"When's Persephone due back?" Vesta asked.

"In the next week or two. If we want to keep Billie in the Underworld, we need to keep her out of Hades' way until she returns. It's our only chance."

"I agree," Vesta said. "I'll speak to Cerberus tomorrow and tell him to keep quiet about Billie whenever he's with Hades."

"He needs to avoid him as much as possible in the next few days, so our beloved god doesn't have the opportunity to ask what he's done about Billie."

"I'll tell him that as well," Vesta concurred.

"Good. Now let's all get back to work," said Aggy as she turned round to continue sorting out her cupboards.

7
A Long Night

Hebe and Artemis sat next to each other in the police station interview room. Their handcuffs had been removed and their possessions were on a small table in a corner of the room. Opposite them was a burly male police sergeant in his mid-40's, together with a small, young female officer looking distinctly nervous.

"Right," said the sergeant. "You've been told your rights, and you don't want a solicitor. Is that correct?"

"Yes," replied Hebe.

"Very well then," continued the sergeant. "This whole interview is being recorded. Are you alright with that?"

"What if we say no?" Artemis responded at the cost of a questioning frown from her sister, since the two of them had agreed Hebe would do most of the talking when they had been waiting in the cells.

"We'll still record the interview."

"Pretty pointless asking us then," Artemis muttered with a shrug of her shoulders.

The sergeant ignored her comment and continued: "Start of interview at 2-05 am, Tuesday 21 May. For your information ladies, I am Sergeant Dufflecoat and this is Constable Cake. The constable is a new graduate recruit to the force, this being her first week as a uniformed officer. She has a degree in Psychology from Durham University. Is that correct, Constable?"

Constable Cake squeaked an almost inaudible "yes," before starting to blush.

Hebe smiled at her. "Your first name isn't Angel, is it?" she asked.

"No, that's me sister," the constable replied, now smiling herself. "I'm called Cherry."

"I bet you've got a brother called Carrot," Hebe said flippantly.

"I have actually. How did ye know?"

Sergeant Dufflecoat gave a cough. "Perhaps we can continue," he said. "Now, can I please have the names of the two of you?"

"I am Lady Hebe Olympiakos, and this is my sister, Lady Artemis Olympiakos."

"Funny; funny; ha, ha. Ha, ha; funny," went the sergeant, sitting back in his chair. "And I'm the King of Siam."

There was dead silence in the room, even Constable Cake unable to muster the slightest of sniggers.

"What's funny?" Hebe asked after a lengthy silence.

"Come on. Stop messing around. Give me your real names," the sergeant responded.

"Those are our real names."

"I don't believe you. For a start, with a surname like Olympiakos, you must be foreign. If you're foreign, you can't be a lady; you can be a countess but not a lady. Only British people can be a lady." The sergeant said this so emphatically that he finished by folding his arms, looking smugly across the table as if to say, "got you."

"You're quite right, Sergeant," Hebe replied calmly. "But we both hold dual nationality, being half British."

Sergeant Dufflecoat's face lost much of its smugness and his mouth gave a small twitch. "Huh!" he responded before continuing on a different tack. "Well, you're clearly not sisters. Just look at you – one of you is tall and dark-haired and the other's small and blonde. No way are you sisters. No way!"

"Yes, we are. Same father but different mothers. Call us half-sisters if you like but we view each other as being proper sisters."

After a short silence, the sergeant went "huh" again before continuing: "I don't believe any of this. Can you prove who you are? Where are you staying for a start? What's your address?"

"We're at the Hotel Savoire in the Strand. We arrived this morning."

"So, if I phone the hotel up, they'll confirm this, will they?"

"I would expect so," Hebe replied.

"Right, I will. What's more, I'll do it here in front of you." The sergeant looked at his colleague before continuing: "Constable, could you please go to the small table where there's a telephone and get the Hotel Savoire on the line. Then hand the phone to me."

Cherry Cake got up, wondering how to get the hotel's number. The police station's operator had gone home at 9pm and Cherry didn't know how to use Directory Enquiries. After fumbling around for a few minutes, she pulled out her mobile and googled the hotel to find the number. She then dialed it on the station's landline before handing it to the sergeant.

"Hotel Savoire, could you please confirm that you have a …… Very well, I'll hold…… Good evening, Night Manager. This is Sergeant Dufflecoat of the Metropolitan Police, South London Section. I'd like to speak to you about two people who claim they're staying at the Hotel Savoire …. I'll give you their names obviously, but I'm unable to disclose why I'm phoning you ……. I recognize you can't talk about your guests for confidentiality reasons, but all I wish to do is confirm certain facts…… Again, I can't tell you why I'm phoning, but this is important police business. Perhaps you would just let me ask a few questions and you can decide if you're able to answer them? ……. Very well, thank you. My first question is – do you have a Lady Hebe Olympiakos and a Lady Artemis Olympiakos staying with you at present? …… You do, thank you. My second question is – are they in the hotel at the present time? …… Yes, I'll hold on …… That's helpful; you've just checked with the front staff, and they were seen to go out about 7pm and no one has seen them return……. Could you please------- ……. I understand that you're not prepared to phone their room at this time, but you're pretty sure they're not back yet…… Next, can you or someone describe them to me please? …. What do I mean? Well, if I were to say that one of them's a small blonde, a bit lippy if you know what I mean; the other's a tall brunette, a bit surly.......... Yes, yes; I'm sorry. I didn't mean to say anything offensive, Mr Night Manager. Perhaps you could just respond to the physical aspects of my description. ...... Yes, I'll hold on ...... Thank you; having spoken to your staff, you can confirm that the size and hair colours of the two guests are as I described. ...... No, no. They're all my questions for the time being. Can you give me your name please? ...... Thank you, and to repeat, I am Sergeant Dufflecoat of the Metropolitan Police, South London Section...... Also, thank you for informing me that you've taped this telephone call and will be playing it to the hotel's General Manager and Director tomorrow morning. ..... Yes, yes. Well, perhaps if you could please apologise to them for my description of your two guests; possibly indicating it was a slip of the tongue in the early hours of the morning....... What was that?....... No, I've not been drinking...... A final point?....... You've just had a note passed to you that there's a message for Lady Hebe from the Palace asking her to contact them in the morning.... Yes, I'll pass it on. .... Thank you. Good night to you as well."

The sergeant handed the phone to Constable Cake who returned it to the small table.

"Everything tickety-boo?" enquired Hebe, trying to suppress a smile, as she stood up. "Can we go home now?"

The sergeant frowned and looked perplexed, his mouth twitching once more. Before he could say anything, Artemis had also stood up and said in an angry voice: "I resent being referred to as surly. And you should feel the same about being called lippy, Hebe."

At this point Artemis got a gentle kick under the table from her sister, who felt the best way of handling Sergeant Dufflecoat was to down-play the incident."

"Well, I am a bit lippy," Hebe said with a smile. "And this evening, Arty, you have been behaving slightly surly. Anyway, let's go home now."

"Just hold on, ladies," the sergeant said, coming back to life. "We've still got a lot more questions to be answered."

"Oh, Sergeant, how long's this going to go on for?" Hebe replied with a sigh.

"Please sit down, Lady Hebe and Lady Artemis, and we'll try and speed matters up now we've been able to verify your identities."

Hebe moaned and grumbled but sat down once more as did Artemis.

"Right," said Sergeant Dufflecoat when everyone had settled down again. "The next item I want to cover is the fact that you are in possession of an offensive weapon."

"What weapon?" Hebe demanded.

"It's in the corner on the table. Your bow and arrows."

"What's offensive about them?" Artemis asked, still angry at being called surly. "They're my bow and arrows and I want to know what right you have to call them offensive. I think they're magnificent and if they offend you in some way, then that's your problem, Mr Policeman!"

"Lady Artemis, let me explain to you how the law defines an 'offensive weapon' in this country. To begin with-------"

"Hold on, Sergeant Dufflecoat," Hebe interrupted. "Do you actually know who my sister is in the world of archery?"

"What do you mean? Not that it should make any difference as far as the law is concerned."

"I think you should know this. It's easiest if I show you on my mobile."

Hebe began to get up but was forestalled by the sergeant. "Please sit down, Lady Hebe. Constable Cake will bring it over to you."

When the mobile had been inspected by Sergeant Dufflecoat and handed over to Hebe, she leant across the table, so the two police officers could see what she was doing. After having accessed various websites, she came to the one she was looking for. During all this time, she was concentrating very hard, and her brain was moving at super-goddess speed as she created a Times of London newspaper article in a matter of seconds. Meanwhile, Artemis just sat there looking perplexed but realising she should say nothing since she didn't know what Hebe was up to.

"There we are," said Hebe. "Read this article about Lady Artemis Olympiakos being a double Olympic and three times World Champion in archery. Also, look at the last paragraph where she explains that she always carries around her favourite bow, together with its arrows, whenever she travels abroad. This was because her last bow was stolen from a five-star hotel in Paris some years ago and she only won silver in her next competition because she had to use a replacement bow. Isn't that right, Arty?" Hebe finished by looking at her sister, at the same time giving her a gentle kick under the table.

"Yes," was all Artemis replied, learning for the first time about having been both an Olympic and World Champion.

Both the police officers read the article twice and then looked at each other. Eventually the sergeant went "huh!" once more as his mouth demonstrated an elaborate array of new twitches.

"I'm not actually sure that disproves anything about being in possession of an offensive weapon," Sergeant Dufflecoat eventually said, somewhat uncertainly.

"It's not offensive!" Artemis retorted aggressively. "If you think it is, then you've clearly got a big personal problem! Don't blame my bow!"

The sergeant gave a little cough. "I was going to say that we should park that issue for the time being and get into the crux of what happened in The Greek Goddess earlier this evening. We've got the account from Sam Slipper, the manager, but haven't yet been able to interview the eleven people currently in A&E whom Sam informs us you both assaulted. What----"

"We assaulted!" exclaimed Hebe. "We were the ones being assaulted! I don't know what cock and bull story you've been told by that Slippery Sam, but it's a load of cobblers!"

"I was about to ask, Lady Hebe, if you and your sister could please tell us your version of events."

Hebe and Artemis looked at each other, the latter giving her smaller sister a nod to indicate she should do the talking – at least initially. Then Hebe set off in an uninterrupted rant which lasted precisely eight minutes, forty-three seconds.

At the heart of Hebe's rant was that she and Artemis were two young women who had just arrived in London. They had read an article about this area of South London being safe and had decided to go off and have a drink in one of the local pubs. While there, they started to play a game of darts. Unfortunately, there were a number of young men in the pub who were clearly drunk and who tried to involve themselves in the darts game. Not only that, but they started touching the two innocent young arrivals to the capital and, despite being rebuffed, this developed into groping – especially with regard to Artemis's bum. This resulted in some of the most tactile gropers being pushed away; they fell against various people and knocked over a table with a load of drinks on it. At that stage other people in the pub got involved and a general brawl took place before the police arrived together with ambulances for the injured.

"So," Hebe finished off. "We were assaulted because the pubs in your district are clearly not safe for young women. What's more, that Slippery Sam chap seemed to be friends with the gang that attacked us. I assume, Sergeant, you're looking into the distribution of drugs that appeared to be taking place quite openly in the bar area, which he seems to turn a blind eye to?" Hebe decided to invent this matter of drugs because she wanted to 'stir the pot'.

"Drugs!" exclaimed Sergeant Dufflecoat. "We've never heard of any drug transactions in The Greek Goddess!"

"Well, maybe some complacency's been allowed to set in. Not by you, Sergeant, but possibly by your fellow officers. Anyway, it may not matter because I assume the pub's licence will be revoked; it being the centre for assaulting young females in the area."

Sergeant Dufflecoat's mouth was twitching at full speed at the end of Hebe's statement. He was busy gathering his thoughts as to how to respond to this statement, which was in direct contradiction to Sam Slipper's account, when Hebe piped up again.

"And what's more, Sergeant," she said: "Do you really believe two weak young girls like us could assault a bunch of big tough young men, so they end up in A&E? It's just not credible! What do you think, Cherry?" She specifically looked at the young constable when asking this final question.

Cherry blushed and muttered "no" before putting her hand to her mouth as she realised she shouldn't have said that. Just as Sergeant Dufflecoat was giving her a disapproving look, there was a knock at the door and another constable came in and whispered in the sergeant's ear.

"Will you please excuse me," Sergeant Dufflecoat said, standing up after he'd heard the message. "I have to take an urgent call relating to this case. Constable Parrot will remain here with Constable Cake until I return. I only expect to be a few minutes."

Forty-five minutes later, the sergeant returned, his mouth twitching incessantly.

"Very well, Lady Hebe and Lady Artemis. That will be all for now. You can pick up your possessions on the table and leave. Thank you for your assistance. There will be no charges at this stage and, if we need to speak to you again, we'll contact you at the Hotel Savoire."

"Why? What's happened?" Hebe asked with a big smile on her face.

"Constable Parrot will show you out," was the only reply she received, with the sergeant doing his best not to look at either of the sisters since he was unable to control his twitching. "Constable Cake; can you please remain here."

Hebe and Artemis speedily picked up their possessions with the former calling out "toodle-pip" in a cheery voice as she left the room. Artemis expressed the hope that Sergeant Dufflecoat would soon be able to get treatment for his hang-up about bows and arrows before following her sister out of the door.

The sergeant sat silently for a while, his mouth still twitching, before he was able to speak. "Cherry," he eventually said wearily. "You're new to the force. Let me tell you what that call was about......"

Sergeant Dufflecoat explained in some detail that he'd been phoned by one of the Assistant Commissioners, who had just received a call in the middle of the night from the Commissioner. Apparently in The Greek Goddess that evening were two elderly ladies who had witnessed the whole affair. They were not involved in the brawl and had left before they could be interviewed. Unfortunately, one of them used to work for the wife of a former Cabinet Minister with whom she was still on friendly terms. For some reason she immediately contacted this person, a titled lady, and told her about what happened. The titled lady herself made a series of telephone calls alleging that two female visitors to the capital were assaulted by a vicious gang in one of the pubs in the force's patch: there being no effective policing in the area. The result was that the Commissioner himself was woken up at home to speak to the Home Secretary, the Mayor, the Palace and at least two major newspapers who were currently sending an army of reporters hot foot over to the station to get the story. He also had the Chairman of the pub chain confirming that he did not want any prosecutions brought since the costs of smashing up the pub were being covered by an anonymous donor. In view of what is likely to be a PR disaster there was a very strong suggestion that Lady Hebe and Lady Artemis should be immediately released without charge.

"So, what I'm trying to say, Cherry," the sergeant said at the end of this explanation: "Is that whatever the law says, you'll find there's 'One Rule for Us and One Rule for Them'."

Cherry sat there, unsure what to reply before giving a slight giggle and saying: "Ye mean Lady Hebe and Lady Artemis are Tories?"

"Huh," went Sergeant Dufflecoat getting up, his twitch having died down by now. "Let's go and meet the press."

●

As Hebe and Artemis walked down the steps of the police station, they were flashed by a taxi's headlights as it drew up. The taxi had the words OCTAVIAN STEGOSAURAS written on its side in large white capital letters.

"Looking for a ride home, luvs?" a voice asked through the open window.

Hebe looked at the cabbie who was a very elderly man with curly white hair, a bushy beard and moustache. "Why not?" she replied.

"Get in ….. Wot's that big stick thing?" he asked looking at Artemis's bow.

"It's a bow," Artemis replied.

"Wot's that?"

"It's for shooting arrows with."

"Cor blimey, one of them things; I know. If you can't get it all in, just stick the end bit out of a window. Not a lot of traffic around at this time of night."

When the two goddesses had got in with a small part of Artemis's bow sticking out of a back window, they set off.

"Where we going?"

"Hotel Savoire," Hebe replied.

"Wot, that place down the Strand? You want me to go to the maid's entrance at the back?"

"We're not maids. We're guests."

"Pardonnez moi! Top nobs, are we? Or should I say, top nobesses?"

Hebe laughed and nudged her sister to give a little smile. "Something like that," she said.

"Been with Sergeant Dufflecoat, have you?"

"We have. You know him?"

"Do I know him? Do I know him? Knew his grandfather and father, didn't I? All coppers in the family. All the same - the Dufflecoats are wot you call yer real and actual...." He paused, trying to find the right words before continuing. "Yea well, yer real and actual right ones, if you know wot I mean."

"Sort of."

"Funny lot, them Dufflecoats. In the real olden days, they were all villains. Yea, right villains, they were. One of them got to be in the last batch hanged at Tyburn; father and uncle before him. Must have had a big family conflab afterwards, I reckon. Decided this villain stuff always ending up with a rope around yer neck weren't a good idea, didn't they? Much better to catch the baduns than being one of them is what they agreed, so they all became coppers instead. That's wot I thinks happened."

"You're probably right," Hebe replied with a yawn, suddenly feeling tired.

"Anyways, wot you seeing Dufflecoat for, miss? Bit of the old Brahms and Liszt, if you don't mind me asking?"

"There was a fight in a pub, and we had to give statements."

"Plenty of that around. It's why I always waits outside the Old Bill's in the early hours, isn't it? Lots of people coming out about now wanting to go home. Good business, you know."

Hebe nodded and looked out of the window as they went over the Thames. "Tell me," she continued after a few minutes: "What's this thing Octavian Stegosauras you're advertising on your cab door? Is it a new film or something like that?"

"Ha!" was the response, together with a laugh. "That's a good un, miss. No, that's me name, isn't it?"

"What! You're called Octavian Stegosauras!" Hebe replied surprised. "That's an unusual name, if you don't mind me saying so. There can't be many Stegosauras's around."

"Not too many Octavian's neither, but that's the real and actual name I got given when I got born. Named after some Roman geezer, you know."

"Yes, he became emperor."

"There you go then. Good name to have, even if I only got as far as being a cabbie. Anyways, I'm quite happy, so no complaints, eh."

"But what about the Stegosaurus bit of your name."

"That's only me name for this year, you see. Last year I were called Rumpelstiltskin, weren't I? The year before I were Grasshopper, but I reckon the best name I ever had were Thatcher. I liked that name; same as that woman Boss Lady who sorted us all out. Tough cookie, she were, but she got respect. Cor blimey, did we not 'arf respect her."

"So, you change your name every year, do you? Can I ask, why?"

"Every year. First of January on the dot. Keeps me young; that's why I does it. Yea, that's why."

"Is it easy to do?"

"Yea. Piece of cake once you've done it as many times as I have. Not easy to change yer date of birth though. In fact, bloody impossible, it is. I've been trying to change mine for years but can't find no way of doing it. Not even the top lawyer nobs can sort it for me, can they? Last one I spoke to told me to piss off cos I were wasting his time. Not very professional, not professional at all, I say."

"Why do you want to change your date of birth?" Hebe enquired.

"Cos, I'm due to be the big three figures in a few months. Licensing authorities are always trying to withdraw my cab licence but can't find no excuse. Every test they give me, I pass which keeps giving them the 'ump, don't it? Anyways, I hear they're about to introduce some rule about not being allowed a licence after you're 100. They're doing it just for me I thinks, so I'm looking to be ten years younger, ain't I? They're yer real and actual right proper bastards them licencing people. That's my considered opinion, that is."

"What will you do if you're not able to make the change?"

"Nothing. I'll just carry on, won't I?"

"Presumably you'll be fined?"

"So wot? I won't pay it and, even if I had to, I'd just have to work longer hours to get the money. So, it'll work against them, it will. Bloody stupid really."

Hebe smiled, yawned again and joined Artemis who had dozed off several minutes ago. A short while later, the two of them suddenly woke up as a large bang was heard from the back of the cab.

"Don't worry about that, girls," Octavian said. "Just the exhaust having a bit of a strop. Does that sometimes, don't it?"

"I see you're not into electric cars then," Hebe replied.

"Not me. I've got these two nieces who've convinced me about this climate change thing. But wot I think is all these governments, they're just going about it the wrong way, that's wot I think. Instead of making us all drive around electric, they ought to stop people having children. It's all us people that is causing this climate change. If there were no people, problem solved. See wot I mean?"

"That's a bit drastic, don't you think?" Hebe replied.

"Not really. No reason why we humans should keep being top dogs in this world, in my 'umble opinion. It all started with them dinosaurs, didn't it? Then they got wiped out by that big rock thing from outer space. So, wot happens but the apes took over. Something must have happened to them because we humans knocked them off their perch. Don't know wot, maybe we could speak Latin or wotever and they couldn't. Anyways, one day some other animal will become world boss instead of us. Bound to happen. That's electrocution, ain't it?"

"Evolution, you mean."

"Yea, that's the word - evolution. The world works by evolution, don't it? After us humans, I reckon the aardvarks are going to take over. Yea, them aardvarks will be the bosses."

"Aardvarks!" exclaimed Artemis, getting involved in the conversation for the first time. "Why aardvarks?"

"Very impressed with aardvarks, I am. Saw a telly programme some years back on the aardvark. I knew afterwards they were the future. Did you know they eat ants? Very useful that. One summer I had millions of ants in my kitchen, didn't I? Couldn't get rid of the little buggers. Went to this pet shop in Mile End to try and buy an aardvark as a pet. Didn't have none. Got offered a hamster or a rabbit instead; even a budgie but said nah to all of them. Had to go to my two nieces, didn't I? They know how to look on these computer things, but they couldn't find me an aardvark to buy. I even went to the BBC head office to see if I could talk to that feller who made the aardvark programme; thought he might be able to help. He weren't in, so I left me number, but he never got back, did he? Anyways, the ants eventually went away when it got cold and never came back, so I didn't need an aardvark then. Still, didn't stop me thinking they were the future like. Yea, them aardvarks will be running the world soon..... Hold on; here we are," Octavian said as he turned into the Hotel Savoire's driveway."

"Thank you," Hebe said as the taxi came to a stop outside the main entrance. "How much do we owe you?"

Octavian paused before replying. "Sorry, luv. Forgot to turn the meter on. Would £25 be alright with you, it being late at night and all?"

"Sounds very reasonable," Hebe replied, handing over £30. "That includes a tip."

"Cor blimey; very generous, miss," Octavian said, getting out of the cab to open the back door. "How long you two staying here, cos if you needs me again, here's me card. I do know how to use a mobile, you know. Very modern bloke for an oldun."

Hebe smiled and took the card which Octavian handed her. "Thank you. Only a couple of days; we leave on Thursday."

"Do you want a lift to the airport?"

"No; we're staying in London for a number of weeks. We're renting a flat in Pimlico, so we'll be moving there. How about you picking us up an 10 o'clock on Thursday morning? We'll have checked out by then."

"Pimlico, eh. That's where one of me nieces lives. Wot's the address?"

"It's in Alderney Street."

"I know it well. Right, I'll be 'ere at 10 on the dot Thursday morning. Wot's yer names in case I get meself asked when I drive up?"

"I'm Lady Hebe Olympiakos and this is my sister, Lady Artemis Olympiakos."

"Bloody hell! Cor blimey! Two proper ladies!" Octavian exclaimed as Hebe nodded. "Not just top nobesses, but top, top nobesses! Blimey!"

The two nobesses had by now got out of the cab, Artemis firmly holding her bow.

"Got everything?" Octavian asked.

"Yes, thanks. Bye Octavian," Hebe replied as she turned round to go into the hotel.

"Bye Octavian," Artemis also said as she followed her sister. "See you on Thursday."

"Bye ladies," Octavian replied as he got into his cab and started driving away. "They're top, top nobesses," he said to himself as he turned right into the Strand. "Yea, yer real and actual top, top nobesses. Blimey! Good lookers too!"

8
Pongo

Billie woke up very early the next day. She hadn't slept well and was in a particularly unsettled mood. She looked at Cerberus who was still fast asleep and wondered what to do. After a few minutes she decided to get up and go outside. The Underworld was quiet as no one seemed to be up and about yet. Billie was pretty sure she could remember the way to the Kitchens, so she set off in that direction.

When she arrived, she could see Aggy through the window of her back room. She tried to push the door open but wasn't strong enough. She stood back and barked "woofy, woofy" a few times. Aggy clearly couldn't hear her since she didn't respond, so Billie kept woofing. A few minutes later, the Head Chef looked out of the window, saw Billie and immediately went over to the door and opened it for the little dog to come in.

"Hello, Billie. You're up early," she said.

"Yes. I couldn't sleep well."

"Have you come for breakfast?"

"That would be nice, but can I have a bath first please?"

"A bath," Aggy replied uncertainly. "Why yes, I suppose so. Is there any reason?"

"I always have a bath in the morning. Is it going to be a problem?"

"Why no; not at all. Let me get a large bowl and heat the water up over the fire I've just got going."

As Aggy was preparing Billie's bath, the small dog moved near the fire to warm herself.

"So, you didn't sleep well," Aggy said. "I suppose that's because everything's new here."

"In part," was the reply. "But sleeping in the same room as Cerberus wasn't easy."

"What! He didn't do anything he shouldn't have done, did he?" the Head Chef asked, quite alarmed.

Billie shook her head. "Oh no; it wasn't his fault. I suppose it's because I've never slept in the same room as another dog before."

"So, what happened?"

"Well, for a start, he snores so loudly; it's really difficult to get to sleep. Then Audrey kept moving around, so when I did manage to get to sleep, I got woken up by the tail hitting me – it was all accidental but ….. you know what I mean."

"Yes, I can see that would be a problem. Anything else?"

Billie frowned but didn't say anything.

"Go on," Aggy said. "I can see something else happened."

"Well…. not really happened," Billie replied reluctantly. "It's just….. Oh, I don't know how to put this without it sounding all wrong, but …..but has Cerberus ever had a bath?"

"I really don't know," Aggy replied, flummoxed by Billie's question. "Can you tell me why you're asking, my dear?"

"It's just that he pongs a lot. I didn't notice it when we were out and about yesterday, but spending the night with him in a room, I couldn't help being aware of his pong. It's really not very nice."

"Morning Aggy," Vesta said as she walked into the back room from the main Kitchens area. She then saw Billie before continuing: "Oh, hello Billie. Is Cerberus here as well?"

"Billie's come by herself," Aggy replied. "She's going to have a nice bath and then have breakfast."

"A bath!"

"Yes; Billie has a bath every morning."

"That's cool!"

"She was asking if Cerberus has a bath from time to time. I'm afraid I don't know. Have you any idea?"

"I don't have a clue. Why?"

"Because he pongs," was Aggy's blunt reply.

"Woofy, woofy. Have you ever noticed it?" Billie now asked.

"No; not really. I suppose we're just used to him."

"Vesta and I have also never spent a night with him in his hut," Aggy added.

"True," Vesta agreed. "Tell me Billie; do we humans also pong to you?"

"No; not really. You're just like the humans in the living world."

"That's probably because we have baths and showers in our sleeping quarters," Aggy said. "But I don't think Cerberus has any arrangements, so I don't know what he does."

"I suspect he doesn't do anything. He's probably never had a bath in his life."

"He might have gone into the river from time to time in the past. But he won't now because of the piranha fish in there."

"So, what are we going to do?" Vesta asked.

"I'm thinking," Aggy replied. She put her fingers into the water, decided it was a nice warm temperature, so took the bowl off the fire and carried it to the table. "Come on, Billie," she said, lifting the small dog up and gently placing her in the bath. "Is that alright or is it a bit too hot or cold."

"Woofy; woofy!" Billie went enthusiastically. "It's perfect. Have you any soap?"

"Here," Aggy replied as she took a bottle of liquid soap from one of her cupboards and began to wash Billie with a sponge.

After a few minutes, the small dog felt totally clean, so she was left to have an enjoyable wallow in the water. Aggy and Vesta went into a corner and had a quiet chat. When they'd finished, Vesta shot out of the door to the Kitchens and the Head Chef returned to see how Billie was getting on.

A few minutes later, Vesta was seen heading off towards Cerberus's hut. Before she got there, she heard loud barking from the jetty.

"What's going on?" she called to Cerberus who was frantically running backwards and forwards over the jetty "woof, woofing" away, while also shouting at the piranha fish in the water.

Cerberus looked up. "Billie's disappeared!" he replied loudly. "I think she might have fallen into the river."

"Don't worry," Vesta replied. "She's with Aggy."

"Aggy! What's she doing there?"

"When I left, she was having a bath. She's probably having breakfast now."

"A bath!" Cerberus exclaimed. "Why's she doing that?"

"It's what lady dogs do."

"How very extraordinary. But why?"

"So they don't pong."

"Really! I didn't know that. Is that why you humans have showers and baths in your dormitories?"

"Of course."

"But men also have them as well. Why's that?"

"Well, everyone pongs, so it's important to keep clean. What do you do, Cerberus? Where do you have a bath?"

"I don't!" he replied somewhat haughtily. "I don't pong, so I don't need a bath."

"How do you know?"

"I've never been aware of any pong from me. That's how."

"But normally people can't smell their own pong."

"That may be so for people and lady dogs, but I'm a gentleman dog. I don't pong!" was the emphatic reply.

Vesta shrugged, unwilling to debate the matter further at this stage.

"Woof, woof!" Cerberus barked. "Let's go and see Billie and have breakfast as well. I could do with a Mars bar."

"Fine," replied Vesta as she set off with Cerberus. "But let's go slowly. We need to discuss something important and

Aggy and Billie need to have their own 'girly chat' without us around."

"A 'girly chat' - what's that?"

"A chat on girly matters."

"Woof! What are they?"

"Things which we girls discuss."

"Like what?"

"I can't tell you. They're private between us girlies. You're not one of us."

Cerberus looked at Vesta in a perplexed manner before replying: "These girly chats, as you call them, are another really extraordinary thing I've just learned. I never knew about them before. We boy dogs don't have chats like you girls."

"Well, that's not surprising since you're the only boy dog in the Underworld, Cerberus."

"Woof! Woof! But I have lots of male friends and I can assure you we don't have these secret private chats between ourselves."

"You probably do, but you're not aware of it."

"Really! So, what sort of things would we boys be talking about?"

"I don't know," Vesta replied. "I'm not a boy, so I can't tell you what you all talk about."

"Woof! You're being very obtuse today, Vesta."

"Obtuse! That's a word I've never heard you use before. Where did you learn that?"

"From my librarian friends, Homer and Virgil. They use it quite a lot between themselves and they've recently advised me to adopt it."

"Very impressive. Do you know what it means?"

"Woof! Woof! Of course, I do. More importantly, do you?"

"Yes," Vesta replied, giving the three-headed dog a smile, "Come on, Cerberus, let's talk about something else."

"Alright. You said that there was something important we need to discuss."

"That's right. Aggy and the rest of us are concerned about Hades. The way you described his instructions about what to do with Billie rather suggests he was telling you to send her back to the world above."

"Umm!" Cerberus muttered. "I've got an answer if he ever challenges me on that. Do you want to hear it?"

"You told it me yesterday, but I'm not sure it sounds totally convincing."

"Woof!" Cerberus didn't say anything more, so Vesta asked him if he really thought it would satisfy Hades.

"Well, it might,"

"But it might not?"

"Woof! I'll argue it very forcefully on Billie's behalf."

"That's cool, but it still might not convince Hades."

"Woof!" Cerberus mulled around, all his heads looking at the ground. He eventually looked up at Vesta. "I wish you weren't so smart," he conceded.

"So, let me tell you what Aggy's plan is."

"Did this come out of a girly chat?"

"No; just a normal chat."

"Well, what is it?"

"Aggy thinks the best way of securing Billie's position here is to enlist Persephone's support. If she takes to Billie, she'll probably be able to persuade Hades to let her stay."

"Woof! That's a good idea. But Persephone isn't here at the moment."

"No, but she's due back soon, so what we thought was that you should try and avoid Hades until her return, so he can't ask you about what you've done with Billie."

"Umm… It may be difficult because I see him most days, usually when Death brings new people to the Underworld."

"All I can say is - try your best."

"But what if I have to see him and he asks about Billie?"

"You'll just have to argue it very forcefully."

"And if that doesn't work?"

"Take your time sending her back until Persephone arrives."

"Woof! Easier said than done!"

"Do your best."

"Woof!"

The two walked along in silence for a while until Vesta again changed the subject. "We met Mrs PorkyPie yesterday evening."

"How come?"

"She was brought into dinner by Mrs No-Messing. She spent all the time on the dinner queue screaming and shouting. When Gigliola served her a plate of pasta, she threw it back all over her. Before anyone could intervene, Gigliola raced round the counter and punched her in the face. There was blood everywhere – some of her teeth were knocked out and we think her nose was broken."

"Woof! Serve her right," Cerberus replied.

"I agree.

"What then happened?"

"Mrs No-Messing pulled her out of the Kitchens and took her away. I don't know what happened afterwards."

By now they had arrived at the outside door to Aggy's back-room. Vesta knocked on the window and Aggy motioned to her to wait a while. After a couple of minutes, the Head Chef opened the door and beckoned them in.

"Woof! Woof! What's all this?" asked a puzzled Cerberus when he looked at the scene in the room.

On the floor was a large vat about four feet high, full of warm water, in which Billie was swimming around. She was clearly enjoying herself and would give occasional 'woofy, woofys'. Aggy, Gigliola and Ming were all in the room wearing thick gloves with Ming sponging Billie every so often. What really surprised Cerberus, though, was seeing three men in the room, all of them eating Mars bars. There was Sisyphus, the former King of Corinth, who had immense muscles, having spent three thousand years until recently pushing a boulder up a hill. With him were two members of the Torturing

Department, Attila and Genghis. They were all friends of his, but he'd never seen them together in Aggy's back room.

"Morning Cerberus," Sisyphus said. "I've never had a Mars bar beforehand. They're really good."

"I agree," Genghis added, but Attila could only nod his head because his mouth was full of gooey chocolate.

"Woof! Woof!" Cerberus barked again as he looked at Aggy, before continuing somewhat aggressively "Why are you giving my Mars bars to them?"

"Don't you adopt that tone with me, Cerberus," the Head Chef snapped back. "They're not your Mars bars. They're supplied to the Kitchens, and we give them to you when you're polite."

"Woof! But if other people start eating them, we'll run out!"

"No, we won't. We've got plenty...." Aggy stopped and looked at Genghis and Attila who had both started sniffing loudly. "What's up with you two?"

"There's a strange smell in here," Genghis replied.

"Yes. It wasn't here a few minutes ago," Attila added.

"Oh, that's Pongo," Sisyphus called out.

"Pooh! Yes," Gigliola agreed, moving over to Cerberus and giving a big sniff before backing away and holding her nose.

"Pongo. Of course," Attila agreed.

Cerberus was looking at everyone, unsure what they were talking about. He saw that Ming and Vesta were also now holding their noses. "Who's Pongo?" he asked.

"You really don't know?" the former King of Corinth asked.

Before Cerberus had a chance to reply, Gigliola burst out laughing. "Why Cerberus, that's the name we call you. It's because you always pong."

Everyone else in the room began to laugh, causing Cerberus to start barking loudly and aggressively as he moved from person to person and growled menacingly at everyone in turn.

"Woof! Woof!" he went. "I do not pong! I do not pong, I tell you! None of you know what you're talking about! Woof! Woof! Stop laughing!" This was followed by more growls and plenty of barking.

Aggy was the first to stop laughing. She took Billie out of the bath and handed her to Ming to dry with a towel. "Why don't you just jump into the bath and freshen up, Cerberus?" she asked. "Then you won't pong anymore."

"Woof! Woof! No way! Firstly, I don't pong and secondly, I don't have baths!"

"Oh, come on Cerberus. It's nice and warm," Vesta added, dipping her fingers into the water.

"No! Woof! Woof! No!"

Having made his point emphatically, Cerberus looked around and saw everyone was now wearing thick gloves.

"Come on, Cerberus," Sisyphus said moving slowly towards the three-headed dog. "Just do it voluntarily."

Cerberus didn't reply but saw the three men moving closer to him. He backed away, but they still came closer.

"Alright then," Aggy called out. "Let's go."

Suddenly, everyone rushed towards Cerberus. Aggy, Gigliola and Vesta each took hold of a head to stop any biting, while the men grabbed his body. Ming, who had now popped Billie on the table, raced round to Cerberus's back and held Audrey just behind the head.

Cerberus was going mad, barking and unsuccessfully trying to bite whatever he came in contact with. He was kicking with his powerful legs but in a matter of seconds found himself lifted up and dropped into the bath. All three heads were submerged at first, but on coming up for air, he again tried to bite the Kitchens staff. Lefty did manage to get one of Aggy's hands in his mouth, but she had thick gloves and merely pulled it out leaving the glove for Lefty to chew. He tried to jump out of the bath, but everyone was pushing him down. Aggy in no time had given out sponges which were being used to wash Cerberus. This went on for a few minutes with the three-headed dog pushed back into the bath whenever he tried to get out. Meanwhile, Billie was resting on the table having a good laugh at everything going on.

"I think that's enough for now," Aggy said after a while as she stood back. "Let's let Cerberus get out."

The others backed away and Cerberus jumped out of the bath.

"Woof! Woof! Grrrr! Grrrr!" he kept going as he moved threateningly from person to person without actually biting anyone. "Woof! Woof! Grrrr! Grrrl! I hate you! I hate you all!"

"Keep calm, Cerberus," Aggy replied. "Here, have a Mars bar," and she threw a Mars bar into Lefty's open mouth.

"I hate you!" he repeated. "You all tricked me! Call yourself friends. Who wants enemies with friends like you lot? Grrrr!"

"Don't be like that," Vesta said as she moved over to Cerberus and stroked him on the back. "Do you want me to dry you with a towel?"

"No!" he shouted, moving away from Vesta. "I don't want any of you to touch me ever again. Never, never, never!"

"Come on, Cerberus," Aggy said. "It was for your own good. You don't pong anymore. Everyone needs a bath from time to time."

"Woof! Grrr! Grrr! I never ponged in the first place! This is all a big trick you've played on me."

The conversation went on like this for a few minutes until Cerberus announced he was going to leave with Billie. He also made it clear that he no longer viewed any of the people in the room as his friends, he was never going to speak to them again, nor would he set foot in the Kitchens from then onwards. He then flounced out, followed by Billie who had been taken off the table by Ming.

"Cerberus is a bit touchy today," Sisyphus said by way of understatement.

"He'll be alright once he's calmed down," replied Aggy.

"Ming and I will go and see him later this afternoon," Vesta said.

"You'd better take him a load of Mars bars," the Head Chef added. "If he's never going to come to the Kitchens again, he'll be going hungry."

"He never thought of that one!" Gigliola said laughing.

•

Meanwhile Billie was having to trot along at quite a pace to keep up with Cerberus's long strides. She was concerned that Cerberus would hold her responsible for his bath, but he said nothing to her about it. Instead, he was considering how to respond to his ducking. As far as he was concerned a serious assault had been carried out on the Head of Internal Security. He'd heard of things called prisons and felt that the Underworld needed to have one under his control. If a prison already existed, then he could put Sisyphus, Attila, Genghis, Aggy, Gigliola, Vesta and Ming into it pending their trial. He'd also heard about 'arrest warrants' and thought they might be useful, although he didn't actually know what they were. He'd have to talk to Vesta about that – she'd probably be able to explain what they were about. He was also aware of a crime called 'conspiracy' and while he also didn't know what that meant, he was sure that given all the people involved in his assault, there must have been a conspiracy. Again, something to talk to Vesta about as well as how trials worked.

As he was mulling over these matters, it dawned on him that Vesta might not be too helpful in answering all these questions. After all, she was one of the people he was going to arrest and put in prison. He'd also said he was never going to speak to her again, so it would be difficult for them to communicate. Furthermore, all the other people involved in the events that day were his friends or rather his ex-friends. He'd always prided himself on the number of friends he had, but now that list was substantially smaller. As he mulled over these points, he felt he should probably go and talk to Homer and Virgil on some of the legal issues, although they might not know much about the law today since one was nearly three thousand years old and the other two thousand. The more he thought about it, the more he wondered if he should make an exception over Vesta – re-instate her as a friend and not put her in prison.

The two dogs were now getting close to Cerberus's residence when they heard the sound of banging and sawing from that direction.

"Woof! What's going on?" went Cerberus before bounding off. Billie did her best to follow but she couldn't keep up.

When Cerberus arrived at his home he found Budiwati nearby, sawing various planks. Budiwati, or Budi for short, was a small but very strong lady who was a master craftsperson, being the Underworld's Deputy Head Builder.

"Woof! Woof!" Cerberus barked angrily as he went up to her. "What are you doing? Woof! Woof! You've made a hole in the side of my palace. Woof! Woof!"

Budi looked up and smiled at Cerberus whom she knew well. "You've come back before I've finished, Mr Cerberus," she said calmly. "I'm carrying out your instructions to create a private annex for Miss Billie."

"Woof! What instructions?" Cerberus demanded. "I never gave any instructions!"

By now an out of breath Billie had run up and Budi moved away from Cerberus and went over to her.

"Are you Miss Billie" Budi asked still smiling.

"Woofy, woofy" was the reply with a nod of the head.

"I'm very pleased to meet you. I'm Budi, the Deputy Head Builder." At that point, Budi bent down and shook Billie's right paw. "I'm here to build you a small annex to Mr Cerberus's home so you can have some privacy."

"Really!" the small dog said, her eyes lighting up.

"Yes, Mr Cerberus------"

"Woof! Woof! What are you talking about?" Cerberus angrily interrupted. "Why have I got a hole in my wall? I don't want a hole! Woof! Woof! Fill it up."

"All as per your instructions."

"What instructions?"

Budi looked at Billie and smiled again. "Mr Cerberus really is very modest, Miss Billie," she said. "He doesn't want to take credit for this generous gesture."

"What generous gesture?" Cerberus snapped angrily.

"Let me explain to Miss Billie, Mr Cerberus, what I'm doing and then at the end you can decide if you want to admit that you initiated it."

"Woof!" went Cerberus and growled. He decided against saying anything more at this stage because he wanted to find out what his instructions were, even if he hadn't given them. This seemed to be another trick being played on him. It just wasn't his day!

Budi calmly explained to the two dogs what she was doing. This involved building a small house for Billie attached to the side of Cerberus's main home. There was a hole between the two about six inches high and wide so Billie could go backwards and forwards. The small house also had its own main entrance at the front. Budi had brought thick curtain material to put across the inside hole and front entrance for privacy. There was also a thick, soft mat for Billie to lie on instead of the hard ground.

"Woof! Woof!" Cerberus said after Budi had finished. "I think there are same flaws in the design."

"Really, Mr Cerberus?" Budi responded. "What are they, please?"

"For a start, the hole into the annex is too small. I can't fit through; you'll have to make it bigger."

"But Miss Billie can get through. It's not appropriate for a gentleman to enter a lady's boudoir. Anyway, you can poke one of your heads through and call to her."

"Woof!" a perplexed Cerberus went. "Well, what about the curtain over Billie's front door? Why's she getting one when I don't have one?"

"I've brought the material to give you one if you want it."

"Have you?"

"Yes."

"And what about a thick, soft mat?"

"I've got one of those for you as well."

"Woof! Woof!" Cerberus barked, unsure what else to say.

Billie's eyes sparkled with delight at hearing everything that Budi had told her.

"So, you can see, Miss Billie," Budi now continued, looking at the small dog, "Mr Cerberus is a very considerate gentleman dog. He realises that a lady dog needs her privacy, and he's arranged all this for you. He is also very modest as well; he doesn't want to take credit for what is being done."

Billie looked at Cerberus and gave him a gorgeous smile. "Oh, Cerby," she said. "You really are wonderful."

The next thing Cerberus was aware of was Billie stretching up and giving Lefty a kiss on the cheek. Suddenly Middly and Righty started barking that they wanted a kiss and Audrey swung round to the front wanting to join in the action. As this love-in was taking place, Budi picked up her saw and continued working on building Billie's annex.

9
Welcome to Pimlico

The shaggy grey horse and cart trotted into the Hotel Savoire's driveway. There were several cars parked in front of the hotel that morning with the only gap available being for a small car.

"Move back a bit, mate," Octavian called out to the chauffeur of the silver-grey Rolls Royce who was standing beside his car.

The chauffeur moved towards Octavian and replied in a superior tone: "You can't park your horse and cart here, my good man."

"Don't you good man me, you young pup! And yes, I can park here 'cos that's wot I'm doing right now, am I not?"

The chauffeur made no reply, but just sneered.

"Are you gonna move yer real and actual posh car back a bit, eh?" Octavian asked as he tapped the horse's back with the reins to start reversing into the small empty space. "Or is you gonna risk us hitting that nice shiny bumper?"

The chauffeur watched the cart moving slowly towards the front of the Rolls. He realised Octavian was serious, so he shouted to him to hold on a while as he jumped into the car and reversed a few feet.

Octavian turned round and gave him a thumbs up. He then blew a horn to get the attention of the driver in front because he needed a few more feet to straighten up. There was no reply, so he blew it again. Still no response which led to Octavian getting off the bench at the front of the cart and ambling over to the bright red Ferrari in front. A young man was sitting in the driver's seat listening to loud music to which he was nodding his head. When Octavian knocked at his side window, he looked up, waved his hand away and then continued to nod to the music.

"Oi, Flash Boy; move up a bit," Octavian shouted while at the same time pushing his hands in a forward movement to indicate what he wanted the driver to do. There was still no response, so the request was repeated in an even louder voice. Again, nothing happened, so Octavian turned round and whispered something in his horse's ear. He then got back on the cart, once more tapped the horse's back and they began to move forwards. When they were within a foot of the Ferrari, the horse gently kicked one of the back wheels. The car shuddered slightly, and the driver got out and shouted angrily as he checked to see if there was any damage.

"No harm done," Octavian said to him. "Just move that flash car forwards a few feet. You've plenty of space in front, so be a bit helpful for once, will you?"

The young man made a V sign at Octavian, before getting back into the car and doing what he'd been asked to do in the first place, allowing the horse and cart to straighten up.

"What's going on here?" called an alarmed George who had hurriedly come out to the front, having observed the proceedings with the Ferrari.

"Nothing to worry yourself about, George," Octavian called back.

"Oh, it's you, Octavian," the Senior Porter said, recognizing the cabbie whom he'd known for many years. "What are you doing with a horse and cart? Where's your black cab?"

"Broken down, hasn't it? This 'ere's me back-up vehicle for emergencies."

"You really shouldn't bring it into the hotel entrance. Anyway, why are you here?"

"I've got me a booking, hasn't I? Ten o'clock on the dot, which happens to be now."

"Who are you picking up?" George asked, keen to see Octavian's horse and cart leave.

"The two top, top nobesses."

"Who are you talking about, Octavian?"

"You know, them two nobesses with the titles. Both proper Ladies; you must know them."

"We have a lot of titled ladies here. Can't you remember their names?"

"Well, they did tell me, but------"

Octavian was interrupted by Hebe who had just come out through the front door, followed by Artemis.

"George, it's okay. Octavian's come for us."

"That's them! Pleased to see you again, ladies."

"How come we've got this horse and cart. Where's your taxi?"

"My apologies to you two top, top nobesses. We 'ad us a bit of a problem first thing this morning, didn't we? Wot happened was-----"

"You can tell us about it once we're on route. George is keen for us to move on."

Hebe could see that George and the two bell boys were hurriedly putting all the cases on the cart. There was a Bentley waiting to park with an irritated driver at the wheel, who was gesticulating at the Senior Porter. Artemis jumped onto the bench next to Octavian and Hebe soon joined her once she'd looked after George and his team.

"Right; all set," Octavian said as he tugged a couple of times on the reins and they slowly moved off, making sure they didn't bump the Ferrari and any other cars in the driveway. "You don't 'arf have a load of cases at the back, if you don't mind me saying so. Wot you got in them – the Crown Jewels, eh?"

"Mainly clothes," Hebe replied.

"Cor blimey, I might have known. You ladies always got tons of clothes, just like them nieces of mine and their girls. We blokes could put all our stuff in a couple of plastic bags....." Octavian paused before continuing: "I hope you don't think I'm being offensive like. I'm always being told off for being politically not right, if you know wot I mean. Bit old fashioned, I suppose."

"No probs. Tell us about what happened to your car?"

"Well, you can see it's a nice sunny day. Bunnykins, that's me horse here, she decides she wants to have a day out, don't she? So, wot she does like is to have a 'how's your father,' and kicks the exhaust on the cab. Fell right off, so I 'ad to take it to Mr Patel, didn't I? He's our real and actual local mechanic down the road, he is; bloody good mechanic, if you'll excuse me French. Anyways, that meant the only way I could pick you top, top nobesses up was in the cart. Hope you don't mind, but it means Bunnykins she gets to have a day out, don't she?"

"We like horses," Artemis said. "And I get a better view of the sights of London."

"Yea, well, we're just coming up to Trafalgar Square and that bloke on the big, long pole thing, he's Nelson. Had a bit of an argy bargy with the Frenchies, didn't he? Showed them not to mess with us on the high seas, he did."

The horse and cart went down Whitehall, passed the entrance to 10 Downing Street and was soon in Parliament Square. By now, Octavian was giving a running commentary like a tour guide. This was principally for Artemis's benefit because, unlike her sister, everything was new to her.

"This 'ere's Parliament, where they makes all them laws, don't they?" Octavian continued as he pointed to the large Gothic building on the South of the square. "Full of people waffling away all the time and collecting big wages. They've all got these expense account things, you know; all their week's groceries and meals out with their mates and girlfriends, they get paid for by us, the ordinary people. We don't have these expense account things, do we? Bloody criminal, in my 'umble opinion. It's us taxpayers coughing up all the time – just not kosher, I say."

"Do you pay much tax, Octavian?" enquired Hebe.

"Well, um, not too much, no. I plan me affairs, you see."

"Do you pay any tax?"

Octavian coughed. "That's a difficult question to answer," he said hesitantly.

"Not really. It's either yes or no. Shall I tell you what I think the answer is?"

"Go on, then."

"No!"

Octavian coughed again. "Well, you could be right. Still, that don't change me argument about all these politicians being on the take. You know wot I'd do with them? I'd get rid of all this Parliament stuff. We've got a King, hasn't we? Let him make all the decisions. After all, that's wot yer kings are for, so the history books tells us. Don't need all these politicians, do we?"

"What about Margaret Thatcher?" Hebe asked. "You liked her. If you got rid of politicians, you wouldn't get the benefit of her running the country."

Octavian thought for a while before replying. "Well, I have to acknowledge, Your Ladyship, you makes a good point, you do. Hadn't thought of that one, had I? Same applies to Churchill, I suppose. He were a real and actual top geezer as well, weren't he? But me, I don't thinks that means you've got to keep a parliament full of all these politicians, just to get a Thatcher or a Churchill. The King, he's a smart feller, ain't he? He's like his mum, the Queen before him. When the King sees someone like them two we're talking about, he goes and makes them Deputy King for a while; that's wot he does. Let's them get on with running the country while he has a bit of a break - spends more time in the garden, relaxing in Margate and doing all them things wot kings do. Anyways, after a time when the Deputy King wants to retire or if he messes up, then the King takes back control again until another Deputy King pops up a few years later. Yea, that's a system that would work, that would. Yea, stands to reason, don't it?"

By now they had travelled halfway down Victoria Street before Octavian turned left into a heavily residential area, including The Gardens. Trotting along Rochester Row they eventually crossed Vauxhall Bridge Road into Warwick Way.

"If you don't mind me asking like, wot you top nobesses gonna do when living in Pimlico?" Octavian enquired as they continued at a slower pace because of the traffic.

"Some sightseeing, but we may even look for a part-time job," Hebe replied.

"A job, eh? Wot you good at?"

"Hunting," said Artemis.

"Hunting! Cor blimey, not a lot of that going on round here, you know."

"We've got an open mind," Hebe said. "Do you know any jobs going?"

"I'll have to have a thinks, won't I? I'll let you know if this old brain of mine comes up with something. You never know, do you?"

"Tell me, Octavian, why do you call your horse Bunnykins?" Hebe asked a short while later as they passed a long row of small shops and cafes."

"Cos that's her name, ain't it?"

"Do you change her name every year, as you do?"

"No. Bought Bunnykins from a farmer in Essex when she were a little un, didn't I? It were the farmer wot give her the name and she's kept it ever since. Me, I can't see nothin wrong with it. Can you?"

"Not really," Hebe said. "Except for the small matter she's not a bunny rabbit."

"Yea, well, I suppose there is that, but does it matter?"

"No. It's fine."

"Good. Anyways, here we are at Alderney Street. Tell us where to stop, Your Ladyships."

"It's at the top near Lupus Street," Hebe replied.

"Call out when we're there, luv."

Alderney Street was quiet at that time of day. The only person near where they all pulled up was a blue-jacketed young woman with an Afro hairstyle who was talking on her mobile on the other side of the road.

All three of them got off the cart and Hebe went and opened a red door on the left of the street. They soon got all the cases into the hallway; Octavian being allowed to carry Artemis's bow and quiver full of arrows. The two nobesses then said goodbye to Octavian, both kissing him on the small area of his cheek not covered by his beard. They promised to contact him whenever they needed a taxi in the future. Finally, Bunnykins was also given an affectionate hug before setting off back home to Whitechapel.

Hebe had rented a fully furnished flat on the top two floors of the white stucco-fronted house. It consisted of two bedrooms, a large living room, kitchen, bathroom and small utility room. She and Artemis spent the next couple of hours unpacking and checking that all the services, such as electricity and gas, were working. This was mainly done by Hebe with Artemis in tow.

"Right; that's all done," Hebe eventually said when everything had been checked and found to be in working order.

"So, what happens now?" Artemis asked.

"We go shopping for food and cleaning materials. Then we come back, and I start showing you how to cook."

"I've never been shopping before," Artemis said. "Being a goddess, I've just told my servants what I want, and they go and get it. As far as cooking's concerned, I-----"

"I know," Hebe interrupted her. "But while in London, you and I are going to behave entirely like human beings. Shopping's not difficult when you get used to it. I'll show you how to do it and also how to use money."

"I don't have any money."

"Don't worry; I'm paying for everything today and I'll show you how money works. Then tomorrow I'll give you five pounds and you can buy something with me next to you."

"What about these things called credit cards?"

"Let's focus on real money to begin with. Once we've mastered that, we'll get onto credit cards. If you feel confident after having watched me for a while, I'll get you your own card."

"Are they difficult to use?" Artemis asked anxiously.

"Just don't worry at the moment, Arty. Today's about shopping with you just watching me and helping to carry the bags back. After that, you're going to have your first cookery lesson. We're eating in this evening."

"Cooking's really complicated! Iris tried to show me how to do it in your kitchen, but I got totally confused. Whenever I'm out hunting in the forests, I just create a fire and heat up the meat over it. These modern cookers are just a nightmare!"

Hebe smiled. "Come on; let's go," she said. "It will all become clearer over the next few days. In a month, you'll probably have your own mobile phone. If Octavian can use one, it will be a piece of cake for the Goddess of the Hunt."

Artemis shrugged as she got off the sofa. "Where are we going?"

"There's a large supermarket a few minutes' walk away. I've got a list of what we want."

"Can I bring my bow?"

"Probably better not to. It will be safe in the flat. I'll put a seal on it as we leave."

•

The following morning, Hebe left the flat early to go and buy a newspaper from one of the convenience stores down Lupus Street. Artemis was in the living room carrying out her daily exercise routine of press ups, stretches and the like. She needed to de-stress, having slept poorly overnight because her mind was full of self-pay tills, bar codes, cash dispensers, nectar cards, receipts and much more. This was before she even thought of the complexities of the flat's Bosch cooker and hob.

On the floor by the front door was a hand delivered letter which had been pushed through the letterbox. It was addressed to Lady Hebe and Lady Artemis Olympiakos, so Hebe opened it and read the following:

Flat 24,
Arkwright House,
The Estate,
Lupus Street.

Friday

Dear Lady Hebe and Lady Artemis,

I hope you don't mind me contacting you, but I'm writing to welcome you both to Pimlico! I am one of Octavian's nieces, who happens to live very near you on the other side of Lupus Street. I wondered if you would like to come round for a cup of tea this afternoon about 3pm? I may well have a small proposition which could be of interest to the two of you. If you could please let me know one way or the other; my mobile number is xxxxxxx.

Kind regards,

Betty Bungalow

Hebe decided to text an acceptance straight away without consulting Artemis. If her sister didn't want to go, she'd go by herself. There was something intriguing about the invite, which she wanted to explore.

By half past three that afternoon, Hebe and Artemis had been sitting for a good half hour in Betty's expensively furnished living room in Arkwright House. They were drinking builders' tea and eating fruit cake while making polite conversation. Betty had also invited a number of her younger friends, whom she referred to as 'her team' and promised to explain what this team did in due course. All the team members had nicknames with the exception of Betty herself. So, the two goddesses met Jade, who had an Afro hairstyle and was referred to as Mopp; then there was Karate Chops with her black belt, Muscles who did weightlifting, Scampi who always ordered the same dish in the pub, and finally Sprog –

real name Chloe who was a shy 18-year-old and clearly the youngest.

Betty did most of the talking for her team as did Hebe for the two goddesses. Ever since she had arrived, Artemis had been in listening and observing mode because everything was new to her. However, she had brought her bow and quiver with her, which led to a short conversation about Artemis's archery talents. Since no one else in the room had ever used a bow and arrow, this topic died out fairly quickly.

After a while, Hebe felt the need to push the conversation along. "It's a real coincidence you're Octavian's niece, Betty, and living so near our flat."

"Well, I can't say it was anything I planned. I've lived here for decades, Hebe. You're the ones who've moved near me."

"Yes, I suppose so. I take it Octavian let you know about us as soon as he dropped us off?"

"He did."

"And he even remembered our names. That I would never have believed possible." In saying this, Hebe looked at Betty knowingly as if to suggest she still didn't believe it was possible.

Betty played a straight bat. "Oh, he didn't," she replied. "All he could tell me was that you were both titled ladies, who'd been staying at the Hotel Savoire. It just so happens that my eldest daughter, who now lives in Bermondsey, was a receptionist there until a few years ago. She phoned up one of her former colleagues who's still there and got me your names. I hope I spelled them properly."

"Oh yes; fine," Hebe replied with a smile. She paused for a few seconds before deciding on a more direct approach. "Your invite mentioned some sort of proposition that Artemis and I might be interested in," she said, enquiringly.

At this, there was a definite stirring within the room as every member of Betty's team made slight adjustments to their seating positions and became noticeably more attentive to the conversation.

"I did and now is as good a time as any to get onto it. In truth, it's the main reason for inviting you both round for tea, much as we want to welcome you to Pimlico. Let me tell you what it is."

Over the next hour Betty explained that she and her sister had been in The Greek Goddess last Tuesday evening, having a drink. They had naturally witnessed the fight and had been very impressed with Hebe's and Artemis's fighting skills. So much so that she wanted to find out more about them since she felt they could be useful additions to her team. She had enlisted Uncle Octavian's support, and he had deliberately waited outside the police station to drive them back home.

Betty then got onto what her team did, which in simple terms was recovering stolen property for a fee, split equally between all the members. They also worked for her small domestic services operation which kept them ticking along between 'recovery jobs'. At the present time, the team was two short since her daughter, Amelia and her cousin's daughter, Sophie had both recently given birth, so they were out of action for a while. Hence, Betty's interest in Hebe and Artemis.

After a considerable number of questions and answers, the Olympiakos sisters were signed up to Betty's team. Artemis was to be known as Bow in view of her archery skills, while Hebe's nickname was HalfPint because that's what she'd been drinking in The Greek Goddess. On the domestic services side, they would each earn £15 an hour in cash, and they could work part-time. As far as the recovery business was concerned, they would participate equally in all fees with everyone else.

"That's all exciting," Artemis said to Hebe as they crossed Lupus Street on the way home from Betty's flat. "But what's all this domestic services stuff we're going to do? I didn't really understand that."

"Cleaning," Hebe replied. "We're going to be cleaners."

"Cleaning!" Artemis exclaimed, as she stopped walking. "You're joking, aren't you? We're goddesses, not cleaners!"

"No, we're not, Arty. We're acting as human beings for a while. Cleaning's one of the things they do."

"But I don't have a clue how to do cleaning. I----"

"Stop moaning. It's not difficult. We've got three whole days for me to teach you. Our first job's not till Tuesday morning."

"If you say so," Artemis moaned. "What are we doing this evening?"

"Cooking, followed by eating. And to cheer you up, I'll do all the cooking, and you can do the eating."

"That sounds better." The two of them had by now turned into Alderney Street; Hebe wondering when she would break the news that it would be Artemis's turn to do the washing up that evening.

10
Holbein

Cedric came out of the lift on the sixth floor of Peter Jones at precisely 10-13am. His appointment was for 10-15 and he'd been asked to be punctual. Being a former military man, that's how he behaved anyway. He turned left at the lift and walked into the restaurant / cafeteria area. Since the department store had only just opened, it was quiet, although within an hour it would fill up and be difficult to find a table. Groups of young mothers with their buggies were a common feature of the famed Sixth Floor.

Cedric walked over to the far corner looking towards Knightsbridge. As he had been told, there was a grey-haired man, smartly dressed in a dark blue suit reading the Wall Street Journal. He was talking to a young blonde lady at the table in front.

The grey-haired man stood up and put out his hand. "Sir Cedric," he said. "Thank you for coming."

"Mr Smith," Cedric replied, shaking his hand.

"May I introduce Miss Jones, my personal assistant."

Cedric turned round and looked at the blonde lady wearing a black dress. "Sir Cedric," she said in a distinctly East Coast American accent as the two shook hands.

"Miss Jones," Cedric replied.

"Please sit down, sir," Mr Smith said indicating a chair opposite his own. "Coffee?"

"Thank you. Cappuccino. No sugar."

"Miss Jones; two cappuccinos please."

The blonde nodded her head and walked over to the cafeteria to get the order. She had left her bag on her table as well as a laptop and a number of papers.

"She will be our gatekeeper," Mr Smith commented. "Sitting at the table in front of us means our conversation will be entirely confidential."

"Very thoughtful. Presumably such an early start guaranteed you would get this location?"

"Precisely."

"I'm naturally intrigued-----" Cedric continued before being interrupted by his host raising his right hand.

"If you don't mind, Sir Cedric, let's wait for our coffee first before we get down to business."

"Very well," Cedric replied before changing the subject: "Are you a regular reader of the Wall Street Journal?" he asked.

"Every day. Do you read it yourself?"

"Occasionally. I'm more of a Times man now; that and the FT at weekends."

"I'm like you – I always read the FT on a Saturday. I suspect you and I, Sir Cedric are members of the last generation to read newspapers, at least in printed form."

"I agree. The younger generation gets its news from the internet."

"Especially social media. Miss Jones, for example, is on Facebook, Instagram, Twitter, TikTok, LinkedIn and You Tube. I suspect she's never read a printed newspaper in her life."

"It's called progress, I'm told," Cedric said with a sigh.

"Yes, that's what people say."

There were a few seconds of silence before Sir Cedric continued: "I take it that Mr Smith is not your real name?"

"You take it correctly, sir. And before you ask, Miss Jones is not my assistant's real name either."

"Thank you. I won't inquire any further. It's what I expected. However, you both have American accents, so I assume you are US based?"

"Not entirely. I'm what's called a Citizen of the World, or what one of your country's former Prime Ministers called a Citizen of Nowhere."

"Yes; pretty derogatory of her."

Mr Smith smiled. "We all know what she meant," he replied.

At that moment, Miss Jones arrived at the table with a tray consisting of two cappuccinos and a small latte for herself. After having handed them out, she went and sat down at her own table with her back to Sir Cedric and Mr Smith.

"I think we can now get down to business," Mr Smith said.

"Yes. As I was saying earlier, I'm intrigued about what this meeting is about. I only agreed to attend because Rodney Smythe was most insistent I should do so. He gave no indication of the subject matter, other than stressing it would be to my advantage. Rodney's been my solicitor for decades; a friend even longer – we were at university together."

"I too have known him for many years, although not as long as you. I'm also a lawyer which is how I know Rodney."

Cedric nodded and smiled at the same time. He'd dealt with many American lawyers in his time and could see how Mr Smith fitted the bill.

"I represent a particular client who wishes to pass on certain information to you as Chairman of The Gallery's Board of Trustees," continued Mr Smith. "For the purposes of our conversation, my client's identity is naturally confidential."

"Understood,"

"Before I pass on the information I'm entrusted with, may I please ask you a question, Sir Cedric?"

Again, Cedric nodded.

"Thank you. Could you please tell me if The Gallery is attempting to sell Hans Holbein's The Three Sisters?"

"I don't know the work myself. I'm aware that we're currently exhibiting a couple of Holbein's on loan from The Royal Collection, but I didn't know we had one of our own."

"You do. It isn't one of Holbein's major works and I believe it was last exhibited by The Gallery more than fifteen years ago. Despite that, being a Holbein it will naturally be worth many millions of dollars."

"We have a lot more works of art in our storage rooms than on the floors," Cedric acknowledged. "It seems to be the case with art galleries all over the world. For some reason, curators want to accumulate all these paintings even if they never get shown to the public. It seems crazy to me, but that's the way it is."

"I agree," Mr Smith replied. "But to get back to my original question, you can't actually tell me if The Three Sisters is up for sale, then?"

"Oh, yes, I can. The answer is - it isn't. At the present time The Gallery isn't selling any paintings. That's our current policy. Is this the reason for the meeting, Mr Smith? Your anonymous client wishes to purchase The Three Sisters from us."

"No it's not, Sir Cedric. Although I'm sure my client would be interested in buying your Holbein if it were legitimately on the market."

"That word 'legitimately' has an ominous sound to it."

"Indeed, sir. Let me explain….. My client has been a major art collector for a long time. As you are no doubt aware, the art world has many dubious dealings----"

"With many dubious individuals," Cedric interrupted. "I haven't been Chairman of The Gallery for long, but I'm well aware of the sector's general reputation. Naturally, my institution is not involved in such practices."

"Naturally," Mr Smith agreed. "However, returning to my client. He occasionally gets approached by some of these dubious individuals, so he hears about some of their dealings. My client is very strict – while he's prepared to deal off-market, he will only do so with principals. Even if a middleman approaches him – and some do quite legitimately - he insists on an early meeting with the principal. To be candid, everything must be above board and every purchase he makes involves detailed research into the provenance of the work of art before it is acquired."

"He sounds like the ideal client to have. I take it he's American?"

"You won't get that out of me, Sir Cedric. Suffice to say that I have international clients in the Americas, the Middle East and Far East."

"I didn't mean to probe," Cedric said. "It was just a question that came out naturally."

"No offence taken," Mr Smith replied with a smile. "Now one more general point about my client's business ethics. He dislikes intensely the activities of some of the dubious individuals we were talking about. In particular, their involvement in stolen works, forgeries and the like."

"I get the general picture."

"Which brings me to why I am here. I have to tell you, Sir Cedric, that my client has been approached confidentially to purchase your Holbein. From what we can gather, it is being hawked around the market to a select group of collectors."

Cedric had kept a straight face while listening to this information. He remained silent for a few seconds before responding: "As I've said, I've never heard of the painting. You are certain it is owned by The Gallery?"

"Absolutely! My client and I have carried out meticulous research both with regard to the original purchase in the last century, where and when it has been exhibited ever since, as well as checking from various sources all the historical records of Holbein sales. Everything points to The Gallery still being the legitimate owner."

"Putting aside legitimate ownership, do you and your client know where the Holbein physically is now?"

"You mean, has it yet been removed from the Gallery's possession?"

"Let's not beat around the bush, Mr Smith. Yes, I'm asking if it's already been 'stolen' – that's the word: 'stolen', and if so, where is it?"

"We don't know. It might have already been stolen or, what sometimes happens, an order is placed for a particular work of art, and then it is physically acquired."

"Umm," went Cedric. "And the person who approached your client is a well-known dubious individual, is he? Please excuse my description, but he's not just some fly-by-night lightweight. You and your client believe he could really get hold of our Holbein, do you?"

"Oh yes, he's a major player. Has been for many years."

Cedric said nothing as he contemplated matters. The American lawyer also remained silent for a while until he decided it was time to continue.

"I recognise this will have come as a major shock to you, Sir Cedric, but may I ask if you are alright?"

Cedric gave a forced smile. "I'll keep my feelings to myself, if you don't mind, Mr Smith. But yes, I am alright. Thank you for asking."

"Good. Is there anything else you wish to ask me?"

"No, I don't think so. .... Actually, yes there is. What else do you and your client intend to do with this information?"

"Nothing because there is nothing else we can do. Unfortunately for you, we've now put the ball in your court."

Cedric sighed and again gave a forced smile. "You have," he said. "But that's my job."

"Another coffee?"

"No thank you. I must be off. Let me thank you for your information, Mr Smith, and also please pass on my thanks to your anonymous client. I take it that you've told me everything, but if any new matters come to light, would you mind please passing them onto Rodney."

"Certainly. One final point which my client has asked me to tell you. This is very general gossip in the art world, but for some time The Gallery has been suspected of not being the most secure of institutions."

"By secure, you mean what precisely?"

"I think I'll just leave it at that, Sir Cedric."

"Very well," Cedric said, standing up to leave.

"Except," Mr Smith continued: "There is some rumour knocking around that a Modigliani, which people thought The Gallery owned, is now in a certain Arab prince's collection."

Cedric stared at the lawyer. His only reaction was to nod before formally taking his leave of Mr Smith and Miss Jones and then hurrying away as he set off for The Gallery.

•

Half an hour after informing The Gallery's Director about his meeting with Mr Smith, there was a loud knock on Cedric's door and Cesare walked in followed by three porters carrying a painting and a large easel.

"Please place the easel there," Cesare said, pointing to a spot directly in front of Cedric's desk. "And then put the Holbein on it for the Chairman to see."

The porters did as instructed and were then ushered out of the room by Cesare.

"So, Sir Cedric," the Director said walking over to the painting and looking at the Chairman who remained sitting at his desk. "I have brought you The Three Sisters as I promised. Look at them – one, two, three," and he pointed as he spoke. "I can double check for you on my adding machine." At this point he pulled a calculator out of his pocket before saying out loud: "One plus one plus one equals three. Here, have a look. Are you satisfied? If you prefer your own adding machine, then I invite you to use it. Please!"

Cedric didn't say anything, but just sighed.

"Also, I would suggest the three girls look like sisters. Do you agree, Sir Cedric?"

Again, Cedric sighed but didn't reply.

"I'll take that as yes. If you stand up and come closer, you will be able to see Hans Holbein's signature. It is here," and Cesare pointed to the bottom right-hand corner of the painting. "On the back is a detailed description of the work of art. Please look at the attached label, it looks many years old, I would suggest. Not something created in the last half hour."

Cedric hadn't moved from his chair while Cesare was speaking.

"Are you going to come and look?" the Director asked him after a few seconds.

"Sit down, Cesare," Cedric said. "I fully accept this is Holbein's The Three Sisters. You don't have to go through all this performance with your calculator and asking me to look at the signature and the like. I accept what you say."

"But you doubted me beforehand!" Cesare responded, now sitting opposite the Chairman.

"That's not true. All I did was tell you about a confidential meeting I'd been asked to have about this Holbein. Given what I was told, the most natural thing to do was to share it with you as The Gallery's Director. What else was I supposed to do?"

"I am greatly offended that you should pay any attention to this fake Mr Smith. It is clear you believed what he said, Sir Cedric."

"No, it isn't clear I believed it, Cesare. However, I viewed it to be of sufficient importance to raise it with you. As Chairman, I couldn't possibly ignore the matter. You must understand that."

Cesare just sniffed and looked out of the window.

"Look, Cesare, you can be in a strop if you like," Cedric said after a rather lengthy silence. "But we have to deal with these difficult matters in a businesslike manner."

"The Gallery is not a business!" Cesare snapped back, now staring at the Chairman.

"Very well; I'll use the word professional if you prefer."

"Are you suggesting I am unprofessional?" was the insistent response.

Cedric sighed. "You know exactly what I'm driving at. Tell me, what is your problem, Cesare?"

"It is that you are bombarding me with all sorts of mysterious allegations. I am told about anonymous bankers and billionaires in the Far East that you refuse to identify. Then a hand-written letter, unsigned about a missing Modigliani. Today, a meeting with someone called Mr Smith, which is not his real name, who has a client – again anonymous – who claims someone is trying to sell him our Holbein. That is our Holbein standing here right in front of you. Have you ever thought, Sir Cedric, that all this is part of a conspiracy to damage The Gallery's reputation. Not only that, but people are taking advantage of you being a new Chairman to sow all this distrust."

"Why would anyone wish to damage our reputation?"

"Professional jealousy. We are at the very top. The only way other galleries can take our position is to cause distrust in the public's mind."

"But none of this is in the public domain."

"Not yet, Sir Cedric. Not yet."

Cedric sat pensively contemplating what Cesare had said. Before he could respond, the Director suddenly shot off: "There is also the Modigliani in the Middle East! That is another stupid thing your Mr Smith said. These matters don't only damage The Gallery's reputation, but also mine! Have you thought of that, Sir Cedric? Have you?" he finished quite insistently.

"I'm very aware how you take this personally, Cesare, but------"

"These issues never arose when Lord Easy-Life was Chairman," Cesare interrupted Cedric. "Have you thought why that was, Sir Cedric? Lord Easy-Life a peer, a lord of the realm. These issues never arose when he led our institution. Why are they happening now? Can you answer me that?"

Cedric didn't bother replying. He knew full well why Cesare had a problem free existence in his predecessor's day. In was all in his name and was one of the reasons why a mixture of parties – the government, major funders and the like – encouraged his retirement.

"So, what do you propose we do about this situation?" Cedric eventually asked The Director after a long silence between the two of them.

"I think I will speak to the other trustees," Cesare replied. "I regret to say, Sir Cedric, that I feel personally under attack by all these accusations being made."

"Excellent idea, Cesare. I've only spoken to one or two of the trustees on a strictly confidential basis. I'll put it on the agenda for the next meeting. You're probably right; it's about time the whole issue was opened up to the entire Board. I've tried to keep it low key in the hope the matters could be resolved quickly. However, that's not happened, so I accept your way forward. We'll have to really emphasise how confidential this is. There must be no leaks."

Cesare frowned as Cedric was speaking. "I did not say it should be raised with the full Board," he said. "I said I feel I should speak to certain trustees, like you on a confidential basis."

Cedric inwardly smiled but kept a straight face. "Oh, I must have misheard you, Cesare. If you prefer to handle it like that, fine. But don't you think we should inform all the trustees?"

"Not just yet, Sir Cedric. Like you, I see certain advantages in keeping it low key. There is also the issue of ensuring no leaks."

"Just as you prefer, but at some point in time we will have to have the missing paintings as a formal Board item."

"Sir Cedric, there are no missing paintings!" Cesare responded forcefully.

"Then please bring the Cezanne and Modigliani to my office, just as you've brought the Holbein today!" was the equally forceful response.

The two carried on in this vein for some time without any resolution. Eventually, Cedric brought the meeting to a close with the words "we agree to differ," before returning to his flat in The Gardens.

•

"So, what do you think will come out of Cesare's discussion with the trustees?" Felicity asked her husband after he'd told her about the events of the day.

"Nothing. Most of them are his mates which he's been instrumental in getting appointed. They've been running galleries and museums the world over to the same low standards as he has."

"What about that woman recently appointed?"

"Dame Pauline. Now, she's different. Spent many years in MI6 before transferring to Whitehall and becoming a Permanent Secretary. She was the one person who helped me drive through the need for detailed systems in the organization. I've already spoken to her, so she's aware of matters."

"Anyone else?"

"One of Cesare's mates and of course got nowhere. He was totally relaxed. Took the view that things went missing for years and then suddenly surfaced again."

Felicity frowned and thought for a while before responding: "You know, Cedric, you're going to have to tell the entire Board sometime. If it blows up and you're found to have kept the information from them for weeks, if not months, you'll be in real trouble."

"I know," Cedric agreed. "I think I'd better speak to Pauline about it later this week."

•

The church clocks had just struck midnight, but they weren't heard by any of the small figures in the air duct system. They were busy trying to prise the grille off the wall at the end of the wall so they could lower themselves into the room.

"Do not make it do ze drop," said the figure overseeing the work as four of his team with crowbars were working to loosen the grille while two others held a rope to stop it from falling.

"No, Adjutant," one of the small men replied.

Suddenly the grille jerked loose, but it was too heavy for the two rope holders and jumped out of their hands, falling to the ground with a clatter.

"Imbeciles!" said the adjutant angrily as he turned round and thumped the two men in the stomach.

A more senior figure came up. "We wait ze few minutes in case someone heard ze noise," he said.

"Yes, Mon Capitaine," The adjutant replied.

After a couple of minutes, the capitaine gave the nod to proceed as planned. Various rope ladders were thrown down and he, the adjutant and a number of the men they had with them shimmied down to the floor below. They were in a large storeroom full of works of art. Some were framed, others on boards or stretcher frames and a few were simply rolled up canvases. The group moved towards a corner by the locked door where they saw a canvas with a yellow sticker on it.

"Zis must be it," the capitaine said. "Ze sticker has ze letter 'C' on it."

"Are we not looking for ze letter 'H'?" the adjutant replied.

"Ze orders got changed at ze last moment."

"You are sure, Mon Capitaine? I was positive it was ze letter 'H'."

"Perhaps we should make ze check..... Soldat," he called to one of the men. "Climb up ze ladder and ask ze colonel if we are looking for ze letter 'C' or ze letter 'H'."

Now it just so happened that the capitaine had chosen a rather overweight, unfit soldat for this task. He was still puffing and panting with the exertion of climbing down the rope ladder, so he thought he would point this out.

"But I have just come down ze ladder, Mon Capitaine," the unfit soldat replied.

"I know," the Capitaine replied. "And you are now to go back up ze ladder and get ze answer from the colonel."

"And am I to come down again with ze answer?"

"Of course. How will we know ze answer if you do not make ze come down to tell us?"

"I could make ze call from above. If I come down, Mon Capitaine, I will have to go back up again when we make ze finish."

Before the capitaine could reply the adjutant intervened. "Soldat!" he hissed angrily. "Do you want to meet ze firing squad?"

"Non!" was the quick reply: "I am on ze way tout suite."

A few minutes later the same soldat returned, again puffing and panting, with the colonel's confirmation that the canvas should be the one marked 'C'. The men down below quickly got it flat on the ground, rolled it over to beneath the duct opening and then tied ropes around it. These were then pulled up by a team of men waiting in the duct under the colonel's charge. When they had secured the canvas, the capitaine, adjutant and the other soldats in the storeroom climbed back up the rope ladders which were raised after them. The grille had also been pulled up and was re-attached to the wall with glue to cover the duct opening.

At nine the following morning two security guards went into all the storerooms as part of their rounds. They found the grille which had again fallen to the ground from the air duct system.

"This is the third or fourth we've found in the last few months," one of the guards observed.

"Yea. Management doesn't spend enough on keeping the building up to date," his companion replied. "These air duct systems should have been replaced years ago."

"They spend all the money on paintings, not maintenance. Got all their priorities wrong."

"Yea. Don't have a clue, do they? Don't have a clue."

11
A Difficult Client

Mopp's mother was Betty's cousin, her father being from Jamaica. The whole family, which included Mopp's younger brother, lived on The Estate with Mopp having worked as part of Betty's team for eight years. She was their driver since she had a blue van, which was used to ferry the other girls around to various clients whenever they had to take their own cleaning equipment and materials.

The blue van arrived just before half past eight on Tuesday morning outside the Alderney Street flat. Mopp called Hebe on her mobile and a minute later the two new recruits came out of the front door and jumped into the van, all three of them sitting alongside each other. Artemis had agreed to leave her bow behind since she and Hebe had put a double shield on their flat which would prevent anyone from breaking in.

"Ey up, Mopp," Artemis said, determined to use her favourite phrase every so often despite Hebe's advice to the contrary.

Mopp smiled as she started the engine and drove off. "Ey up, Bow," she replied. "You must have spent some time Up North, although I thought you were from abroad."

Artemis looked at Hebe, unsure what to reply.

"We've both been lots of places," the smaller goddess replied. "How did you home in on the north?"

"I once had a boyfriend from Manchester. He was always saying 'ey up' to me. But he's history now."

On the way to Hebe's and Artemis's first client, Mopp gave them a detailed briefing. Betty had felt obliged to let them know that they were going to work for a very difficult man, who had complained about everyone else on the team. It was the reason why the two newcomers were going to clean his flat. He kept demanding new people from Betty and they were the only ones Betty had.

"But we'll probably get fired as well after our first visit," Hebe said after listening to Mopp.

"Yes, probably," Mopp agreed. "But what else can Betty do?"

"Why doesn't she suggest he gets a different firm?"

"I think he's tried every firm in Central London over the years, and we're the only one left. Betty tries to walk away every so often, which makes him panic, so he offers to pay a lot more each time. It's really good money, so we keep sticking with him a bit longer. It's okay, provided you've got a thick skin which is why Betty was keen on the two of you. She wouldn't let Sprog work for him; she's too young and sensitive at present. She'll be alright in a few years."

They were now driving along Knightsbridge. Soon Mopp turned right into an underground driveway below a large modern block of flats. She stopped by the intercom and spoke to the concierge team who opened the electronic doors so they could drive into the basement car park. Once inside, she parked the van in an empty space and the three of them got out.

"Now it's time to get kitted up," she said, after opening the van's back door and beginning to hand out various items to her two companions. "Remember, you're to call each other Bow and HalfPint all the time upstairs; no using real names. It's Betty's fundamental rule in front of clients. She wants complete anonymity for her team. The only person whose real name is used is hers."

"Okay," Hebe said while pulling on a cream-coloured gown.

By the time one of the concierges had come down to escort them to their client's flat, Mopp, Bow and Half Pint were all wearing large medical facemasks, goggles, hairnets, gowns and gloves. Mopp also had a number of polythene foot coverings for when they got upstairs. Between them they carried a vacuum cleaner, ironing board, iron and a bucket full of cleaning materials.

"By the way," Mopp said as they were in the lift. "I forgot to tell you that he speaks in a funny way."

"What do you mean?" Bow asked.

"You'll soon find out."

Getting out of the lift on the fifteenth floor, the concierge turned left, walked over to a door at the end of a short corridor and pressed the doorbell. Half a minute later, Betty's three girls were face to face with Mr Panos Pantaloonos. He was a slim man of medium height. He had long, straggly grey hair and a small goatee beard. He was wearing baggy brown trousers and a dark green jacket. While he wore a face mask, he didn't have goggles, hairnets, gloves or gowns as the cleaning team did. He was, however, resting on a walking stick.

"Mr Pantaloonos, may I introduce------" Mopp began before being interrupted.

"Shoes!" the client barked, pointing to the team's feet.

"Of course," Mopp replied, giving out the polythene foot coverings to Bow and HalfPint, as well as putting on a pair herself. The concierge had by now retreated back to the lift where he remained, staring into space.

Mopp proceeded to introduce the two new cleaners. Panos didn't say anything until she had finished, at which point he stood aside, pointed at HalfPint and called out the word "Move!" to her. She walked a few feet into the hallway and then heard the instruction "Stop!", so she promptly came to a halt. Bow tried to follow her, only for Panos to shout out "No!" He then limped over to a nearby table, took hold of a disinfectant spray, and proceeded to give HalfPint's clothes a thorough clean, while avoiding her neck upwards. He also sprayed the contents of the bucket she was carrying full of cleaning materials.

"Move!" he barked again, so HalfPint walked further into the flat before again hearing the order "Stop!" Panos then pointed to Bow, called out "Move!" and went through the same routine with her and Mopp. When this was completed, he pointed at the front door, shouting "Shut!" to Mopp who did as instructed. Panos then looked at Mopp again, saying in a slightly quieter tone "Show!" before he went into the living room, sat on a chair and picked up a book to read.

Mopp then spent the next twenty minutes showing HalfPint and Bow round the apartment, including how all the kitchen appliances worked. It was actually a magnificent home consisting of three reception rooms, four ensuite bedrooms, as well as a large kitchen, utility room and cloakroom. The living room, dining room and main bedroom had direct views of Hyde Park with the other rooms looking towards Knightsbridge and Chelsea. There was one room which they could not enter; this was the third reception room which was locked with three sets of bolts and padlocks as well as a code lock. Mopp explained this had always been the case and it was just accepted that no cleaning was done in this room.

When Mopp had completed her tour, the three girls went into the living room to see Panos.

"Finished?" he asked.

"Yes, Mr Pantaloonos," Mopp replied. "I'll go now and I'll collect HalfPint and Bow in the underground carpark at one o'clock."

"'Silence' and 'test'?" he barked enquiringly.

"I'll cover them now in front of you, if that's alright?"

"Speak!"

Mopp proceeded to tell HalfPint and Bow that they should only speak about work matters between themselves; Mr Pantaloonos wasn't prepared for them to have any 'girly gossip'. Also, there was to be no use of mobile phones. They were there to work and to do nothing else. When it came to the word 'test', they should know that Mr Pantaloonos had noted various matters which needed cleaning in the flat. When they were finished, he would check if they had been dealt with and would give them a score.

"Is there anything else you want me to cover, Mr Pantaloonos?"

"No!" he rasped without looking up from his book. "Go!"

At this point, Mopp said goodbye to the others and walked into the hallway. Just as she was walking through the front door to leave, Panos shouted out the word "Shut!" to remind her to close the front door behind her, which she slammed extra hard so he would hear. The concierge then escorted her down in the lift and out into the car park.

"Work!" Panos suddenly called to HalfPint and Bow who had followed Mopp into the hall. "Now!"

The two goddesses unpacked all the cleaning materials in the kitchen, filled the washing machine with the laundry from a basket placed nearby, set up the ironing board and then started giving the flat a thorough clean. When they were together and well away from Panos, Bow raised a finger to her head which she twisted slightly to suggest the word 'nutter'. HalfPint nodded in agreement.

Time passed quickly. HalfPint or Hebe was used to cleaning since she and Iris did all the work in their bungalow on Mount Olympus. She had spent the last three days teaching Bow the basics with the result that the Alderney Street flat had been cleaned six times in that period. Bow was now quietly confident in what she was doing, but looked to her sister to take the lead, especially when it came to working the appliances. Every so often, Panos would limp out to look at what they were doing. He didn't say anything, but just stood and stared at them for about a minute on each occasion before returning to his book in the living room. However, at 11 in the morning, he went into the kitchen and poured out two glasses of water from the tap. He then called out "Come!" to the two cleaners who were in his bedroom. When they arrived, he pointed at the glasses and said "Drink!"

"What is it?" Bow asked.

"Water."

"Where from?"

"The tap."

"Why?"

"Rest. Two minutes. Drink!"

Bow looked at HalfPint, wondering if this was some sort of trick. Her sister shrugged, took a sip, which tasted perfectly normal, so she drank the rest. Bow followed suit and then said, "Thank you." Panos just nodded, barked out "Work!" again and then limped off.

By late morning, Bow and HalfPint only had the living room to clean.

"Can we do in here please, Mr Pantaloonos?" HalfPint asked, appearing in the doorway.

"Come!" was the reply before Panos got up and went into the dining room to sit.

As they had gone through each room, Bow and HalfPint had looked for Panos's so called 'test' items which they viewed as 'traps'. They'd found various ruffled pieces of paper and small coins under some of the beds and on top of two of the high cupboards in the kitchen. There were also marks on some of the mirrors and mats, which were so obvious that the two sisters wondered what they were missing. In the living room, despite moving all but the heaviest furniture, they could only find another ruffled piece of paper under a large sideboard. This was too heavy for them to move, so HalfPint used the vacuum's suction to try to retrieve it. Unfortunately, it was too far back, so she had to crawl under the gap below the sideboard, got her bottom stuck because it was only a few inches high, so Bow had to pull her out.

"Did you get the paper?" Bow asked.

"No; it's too far back."

"Let me try."

Bow didn't get stuck and because she had longer arms than her sister, she managed to retrieve the paper which she binned in the kitchen.

Just before one o'clock, Bow and HalfPint went and told Panos they'd finished.

"Wait!" he rasped as he hobbled out of the living room. He returned a minute later with a periscope. "Follow!" was the next instruction as all three of them went from room to room. Panos pressed various buttons to adjust the size of the periscope as he looked on top of cupboards, underneath various pieces of furniture, as well as to their side. He also looked for marks on the floor and mirrors, all the time making his own mental calculations. When he had finished, he went to the intercom in the hall and barked "Come!" at the concierge. He then stared at Bow and HalfPint without saying anything.

"How did we do, Mr Pantaloonos?" HalfPint asked after a lengthy period of silence.

"Six!" he barked.

"What does that mean?"

"Pass!"

"Pass!" Hebe exclaimed, giving her sister a broad smile. "So, what happens now?"

"Go!"

"And do we come back on Friday?"

"Yes!"

Shortly afterwards the concierge pressed the doorbell. Bow and HalfPint went to collect the vacuum cleaner, ironing board and cleaning materials before saying goodbye to their new client and being escorted in the lift to the basement.

"How did we manage to pass?" Hebe asked, still smiling.

"I don't know," Artemis replied with a groan. "I wish we'd failed. I was rather hoping we'd get fired like everyone else."

"Oh, don't be a misery guts. It wasn't that bad."

"Yes, it was. He's a complete nutter. I don't know how I'm going to cope with another morning of that guy. If he tests us again, we'd better make sure we fail."

"It will be better from now on. We've convinced him we're up to the job, so he's bound to give us an easier time in the future. Look, there's Mopp," and Hebe pointed to the blue van in the middle of the carpark.

●

"Are you another one of yer real and actual top nobesses?" Octavian asked as he was driving down Park Lane.

"What's a top nobess?" Iris replied.

"You know, like them ladies I'm taking you to. Got proper titles, both of 'em. Have you got a Lady title, if you don't mind me asking?"

"Well, yes I suppose so. I do have the title of Lady."

"Then Bob's yer uncle. That makes you a top nobess."

"Good," Iris replied, not really sure how to respond.

Octavian continued to drive down Park Lane, round Hyde Park corner and towards Victoria and Pimlico. Hebe had asked him to pick Iris up at the Bayswater stables where she'd left the chariot and horses, having just arrived from a short trip to the Underworld. The three goddesses were all going to the theatre that evening and Iris would stay with Hebe and Artemis for just one night before setting off back to Olympus.

"That nice Lady what's her name," Octavian continued. "You know, the little 'un, she says-----"

"You mean Hebe," Iris interrupted.

"Yea, that's her; Lady Hebe, she says you all going to see Shakespeare this evening, didn't she?"

"We're off to see Macbeth at the Globe. Do you like Shakespeare?" Iris responded.

"No; not really. Don't understand wot them actors are on about, do I? Bit surprising really, cos I'm a bit on the old side, you see. I reckons I were probably born just after him being around, if you know what I mean, so I should understand how they talk. Trouble is, I don't. Bit of a mystery, I suppose."

"Can I ask how old you are?"

"I'll be a hundred later this year," Octavian said proudly.

"If Shakespeare were still alive, he'd be four or five hundred years old."

"Cor blimey! I'm not that old! No wonder they speak all odd like in them plays of his. How come anyone today can get what they're on about. All sounds like yer real and actual Double Dutch, it does."

Iris and Octavian continued to have a learned discussion about Shakespeare until they arrived at Alderney Street. Octavian then went off for tea with his niece Betty, saying he'd be back later to take the three top nobesses to the theatre.

The Globe Theatre is on London's Southbank. It was constructed towards the end of the 20th Century as a close replica to the original Globe Theatre playhouse in Shakespeare's day. The original was destroyed by fire in the early 17th Century, rebuilt and then eventually demolished some years later. The new Globe Theatre was very much the brainchild of Sam Wanamaker, the actor and director, and every year hosts a number of Shakespearean plays as well as others in the same historical vein.

The theatre's exterior is black and white in the Tudor style. It is circular with an open roof over part of the stage as well as the 'pit' where the audience can stand. For those who have booked seats, there are three levels or galleries where people sit on wooden benches. For experienced Globe theatregoers, the trick is to buy tickets on the back row in the Lower or Middle Galleries where you can lean against a wall. It's also important to have a cushion to sit on, since discomfort is guaranteed if you're sitting directly on a wooden bench for two or three hours.

Hebe knew the Globe well and had bought ideal back row tickets in the Middle Gallery which directly faced the stage. She'd also ensured they were all sitting on comfortable maroon cushions that the theatre rented out.

For the first twenty minutes, Artemis tried to concentrate on the performance. However, she was having difficulty understanding the language despite reading the play with Hebe and Iris before coming to London. She did, though, find the programme interesting, especially the bits about witches. It also had a synopsis, which was some help. After a while she again focused on the performance but soon found her gaze wandering to the galleries on the right and left. Suddenly, she saw a man with a dark green jacket, wearing a facemask whispering to a male companion on his right. Artemis kept looking at the pair until she was positive it was their Knightsbridge client.

Iris was sitting between her friends, so Artemis tapped her on the shoulder, whispered the word 'nutter' while at the same time pointing to Hebe and then towards the right side of the Lower Gallery. Iris wasn't sure what Artemis was on about, but she did as she was asked.

"What have I done now?" Hebe whispered back to Iris. "Why's she calling me a nutter?"

Hebe could also see that Artemis was gesticulating towards her right, so she had a look, couldn't see what the matter was, shrugged her shoulders and focused again on the acting.

Half an hour later, the three of them were walking down the stairs to the yard at the start of the interval.

"What was all that about?" Hebe asked Artemis.

"Didn't you see him? The Nutter's here."

"Who? Mr Pantaloonos?"

"Yes; on the right in the row below us. Talking to someone."

"Are you sure?"

"Positive."

"Well, let's see if he's downstairs. But does it matter?"

"It's weird!" Artemis said, before hurrying downstairs ahead of her friends.

Hebe and Iris went off to buy three chocolate ice-creams, Artemis having disappeared in the crowd looking for the Nutter. She eventually returned just as Hebe and Iris had paid.

"Here's your ice-cream," Iris said handing Artemis a tub.

"Thanks..... I've found him. He's over there in the corner. Come and have a look, but make sure he doesn't recognise us."

Iris and Hebe followed Artemis, working their way between other theatre goers in the packed yard. In due course Artemis stopped, turned her back to the corner and then gesticulated to the two others to look behind her. Iris just looked out of curiosity, while Hebe wanted to see if her sister was right or just imagining things.

"I agree," Hebe eventually said. "It's him. He's even resting on his walking stick."

"Don't you find it weird?" Artemis said.

"Why?" Hebe replied. "He's allowed to go to the theatre. It's just a coincidence we're all here."

"Why don't you go and say hello?" Iris asked.

"No! No! No!" Artemis exclaimed, frantically shaking her head. "No! No! No!"

A perplexed Iris looked at Hebe.

"Probably best not to," she said. "We've got assumed names when we work to keep us anonymous. Also, he wouldn't recognize us because we have to wear masks, goggles and hairnets when we're in his flat."

"That's because he's a nutter," Artemis added. "Did you notice how he seemed to be speaking in long sentences whereas he just barks out one or two words to us?"

Hebe shrugged, suggesting she didn't think it was a big deal.

"Come on," Iris said. "Let's go back to our seats for the second half."

In Octavian's taxi returning to Alderney Street, Artemis kept talking about how weird it was that the Nutter was at the same performance as them. Since she got little response from Iris and Hebe, she then went on to bemoan the fact that she still didn't understand much of what the play was about.

"Except that Lady Macbeth," Artemis continued. "She was the one character I think I got. She reminded me of Hera. The two seemed to have a lot in common."

"But Lady Macbeth's a horrible person," Hebe responded. "You can't honestly say my mother's that bad."

"Yes, I can!"

"How come?"

"She did actually try to harm, if not kill, my mother, my brother and me, or have you forgotten?"

As Hebe pondered the extent to which she should defend her somewhat difficult Mother, Iris decided to contribute to the discussion.

"Arty does have a point, you know, Hebe," she said.

Hebe reflected for a few seconds before shrugging her shoulders and saying: "Yea, I suppose so."

12
Old Friends

Hebe and Artemis were walking in front of Victoria Station when something sped a few feet over their heads. They looked up, as did a number of other people, and saw a reddish object circle round a double-decker bus before coming back slowly towards them. It hovered a few feet in front of the two goddesses and made a 'toot, toot' sound.

"Hebe! Hebe! Hiya!" a voice shouted from the object. "It's me, Rach! You remember, Rach from Lilliput!"

"What are you doing here?" Hebe replied, recognising Einstella, otherwise known as Rach, the Head of Special Projects on the island where adults were rarely taller than six inches. She was sitting on her dark red miniature Vespa scooter which could both hover and fly.

"I'm in London for a few weeks. I only arrived yesterday, but heard you were here as I called in on Olympus to see Tots beforehand. She said you'd just left for London as well and gave me your address. I was going to look you up in a few days' time. Is this your sister, Artemis?"

By now Rach had taken off her helmet and goggles. She still had spiky, multi-coloured hair, wore rings in both her ears and nose, and had tattoos on her face and arms.

"Hello, Rach," Hebe's companion replied, deciding to introduce herself. "Yes, I'm Artemis. I've heard lots about you."

As the three of them were talking a large crowd gathered around in front of the station. The crowd was intrigued by the small figure sitting on a scooter hovering about six feet from the ground. Once they heard the word Lilliput many of them remembered the small island where the 'little people' lived.

"We can't talk here," Hebe said becoming increasingly aware of the growing crowd which had now spilled onto the bus station concourse. A couple of policemen were seen in the distance walking over to look at what was going on.

"Why not?" a male voice shouted from the crowd in response to Hebe's comment.

"Yes; why not?" an elderly woman carrying a supermarket bag called out as well. "It's interesting listening to you, whoever you are."

There were various other comments of support, so Hebe hurried Artemis and Rach away to the side of the station. Some of the crowd followed them but when they were out of earshot, Hebe said: "Let's all go back to our flat and have a proper chat there."

"Okey-dokes," Rach said.

"It's probably better if we go separately," Artemis suggested. "Some of these people look like they want to follow us."

"Yea," Rach agreed. "It's me and my flying scooter they're interested in. You're at the top of Alderney St, aren't you? I've looked it up and got it on my sat nav."

"It's only about a ten minutes' walk," Hebe said.

"I'll be there in two," and Rach sped off into the sky to avoid the high buildings.

Hebe and Artemis soon lost the crowd who were not interested in them once the flying mini scooter had disappeared. As they walked along Hebe filled her sister in on some of the facts about Lilliput which she didn't know. Being the Goddess of the Hunt, she'd never had any reason to visit the island although she had heard a fair amount about it from some of the other gods and goddesses. In particular, she was aware of the central role played by Lilliput in the recent conflict between Poseidon, the God of the Seas, and Mars, the God of War. Both Hebe and Rach had been actively involved in this conflict supporting Poseidon.

Lilliput is an island on the eastern side of the Indian Ocean. It was first visited by 'normal sized' mankind about three hundred years ago. In order to stop it being overwhelmed by tourists, the gods numb the memories of people who have visited the island or who come across Lilliputians elsewhere. They also ensure that anything written about them disappears from the page very quickly. The inhabitants do though have a number of dealings with the outside world since Lilliput has for some time placed considerable emphasis on education, especially science. This resulted more than fifty years ago in Lilliput College being established as part of Cambridge University where bright students from the island go to study. So they can be properly integrated into the community, the gods have made an exception to the general rule about people's memories being numbed if they come across Lilliputians. Everyone within the town remembers the little people and their dealings with them up to a distance of five miles from the Market Square. Once they go out of that area, they forget them within a short while.

The Lilliputians also keep embassies in all the major capitals with the one in London being on Duck Island in St James's Park, near to Whitehall, 10 Downing Street and Buckingham Palace.

Rach herself is part of one of the leading families in Lilliput. Her grandmother is the Empress, mainly a ceremonial role to which she is elected. Similarly, her father is the country's Chief Scientist, her mother is a leading cardiologist and one of her uncles is a cabinet minister. Rach works for her father and runs Special Projects which deals with cybersecurity as well as a certain amount of electronic eavesdropping or hacking of computer systems – principally those belonging to unfriendly governments or organisations. She knows England well, having been educated at Lilliput College over many years and still visits Cambridge and London at least once a year.

When Hebe and Artemis arrived at the top of Alderney Street, Rach was whizzing backwards and forwards on her scooter, occasionally getting perplexed looks from the few passersby in the street.

"We'll go inside first, Rach," Hebe said opening the front door, "and open the third-floor window. You can fly straight in and come to a halt on the large dining room table."

"Okey-dokes!"

Two minutes later, the two goddesses were sitting on comfortable chairs with Rach sitting on the edge of the table drinking a cranberry juice which Hebe had poured into a thimble.

"This looks a super-cool place," the Head of Special Projects said, looking at the pictures of the South of France on the walls. "How long are you here for?"

"A few weeks or months. We haven't decided yet," Hebe replied. "What are you doing in London?"

Rach explained she was involved in a research project with Imperial College, so expected to be here for about a month or two. Athene had set up Cambridge type arrangements on the Imperial site in Kensington, so people's memories weren't numbed until they left campus. This was her second visit in the last year; she had her own room in the college, but normally stayed at the embassy in St James's Park. While everyone at Imperial was really friendly and helpful, they didn't have the arrangements for socializing with the little people which Cambridge had, so she preferred to stay overnight with her fellow Lilliputians. Anyway, she knew the Ambassador well, having stayed at the embassy many times before.

"I really like this miniature scooter of yours," Artemis said, changing the subject. "Did you fly all the way from Lilliput on it? I've heard you're great at inventing all sorts of machines."

"Nah. This is my city run around, which I brought as luggage on the BA flight from Indonesia. It's an upgraded version of the one I had when you were on Lilliput, Hebe, and we were all zapping Lord Mars and his Tyrant friend."

"And you're allowed to fly it around London?" the smaller goddess asked. "You've got some permit or whatever, have you?"

"I don't know. I've left that to the Ambassador."

"I bet you haven't."

"You're probably right," Rach said laughing. "But I'm sure they can't catch me. Also, I've got diplomatic immunity for my visit."

"But what about these other scooters you've made in the last year?" Hebe continued. "When you come to Olympus, you have a really powerful model."

"Yea, it can resist all the air currents. I only ever use it to come and see Tots when she's staying with you. Never thought of travelling to another country on it. I prefer to travel by BA; it's more comfortable. I'm still trying to design a miniature submarine to visit the Sea Cavern, but it's more complicated than I expected."

"Rach is a little genius," Hebe said looking at Artemis.

"Nah; not really. I'm a scientist. It's what we do - invent things."

After a few more minutes, Rach stood up, saying she had to go to Imperial College to meet her fellow researchers for a couple of hours to plan the next few weeks.

"But why don't the two of you come round to Duck Island for tea if you're not busy this afternoon?" she suggested as she was putting her helmet and goggles back on. "We've got arrangements at the embassy to look after big people just like on Lilliput."

Hebe looked at Artemis, who said: "Sure. Why not."

"Come about 3 o'clock. If the Ambassador's around, I'll introduce you. Also, and I've been saving this one up for you, Hebe – an old friend of yours is there."

"Who? Is the Empress in London?"

"Nah! Think of the words 'you 'orrible little man'" Rach said, then burst into laughter.

"No way!" Hebe squealed and then also started laughing. "What's Sergeant MacGobo doing in London?"

"He's only been here about a month. He's the London embassy's Military Attaché."

"You're kidding. As a sergeant?"

"He's now Acting Captain MacGobo."

"But why? He's the last person in the world I'd expect to be a diplomat."

"I don't really know. The Regiment didn't seem to have a lot going on after defeating Mars and The Tyrant, so I suppose someone suggested he should get some experience of the outside world."

"Is he the one who came to the Dog and Duck to arrest you that evening?" Artemis asked, looking at her sister. "The one who got, what's that phrase Octavian used - Brahms and Twist?"

"Brahms and Liszt; Oliver Twist. Yea; that's him."

"Oh, I've got to see him again!" Artemis said firmly and then also laughed.

"What's all this?" Rach asked.

"It doesn't matter," Hebe replied. "So, if we come, will he be joining us for tea?"

"We're definitely coming!" Artemis said before Rach had a chance of replying.

Hebe shrugged. "I suppose so," she said. "Has he changed at all, Rach?"

"It's difficult to say. I only saw him for a few minutes yesterday. I think he's probably bored out of his mind. Anyway, I'm sure he'd love to see you again."

"As you'll love to see him too!" Artemis said, continuing to laugh.

Hebe pulled a face, said goodbye to Rach and confirmed she and Artemis would be at Duck Island at 3 in the afternoon. A minute later the miniature scooter and its driver flew out of the window, going 'toot, toot' as they both went down Alderney Street.

•

"This is really wonderful," Artemis said as she and Hebe walked through St James's Park. "We must go right round the lake after we've been to the embassy."

"You can't go hunting, you know."

"I don't want to hunt!" Artemis exclaimed. "I want to explore all the wildlife. I love the swans."

"It's the pelicans that are the real feature. Anyway, here we are."

The two of them had arrived outside a small house on the edge of the lake. Suddenly, Rach's flying scooter, which had been hovering nearby, appeared going 'toot, toot'.

"Come this way," she said as she motioned them along to the side. One of the gardeners was waiting for them by a gate which he opened and took them over a small bridge onto Duck Island. "The embassy's the far side."

Rach continued to lead the way, still on her scooter. "The captain's waiting for you in the garden. I think he's really excited at seeing you again, Hebe, but he's trying not to show it. The Ambassador's out, but you can always meet him another time."

The three of them continued along a narrow-wooded pathway until they passed the embassy, a modern red-brick building, before coming to a large lawn. In the middle was a platform about five feet high with a ladder on the side, in front of which were two chairs for two normal-sized human beings with a table in between.

"I'll leave you here," Rach said, zooming off on her scooter before either of the goddesses could reply.

"Stop slouching, you miserable, lazy, good for nothing, rattlesnake's backside," a voice shouted from the top of the platform. "Stand up straight! Shoulders back! Stomach in! Chest in front! Face looking straight ahead! Do it now, Private!"

Artemis suddenly got the giggles as she and her sister approached the platform. At the top was a small well-built man, wearing a dark-grey lounge suit which had a full row of medals on the top left.

"Is you talking to me, Captain?" Hebe asked.

"Of course I is talking to you, Private MacHebe! You is still the same 'orrible little man, you always was!"

"Oh, I thought you might be speaking to my sister, Artemis." Hebe then looked at her sister before continuing: "Stop giggling, Arty. Let me introduce you to Acting Captain MacGobo of the Argyll and Sutherland Highlanders Regiment. Captain, this is Lady Artemis, Goddess of the Hunt, which is why she always carries her bow and arrows with her."

Suddenly, the figure on the platform adopted a different tone. "My Lady Artemis; very pleased to meet you," he said before saluting and then bowing to her, before making a final salute.

"Captain," Artemis managed to reply, having now got her giggles mostly under control. "I've heard a lot about you. We also met once when you came to Olympus to have a few drinks with us in our local pub. That time when you had an arrest warrant for Private MacHebe."

Captain MacGobo blushed as he recalled this embarrassing incident when he got well and truly Brahms and Liszt.

At that moment a mass of servants came out of the embassy carrying large trays with two human size teacups, a teapot and a jug of milk on top.

"Here, let me help you," Hebe said, taking the tea-set from the little people and putting it on the table. "Thank you."

"I has arranged tea for you, Lady Artemis, and the private."

"Thank you, Captain," she replied. "Do we sit here?"

"Certainly, my Lady...... That doesn't apply to you, Private!" Captain MacGobo suddenly shouted at Hebe as she also sat down.

"Look!" Hebe shouted back at the captain for the first time in their relationship. "You is pissing me off!"

"Why is that, Private?" the captain shouted back at her in an equally loud voice.

"I'll tell you why! Firstly, I has stopped being a private; I has got myself promoted to lance-corporal! Secondly, I is no longer in the regiment; I has left! Thirdly, I want to be called 'she' now, not 'he'; I is a goddess! Fourthly, my name is no longer MacHebe; it is Hebe!"

There was a dead silence for a few seconds before Captain MacGobo responded: "Has you finished now, Private?" he asked in a firm tone. When he didn't get a reply he continued: "Let me set you right on certain matters, you deformed pea brain. You is only a lance-corporal on Lilliput; everywhere else you is a still a private. Secondly, once you has been in the regiment, even if you has left, you can always be called up in an emergency which is what I is doing now. If you didn't read the small print when you signed up, that is your own dimwit fault! Next, you enlisted as a 'he' so you is staying a 'he'; changes is not allowed. The same applies to your name; we cannot has people changing their names whenever they want. You was MacHebe; you stay MacHebe! Understand, Private?"

"Captain MacGobo, may I say something?" Artemis intervened.

"Certainly, My Lady," the captain replied followed by a salute.

"We came here for a nice friendly cup of tea. Can't we have that, with you and my sister sorting out your issues another time?"

Captain MacGobo took a deep breath as he thought about the matter. He was aware that this proposal was being made by a goddess, so he did finally say, although in a slightly reluctant tone: "I suppose there is rare occasions when the senior ranks mix informally with the lower ranks. We could perhaps treat today as one of them days."

"That seems------"

"Let me say something," Hebe interrupted Artemis. "Here's the deal, Captain; take it or leave it. You can call me private, but I is going to call you sergeant. I'll rejoin the regiment if it really is an emergency – but you has not told me what the emergency is yet. Finally, if you want to call me he and MacHebe, that's okay, but other people is going to call me she and Hebe. All of this is conditional on you giving an honest answer to one question and me believing your answer."

"What's that?"

"Is you happy being a military attaché and an acting captain?"

"No, I bloody is not!" was the very prompt answer.

"Ah!" exclaimed Hebe with a laugh. "I believe you! Does you agree to my deal then?"

"You bloody know I does, you piece of rat's liver."

"Good. Then why doesn't you sit down on your chair and tell us how come you've been made a diplomat and what you doesn't like about it."

It took a long time for Hebe and Artemis to coax Sergeant MacGobo, as we will now call him, into admitting how he had ended up as the Military Attache in the Lilliputian Embassy in London with the rank of acting captain. The Argyll and Sutherland Highlanders Regiment had been approached for an exceptional individual to take on a special mission. Apparently, the Empress had let it be known that she thought the sergeant would be the ideal person for the role, so he had volunteered without knowing what he was signing up to. Since he was the only candidate, he was naturally chosen and only then did he learn, much to his disgust, that he was to be a military attaché. Since this was viewed as an important appointment, he needed to be an officer, so was elevated to the rank of acting captain.

Hebe laughed after hearing the eventual explanation. "Did you ever find out why the Empress wanted you to be appointed?" she asked.

Sergeant MacGobo shook his head. "Not really. I did 'ave an interview with her, but all I got was how it were felt to be important to broaden my experience, whatever that means, for more challenging roles in the future."

"Sounds like you was done, Sergeant," Hebe said, laughing again.

"I does not like that accusation, Private!" MacGobo snapped back.

"No, but it's true, isn't it?"

"Yes," was the gruff reply.

"So, what don't you like about the job?" Artemis asked.

"I does not like just about everything. For a start, all these cocktail parties where I has got to stand on a high table, so I is able to talk to all the other military attaches. All we do is drink champagne; never any beer 'cos we is meant to be posh."

"And what about your uniform?" Hebe asked. "Why is you wearing a suit and not a proper uniform?"

"That is another bloody stupid thing about this job. All Lilliputian military attaches everywhere in the world have now been told we has to wear suits whenever we is in company."

"Why? That sounds daft."

"I does not know why. Also, for the first time I can remember, Private, I is in agreement with you despite you being a totally useless ferret brain."

"Thank you for the compliment, Sergeant," Hebe replied. "But moving on, what's this emergency you've got which is letting you call me up?"

"I regret to say, I needs your help, you useless tosspot. As well as being the Military Attaché, the Ambassador has put me in charge of embassy security. He does not think the existing security team is much good. He wants some military discipline instilled in them"

"So, what's that to do with me?"

"I is about to tell you, Private. Do not interrupt me in full flow…. The Ambassador is right, the security lads are a motley group of totally useless gits. I has run a number of training sessions, but it is very hard work, it is. Now, if you was in attendance, participating in this training, then they would have an example to look to. That is why."

"But how would it help having me as I is a totally useless ferret brain? Surely, you does not want them to turn out like me, does you, Sergeant?"

"No, I bloody does not, Private. But there is a difference between you and them."

"What's that?"

"Stop saying 'what's that', you six-nosed hyena's swollen bile duct, when I is about to tell you!" the sergeant snapped back. "You is quite right, you is a totally useless ferret brain. But.... and this is a big but, you is a trained, totally useless ferret brain. Them other lot is just totally useless ferret brains; at least with you setting an example, I might stand a chance of turning them into trained, totally useless ferret brains. That would be a big advance, that would!"

By this time, Artemis had to stand up and walk around, so Sergeant MacGobo couldn't see her giggling again. Hebe, however, was able to keep a straight face.

"So, you really does need me," Hebe said with a smile.

"Desperate situations does require desperate measures," was all she got in reply.

"Oh, come on, Sergeant; can't you be nice to me, just for once?"

Sergeant MacGobo gave a grunt but nothing more.

Hebe continued to smile at him, while he looked everywhere other than in her direction. "Alright," she eventually said. "When does we start?"

"This Friday morning at nine o'clock. For one hour."

"No can do. Artemis and I have another job every Tuesday and Friday mornings. How about Saturday at nine?"

"Agreed, Private. Be here five minutes early for a debrief."

"Okay. One final point, Sergeant. What is you going to pay me?"

"Pay! What does you mean by pay?"

"Money; wages. That sort of thing."

"Was you paid when you was fighting Lord Mars and The Tyrant?"

"That was different. Times has changed. I work for money now."

"How much does you want?"

"Twenty pounds an hour. That includes a premium for weekend work."

"Huh!" MacGobo replied. "I'll speak to the Ambassador on the matter."

"I'll expect you to have a nice shiny twenty-pound note for me when I arrive on Saturday morning. Otherwise, I won't be staying long."

"I does not like your attitude these days, Private. You always was a cheeky, little bugger, but the threat of a firing squad kept you under some sort of control. I has been told I can't get you shot in England, or I'll create a major diplomatic incident. You is taking advantage of your situation here, but don't think you can totally get away with it. I is still the same old Sergeant MacGobo at heart, even though I is an acting captain. Does you understand?"

Before Hebe had a chance to reply, Artemis returned to her chair, having again got her giggles under control. "May I come along as an observer?" she asked as she sat down.

"Certainly, Lady Artemis," the sergeant promptly replied. "Has you ever given any consideration to joining the Highlanders, My Lady? We can offer you a rewarding career and I'm sure you'll very quickly become an officer, given your excellent credentials."

"Hey! Why's she becoming an officer? What about me?" Hebe shouted.

"Don't you question the promotion decisions in the regiment, Private. I has told you before….."

The conversation carried on in this vein for a few more minutes until Artemis stood up, saying she and Hebe had to leave. She agreed to give careful consideration to Sergeant MacGobo's kind offer and would give him an answer on a future occasion.

As the two goddesses walked around the park looking for the pelicans, Artemis said she thought Sergeant MacGobo had been really pleased to see Hebe.

"Yea, I agree," Hebe replied with a laugh. "He's mellowed a bit."

"And you enjoyed meeting him as well, didn't you?"

Hebe took a few seconds to reply. "Yea; I suppose so," she eventually said. "And I'm getting twenty pounds out of him on Saturday morning as well."

"I think I'd better sign up if I can get the same deal."

"You should ask for more if you get made an officer. Boost our household income!" And the two of them burst out laughing as they hurried towards the pelicans they could now see in the distance.

13
Escape Plan

The light in the Underworld was the same during both the day and the night; it was simply dull all the time. There was, however, a difference in the human activity which was a feature of 'life' underground. Put simply, during the day, people worked; at night they were in their dormitories, asleep. Except tonight two figures were moving furtively towards a large wooden warehouse structure.

The taller figure wore a green waistcoat and a maroon velvet jacket. He had a dark blue tricorn hat on top of his head and a black eye patch over his left eye. His most startling feature though was a thick green beard, which stood out against the rest of his hair, a mixture of brown and grey. His companion was a shorter and stouter man, with a beard of a few days' growth and a face with a permanent growl. His jacket was also velvet, but black, while his head was covered with a tatty brown hat.

When they arrived at the warehouse, the green-bearded man pulled out a key from his jacket pocket and quickly opened the large wooden door. Only when the two got inside with the door closed behind them did they speak.

"Do you know your way around this dump, Greenbeard?" the stouter man asked.

"Not well. I only deliver stuff to Fagin, and he puts it away. But on occasions he's let me help him carry some of the heavy items."

"That sounds like him," the other growled. "Always getting someone else to do the hard work."

"He's not so bad."

"Yes, he is. I knew the greedy, conniving bastard up above. I'm surprised he let you have the key to his warehouse."

"He didn't want to, but I threatened him."

"How?"

"I told him you'd want a little word with him if he didn't give it to me. He's scared stiff of the name of Bill Sikes."

"He's reason to be!" was the growled reply. "I murdered the wrong person in Nancy. Should have been Fagin. The police wouldn't have been so keen to find me. I'd have been doing them a favour cutting the nasty little bastard's throat. Still, he soon ended up dangling from a rope outside Newgate, so that was one consolation. Laughed my head off the day he arrived in the Underworld, and I found out what had happened. Got the same punishment here as me from Hades."

"And me," Greenbeard added. "A day in a cauldron of boiling water every month. Courtesy of Ivan."

"Bugger Ivan! And bugger Hades!

"Don't forget Satan; he runs the Torturing Department."

"Bugger him as well!"

"Aye; bugger them all! But come on - we're here to get out of this hell hole."

"You lead the way. This place looks as if it goes on for miles. What's it called again – The Unwanted Goods Warehouse?"

"That's right. Follow me; from memory we should find some useful stuff down this way."

The Unwanted Goods Warehouse was where goods were stored that new arrivals brought with them. These were items which wouldn't be needed in the Underworld, ranging from mobile phones to Rolex watches, ski boots, footballs - effectively anything which people had in their possession when Death came to collect them. All these goods were simply placed in this ever-growing warehouse, which was under the stewardship of Fagin, since he was by nature a hoarder. Greenbeard, a former pirate operating in the Caribbean, was a member of the Carrier Department, responsible for transporting goods around the Underworld. This sometimes involved the dead's unwanted possessions, so over the years he'd got to know Fagin.

"This is the area," Greenbeard said after the two of them had walked down various aisles with stacks of goods either side. He then moved quickly to his right and pointed at what looked like a large pile of wooden sticks. "I thought these could be useful."

"They could be," Sikes replied picking up one of the sticks and firmly moving it around as if he were striking something. "What is it?"

Greenbeard shrugged, then picked up another stick and looked down the side. "It's got some label on it."

"What does it say?"

"Baseball bat."

"What's that?"

"I don't know, but does it matter? It looks ideal for our purposes."

"It does that. No need to look for anything else with these. Let's take them. Have you got a place where they'll stay hidden?"

Greenbeard nodded. "Leave it to me," he replied.

"I assume we're still four. You've not let Fagin in on our plans, have you? The grubby little bastard doesn't expect to join us, I hope."

Greenbeard shook his head. "He wanted to know why I wanted the key, but I just kept mentioning your name and he shut up."

"The sneaky scumbag may start spying on us. If I catch him, I'll spill his guts out."

"Aye, I do believe you would. Come on, let's go."

They each picked up two baseball bats and started walking back to the warehouse door.

"I still don't like the other two who are involved in this," Bill Sikes growled as they went along. "We'd be better off just you and me together."

"We've had this discussion, Bill. The woman comes with us!"

"She's your new lady friend. Don't get carried away with her; I wouldn't trust her an inch."

"Aye, I know that's your view, but she comes!" Greenbeard again reiterated. "We've already mapped out our future together when we're out of here."

"So, why's Fairy involved? What good's that boy to us?"

"On that I might agree with you, but the Marchioness insists he comes, so end of debate."

"What does she see in him?"

"They've become friends. They work together in the laundry; he's technically her boss. Also, Fairy's the one who came up with this plan, so she feels we're sort of beholden to him."

Sikes growled. "Rubbish. Every man for himself, I say. Anyway, what's he going to do when he gets out? He's going to get an almighty shock after spending the last few thousand years down here."

"Aye, I suspect we all will. That's a strong reason for having the Marchioness with us. She knows how things work upstairs."

"Means nothing to me! I told you; we're going our separate ways as soon as we get out. Just you make sure Fairy does as well."

"He will. It's all been discussed."

"I'll believe it when I see it. I'd put money on the scared little mouse trying to cling on to you and your Marchioness."

Greenbeard just nodded and said nothing more until they reached the door. "Right," he whispered as he opened the door. "Silence now. We'll all meet in the dining room at midday."

"Agreed," Sikes growled as he followed his companion out of the door.

•

Billie was walking towards the Kitchens. She did a lot of walking now she was in the Underworld and was definitely getting both fitter and stronger. When she had been with the Marchioness, she'd been carried around everywhere, but now she walked and sometimes even had a little run, although not too far yet. She talked a lot to both Vesta and Gigliola about sensible eating and the importance of exercise since both were converts. Even Ming, who had lived in a world where such considerations were non-existent because life had been all about survival, was signed up to this health regime. Billie thought it was strange because everyone was dead, but they didn't behave like they were!

Everything had also become a lot calmer as far as Billie's position in the Underworld was concerned, so she was no longer stressed any more. This was all due to Lady Persephone who had returned from Olympus to be with Hades for a few months. Persephone had immediately taken a great liking to Billie, no doubt influenced by Aggy, Vesta and many others, and had agreed that the small dog should remain in the Underworld and not be returned to the world above. Billie gathered from Cerberus that Persephone had got Hades' agreement to this by threatening to withdraw certain marital rights if he took a contrary view. Cerberus didn't know what this withdrawal threat meant - Billie did but thought it wasn't necessary to explain it to the Head of Internal Security.

Since she was now a permanent member of the Underworld, Billie had to have a job. It was decided she should work for Cerberus in the role of 'Intelligence Gatherer'. Neither of them were quite sure what this involved in practice, so Billie decided she'd go around everywhere, listen to what people were saying, and every evening would give her boss a debrief. Dear Cerberus was always interested in listening to what the little dog had to say. Billie had first found him a bit rough and unsophisticated, but she'd now become quite fond of him. He also tried to do things to please her, especially having regular baths. These took place once a week and Cerberus clearly didn't like being covered in the water, but Vesta had told him that Billie wanted him to have baths, so he did so reluctantly. He was also given a Mars bar at the end, which was another incentive. What's more, no one called him Pongo anymore – Billie had found it funny at the beginning but had to admit it was all a bit unfair, so she was pleased when the name got dropped.

Billie and the Marchioness had seen each other a few times. The little dog still called her by her titled name despite her now being called Mrs PorkyPie in the Underworld. Similarly, the Marchioness couldn't get used to the fact that Popsy had become Billie, so the two of them continued to call each other by the names they had in the world above.

Quite soon after their arrival in the Underworld the Marchioness accepted that she couldn't look after Popsy anymore. They both agreed it was best if Popsy made her own way, especially since she already seemed to have a number of important friends such as Cerberus, Aggy and her key kitchen staff. Having reached this decision, the Marchioness kept saying that she would love Popsy forever and ever, which the little dog didn't really believe. However, she reciprocated by saying she'd also love her former mistress forever as well, which she knew full well was a total fib, but she said it anyway.

By now Billie had entered the dining room where people were eating their lunch. She spied the Marchioness at a table in the distance sitting with a teenage boy whom she'd befriended. He always wore a blue tunic and had a silly gold fez hat on his head and went around with a snooty expression. Just as Billie was looking at them, two men came and sat down at the same table. Billie recognized Greenbeard, the Marchioness's new gentleman friend, and Bill Sikes. She didn't mind Greenbeard and could see why her former mistress had become attached to him. He was a bit coarse and lacking in manners, but he treated her well. Most importantly, he was strong and powerful and could provide her with an element of protection, which she would need since she was good at rubbing people up the wrong way. But Bill Sikes was a totally different matter. He was a nasty, vicious brute, always snarling at everyone. He'd once kicked Billie on the right shoulder, leaving her with a big bruise which took several days to clear, despite Aggy's special ointment. Billie had seen him with the Marchioness as well as the other two on a number of occasions recently and wondered why. She decided to go and settle down under the table and have a good listen, making sure she kept well clear of Bill Sikes's boots.

"I still don't understand why we have to wait for Death to return before overpowering the ferryman and making our escape," the Marchioness said.

"I agree," the teenage boy concurred in a whining voice. "What I'm trying to do is get back to the outside world and then move to Olympus. Nothing else."

"Fairy, I thought you had a score to settle with Death like the rest of us," Bill Sikes growled.

"I do. More than anyone here."

"Aye; why's that, lad?" Greenbeard asked in a neutral tone.

"I thought I'd told you all-----"

"Then tell us again, Fairy!" Sikes interrupted.

"You all know I am the great Pharoah Tutansillytwerp. When I unfortunately died from a snake bite, Death brought me to the Underworld instead of my rightful place on Mount Olympus."

"Why's it your rightful place?"

"Because I am a god. All we pharaohs are gods and go to Olympus. I told Death when he was bringing me here, but he didn't pay any attention."

"It was very wrong of him, I agree," the Marchioness said, taking the young man's side. "And you have a very legitimate grudge against Death, but you're not letting it interfere with your key aim which is to leave the Underworld and then go on to Olympus. I also feel greatly aggrieved towards Death, but I'm not in the camp of wanting to beat him up just to get my revenge for bringing me here."

"We've discussed this already, my love," Greenbeard said, taking the Marchioness's hand. "And agreed we wait for Death and deal with him. Bill and I won't feel right until we break all the bones in his body. To me, beating up Death is at least as important as getting out of here."

"Why?" Fairy asked.

"I'll tell you, lad. In my day, the authorities had many ways of dealing with us pirates. I was caught in the Caribbean after a fight with a Royal Navy frigate, and then brought back to London to be tried. Sentenced to death, which was what I was expecting. On the morning, I was taken down to the Thames with two other pirates and we were all pegged out on our backs waiting for the tide to come in, which it did over the next few hours. It drowned my companions, but I was a bit further back and water got into my mouth when I opened it, but it didn't rise quite enough to cover my nose, so I kept breathing. Death came along, smiled at me and then went away because the tide started to go back. By that time, you're cold, sodden and just want to get the whole thing over with. This happened two more times and I was screaming with frustration. The second time Death came and had a chat, said he'd had a pint in The Prospect, thought he'd go back and have another and collect me later. Well, it wasn't until the fourth tide that I drowned properly. Had to wait until the second day, all because bloody Death liked to have a few at the Prospect. So, that's why I want my revenge on the black-cloaked skeleton."

"But---" Fairy started to speak before Sikes interrupted him again.

"Shut it, Fairy!" he growled. "Greenbeard's given his reasons and that's why we're going to smash Death to bits. I hate Death as well for bringing me here instead of letting me get away. If you don't want to be part of it, then we'll go our separate ways. You and the Marchioness work out your own plan to get out of here and leave me and Greenbeard to do it our way."

"No," the Marchioness said. "We're all going together. We'll do it your way, Bill."

"Yes," Greenbeard concurred.

"But---" the Fairy began again, before being interrupted by the Marchioness.

"Tuts, please don't argue," she said putting her hand on his. "We're all in this together and it will be fine. Greenbeard and Bill have it all worked out."

"I thought I was the one who came up with the idea of the escape," was the sulky reply.

"And so you did," the Marchioness said soothingly. "And the other two have fleshed out the detail. It's as we discussed before, isn't it?" She looked at the two older men, both of whom nodded their heads.

"Aye," Greenbeard replied. "We wait behind one of the large boulders near the ferry. What normally happens is Death takes the new arrivals to meet Hades once they arrive. Charon then goes off for a while before coming back to pick Death up once he's returned from Hades. At that point we pounce. Bill and I have got hold of four of these big stick things called baseball bats, which we'll use to bash both Death and Charon. We then get on the ferry and punt it back along the river to freedom."

"Who's going to attack whom?" the Marchioness asked. "If you and Bill both want to beat up Death, that leaves the ferryman to Tuts and me. I'm not sure that's a good idea."

"No!" Bill growled. "I'll take Charon with the Fairy. You and Greenbeard can deal with Death. While I hate the bony bastard, I'm happy for the pirate to dish out revenge for the two of us."

"And you, Tuts have got to make sure you get hold of the ferryman's pole," the Marchioness said.

"Aye: without it we're stuffed," Greenbeard added.

"So, when do we do this?" the Fairy asked, now accepting his involvement in the project.

"The day after tomorrow," Greenbeard replied. "The ferry normally arrives about an hour after breakfast. We all meet behind the boulders in good time beforehand. Can everyone find an excuse for getting off work that morning?"

The other three all nodded.

"Then, that's it. We're all agreed," the pirate said before continuing: "One final point none of you have raised is why we don't make our attack as soon as Charon and Death arrive instead of waiting for Death's return from Hades."

"So why don't we?" Fairy asked in a surly voice.

"Bill and I have discussed this. Too much risk. We don't know how the new arrivals will react; they might get involved in the fight. Also, that beast Cerberus is often at the jetty when the ferry arrives. From observation over the years, he's never around when Death returns."

"Makes sense," the Marchioness concurred.

"I've got a final point as well," Bill Sikes growled. "Once we're off the ferry, we all go our separate ways. I don't want any of you hanging around me."

"Greenbeard and I are going in for luxury living," the Marchioness responded. "Once we dig up all his treasure he's left in the Caribbean.

"Aye," the pirate concurred. "I still remember exactly where it is. Not something you ever forget. But what about you, lad?" he asked looking at the Fairy. "Have you worked out what you're going to do?"

"I do not have to," was the dismissive response. "I am a god, and I will soon find my followers who will assist me to go to Olympus to join my fellow immortals."

"Are you sure about that?" Greenbeard asked. "I seem to have come across a lot of you fairies in the Underworld. I've not heard of any who've gone to Olympus."

"They are not of the pure blood, like me. My people will be waiting for me."

Bill Sikes gave a wicked smirk but decided not to say anything. It would be fun for a few minutes watching the pathetic little boy's reaction to what life looked like in the modern world. But he wouldn't hang around too long; he'd be off well before the Marchioness took pity on Fairy and insisted he should join up with her and Greenbeard. He had no doubt that would be the outcome, and he doubted the pirate would say no. After all, she was the one person who knew how to deal with the 21st Century and the others would quickly realise how dependent they were going to be on her. Even he, Bill Sikes, would struggle, but he was a loner; he'd take his chances!

As these thoughts were going through Sikes's mind, Billie very quietly slipped away unnoticed from under the table. She walked quickly out of the dining room before running as fast as possible, occasionally barking "woofy, woofy." She had to find Cerberus as soon as possible. This was exactly the sort of information he needed to know. For the first time since she'd arrived in the Underworld, Billie understood what being an Intelligence Gatherer was all about and how important it was. She now really did have a key role to play in the Underworld.

14
The Park

St James's Park is the most central of all London's parks. It covers the area between Buckingham Palace in the west and Horse Guards Parade, together with the major offices of state, in the east. To the north is The Mall and to the south there is a tree-lined avenue, Birdcage Walk, which links the Palace to Parliament Square.

Many people regard St James's Park as the most attractive of all the Royal Parks. It isn't as large as Hyde Park or Regent's Park or even Victoria Park in the East End, but it has a large lake with an abundance of wildlife. There are currently six pelicans which always interest the tourists, a fair number of swans, including black swans, geese, ducks, herons and many other birds. As well as the pelicans, tourists often gravitate to the parakeets who are quite prepared to eat apples out of their hands, allowing friends and family to take photographs which invariably appear on Facebook, Instagram and other social media sites.

The lake can be crossed in the middle by the Blue Bridge. There are two islands at either end. Near Horse Guards is Duck Island which is by far the larger. It has a land bridge allowing the Royal Park staff access since they have their base there; this also includes a pen where the pelicans are taken for protection whenever bird flu breaks out in the UK. In addition, Duck Island houses the Lilliput embassy, being a handy location close to Whitehall and in particular the Foreign Office. The other island, West Island, is near to Buckingham Palace; it is not connected in any way to the land and is less frequently visited by the park's gardeners. The result is that it is wilder than Duck Island, although this doesn't prevent it from being frequented by the park's wildlife.

Emily was again staying with her grandmother in The Gardens. When it was a fine day, the two of them would often visit St James's Park as they were doing that morning. Lady Felicity had arranged to meet one of her friends at the cafeteria for coffee, giving Emily the opportunity to wander round the park with her camera and her mobile, taking photographs of the different birds as well as the stunning flower beds which were a feature at this time of year.

"What have you got there?" Mrs Moncrief, her grandmother's friend, asked Emily as the three of them were sitting at one of the cafeteria's tables.

"It's a strawberry milkshake, my favourite," Emily replied. "Have you ever had it?"

"No; is it good?"

"Scrumptious. You should try it sometime."

"Maybe I will, but I tend to be a coffee person like Grandma."

Emily turned her nose up. "Boring," she said before taking another large suck from her straw.

"Are you going off to see your pelican friends soon?" Lady F asked her granddaughter.

"Yes, Grandma, but I want to finish my milkshake first. Then can I have a banana one please, which I can drink while I go round the park?"

"Emily; you can't consume two! They're fattening. You won't have any room for your lunch."

"Yes, I will Grandma. Anyway, if you don't let me have another one, I'll just have to sit here and then you and Mrs Moncrief won't be able to have the adult conversation I know you want to have."

"What would you do with her?" Lady F asked, looking askance at her friend.

"I think I'd buy her that second milkshake," Mrs Moncrief replied, unable to suppress a large smile.

Lady F mumbled something inaudible but got up, and taking her granddaughter's hand, went off to order a banana milkshake. When it was made, she handed it to Emily and sent her away with all her photography equipment, telling her to be back promptly by 11-30am.

"She's gone to see her favourite pelican," Lady F said after returning to her table.

"I love the St James's Park pelicans," Mrs Moncrief replied.

"So do I, but sometimes Emily gets carried away. She kept claiming this pelican of hers could speak English, so I asked to be introduced to him. Not surprisingly, when we all met up, I only got all sorts of pelican noises but no words of English or any other language. The good thing is she doesn't go on about the conversations she has with him anymore."

"How old is she?"

"Ten, but she'll be eleven in a few months."

"She'll soon be a teenager, Felicity; then you'll have far worse problems than talking pelicans. My eldest grandson's fourteen and he's no longer the lovable boy he was a few years ago."

"I'll be ducking out then. I decided some time ago that Emily's teenage years will be for her parents to deal with."

As the two grandmas were discussing Emily's future prospects, she was walking around the lake taking various photos of the different birds. She was, as Lady F had predicted, looking for her favourite pelican, the youngest one in the park, who had become a particular friend of hers in recent months. She'd turned left from the cafeteria, walked all the way round the Horse Guards end of the lake, then the entire south side, came to West Island and only then did she see her feathered friend sauntering around on the pathway. He was near a bench where two middle-aged men seemed to be having a rather intense conversation.

"Hello Elvis," Emily said, going up to the pelican and giving him a broad smile. "Are you going to talk to me today?"

"Oh, hi there Emily. Of course, I'll talk to you if you're by yourself. You've not brought your grandma with you, have you?"

"She's in the cafeteria with a friend of hers. You know, you made me feel really foolish when I introduced her to you, and you wouldn't speak to her. I'd promised her you would beforehand. She didn't believe me at the time but agreed to come and meet you. When you stayed silent, she just decided I was a silly little girl who made things up to get some attention."

"I'm sorry, I didn't mean that to happen. I should have told you I only speak to children and then only the ones I really like."

"That's nice, Elvis. So, you really like me?"

"You're my favourite girl."

"I'm pleased. Anyway, I've just spent ages looking for you. I didn't think you came to this end of the lake much; you're normally near Duck Island."

"I'm a bit worried about what's happening up here. The swans, especially the young ones like me, have been getting very aggressive recently. I've just had a big argument with Slasher and Spike; I wanted to visit West Island, but they wouldn't let me come ashore."

"Don't the pelicans and the swans get on?"

"No, not really. I think they're jealous of all the attention we get from the tourists compared to them. According to Sir Peregrine, our senior pelican, it's always been like that. Also, he doesn't get on with Sir Sigmund, the senior swan, so that doesn't help matters."

"Why do you want to go onto West Island? It looks all wild and a bit of a dump."

"I suppose I'd like to see why the younger swans are spending so much time there. Also, I'm sure I've seen some of the little people on the island, but when I speak to the ones I know on Duck Island, they say they never go there."

"Now you mention the little people, I remember them. I'd forgotten they live on Duck Island."

"In their embassy. That's the Lilliput embassy."

"Lilliput, that's the name. It's in a book called Gulliver's Travels. I've got it to read at home but haven't started it yet. I much prefer reading about wizards and things like that."

"I don't know what wizards are," Elvis said. "But I'm sure we've not got any in the park."

"No, I don't think they come here....." Emily then paused before continuing: "Tell me, Elvis, does it matter if the swans are spending time on West Island? After all, you pelicans have Duck Island which looks much nicer."

"No, not really, although I just get the feeling something's going on. Anything Slasher and Spike are involved in tends to result in trouble."

"Have you told the other pelicans?"

"I've spoken to Sir Peregrine, but he doesn't seem to be concerned. Still, I'm going to keep a bit of an eye on things in the next few days."

"What shall we do now?" Emily asked, wanting to change the subject. "Can I take some photos of you?"

"Alright. Get them in quickly. I can see a party of tourists coming our way and they'll all start clicking their mobiles soon."

Emily got her phone out and took a number of photos of Elvis in front of the bench where the two men were still involved in their serious conversation. He then started walking along the pathway, so she took a video of him. Various tourists came along and began to crowd Emily out. Elvis was his normal courteous self, adopting different poses for them. After a while, he squawked, looked directly at Emily, gave her a wink and then took off into the air as he flew part way across the lake to join two of his fellow pelicans who were fishing near the Blue Bridge.

Emily looked at her watch and decided to return along the pathway back to the cafeteria. Grandma had promised to take her for a burger and, while she quite liked Mrs Monkey as she called her, she was an old person so she hoped she wouldn't be joining them.

"Grandma, Mrs Monkey," Emily called when she got into the café. "Look what I-------"

"What did you say?" Lady F angrily interrupted her granddaughter as she reached their table.

"What do you mean?" Emily replied unsure why Grandma was standing up and looking so fiercely at her.

"What did you call Mrs Moncrief?"

"Ooh!" the ten-year-old said, putting her fingers to her lips as she realised what she'd said. "I'm sorry, Mrs Moncrief; it just sort of slipped out."

"Just sort of slipped out!" her grandmother exclaimed. "How dare you use cheeky names to refer to my friends. We don't call you Empty-Head Emily or any other rude names, although that's what you are at times!"

Tears began to well up in Emily's eyes, so Mrs Moncrief took hold of her hand, encouraged her to sit down next to her and gave her a hug.

"Don't worry, Emily," she said. "I've been called a lot worse things than that."

"I'm sorry, Mrs Moncrief. I didn't mean to use that word."

"Would you like me to get you another milkshake?"

Emily looked nervously at her grandmother.

"Perhaps an orange juice," Lady F said, still looking angry.

"Yes," the young girl mumbled. "That would be nice."

"I'll get it," Lady F responded and turned round and marched off to get Emily's orange juice. She didn't want to be alone with her granddaughter until she'd had a few minutes to calm down.

By the time Lady F returned to the table, she was more settled. She found Emily showing Mrs Moncrief the photos she'd taken during her walk; the two of them chatting happily together.

"Felicity, you must look at Emily's picture show. What a talented young lady you have as a granddaughter."

"Did you see your pelican?" Lady F asked with a slightly forced smile.

"Yes, Grandma."

"He's called Elvis, I'm told," Mrs Moncrief said enthusiastically. "There are loads of photos of him and also a video of him walking along the pathway….. Come on, Emily, show Grandma."

Emily pulled her chair next to her grandmother's and slowly went through the various photos. She gave a running commentary, starting with the geese and ducks at the beginning of her walk until she found Elvis. Then Grandma got bombarded with shot after shot of Elvis in all his different poses, followed by a video.

"Can you just go back to the photos on Elvis," she said at the end. "There are a few about half-way through I want to have another look at."

Emily clicked back until Grandma suddenly called out "Stop." She looked hard at the photo, asked to see the next two and then went back to look at all three again.

"What's up, Grandma?" Emily asked.

"Yes, you look as if you've seen something interesting," Mrs Moncrief added.

"I recognize one of the people on the bench behind Elvis," Lady F replied looking up. "Cesare Shiftyopolous, the Gallery's Director."

"Is he the one Grandpa calls Shifty?" Emily asked.

"Emily!" Grandma snapped.

"I don't think you ought to reply to that, Felicity," Mrs Moncrief said with a laugh. "Can I have a look, please?" Emily showed her the three photos. "Shifty seems to be a pretty good name from what I can see of him," she said after a while. "But who's the strange man he's talking to?"

Lady F shook her head. "I've never seen him before, but yes, he does look a bit weird wearing a mask in the open air." Then after a pause she looked at her granddaughter. "Poppet," she said. "Whereabouts did you take these photos of Elvis."

"Over there," Emily replied, pointing to her right. "The other end of the lake near Buckingham Palace."

"How do you all feel about us taking a walk in that direction?" Lady F asked, standing up.

"I've got to go now," Mrs Moncrief replied. "But you two go ahead."

"I'll show you, Grandma," Emily said as she also stood up. "I don't want to finish my orange."

The three of them set off in different directions. When Emily and Grandma reached the bench at the far end of the park, it was completely free. They looked around for Cesare and his companion, but there was no sign of them.

"Let's walk back this way," Lady F said, pointing to the steep pathway leading to Birdcage Walk. "We'll head back to Victoria and call in somewhere and get a burger."

"Yummy!" Emily replied, pleased that Grandma wasn't going to deny her a burger as a punishment for calling her friend, Mrs Monkey.

At the top of the pathway, Emily suddenly took hold of Lady F's arm. "Grandma!" she said excitedly. "That's him; the man who was with the person you know."

"Where?"

The two of them quickened their pace, reached the roadside and saw about fifty yards away a man limping towards a taxi he'd just called. He had a stick, was wearing a dark green jacket and when he turned to get into the cab, they could see he had a face mask.

"Yes," Grandma said. "That's certainly the person in your photos."

"Do you know who he is?"

"No, but I'd like to find out. I just wonder what Cesare's doing meeting such a person in the park."

Emily felt it all seemed a bit shifty, but thought it better not to say so, given her earlier Monkey comment.

•

"Grandma, I've sent you an email with those 3 photos you asked me for," Emily called from the hallway to Lady F who was sitting in the living room.

"Thank you, my dear."

Emily went into the kitchen to see Chloe.

"Did you enjoy your burger?" Chloe asked, busy cleaning the kitchen surfaces.

"Uh huh. Burgers are my equal favourite meal with pizzas. Do you like burgers, Chloe?"

"Yes, but I don't eat them very often. They're fattening, not good for my figure."

"Oh, I don't worry about that. Mummy says I will when I get older, but I'm not sure I understand why. Something to do with boys, she says."

Chloe just smiled. "Did you go to the park beforehand?" she asked.

"Yes; that's why I've come to see you. I took loads of photos. Do you want to see them?"

"Please," Chloe replied putting down her cloth. Emily pulled out her mobile, clicked on Gallery and handed it to Chloe.

"Just keep clicking away. I've taken over thirty as well as a video of Elvis, my pelican friend."

As Chloe was looking at the photos, Emily decided to tap her for some career advice.

"Do you like your job, Chloe?" she asked.

"What, cleaning? Yes, it's fine; at least when I work for nice people like your grandma."

"She doesn't call you a cleaner. She views you as her housekeeper, which sounds a much better word."

"It's a bit posher, but the work's still the same."

"Do you think I should be a housekeeper or a cleaner when I grow up?"

"No! You're a clever girl. You'll end up doing something much more interesting."

"Grandma thinks you're clever, Chloe. Anyway, I'm beginning to think about what I should do when I grow up. Mummy wants me to be a lawyer like Daddy and Daddy wants me to be a doctor like Mummy, so it gets a bit confusing."

"What do you want to be?"

"Oh, that's easy. I want to be a spacewoman. I'd like to have my own spaceship and go travelling around the planets saying "hello" to all the people who live there."

"Well that certainly sounds a lot more fun than being a cleaner."

"Or a boring lawyer or doctor….. Look, you're at one of the photos Grandma's really interested in," Emily said, changing the subject as she saw Chloe was looking at Elvis and the two men on the bench. "It shows someone called Shifty that Grandpa knows. He's the one on the right. Have a look at the next two as well."

"He's not really called Shifty, is he?"

"No, that's just a nickname. Have a look at the person next to him. They were having a talk, and Grandma wants to know who he is. He looks a bit weird wearing a mask in the open. He can't walk very well either; that's why he's got a stick."

"Let me look at them again," Chloe said, now interested.

After a couple more minutes, she asked Emily to let her have copies of the two men on the bench. She then went to the living room and knocked on the door.

"Come in, Chloe."

"I'm sorry to disturb you, Lady F, but Emily's been showing me her photos of the park. That gentleman, the one talking to Sir Cedric's friend, I think Auntie Betty might know who he is."

"How come?"

"Well, I've never met him, but Auntie Betty's got a client she and the other girls often talk about. He's got a dark green jacket, always wears a mask and has a stick 'cos of his limp."

"Right!" Lady F said determinedly. "That's the only lead we've got. Well done, Chloe. Let's send Betty the photos and I'll also phone her up." She started looking at her phone for the photos but was soon interrupted by Chloe.

"I've got them, Lady F. I can send them to Auntie Betty."

"Fine; it saves me locating them. I'll phone Betty as soon as you've done so."

Half an hour later Betty Bungalow and Lady F were ensconced in the living room with the door firmly closed. They would both have liked to include Chloe in their meeting, but she was instead given the job of making sure that Emily didn't eavesdrop.

"It's not fair," Emily whined to her grandmother as she was shooed into the kitchen once Betty had arrived. "I'm the one who took the photos, so I should be included in your meeting."

"I promise to tell you what we've discussed afterwards."

"But why can't I listen in now?"

"Afterwards, Poppet. You've done a really good job, but there's a lot of detail we need to go through which you wouldn't be interested in."

"Yes, I would."

"Go with Chloe. She'll give you a big piece of sponge cake."

"I don't want any sponge cake. I want to be part of the meeting."

"No," Felicity said, deciding to close the door and not argue any more.

"It's just not fair!" Emily said as she looked at Chloe who'd been standing nearby. "It's not fair," and she stomped off along the corridor to her bedroom.

In the living room, Betty confirmed that the photos were of Panos Pantaloonos, one of her clients. She also told Lady F what little she knew about him as well as the difficulties he caused all her staff.

"So, does he actually do any work?"

"I don't think so," Betty replied. "He seems to be retired and just spends his time reading books in his flat. He does go out occasionally because I once saw him go into Harrods about a year ago, but whether he goes to other places, I don't know."

"You know what I'm thinking?"

"You suspect he might be involved in these art thefts from the Gallery."

Lady Felicity nodded. "I know it's a long shot but isn't it the only clue we have at the moment?"

"Yes," Betty agreed.

"So, what do we do?"

"I think we should keep a watch on his movements. We can't do it twenty-four hours a day, but we can do something."

"Have you told all your girls about the Gallery thefts yet?"

"All, except the two new ones – the sisters of your friend."

"They're the ones actually working in his flat at present, aren't they?"

"Yes, I can't change them because Mr Pantaloonos won't have any of my others."

"So?"

"I'm not sure. I'm reluctant to tell them everything because I don't know them well enough yet. But they've got to be involved somehow. Can I think about it?"

"Over to you," Lady F replied. "You're the operator in our team."

•

It was after ten at night when Sir Cedric walked into the living room to join Lady F.

"I've spent over two hours searching the internet for Panos Pantaloonos. I can't find a thing about him," he said wearily.

His wife closed her laptop. "The same here. I've just had a text from Betty; she got two of her younger girls onto it as well as herself. Everyone's drawn a blank."

"Perhaps Panos Pantaloonos isn't his real name."

"Perhaps."

"Also, I've been wondering if we're seeing 'reds under the beds' on this one. Suppose Cesare just sat on the bench and got talking to a stranger."

"Or they could be genuine friends who arranged to meet up. Cesare is allowed to have friends like everyone else."

"Yes," Cedric said and then sat silently contemplating matters.

"But then of course it may not be totally innocent," Felicity said after a while.

"Yes," Cedric agreed again.

"What do you honestly think, Cedric – not just about this Panos character, but about the whole question of The Gallery?"

"That's a question I ask myself ten times a day. I don't know what to think about Panos, but on the bigger question, it may be I'm seeing 'reds under the beds' on that one as well. For example, the Cezanne hanging on a wall thousands of miles away may actually be a fake. But my instincts tell me something fishy's going on. Ask me to prove it and I can't – but that's what I think."

"And Cesare?"

"That's what I can't decide on. He may be involved in funny business, or he may not, and things are just happening around him he's not equipped to handle. I simply can't tell with him."

"His shifty personality doesn't help."

"Oh, he's shifty alright. That's a hundred percent certain." Cedric stood up before continuing: "Come on, let's go and join young Emily in the Land of Nod."

15
Mysterious Visitors

Mopp no longer accompanied Bow and HalfPint up to Panos's flat, so when the concierge had collected them from the basement car park, she walked over to a white van parked about twenty yards away. She'd recognized the number plate when she drove in and wanted to find out what it was doing there. As she approached from the side, she heard music and saw a man in the driver's seat looking at his mobile phone. She rapped hard on the window giving the occupant an unexpected start. He looked at her before turning down the music and lowering his window.

"Hello Terry," she said in a crisp voice. "What are you doing in a posh block of flats in Knightsbridge?"

"Oh hello, Jade," Terry replied. "I could ask the same of you."

"You answer my question first."

"Oh um… just business, you know."

"No, I don't know, Terry. I've never been able to work out what you and your brothers do."

"That's because we've lots of different business interests," he said with a smile.

"Yea, yea."

"So, why are you here?"

"Dropping off a couple of our cleaners for one of the flats. We at least have proper jobs."

"What do you mean by that?"

"Work it out." Jade looked at the passenger seat before continuing: "Why do you want a rug in your van on a hot day like today? Hold on …. There's something underneath which moved, I'm sure. Have you got a mouse?"

Terry looked slightly guilty. "No," he mumbled. "You must have imagined it."

"No way! Come on, what is it?"

"Nothing."

Jade looked at him sceptically. "You're up to something, I know. Still, keep it secret, if you want......" She waited for a response but when she didn't get one, she just said "I've got to go. Try and behave yourself, Terry," before turning round and walking over to her van.

"See you, Jade," Terry mumbled before closing the window.

A small head popped out from under the rug.

"You are ze imbecile!" it said, clearly annoyed.

"What do you mean?" Terry asked.

"You play ze music too loud. It draws ze attention to us. You have been told to keep under ze radar, as you English say. Imbecile!"

Terry shrugged his shoulders, turned the music on and picked up his mobile once more. He really wanted to take hold of this small man, called the Adjutant, and squash him, but he didn't dare. His two elder brothers would really beat him up if he did, just as they'd been doing all his life. After all, they had a really good deal working for these small people - they'd go mad if they lost it!

Meanwhile upstairs on the fifteenth floor, Panos Pantaloonos had opened his front door to let Bow and HalfPint into his flat. After having gone through the normal routine of inspecting and then spraying them with disinfectant, he stood aside to let them in.

"Kitchen!" Panos barked. "Work! Living room - entry verboten!"

"Don't you want to punch him on the nose?" Bow said to her sister once Panos was out of earshot.

"Yea, but we'd better not. Betty earns good money from him."

"I'd pay good money to punch the Nutter on the nose," was the tart reply as Bow opened the ironing board.

"Why can't we go into the living room. Has he got guests?"

HalfPint stepped into the hall. She could hear voices but couldn't make out what they were saying. "Yes," she said when she returned. "Let's do the bedrooms and bathrooms first. Perhaps they'll have gone once we've finished them."

"Lead the way."

In the living room, Panos was sitting on a comfortable armchair opposite three small figures sitting on a sofa. Two were wearing black berets on their heads, while the one in the middle had a tricorn with a gold braid.

"You were saying, Marshal?" Panos continued the conversation they were all having before he'd got up to let the cleaners in.

"I was ze saying, Monsieur Pantaloonos, zat we are getting to have ze concerns wiz ze monetary flows which are moving not in ze direction of us. I emphasise the word 'not'. It is ze big concern at ze embassy and in ze government. We are not ze happy."

"Haven't we had this discussion before?"

"Maybe, but still ze issue exists. We have done ze work; we must be paid ze money! You must pay us now. Now, I emphasise. Now!" the Marshal finished forcibly.

Panos sighed. "I've told you before that no one can be paid until the paintings are sold," he said. "It takes time to find a buyer for these works, especially when it is all being done highly confidentially."

"But it is taking ze too long, Monsieur Pantaloonos. As we all know, ze rewards are split zree ways. We have done our job, it is you zat needs to make ze sales. We are not happy at ze speed you work."

"We have four paintings still to sell and I am making progress on all of them."

"Do we agree it is four?" the Marshal asked looking at his companion to the right. "What are zese paintings?"

"Zere is ze Canaletto, ze Gaughin, ze Turnip, ze van Duck and ze 'C.'"

"Zat is five!" the Marshal exclaimed and then stared at Panos. "Why do you say it is ze four, Monsieur? What is ze explanation?"

Panos sighed again. "Firstly, let me correct the colonel," he said. "It is Turner, not Turnip, and van Dyke, not van Duck."

"But it is still ze five the colonel spoke about," the Marshal replied. "How do you account for ze difference? Where is ze painting number five? Speak now, I do ze insist!"

"Marshal, the colonel is quite right. I omitted the last work of art because I have only just received it. The 'C' that he talks about is the Constable."

"Zat is quite right," the third member of the party said. "We zought we were going to obtain ze Holbein, but at the last moment it was ze Constable."

"Now I remember, Capitaine," the Marshal replied. "We do not have ze proper understanding of why zere was zis change. It does not make us happy, Monsieur Pantaloonos. Ze Holbein was worz ze much more zan ze Constable."

"I agree, Marshal," Panos said. "However, I gave a lengthy explanation to the colonel at the time."

"Please to repeat, Monsieur."

"Some last-minute questions were being asked about the Holbein at The Gallery. That meant that major suspicions would have been raised if it disappeared. Since all arrangements were in place for the operation that night, it was decided to go ahead but to take another painting. The Constable was the most convenient choice with little time to spare."

"But it is of ze less value zan ze Holbein."

"Correct, but that's life."

"Maybe," said the Marshal. "But we are not ze happy."

After an awkward silence, Panos suggested that he should give a detailed account of the discussions he was having about the sale of the various works of art, which the Marshal agreed would be useful.

Half an hour later, Panos phoned for a member of the concierge team to escort the Marshal and his two companions down to the carpark. When the doorbell went, the four of them came out of the living room just as Bow and HalfPint were in the hallway. The smaller goddess was in the front, and she immediately spun round and put a finger to her lips to indicate that her sister should say nothing. Panos saw they had seen the little people so when he had closed the front door, he turned round, looked at the two cleaners and shouted "Forget!" followed by "Work!" and pointed to the kitchen.

During the rest of the morning, Bow was agitating to finish because she wanted to leave so they could talk about the three little people.

"We're done," Bow said just after 12-30pm.

"We can't go yet," HalfPint replied. "We're meant to be here until one. Anyway, we need to have a final look for any items we might have missed."

"You mean tricks cunningly planted to catch us out?" Bow whispered.

"Sssh! But yes."

"Okay, but let's hurry up."

"Look, we have to stay another twenty-five minutes, so let's do it properly."

The two went round the flat together as they carried out their final double-checking routine. They then followed Panos as he reviewed their work. When he'd finished, there was a lengthy silence as they all stood by the front door.

"How did we do, Mr Pantaloonos?" Bow eventually asked as she was getting frustrated waiting for the score and was desperate to leave.

"Five!" he barked.

"Five!" Bow exclaimed as HalfPint also groaned. "Does that mean we've passed or failed?"

"Borderline!"

"So, what happens now?"

"One more chance!"

"And what if we get five again?"

"Fired! Two fives together equals fired!"

Just at that moment, the concierge arrived and Bow and HalfPint left. When they got down to the carpark, they put the vacuum, ironing board and other materials into the back of Mopp's van. They asked her to drop them off at Constitution Hill as they'd like to walk the rest of the way.

"So, what are Lilliputians doing at the Nutter's flat?" Artemis asked as soon as they'd got out of the van.

"I don't know," Hebe replied. "I didn't recognize any of them. They weren't in any of the sergeant's training sessions, or at least I didn't see them."

"I agree; they definitely weren't there. But then the Nutter wouldn't have a meeting with just security staff. Do you think one of them was the Ambassador?"

"Nah. Anyway, they seemed to be wearing uniform, but I didn't recognize it."

"Shall we walk over and see Rach and Sergeant MacGobo? They'll know who they were."

"Let me phone Rach up first. She might be at her college."

"When am I going to get one of those mobile phone things?" Artemis asked as she watched Hebe waiting for Rach to answer.

"Next week. It's all in the masterplan."

•

Just after 5pm Hebe and Artemis arrived at Duck Island for a meeting with Rach and the sergeant. A gardener was waiting for them by the gate, which he unlocked to let them in. They then made their way to the embassy and again found Sergeant MacGobo on his platform with Rach sitting on her scooter by his side.

"You is getting into bad habits, Private!" were the friendly words greeting them as they walked across the back lawn. "You is five minutes late, you lazy little one-legged ostrich! If you is not five minutes early, you is late!"

"Does the same compliment apply to Lady Artemis, Sergeant?" Hebe asked.

"No, of course it does not! I is directing my words at you, you squashed-nosed, over-weight stupid water rabbit!" Sergeant MacGobo then looked at Hebe's sister, bowed to her and said: "My Lady Artemis; delighted to meet you once more."

"Thank you, Sergeant MacGobo. And I'm very pleased to see you too," Artemis replied, no longer bursting into uncontrollable giggles in the sergeant's presence, but unable to suppress a smile.

"Let's move on," Rach said, deciding to intervene in the conversation. "Tea's waiting for you on the table when you sit down, but you'll have to pour it out yourselves. Then shoot away."

Sergeant MacGobo flinched. "I does not like that phrase, Miss Rach," he said. "What with being a military man, when it's proposed to the people in front of me."

"I do," Hebe said. "You've got your bow and arrows, Arty. Fire one at the sergeant; the Empress's granddaughter just gave you permission."

Artemis raised her eyebrows. "Come on, let's stop messing around. We've got important things to discuss. Will you explain why we're here, Hebe, or shall I?"

"I'll do it. You pour the tea." Hebe then looked at the two little people on the platform and continued: "How well do you know the Lilliputian community in London?" she asked.

"What community is you talking about?" the sergeant asked.

"All the people from Lilliput who is in London."

"They is all in the embassy."

"But don't some Lilliputians come to London on non-embassy business? Also, where do all the staff live?"

"The only person from Lilliput on non-embassy business we know about is me," Rach said. "And I live most of my time in the embassy even though I've got my rooms in Imperial. All the embassy staff do the same, I think."

"Yes, they does," Sergeant MacGobo confirmed. "I sense, Private, you is asking these questions for a reason. That being my military brain at work."

"I get the same feeling," Rach said. "What's going on?"

Before Hebe had a chance to reply, Artemis jumped into the conversation. "Isn't it obvious that those little men we saw this morning must be from the embassy, Hebe?" she directed at her sister.

"What little men is these?" the sergeant asked frowning, while Rach gave him a concerned look.

"Do either of you know someone called Panos Pantaloonos who lives in Knightsbridge?" Hebe asked.

The two Lilliputians both shook their heads. "Does you think he comes from Lilliput?"

"No," replied Hebe. "He's a normal size human. Artemis and I work in his flat occasionally. We were there this morning and found he was having a meeting with three Lilliputians."

"Three Lilliputians!" MacGobo exclaimed. "Is you sure?"

"We're absolutely sure," Artemis replied.

"Were they men or women?" Rach asked.

"All men," Hebe answered, then after a short pause, she said: "Neither of you know anything about this, do you?"

"Not me," Rach said, shaking her head.

"I does not neither," the sergeant added.

"Perhaps it's something the Ambassador's dealing with," Artemis suggested. "He might have been at the meeting."

"No, Lady Artemis. Firstly, the Ambassador he were in his office all morning. Secondly, given my security role, I is informed on all issues we is dealing with. This Pantopolopolumis gentleman, is not on my radar, if you understand. That being a military term I is using from time to time."

"It's Pantaloonos," Artemis corrected.

"Well, whatever his poxy name is, we does not know about him here in the embassy."

"What did these Lilliputians look like?" Rach asked.

"That is a very good question, Miss Rach," the sergeant complimented her. "I is about to ask that very question myself."

Hebe looked to Artemis to reply: "Clearly about your height. They seemed to be wearing dark suits, which Hebe thinks looked like uniforms; they also had black things on their heads."

"Berets," Hebe added.

"Except the one in front, who seemed to be the leader. He was wearing some sort of square looking hat."

"I'm sure it was a tricorn. It had three sides."

"What!" exclaimed Sergeant MacGobo. "There were a little man with a black tricorn on his head!"

"That sounds like the Marshal!" Rach added excitedly. "In London now."

"So, I take it you do know them?" Hebe asked.

"The Marshal's the Head of the Blefuscu's military. The top geezer. Definitely not from Lilliput."

"What's Blefuscu?" Artemis asked.

"I'll answer," Hebe said, putting a hand up towards the platform to stop everyone speaking at the same time. "Blefuscu's an island near Lilliput. It's also got little people, and I think the same rules apply with humans – they forget their existence within seconds of them disappearing from sight. I've not been to Blefuscu for over a hundred years. They're traditional enemies of Lilliput and the two countries have fought wars against each other for about a thousand years. Personally, I don't like the Blefuscudians; they're arrogant and rude, always looking for an argument or a fight....... Is that about right?" Hebe finished, looking at Rach and the Sergeant.

"That sounds okey-dokes to me," Rach answered.

"But what were they doing in the Nutter's flat?" Artemis asked.

"Who's the Nutter?"

"Panos Pantaloonos," Hebe replied.

"Lady Artemis's question is also the question I too is asking myself," Sergeant MacGobo said with a worried expression on his face. "In fact, I wants to know what the Marshal is up to in London. Also, who his two companions is. Can you describe them?"

Hebe shook her head. "We only saw them for a few seconds. All that we really noticed was their black berets."

"They is undoubtedly military men. It is all very concerning, it is."

"There's also the matter of the Nutter," Artemis said, looking at her sister. "How come he can have a meeting with the little people in his flat if he's meant to forget them when they're not there. Did they just turn up and ring his bell?"

"I don't know," she replied, shrugging her shoulders. "Lots of mysteries, although I have heard of instances where people don't forget the little people without any real explanation."

The four sat in silence for a while before Rach said in an unusually authoritative tone: "Fergus, I think we need to tell them what's going on."

"Fergus!" exclaimed Hebe. "Who's...... Oh no, it's you," and she pointed at Sergeant MacGobo whose face had begun to colour up, while she burst out laughing.

"I does not like that name," the sergeant growled.

"Where did it come from?" Hebe asked.

"Grandma," Rach answered. "Every diplomat has to have two names, unlike just the one we have on Lilliput; so Grandma chose Fergus for the sergeant or captain."

"Then I'm going to call you Fergus from now on," Hebe said, still laughing while looking at the small man on the platform. "It's a good Highlander name."

"You is bloody not, you snivelling cross between a hyena's intestines and a cockroach's stuffed nose. You is to keep calling me Sergeant or even Sir. I has noted you has not once called me Sir since we met in London."

"We'll see," Hebe replied. "Anyway, what's all this you want to tell Artemis and me?"

The sergeant looked at Rach before saying "I is not sure, Miss Rach. I is not sure."

"Oh, come on, Fergus, it's okey-dokes. They're friends; after all, Hebe's in your regiment."

"I accepts what you says about Private MacHebe, but...."

"You've got a problem with me, haven't you?" Artemis said, aware that Sergeant MacGobo was staring in her direction.

"Lady Artemis, I has the greatest respect for you, but....."

"Would it help if I joined your regiment?"

"Arty, don't be nuts," Hebe said. "You'll get called all sorts of names by the sergeant."

"How about it, Sergeant?" Artemis asked.

"That would help; yes it would," was the reply. "But I is not able to offer you the rank to which you is entitled, being only an acting captain."

"What rank's that then?" Hebe demanded, sensing she wasn't going to like the answer.

"General."

"General!" screamed Hebe. "How come she gets to be a general and I'm only a private or a lance-corporal?"

"You shut your big gob, Private! I has told you before, promotion decisions is none of your bloody business, you pathetic toe rag!"

"I demand to see------"

"Ssh, Hebe" Artemis interrupted her. "Listen to me everyone…. Sergeant, I'm only prepared to join your regiment if I come in at the level of private, like my sister."

"Really!" exclaimed MacGobo.

"Really."

"You're the Nutter now," Hebe muttered.

"Shut it, Private!" the Sergeant shouted.

Over the next few minutes, Lady Artemis Olympiakos was enlisted into the Argyll & Sutherland Highlanders Regiment under the name of Private MacArtemis.

"Fergus, can we now get on and tell Hebe and Artemis what's going on?"

"I is now happy to do so. I is feeling a lot more comfortable."

Between them, Rach and Sergeant MacGobo gave a detailed account of the real reason they were in London. There was always tension between Lilliput and Blefuscu, but in recent months it had been rising at an alarming rate. The Blefuscu navy was harassing the Lilliput fishing fleet, ramming a number of boats and sinking one of them. Shells were also being fired into Lilliput's territorial waters and there was evidence of a significant increase in Blefuscu's munitions production, which was being funded from unknown sources since the country was not as wealthy as Lilliput. Perhaps most alarmingly, Rach's surveillance team in Special Projects had picked up communications about possible attacks on Lilliput interests overseas. This really meant embassies, although there was also concern about Lilliput College in Cambridge.

The limited evidence to date suggested that London was probably the main target which was why Rach and Sergeant MacGobo had been sent there. Rach did have a genuine research project at Imperial College, but she'd also set up a small unit to carry out a more intensive surveillance operation than was possible from several thousand miles away. She'd brought two members of her team with her who were based full-time in the college. She had also enlisted a small number of her Imperial colleagues into the unit, telling them enough to be interested in participating, but not the full story.

As far as Sergeant MacGobo was concerned, he'd been sent as the embassy's Military Attache to see if he could pick up any useful information in the diplomatic circles. More importantly, he was to provide any 'muscle power' if needed to support Rach.

"So, you see," the sergeant said at the end of this explanation. "The arrival of the Marshal in London does tell us something big is going on. Anyone he meets is to be of considerable interest to us."

"Which means this Panos guy is a number one suspect," Rach added.

"But a suspect for what?" Artemis asked.

"We does not yet know, Private," the sergeant answered.

"But we're going to have to find out," Rach said. "And that's why we need your help."

"Blimey!" Hebe exclaimed. "We're going to become spies! So, what happens next?"

"We is going to take a deep breath and apply a military solution," Sergeant MacGobo answered. "Today is Friday and tomorrow morning we has another training exercise. After that, I propose we has a detailed planning meeting. Much as I dislike involving him cos he is not a military man, we has got to speak to the Ambassador this evening."

"And I'm going to phone Grandma," Rach added.

"So, we do nothing more today?" Hebe enquired.

"Nothing more, Private. But we has got us a busy day tomorrow."

•

As Hebe and Artemis walked back through the park towards Pimlico, they reflected on the events of the day.

"I didn't know what to expect from my visit to London," Artemis said. "I thought I was going to experience normal life in a big city. However. I get the feeling that what's happening to us isn't quite what happens to most normal people."

"Yea, that's probably right, but it's fun, isn't it?"

"I suppose it depends on what comes next. Whatever it is, it's bound to be a big surprise. After all, I got up this morning to do our cleaning job at the Nutter's flat and have ended the day enlisted as a private in Lilliput's Argyll & Sutherland Highlanders Regiment. I bet that's not happened to anyone else currently walking in the park."

"And tomorrow we're going to become spies."

"On that matter, we've got an important issue to address. If we're going to watch the Nutter, which is what I suppose our job will be, we'd better make sure we don't get fired. Another five score and we're out."

"Good point. It's obvious we got done today because of the kitchen. We didn't clean the microwave or the toaster; also those marks in the sauces cupboard."

"That last one about the cupboard was because we were rushing. The microwave and the toaster, he's never used before, so we just didn't look."

"I think when we get back we should both create our own really detailed list of everything to check next time we're in the flat," said Hebe. "We'll then compare notes and create a combined master schedule and make sure everything's ticked off next Tuesday. We can't afford to get fired."

"Betty won't be pleased if we do."

"I'm thinking about the sergeant. He'll court martial us."

"But he can't put us in front of a firing squad."

"Not officially," Hebe said. "But knowing him, he might find a way."

16
The Plan in Action

"I'm very distressed," Death said as he stood in front of Hades' throne. "This has never happened to me before."

"Just don't worry about it, Death. We've got it all under control. All you have to do is walk back to the ferry and leave the rest to us."

"Shouldn't I have an armed guard?"

"No need; the attack's going to take place at the jetty. The four scoundrels want to escape from the Underworld."

"But why? Don't they like it here? I always thought you looked after them pretty well in the circumstances."

"What circumstances?"

"The fact they're dead."

"That's what they don't seem to like very much."

Death stood silently reflecting on matters. "What I don't understand, Hades," he eventually said: "Is why you just don't detain these so-called scoundrels now before they begin their attack?"

"We want to catch them red-handed, then we can give them a proper punishment. It will be an example to anyone else who wants to try to escape."

"But you're using me as bait."

"No, I'm not!" Hades exclaimed. "All I'm doing is telling you that something unusual is going to happen today while you walk back to the ferry. A walk you carry out every day. I'm also telling you how we're going to deal with this unusual matter, so it shouldn't be a concern."

"Umm..." Death responded, not entirely convinced. "Can you please repeat what's going to happen and how you're going to deal with it."

"Fine," Hades replied, suppressing the groan he wanted to give because he'd already gone through the matter twice already. However, he did accept that it had all come as a big shock to Death, so he needed to be tolerant. "As I explained earlier, we've found out that four people are going to try to escape from the Underworld by attacking you and Charon at the ferry as you return today. Those four people are the pirate Greenbeard, Bill Sikes, Mrs PorkyPie and Pharoah Tutansillytwerp----"

"An unusual grouping," Death interrupted.

"I agree, but that's who they are."

"And you say the reason why they're waiting for me to return instead of just over-powering the ferryman, is so they can beat me up and break my bones?"

"Unfortunately, yes."

Death took a deep breath. "That is why I'm very distressed. You do understand, don't you, Hades?"

"I do," Hades replied with a slight sigh. "But as I keep saying to you, no harm will come to you or Charon. We have a team seven strong to intercept them before they reach you. It'll be the scoundrels who get a good beating.

"The team being?"

"Me, Persephone, Sisyphus, Attila, Genghis, Cerberus and Billie."

"Umm…" went Death again. "Are you sure this team's up to the job. With great respect to Lady Persephone, she's a girl."

"No, she's not!" Hades shouted back at Death. "My wife is a goddess with great powers. She's also recently been building up her muscle strength at fitness classes while on Olympus. They're run by Totty; you remember that young lady that caused you and Poseidon to have a slight disagreement a little while ago."

Death frowned, remembering full well how The Sea God refused to let him bring Totty to the Underworld despite the fact she'd drowned. However, he didn't want to think about the matter now; there were far more important things currently on his mind.

"So, who's this Billie person?" Death asked instead.

"She's the little dog who came with Mrs PorkyPie. She used to be called Popsy Something-or-Other."

"Well, you can't include her!" Death exclaimed. "She's a tiny little thing. She won't be any good in a fight."

"Okay, let's call it a team of six and a half," Hades responded. "But then there's also you and Charon. You've got your scythe and Charon's got his pole. That's enough to take out two of the scoundrels without any help from the rest of us."

"But I've never used my scythe. I only carry it around for show."

"Then now's the time to put it to some practical purpose."

"How?"

"How what?"

"How does it work?"

"You mean you don't know?"

Death shook his head, so Hades stood up from his throne. "Here, hand it to me and I'll show you."

Hades took hold of Death's scythe in both hands and then swept it firmly about a foot above the floor. "There, that should cut off their legs," he said. "Now, let's lift it higher up and make the same stroke...... There again, that's the head off. It really is as simple as all that. You try it."

Hades handed back the scythe and got Death to practice his sweeps. "See, it's not difficult," he said after a while, once he was satisfied his pupil had mastered the correct technique.

"Good," Death said, feeling better prepared to protect himself than a few minutes earlier. "So, what happens now?"

"You wait here and count to five hundred, while I race off and join the others in hiding near the ferry. I'll have to go the back way, so I'm not spotted. Then you follow your usual route to the ferry; once you arrive the fun and games will begin."

"Fun and games," Death repeated, confused. "I don't understand."

"Don't worry about it. It's merely a turn of phrase."

"What! For me being beaten up?"

"Come on, you know what I mean. Just behave perfectly normally and it will be fine. The last thing you should do is give any indication you're expecting something to happen." Before Death had a chance to reply, Hades got up and said: "Look, I must be off; see you later."

The god walked to the doorway behind his throne, leaving Death to reluctantly begin counting to five hundred before setting off to meet what he still felt might be his doom.

•

Earlier that day, the Marchioness and the three others started to put their plan into action. Interestingly, there was also another plan being implemented that they didn't know about.

The Marchioness emerged from the Women's Quarters and walked over to the Young Men's Dormitory. She was followed at a distance by Vesta. The Marchioness found Fairy waiting for her and the two set off together for breakfast. Ming had been watching Fairy from the nearby doorway of the Young Girls' Dormitory. She and Vesta joined up and then trailed some way behind the Marchioness and Fairy as they walked towards the Kitchens and the Dining Room.

Bill Sikes and Greenbeard came out of the Men's Quarters together and also set off for breakfast. Billie had been lying unobserved by a nearby wall waiting for Sikes, so she proceeded to follow the two men. Sisyphus had been assigned to watch Greenbeard. He came out of the building about a minute after the two men, saw Billie ahead of him but still decided to follow them, just in case the two conspirators went their separate ways. He was a long way back and ambled along looking as if all he was doing was heading off for breakfast.

In the Dining Room, Sikes and Greenbeard sat at a separate table to the Marchioness and Fairy, all four of them under observation from their watchers who were also having breakfast. This included Billie who was gnawing at a small bone near Sisyphus.

The two grown men didn't spend long over their meal. They soon got up and were now followed by Attila and Genghis who had been talking together at the far end of the room, while slyly keeping an eye on the pair. Greenbeard led the way to The Carrier Department where he'd stored the baseball bats under a tarpaulin in a back room which was rarely used. He and his companion took the bats and then set off, taking a roundabout route towards the ferry. This was because they wanted to pass as few people as possible who might ask awkward questions about what they were doing. Neither of them looked round to check if they were being followed. They were practiced hands and knew full well that continuous backward glances would suggest they were doing something suspicious. Anyway, it was unlikely they would have seen Attila and Genghis who were well behind them and were also experienced enough not to be spotted.

When the Marchioness and Fairy left the Dining Room, they headed straight towards the ferry. This time they were followed by Sisyphus who was trailed by Cerberus and Billie; as they went along the three of them swapped positions, taking it in turns to be the lead follower. This was useful because the two they were tracking frequently gave fearful looks over their shoulders, but generally spotted someone different each time. When the Marchioness and Fairy were near the ferry, they went and hid behind a large rock about twenty yards from the landing area. This entire part of the Underworld consisted of a number of large rocks. Cerberus, who knew it intimately, led his companions to another rock over on the far left-hand side where they took cover.

As expected, Bill Sikes and Greenbeard arrived in due course. They came from the direction Cerberus had expected, so he, Billie and Sisyphus were well out of sight. Attila and Genghis had stopped following the two men before the rocky area; they both moved over to a derelict building where they waited.

Within a short while Billie arrived, having run at full speed.

"Woofy, woofy," she managed to bark, before having a good pant. "They're all together." She panted again before continuing: "Follow me. We've got to go a roundabout way."

"Come on, Billie, I'll carry you," said Genghis as he picked up the little dog. "You tell us which way to go, but quietly."

"Woofy," was the almost inaudible response.

Billie's job was to run backwards and forwards to make sure everyone got into position without the prospective escapees observing them. As they waited for the ferryboat to come in, Billie's next mission was to go to the palace to collect Persephone, again bringing her in a circuitous route to join the others. While she was doing this, Sisyphus crept between the rocks to reach Cerberus's hut. The day before he had left five quarterstaffs there; each one being about seven feet in length with metal tips at both ends.

Persephone had not arrived by the time Charon punted the ferryboat alongside the jetty bringing three new arrivals, together with Death. However, Sisyphus had returned and he, Attila and Genghis were now fully armed with their quarterstaffs in case the other side decided on a change in their plans. This could involve an attack now instead of waiting for Death to return from Hades. Cerberus had slunk off a little while ago and just as everyone began to disembark, he ran up to the group barking very loudly.

"Woof! Woof! Give us a Mars bar or I'll bite yer bums!" He then went up to the smallest new arrival, an elderly, grey-haired woman in her mid-80's and growled menacingly, all three of his mouths showing their sharp teeth.

She screamed as did her two aged male companions as they backed away. For the next few minutes, Cerberus deliberately behaved very aggressively, barking and growling and threatening to bite everyone's bums, generating all sorts of terror amongst the new arrivals. Death eventually intervened and threw Cerberus a Mars bar, which calmed him down somewhat.

"Woof! Woof! I'll walk with you to the palace," the three-headed dog said in a loud voice just as the group set off with Death. "I've then got to go to the Kitchens before doing a full day's tour of the entire Underworld. I won't be back at the ferry until this evening."

Cerberus then proceeded to go up to the elderly, grey-haired woman. All three heads gave her a warm smile, and he set about explaining that he was called Cerberus, and he was the Head of Internal Security in the Underworld. He stressed that despite his official role, he was really a friendly sort of dog deep down. He very much hoped he and the elderly lady, who turned out to be called Agnes Wainwright, a retired teacher from Newport Pagnell, would become firm friends very soon. In fact, if Agnes had any questions or if there was anything which she needed, he would be very happy to help her. He told her about his number 2, Billie, a chihuahua who shouldn't really be in the Underworld but was allowed to stay. Agnes also heard all about Vesta, Ming and Aggy and many more of Cerberus's friends, and just before they reached the palace, she was introduced to Audrey, the snake's tail who gave her a friendly smile followed by a loud hiss about six inches from her face. By this time, poor Agnes was in need of her daily medication, as she wondered if she wasn't really dead after all, but in some strange mental institution she'd read about in the Walsall area.

Cerberus didn't go on his tour of the Underworld, but instead returned unobserved to the ferryboat area. He didn't join his companions, as his role was to position himself behind another large rock on the far side of the jetty. This was all according to the plan which he and the others had meticulously worked out the day before. Not surprisingly, as Head of Internal Security, he viewed it as the Cerberus Plan, although in reality it had been formulated by Hades with useful input from the others.

Persephone arrived, carrying Billie. The goddess was given a staff like the others and waited silently out of sight. Billie, after a short rest scampered back to the palace. She'd been shown where to wait for Hades the day before - a small room just behind the throne room. Vesta had left a bone, together with a bowl of water, for her to nourish herself before the battle between 'the good guys and the bad guys'.

Everyone now waited. The conspirators were behind their rock, unaware that there was another group watching them concealed by another rock. There was also Cerberus located somewhere in front of them, remaining very quiet and still for once. Nothing was going to happen until Death and the ferryman arrived.

"Come on, Billie," Hades said as he came out of the throne room and picked up the little dog. "Let's get moving."

"Woofy; woofy," was the response. "We've got to go the back way."

"You just tell me where to run."

"Woofy!"

Hades ran at full speed with Billie in his arms. Every so often he would stop, look at the small dog for confirmation they were following the right path and then carried on. As they approached the ferry area, all communication was by head movements with no words being spoken and certainly no "woofy, woofys." Gods can move very fast when they want to and today Hades wanted to, so he soon joined his wife and the others behind their rock.

They didn't have to wait too long for Charon to arrive once more with his ferry. He drew up by the jetty, tied up the boat and walked ashore, stretching his legs for a few minutes. At that point, Hades, Persephone and their three companions put on black balaclavas, and they all now looked down the pathway to the palace, anticipating Death's arrival at any time.

Death himself had been walking slowly, since he was becoming increasingly fearful with each step he took. He thought it was all very well for Hades to tell him to behave normally, but it wasn't easy knowing he was going to be the subject of a violent assault. Still, he had his scythe, and he kept swinging it around, which was precisely what he shouldn't be doing since he'd never done so before. Anyway, he realised this as the ferry came into sight, so with a super-human effort – which was also unusual as he wasn't human – he managed to hold it still as he got closer to the jetty.

With a tap on the shoulders from Greenbeard, the planned escapees suddenly leapt into action as they emerged from behind their rock. They charged silently as two groups, with Greenbeard and the Marchioness heading towards Death as the others went for Charon. To their great surprise, Cerberus suddenly came bounding out at great speed from behind his rock, barking like mad.

"Woof! Woof! Woof!" he went, followed by innumerable barks and growls as he raced past Death and launched himself into the air and knocked Greenbeard over before he had a chance to raise his baseball bat.

"Aaaah! Aaaah!" screamed the Marchioness, shocked at the sudden appearance of the large dog. "Aaaah!" She still had some fight within her, though, and raised her baseball bat, ready to bash Cerberus on all three heads. However, she hesitated because she couldn't be sure whom she was going to hit. This was because Cerberus and Greenbeard were continuously rolling around on the ground, the pirate thumping Cerberus as many times as possible as well as trying to push him off, while Cerberus was biting large bits out of his adversary's arms and legs. The Marchioness kept positioning herself for her hit, but then something extraordinary happened which was definitely not in any plan.

There was now a lot of shouting, screaming, barking and growling in the whole ferryboat area. As for Death, he had reacted spontaneously to the start of the attack by swinging his scythe round at head height. He was like a whirling dervish in a trance, unable to control his actions. His feet drew him closer to the fighting with his scythe continuing to swing. Suddenly it felt a slight resistance as it moved through the air, because it had just cut off the Marchioness's head. Since she was already dead, it didn't stop the rest of her body from standing up and waving the baseball bat around until she received a painful thump on the back from Persephone's quarterstaff. She toppled over on her stomach where she remained prostate.

By now, Death's scythe was continuing to make its presence felt on proceedings. Having decapitated the Marchioness, it then went on to cut off Lefty, which was the name for Cerberus's left head. This caused the Head of Internal Security to go berserk with the pain and, amidst much barking, he jumped off Greenbeard and attacked Death knocking him over. By now Sisyphus had arrived on the scene with Persephone. He decided there was only one course of action which was to knock everyone out, so he bashed Cerberus on both heads with his staff and then did the same with Death. Meanwhile, a much-mauled Greenbeard had begun to get up but Persephone, following Sisyphus's example, brought her staff down on his head and he collapsed on the ground, totally inert.

Bill Sikes and Fairy were also having a tough time in attacking Charon. Before Sikes managed to reach him, he felt a sharp pain and jolt on his left side as a couple of ribs broke from Hades' staff. Another whack on the other side and he was face down on the floor. He tried to get up, but his head got no further than Genghis's foot which smashed into his face, breaking his nose and a number of front teeth.

Fairy soon realised things weren't going to plan, so he stopped midway between the boulder and Charon. He was about to turn round and flee, when strong arms lifted him off the ground. It only took Attila a dozen paces before he threw the young pharaoh into the river where he was soon feasted on by a number of grateful piranha fish.

Charon's brain tended to work slowly, so it hadn't told the rest of his body how to react to all this nearby violence. When it cranked into action, it realised that whatever had been going on was all over. Charon just surveyed the scene and looked at Hades.

"Will Death be going back today, or will he be staying here?" he asked.

"He'll be going back," the god answered. "Stay here, Charon, and I'll fix him up before he leaves."

Billie had been determined to join in the fight, but everything had happened so quickly that she didn't have an opportunity. She'd been determined to bite Bill Sikes in the groin as revenge for the hard kick he'd previously given her. But when she went over to him on the ground, she felt he'd suffered enough that day, so she turned round and went to look at the Marchioness's head which was on the ground.

This head was fully conscious and functioning despite not being attached to its body. It had been screaming and shouting loudly in frustration at the failure of the conspirators' plan. When it saw Billie in front of it, a loud wail of "traitor!!!!" was directed at the small dog.

"I'm sorry," Billie replied quite sincerely, her eyes beginning to water.

"Come away, Billie," Persephone said as the goddess picked her up. "She's not worth it."

"Traitor!!!!" was again screamed. "Traitor!!!!" At that moment Genghis's foot again came into action and kicked the Marchioness in the mouth as he'd done with Sikes.

"That will shut her up," he said.

By now everyone had taken off their balaclavas.

"Pull Fairy out of the water," Hades said to Attila. "Let's take stock of where we are."

Cerberus and the Marchioness were both lacking heads; the Head of Internal Security was also unconscious as was the pirate. Bill Sikes and Fairy were conscious but badly injured, the piranha fish having begun to strip the flesh from the latter's legs. The two of them were crying out in pain, but the noise was not as great as when the Marchioness's mouth had been functioning.

Hades and Persephone decided to partially rectify matters using their divine powers. Hades had strong healing powers because each day he was dealing with the results of the actions of The Torturing Department. Persephone had acquired her skills from her mother and aunts on Olympus.

The two gods went over to an area by themselves, raised their arms and a purple fog surrounded them. Hades quickly emerged and dragged the Marchioness's body and severed head into the area, followed by Cerberus and Lefty. Within twenty minutes the fog lifted, and a fully intact three-headed dog bounded towards the others.

"Woof! Woof!" he went. "Did we win?"

"Woofy; woofy," replied Billie, giving him a smile before kissing Lefty on the cheek. They then moved away a little distance and had a doggie chat.

The Marchioness was also no longer headless, although Hades had decided not to fix her mouth for a few days, as punishment. She whimpered as her hands were tied behind her back and was then left standing under Sisyphus's control.

Bill Sikes and Fairy were also now tied up, having been left as they were. Sikes's ribs would have to heal themselves and his mouth could wait a few days before it was fixed, just like the Marchioness's. The same applied to Fairy's legs.

Another purple fog was created for Greenbeard with Hades and Persephone bringing him back to consciousness and healing his fractured skull. The multiple dog bites from Cerberus were also left untended as a temporary punishment.

Death was dealt with last of all. Hades wasn't sure how to bring an unconscious skeleton back to 'life,' but he and Persephone managed to do so over the next half an hour. Death had a lot of questions and a lot of opinions to voice on the fact he'd been attacked and injured, which was contrary to Hades' assurances. The god wasn't in the mood for any discussion at that time, so he told him he'd give a full account of what happened the following day, and then passed him over to Charon to take away.

"Right," said Hades walking over to the others once the ferryboat had left. "Let's escort these villains back to the palace. We'll put them in a cellar for the night and work out what to do with them tomorrow."

As they were walking along, the Marchioness looked at Greenbeard and snarled through her broken teeth: "So your stupid plan didn't work!"

The pirate gave no reply, but Persephone who was nearby, looked at her and said with a smile: "No, but ours did."

•

The next morning there was a large crowd in the square outside the palace. Everyone was focused on the wooden pillory which had been erected overnight by members of the Building Department. Currently there were four heads sticking out of the larger holes and eight hands visible from the smaller ones. There was a large table on one side of the pillory where Vesta sat with a parchment and quill. Ming was next to her looking after a vast quantity of eggs, tomatoes, turnips, potatoes, apples, oranges and many other types of different fruit and vegetables. There was even more fruit in a number of baskets by her side. Finally, Gigliola was standing in front of the pillory, supervising matters.

"So, how does it work, luv?" a tubby lady asked Vesta in a cockney accent.

"You give me your name, then Ming will give you whatever you want from the table. After that, you go and throw it at one of the heads."

"And does that mean Hades lets me off my next monthly punishment for all the naughty things I did while alive?"

"Yes, but only if you hit a head."

"But if I miss, I don't gain anything?"

"You won't miss, Mrs Carver," Vesta replied. "For a start, you can have as many throws as you like. Also, Gigliola will make sure you stand very close."

"Count me in then, luv. I'll take one of them eggs. I'm going to chuck it at that PorkyPie woman, who keeps calling herself a Marchioness. Stuck up silly cow."

"A very good choice," Vesta replied.

"Here's your egg," Ming said handing Mrs Carver a large brown egg. "And I agree with Vesta on your choice."

"Thank you. Where do I go now?"

"To Gigliola."

Mrs Carver moved over to the Italian chef who showed her where to stand, which was about two feet from the Marchioness's face; she then took aim and proceeded to hit the face right between the eyes.

"Good shot, Mrs Carver. Would you like another go?" Gigliola said

"I would."

"Here you are," Ming said standing up from the table and walking over in front of the pillory. "I've brought you an entire box."

Mrs Carver nodded. "This is great fun," she loudly proclaimed as she now scored a direct hit on the nose.

Other than grunting or squealing with pain, the four conspirators said nothing all day. After all, there was simply no use mouthing off – their brilliant plan had failed.

17
Surveillance, Lilliput Style

Rach arrived on her scooter after the Security team's training session. She landed on the platform and handed Sergeant MacGobo a flask.

"Black coffee," she said. "Plenty of sugar. How much sleep did you get?"

"I has got three hours. What about you?"

"I haven't been to bed. I'm going after this meeting."

"You look knackered," Hebe said from her chair where she was sitting next to Artemis. "What's happened?"

"Everything. Shall I explain, Fergus, or will you?"

"You, Miss Rach. You is more up to date than I is, since I does not know about events since I retired to bed."

"Okey-dokes," she said before looking directly at Hebe and Artemis. "This is what happened since we last saw the two of you. Fergus and I decided we had to somehow plant bugs in the Blefuscu Embassy, so we went to see the Tosspot on----"

"The Tosspot being Miss Rach's name for the Ambassador," interrupted Sergeant MacGobo.

"Well, he is," Rach continued. "Anyway, he didn't like the idea of bugs at all, even though we told him about the Marshal being over here. So, we had a big row but couldn't shift him. He was just totally paranoid about the possibility of a big diplomatic incident if the bugs were found."

"The Ambassador not being a military man, you see, Privates MacHebe and MacArtemis," the Sergeant added.

"As well as being a big prat and a tosspot. So, after our big row I went and phoned Grandma in Lilliput. Fortunately, it was daytime there, so I didn't wake her up. She was really concerned once she heard about the Marshal being in London. That spelt real trouble as far as she and everyone else, but the Tosspot, were concerned. What then happened over the next few hours was Grandma immediately contacted the Prime Minister who called an Emergency Cabinet Meeting. Fergus and I were on the speakerphone during part of it. They ended up giving the okey-dokes to bugging the embassy and also Panos's flat, which I should have mentioned at the beginning, as well as everything else we wanted to do."

"All very satisfactory," Sergeant MacGobo added. "Except the Ambassador, he is not at all happy. The Foreign Minister he is on the phone to him straight after the Cabinet Meeting and tells him what is decided. He does not like it one bit; not one bit."

"Woke the Tosspot up," Rach added. "He's in a right Edwin Drood with us."

"Glory be!" Hebe explained. "You speak rhyming slang, Rach."

"Yea, you've got to at Imperial. They're right into it."

"What does right Edwin Drood mean?" Artemis asked.

"Right Edwin Drood; right mood," Hebe replied, before looking at the platform and continuing: "So, what next?"

"Then Fergus went to bed."

"No, I did not, Miss Rach. I----"

"You're quite right, Fergus. You took a call from Colonel MacPonsibl who confirmed that six members of your Regiment were being sent to London super-fast, which is what you asked for at the Cabinet meeting."

"That is correct, Miss Rach."

"Then you went to bed." The sergeant coughed at this point to indicate he accepted Rach's statement. "I then went round to Imperial----"

"What time was it?" Artemis asked interrupting.

"About three in the morning. I woke up the entire team in the small surveillance unit I told you about - the two Lilliputians and the three big people. They weren't happy about being dragged out of their beds. Anyway, it was important! I told them what was going on and what we were going to do, found out we were only about two days away from breaking into all the embassy's systems and agreed what extra resources we needed. I then came back here, had loads of telephone calls with Father and various members of Special Projects before going for breakfast."

"Is any more Special Projects people coming to London?" Sergeant MacGobo asked.

"Yea; ten. They're travelling on the same flight as your Highlanders. By the way Fergus, we'd better go and tell the Tosspot. They should be arriving on Monday morning and he's going to have to find accommodation for them."

The Sergeant coughed, imagining the Ambassador's reaction to that news.

"Who's Father?" Artemis asked, having listened to everything Rach had said.

"Professor Archimelock's my dad. He's also Lilliput's Chief Scientist," Rach replied.

"Everyone's connected somehow on Lilliput. It's just like Olympus," Hebe added.

"Okay," Artemis said, nodding her head. "So, what happens now?"

"That is what we is coming onto…." Sergeant MacGobo began.

•

In the early hours of the morning, two figures in tracksuits jogged gently through Hyde Park. The taller one was carrying a bow and a quiver; the smaller one was holding her hands against her two breast pockets so whatever was inside didn't fall out. Both joggers had large bags on their backs.

They came to an area in the middle of the park which was fenced off with a hedge growing behind high grilles. There were plenty of tall trees both in the fenced off area and its surroundings. The two joggers stopped and looked around, listening for any noise. When they were satisfied they weren't being disturbed, the smaller jogger unzipped her breast pockets and took out two small figures which she placed on the ground, kneeling so she could speak to them.

"Are you two okay?" MacHebe asked in a whisper.

"I should have come on my scooter," Rach said. "I don't get shaken up as I do in your pocket."

"Well, we're here. I did my best to keep you stable."

"I'm okey-dokes really. No probs. What about you, Fergus?"

"I has been in worse situations," he replied. "Being a military man, you understand."

MacArtemis bent down. "Are we ready to go ahead?" she also whispered. "We've spent the last day and a half observing the whole area and I can't see anything's changed. There's enough light from the moon, so I can see what I'm doing,"

They all looked at each other and nodded. Rach then pulled out her small mobile and sent a pre-arranged text message. A minute later, she got a reply, telling her what she wanted to know. She then turned off her mobile.

"Right," she said." The team's just knocked out their security system, so none of the alarms and sensors are operational. Let's hope we can get in and out before they notice."

MacArtemis nodded, stood up and moved towards a nearby tree. MacHebe joined her and they both now took off their backpacks and pulled out two thin but very strong ropes. Artemis attached the ropes to two arrows, took hold of her bow and shot the first arrow so it hit the tree trunk about thirty feet above the ground. She then shot the second one which struck next to the first. Pulling firmly on one of the ropes, MacArtemis confirmed it was secure. She then went over to the two Lilliputians and now put them into her breast pockets.

Suddenly, Sergeant MacGobo's head popped out. He looked at MacHebe and whispered: "Private, what is you going to do if someone comes?"

"I'll run away and hide," she replied.

"Very helpful," her sister muttered before pushing the sergeant back into her pocket.

Within seconds the goddess, with her bow on her back, was pulling herself up the rope until she reached a thick branch a few feet below her arrow. She then moved over to the second arrow and pulled up the rope attached to it, the free end of which she tied to the tree trunk. Dislodging this second arrow and once again drawing her bow, she shot it over the fence, so it hit a tree in the distance.

The next thing MacArtemis did was to pull up the first rope, which she detached from its arrow. Securing her bow between some nearby branches, she wrapped this rope over her shoulder, tightened the other rope between the two trees, took hold of the cord and then slid off the branch. MacArtemis was extremely strong and as soon as she was hanging over the ground, she began to pull herself slowly along the rope. It was about twenty yards to the next tree, but she reached it with little difficulty. Sitting on a branch, she took off the rope she was carrying over her shoulder, tied it to the branch and dropped it to the ground. She then pulled Rach and Sergeant MacGobo out of her pockets and gave them a thumbs up.

"Well done, Private," the sergeant couldn't resist whispering which received an angry frown from MacArtemis who put a finger to her lips.

The tree they were sitting on was near a small building about six feet high. This was the Blefuscu Embassy in London, consisting of three stories. Rach pulled out her night binoculars, checked that a number of top floor windows were half open due to the summer heat, identified the window they should go through and indicated to her two companions to move ahead. Artemis put the two Lilliputians back in her breast pockets and silently climbed down the rope. At the bottom, she stood on the ground and took Rach, who was now wearing a mask, out of her pocket first. Rach pointed to the partially open window and MacArtemis put her on the ledge so she could climb through. She then did the same with the sergeant, also now masked, before hauling herself back up the rope.

MacArtemis sat on a branch, pulled up the rope and waited silently. From last night's detailed observations, they'd identified the embassy guards did a quick round of the grounds and building every sixty minutes, precisely on the hour. They were working on the assumption this pattern would be repeated tonight. It was now two-fifteen in the morning; the two Lilliputians had thirty minutes to do their work before returning to the window when MacArtemis would again drop down to the ground to collect them before they all got away.

Inside the embassy building, Rach and Sergeant MacGobo found everything as expected. Lilliput's Ministry of Foreign Affairs had acquired a detailed plan of the interior two years ago which had been poured over in the last twenty-four hours by the team on Duck Island. When the two Lilliputians had climbed through the top floor open window, they found themselves on a landing. They both pulled out their torches and quietly went down the stairs to the ground floor. They'd decided on the rooms they were going to bug – the meeting rooms, the Ambassador's office and the offices of the senior staff. To their surprise, only the Ambassador's office was locked. Sergeant MacGobo was an expert at picking locks; he pulled out his tool kit, found the lock was very rudimentary, and within a minute had opened the door. The two of them went into the room and attached three small discs with self-adhesive gum under two chairs and the large table in the middle of the room. They then went out, the sergeant closing and locking the door silently before they went into the other offices and meeting rooms to leave their concealed discs.

Within twenty-five minutes, the two of them were back on the top floor landing. They had decided against trying to get into the Ambassador's private apartment which was on the same floor since it was too risky. Instead, their job done, Rach climbed back out of the open window and sat on the ledge waving to MacArtemis to get her attention. The goddess was watching for her, waved back to indicate she was coming and dropped the rope once more. When she was on the ground, she put Rach and Sergeant MacGobo, who was now also on the ledge, in her breast pockets and climbed back up again. MacArtemis then pulled herself, with the first rope over her shoulder, across the twenty yards to the tree outside the embassy compound. Once there, she attached the rope she was carrying to the tree, retrieved her bow and quiver, and climbed down to the ground, where she took the two Lilliputians out of her pockets, and left them with MacHebe, together with her archery equipment.

MacArtemis now had one more task which was to retrieve the arrow in the tree overlooking the embassy as well as the rope between the two trees. She stood by her agreement with MacHebe not to use any of her goddess's powers while in London, which would have been the easiest way of dealing with the matter. Instead, she climbed back into the tree, undid the rope-end linking the two trees and then clambered as high as possible. She'd deliberately used an arrowhead which allowed her to dislodge it at an angle. She pulled the rope from all angles, working away at loosening the arrowhead. After a few minutes, she felt it coming free; one more strong tug and it fell to the ground near the embassy building together with the attached rope. MacArtemis tried to pull it over the hedge, but it got stuck so she had to shake the rope for a couple of minutes before it became free. Eventually she released it, drew it towards her in the tree before dropping both arrow and rope onto the ground. She then climbed down from the high branches, took hold of the remaining rope hanging down to the ground and quickly let herself down to her companions. Finally, she yanked on this hanging rope very hard from an acute angle and it too came away from the tree.

The four of them quickly packed everything away so there was no evidence of their activities. Rach and the Sergeant again settled in MacHebe's two breast pockets, and she and MacArtemis jogged back the way they had come an hour ago. As they set off, they heard shouts from the Lilliput embassy compound, the loudest of which was "ze alarms, zey are not working!" suggesting that the security system failure had now been identified.

•

Bow and HalfPint were in Panos's flat for the first time since they had received their lowly 5 score. They were both well aware they had to beat it today or they would be fired like all the other members of Betty's team. The two of them had created detailed lists of what to check and had ticked the items off as they went along. They then repeated the exercise, quite prepared to double-check each other's work.

Rach had given them a number of discs which she'd specially made as large as possible, since the Lilliput size discs were too small and not powerful enough to be effective in tall buildings with thick walls. When Panos was not around, Bow and HalfPint had attached three of these discs to the underside of furniture in the living room and two each in the dining room and the main bedroom. HalfPint had also taken quick photos of Panos's broadband hub as well as the card showing his network and password. Rach's team would be able to find this information in due course, but these photos would save them time.

HalfPint felt everything was going well but Bow had been anxious all morning. She hadn't slept well and was just worried that they'd get another 5 score or less. She was also uncomfortable with Panos's behaviour since he'd smiled when they arrived and had even grunted "Morning" to them both. HalfPint had responded with her own cheery "Good morning, Mr Pantaloonos," but all Bow had been able to say was "Ey up." As the morning progressed, Bow became increasingly disconcerted. Panos was walking around the flat a lot, instead of just sitting in the living room reading as he'd done on previous days. He seemed to have a smirk on his face most of the time as if he was anticipating giving them a score of 'zero' when they left. Whenever Bow was walking along the corridor linking the rooms, Panos would pass her. Sometimes his smirk turned to a smile and involuntarily Bow would give him an 'ey up'. She liked 'ey up' as a phrase and was still determined to use it occasionally whatever her sister said about it being 'northern'. The only good thing about today was that Panos didn't seem to mind.

It was late morning and nearly time to go. Bow was in the living room carrying out a final triple check on a few matters when Panos walked in and sat down on his normal armchair.

"Stay!" he barked, as he could see Bow was beginning to move out of the room. "Work! Finish!"

"Ey up," Bow replied as she continued with what she was doing.

A short while later, the word "English?" rang in her ears. She looked up at Panos and nodded, giving him another 'ey up'.

"Where? Born?" he demanded.

"Ey up," Bow said unsure what to reply.

"Town? Born?"

"England."

"No! No! No! Town?"

"Ey up."

"Town? Town? Town?"

Bow could sense Panos's growing frustration, and she suddenly began to feel increasingly nervous. The only town she knew was London, so that's what she answered.

"London!" Unfortunately, Panos knew 'ey up' was a phrase used in the North, so he barked out: "Ey up. North! Explain!"

Bow was now at a complete loss, so she decided to try her other favourite phrase and said *"Oggy Oggy Oggy"* to Panos.

"Oggy Oggy Oggy" he shouted back at her. "Meaning?"

Bow didn't know what it meant, so for reasons she couldn't work out she suddenly said the word 'Manchester'. It was totally unrelated to *Oggy Oggy Oggy*, but Bow remembered Mopp referring to it as a place in the north, so it just came out.

Panos looked slightly relieved. "Manchester!" he exclaimed. "Born Manchester?"

"Ey up."

"Red or blue?" Panos demanded.

Bow didn't know what he was talking about. Since she spent a lot of time amongst the greenery of forests, she replied "Green."

"Green!" Panos shouted at her. "Green! Fool! Meaning? Meaning? Meaning?"

"Oggy Oggy."

"Fool! Fool!"

Bow had had enough. She was a goddess, and she wasn't prepared to have someone shouting that she was a fool. She got up to punch Panos, but just at that moment her sister walked in, having heard raised voices.

"Is everything okay?" she asked.

"No!" Panos shouted before repeating the word "Fool!"

HafPint could see that Bow was going to do something stupid, so she pushed her into the kitchen without saying a word. Fortunately, Panos hadn't noticed he was about to be thumped, so over the next few minutes, HalfPint was able to calm matters down with him. She explained that Bow was very nervous and sensitive. She wasn't used to conversing with important, intelligent people like Mr Pantaloonos and often panicked in difficult situations. HalfPint confirmed that Bow had been born in Manchester, but then lived in the countryside. She liked the greenery of the country and, unlike her half-sister, had only recently come to London. That was probably why she'd said the word 'green'. Also, she wasn't interested in football, so had no affiliation towards either the red of Manchester United or the blue of Manchester City.

After having concocted this story about Bow's past life, she went into the kitchen, closed the door, and managed to talk her sister out of using the long sharp knife she'd taken from the cutlery drawer to cut Panos into a hundred pieces.

Having completed her double diplomatic mission, HalfPint went and told Panos she and Bow had finished and would await his verdict on their work by the front door. A few minutes later, having completed his inspection, he joined them.

"Eight!" he barked. "Back Friday! Go!"

Just at that instant the concierge rang the bell, having already been called by Panos to escort them to the car park.

"Don't say anything about it," HalfPint said while they were in the lift. "Not even with Mopp. We'll sort it out when we get home."

•

It was early evening and Rach and Sergeant MacGobo were feeling pleased with themselves. The six Highlanders had arrived the previous day, as well as the members of Rach's Special Projects team. Together with a number of the embassy's security personnel, the Highlanders would be physically watching the Blefuscu embassy twenty-four hours a day.

As far as Rach's team was concerned, she had taken over a large meeting room at the embassy which was where the new arrivals and their computer equipment were already installed. The Imperial team had now fully broken into all the Blefuscu embassy systems, so the people in this meeting room would be monitoring all its digital communications, as well as listening to the conversations picked up by the bugs planted two days ago.

Panos's flat was subject to a similar surveillance routine. The large discs left by Hebe and Artemis that morning were working well; also, it had taken Rach no more than an hour to break into his computer. The small team at Imperial of normal sized people and Lilliputians, who were already in place, would remain on campus and be responsible for monitoring Panos. Ideally, Sergeant MacGobo would have liked to watch his movements twenty-four hours a day as well, but it wasn't considered practicable. As a compromise, it was agreed that if the monitoring team picked up that he was going somewhere considered 'interesting', the two goddesses would be alerted, and they would decide what to do at the time.

Artemis was also feeling much better. Hebe had told her to focus on the positives – the Nutter had given them a score of 8, meaning they would keep their jobs; and now all the surveillance arrangements had been put in place. She was currently enjoying the totally mindless exercise of marching up and down the Lilliput embassy back lawn with Hebe and all the recently arrived Argyll & Sutherland Highlanders, together with members of the security staff. Sergeant MacGobo had decided that it was time to get his troops doing some square bashing, something he'd missed since being appointed Military Attache. Being members of the regiment, Privates MacArtemis and MacHebe were ordered to participate, but in view of their greater size, the two of them marched over a larger area than the Lilliputians. As they started off, for no reason at all other than showing who was boss, the sergeant shouted from the platform that they were a couple of good for nothing, putrid, six-nosed weasel's deformed kidneys. This made MacArtemis feel good – she knew she was now an accepted part of the regiment.

As they were marching backwards and forwards MacHebe encouraged MacArtemis to chant *"Oggy Oggy Oggy!"* to which she replied *"Oi Oi Oi!"* Soon some of the other members of the regiment and security staff were joining in. Sergeant MacGobo didn't seem to mind the chanting; after all, it was a good way of creating comradeship and he noticed that everyone's marching suddenly seemed to be a bit sharper. Rach heard the noise from her meeting room, looked at what was going on and was soon on the platform. She was very quickly chanting away louder than anyone. After a couple of minutes MacHebe took over the lead from her sister and then Rach muscled in on calling out *"Oggy Oggy Oggy"* as she danced around the platform pumping her right fist in the air.

The Ambassador couldn't work because of the noise in the garden, so he watched what was going on from his study window. He wasn't the complete prat or tosspot Rach made out. After all, he was a diplomat, forever focused on downplaying and avoiding conflict. However, he now accepted that the powers that be on Lilliput had taken a different view – they had made it clear he had to support his Military Attache and Rach in whatever they were doing. As a member of an older generation, he didn't totally approve of everything about Rach, especially her being a punk. But he did recognize she was a highly intelligent young lady with immaculate connections amongst the Lilliput establishment. He also felt it was 'a dead cert' she would become Empress in thirty years or so. There was just no one else to rival her.

While all this marching and chanting was taking place, the six pelicans decided to pay a visit to the embassy. They stood on the edge of the lawn and soon they were joining in with the *Oggy* chant; the youngest, Elvis, being the most vocal. Even Sir Peregrine found it catchy although he did little more than mumble the *Oggy* words. He wondered how many of the chanters knew the origins of the chant; something to do with Cornish pasties he believed, although he'd never eaten any. He was reluctant to change from his fish diet at his age, but he might encourage Elvis to try a pasty and tell him what it was like – he accepted you had to be prepared to move with the times!

Just then Rach launched off again, accompanied by her fellow chanters:

>"*Oggy Oggy Oggy!*
>*Oi Oi Oi!*
>
>*Oggy Oggy Oggy!*
>*Oi Oi Oi!*
>
>*Oggy!*
>*Oi!*"

and so it went on.

18
Mutual Disclosures

Betty had been in a dilemma for some time over how much to tell Hebe and Artemis about the missing paintings from The Gallery. After discussing the matter with Mopp, she decided she had to tell them everything as they were the two people working in Panos's flat. Her only reservation had been that she didn't know them well, although they came recommended by Lady Felicity, being sisters of one of her good friends.

Having made her decision, Betty arranged to call with Mopp at the Alderney Street flat the following morning. It just so happened that Uncle Octavian was also expected at the flat at the same time since he was driving Lady Iris, who was again in London, to Hampton Court for the day. Betty had heard a lot about Lady Iris from Octavian, and he'd asked if he could call round at The Estate before picking her up, for a haircut and for his niece to make sure he was generally presentable.

When the three of them arrived at the Alderney Street flat the next morning, Octavian insisted on coming up the stairs. Since the entrance to the flat was on the third floor, he was puffing a bit when he arrived.

"You needn't have come up, Octavian," Hebe said inviting them in. "Iris is nearly ready, and she could have come down to you."

"Cor blimey, no way," was the firm reply. "I've come to carry Lady Iris's bag for her, me being a real gent, if you know wot I mean."

Hebe raised her eyebrows. "She's only taking a small bag, you know. The two of you aren't going off for a naughty weekend, are you?"

Octavian blushed. "I like to behave proper like wot with Lady Iris being a real and actual top, top, top nobess."

"Why does Iris get three tops for being a nobess, while Artemis and I only get two?"

Just at that instant, Artemis walked into the living room where the others had congregated.

"You're looking very smart today, Octavian," she said. "You've had a haircut, and I like your suit. Is it new?"

Betty decided to come to her uncle's assistance, since his face was starting to redden, and he was clearly feeling uncomfortable. "He popped round to my flat before we came here and I made sure he was looking tidy," she replied on his behalf.

"Well, I approve! Let me tell Iris you're here."

"I'll do it," Hebe intervened. She went into the hallway and, feeling mischievous, called out: "Iris, your date's arrived!"

As Octavian continued to glow, all eyes were turned to the doorway as steps were heard on the stairs. Iris soon walked in; she was wearing a Calvin Klein cream dress with a rainbow-coloured shawl. Her hair had recently had a perm, and she'd just put on her lilac lipstick. As Hebe had predicted, she was only carrying a small Hermes bag.

After having been introduced to Betty and Mopp, Iris moved over to Octavian.

"You look very presentable today, Octavian," she said. "Are we ready to go?"

"Lady Iris," he replied with a slight bow. "You look smashin, if you don't mind us saying so."

"Why, thank you," she replied with a smile. "May I take your arm down the stairs?"

"Certainly," Octavian replied proudly.

The two said their goodbyes and went through the front door which Hebe had opened for them.

When they had reached the bottom of the first flight of stairs, Hebe called after them: "Any particular time you expect to be back this evening, Iris, or won't we see you until the morning?" She quickly slammed the door before Iris had a chance to reply and went off to make coffee for the others.

A few minutes later the four of them were sitting in the living room, drinking flat whites. Betty was wondering how to begin the conversation when Hebe piped up: "Have you come to give us the boot, Betty?"

Betty laughed and took advantage of the opening which she'd been given. "Not at all. In fact, quite the opposite. By the way, I'm going to call you Hebe and Artemis today and Mopp's real name is Jade."

"But I still want you to call me Mopp," Betty's companion said. "Everyone at home and on the Estate does."

"Okay," Hebe said before looking directly at Betty. "So, what's this all about then?" she asked.

"You may remember I told you that our little group didn't just provide cleaning services, but we also recovered stolen property. Well, we've now got a big job involving tracking down stolen artwork from a major national institution. Let me tell you about it as it might just involve Mr Panos Pantaloonos. We're not sure of that, by the way, but it's the one lead we have."

"The Nutter!" Artemis exclaimed.

Betty looked up, confused until Mopp said: "It's Artemis's name for Panos."

Betty nodded before continuing.

Over the next quarter of an hour, Betty explained about her long-standing relationship with Sir Cedric and Lady Felicity Brassington-Bear. She then went on to explain that Sir Cedric was now Chairman of The Gallery and how he'd been informed on a confidential basis about missing, and most likely stolen, paintings from the institution. The Gallery's Director, Cesare Shiftyopolous, with whom Cedric had a less than positive relationship, was highly dismissive of the whole matter and was doing little to follow up the Chairman's concerns. Betty had been told about all of this many weeks ago and had been asked to help, but there were really no clues until a recent sighting, caught on camera, of Cesare and Panos together in St James's Park.

"Panos in the park!" exclaimed Hebe. "What was he doing there?"

"That's what we'd like to know."

"Have a look at this," Mopp said, pulling out her mobile and moving over to Hebe and Artemis to show them one of Emily's photos of Elvis and the two men sitting on a bench.

"It's him!" Artemis suddenly exclaimed. "He's the one we saw with the Nutter at the Globe! I'm sure he is!"

"I agree," Hebe said after a few seconds of careful consideration.

"What's this?" Betty asked.

"We went to the Globe theatre one evening and saw Panos sitting with some guy, but we didn't know who he was."

"Now we do," Artemis said. "It was him, What's-his-name."

"That's really important news," Betty said. "One of our concerns was it was just a chance meeting between the two in the park; a couple of men sitting on a bench saying a few words to each other. Now it's clear they know each other."

"Betty; there's also Terry Grabbit being in the Knightsbridge flats carpark that morning," Mopp said. "It all seems a bit of a coincidence."

"I'm not sure about that one," Betty said. "There are over a hundred flats in the block and the Grabbits pop up everywhere in Central London."

"Who are the Grabbits?" Hebe asked.

"Three crooked brothers who live on the Estate," Mopp said. "Wherever they go, they're normally involved in some sort of dodgy activity. I found one of them parked below the flats when I dropped the two of you off one morning."

"Well, whether the Grabbits are involved or not, we've found out enough today to keep a close eye on Panos," Betty said.

"So, what's the plan?" asked Hebe.

"Just a minute," Artemis intervened before anyone else could respond. "I'd like to have a private word with you first, Hebe. Can we go upstairs?"

"Yea, okay. Hope you don't mind," Hebe said looking at the two visitors. "We'll only be a couple of minutes."

"That's fine," Betty said.

As soon as the two sisters were in one of the top floor bedrooms, Hebe looked at Artemis and said: "I know what you're going to say, and I agree."

"We tell them everything?"

"Yes."

"Will they believe us?"

"Dunno, but let's go and find out."

"Okay."

Back in the living room, Mopp's immediate reaction was to exclaim: "That was quick! You've only been gone seconds."

Hebe smiled and looked at her sister.

"You go," Artemis said. "You know them better than I do."

Hebe now turned to Betty and Mopp, her smile still on her face. "Have you two ever read Gulliver's Travels or seen the film?"

"I think I saw the film or the story on TV when I was young. Some fairy story about little people," Mopp replied.

"I sort of know the story," Betty added.

"It's not a fairy story," Hebe replied. "It's real."

At this point, Mopp exploded with laughter, claimed Hebe was either having them on, or she'd just taken magic mushrooms or something similar in the short while she'd been upstairs. Hebe sat silently, no longer smiling, but looking serious as did Artemis. After having exhausted herself with all sorts of comments about Hebe just messing around, Mopp ran out of things to say. She looked at Betty who was also sitting quite poker faced.

"I'd like to hear what you girls have to say," she said. "There's something in the back of my mind telling me it's all a bit more real than Mopp's making out."

"Oh, come on, Betty! It's all make-believe."

"Let's listen to Hebe," was all Mopp got in reply.

Just as Betty had given a detailed explanation of the theft of art works from The Gallery, Hebe spoke about the little people who had first been recorded in Gulliver's Travels. Her three companions were all aware of the serious tone she was adopting – there were none of the light-hearted flippant remarks that she tended to make.

Hebe dealt with a number of matters, the first one being who the little people were. She specifically addressed the fact that most people forgot about them within a few seconds. No one knew why, just as there was no explanation as to why a few individuals, principally residents of Hebe's and Artemis's home country, didn't have this memory loss. She suggested that genetics might be a factor, but admitted it wasn't scientifically proven. Having given this totally made-up explanation which avoided mentioning that she and Artemis were goddesses, Hebe went on to her second point which was where the Lilliput and Blefuscu embassies were in London, being in St James's Park and Hyde Park respectively. This led to a brief description of the historical enmity between the two islands, Hebe making it very clear where her sympathies lay.

When it came to hearing about senior members of the Blefuscu military being in Panos's flat one morning, even Mopp became attentive. This naturally led onto the surveillance regime which had been established by the Lilliputians on both the Blefuscu Embassy and Panos's residence.

"You mean you've bugged the Knightsbridge flat!" Mopp exclaimed. "As Octavian would say: 'Cor blimey'."

Hebe nodded. "So that's where we are. It looks as if all roads lead to Panos."

There was dead silence in the room after Hebe had finished. Mopp still didn't really believe any of it, but she'd been watching Betty while Hebe had been talking. There was such a serious look on her older relative's face that she decided to refrain from making any more comments at this stage.

"Do you have anything to add?" Betty asked after a while, looking at Artemis.

"No. I agree with everything Hebe's said. My only suggestion is that we should all go round sometime to Duck Island where the Lilliput Embassy is. We can show you it really exists, and you can meet some of the little people."

"I think that would be very helpful as far as Mopp is concerned," Betty replied. "For me as well, although I must say, I'm inclined to believe you both. The more I listened to you, Hebe, the more distant memories came back into my head. I'm sure I've met some of the little people. I can't recall where or when precisely except it was a long, long time ago."

"Betty!" exclaimed Mopp, "You can't be serious!"

"I am, but the best way of proving it is for us to take up Artemis's suggestion. Do you agree?"

"Fine. When?"

"How are the two of you fixed about five o'clock this afternoon?" Hebe replied. "The little people I want you to meet should be there then."

Betty and Mopp both nodded.

"Won't we forget it all soon afterwards?" Mopp asked getting up to leave.

"Yes, but when the subject gets raised again, you'll recall a lot of it because it will have been recent," Hebe replied.

"Whatever the outcome of this afternoon, we now need to put in place a proper watch on Panos," Betty said as she walked into the hallway. "I'll organize a full team meeting on how we do it in the next couple of days."

"And I'll pick us all up in my van just before five today," Mopp added as she and Betty started walking down the stairs.

•

"We need to talk about the Nutter," Artemis said.

"We're always talking about him," Hebe replied.

"This is important."

"Well, if it's important, let me finish my muffin first so I can concentrate properly."

"That's the third muffin you've had this morning."

"So what? Anyway, sitting here in this café opposite Panos's flat is hard work. I need the energy."

Artemis raised her eyebrows but didn't bother replying. She did feel some sympathy for Hebe's comment. This was the third time in a week the two of them were on 'watch duty' and they'd been there for nearly three hours; it would be another sixty minutes before Karate Chops took over from them.

"Alright," said Hebe, licking her fingers. "Muffin's gone, and you've got my full attention. What is it?"

"I've been thinking a lot about the Nutter. He reminds me of Pan, and I wondered if you'd noticed the same resemblance."

"You're kidding!"

"No. Haven't you noticed any similarities?"

"I can see a lot of differences. The fact he doesn't have any horns, being one. Then, Pan had goat's legs, but Panos seems to have two perfectly normal legs."

"We've never seen the Nutter's legs because he's always wearing trousers."

"That's not all that surprising, is it? After all, that's what people in the 21st Century do. Even you and I are in jeans."

"He's got a limp."

"Well, that doesn't turn him into a goat, does it?"

Artemis shrugged. "There's something in his look which brings back memories of Pan."

"We don't get much of a look at him because of that big mask he's always wearing. Also, Pan had a great big beard, while Panos only has a small goatee."

"It's his eyes."

"I didn't really know Pan. Did he have any special feature to do with his eyes?" Hebe paused and getting no reply continued: "Come on, Arty. Don't you think you're being influenced by his name being Panos? Take off the last two letters and you get Pan. It's just word association."

"I'm not sure."

"Alright, let me bring up some other points. Wasn't Pan a randy devil, always chasing female nymphs? You're not telling me he's been making advances towards you when I've been in another room, are you?"

"Don't be ridiculous. Look, I agree Pan was always chasing females. I used to come across him a lot in the countryside and tried to avoid him for exactly that reason. But the fact the Nutter isn't flirting with us doesn't stop him reminding me of Pan."

"Wasn't our fellow god always playing the flute. I've seen no evidence of Panos being musical, have you?"

"Maybe. I was clearing out one of his top cupboards and I did come across a very old flute."

"There could be all sorts of reasons for that. Maybe his mother or father played the flute, and he inherited it. He's possibly kept it for sentimental reasons or maybe he's just forgotten all about it."

"Everything you say is right, but….."

"You're not saying Panos is actually Pan, are you?"

Artemis shook her head. "No, Pan's dead, I know. The only god ever to die, although I never knew how it happened."

"I think the only person who definitely does is our father. I used to ask him about it a long time ago, but he always refused to talk about it. Not even my mother knows, although she suspects Uncle Hady and Uncle Posy might."

"Why wouldn't Zeus tell Hera?"

Hebe shook her head. "I don't know. Perhaps it was some sort of male thing, but really I haven't a clue."

"Where was he buried?"

"I don't know anything more about him."

"Maybe he never died," Artemis speculated.

Hebe sat pensively for a while. "What made you say that?" she eventually asked.

"Pure speculation. No particular reason."

Hebe frowned and continued deep in thought.

"Why have you become so serious all of a sudden?" her sister asked.

"It's just you raising the possibility of Pan not actually being dead. I don't want you to get all excited by this, but Mother used to wonder the same thing."

"What! You're kidding? Why?"

"I can't help with that. Not even she knew why she thought it. I suppose it's just that the whole matter was shrouded in so much mystery; Father always refusing to say anything about it."

"So, I may not be crazy after all?"

"Yes, you are if you really think Panos is Pan." Artemis shrugged before Hebe continued: "Look, I've just thought of another reason why he can't be. If Panos really was a god, he wouldn't need all those locks and bolts on that secret room of his. He'd just create a shield over it so no one could get in. Even the weakest of gods can seal off a room like that. There's no evidence at all of any godlike powers being exercised in Panos's flat."

"I can't argue with you. All your points are logical, Hebe..... It's just that Panos reminds me of Pan. I can't help it – he just does."

"What about his voice? Does he talk like Pan?"

"Not really, but then we only hear Panos barking out single words at a time."

Hebe nodded her head in agreement. "Well, I suppose all you're really saying, Arty, is that Panos reminds you of Pan. Given there are billions of people in the world, it's probably not surprising that someone looks a bit like Pan. Also, he had a number of children, so maybe Panos is related to him with about a hundred generations in between. That's possibly one reason for the similarities."

"I suppose so," Artemis said reluctantly before looking up at the café door. "Look, here's Karate Chops. She's arrived early."

"Released at last!" Hebe replied thankfully.

19
Alarming Information

Artemis was sitting in the living room watching television when she suddenly heard a 'toot, toot' at the window. Just as she looked up, there was another 'toot, toot' from Rach's Vespa which was hovering outside.

"Let me in," Rach shouted as she waved her arms frantically.

"What's the matter?" Artemis asked, opening the window to allow Rach to fly inside and land on a table.

"You've got to hear this. Mega-urgent; we're about to be zapped! Mega-zapped! Where's Hebe?"

"In the supermarket doing some shopping."

"You need to hear it together. I'll go and get her," Rach said, her Vespa rising in the air and flying out of the window before Artemis had a chance to reply.

The goddess frowned, wondering what the panic was all about. It would have been easier just to phone Hebe on her mobile. Still, it didn't matter; Rach would find her within a few minutes.

The Vespa sped down Alderney Street, turned right down Warwick Way and then left into Wilton Road. Once she reached the supermarket, Rach hovered in the air until someone walked out, opening the automatic doors. The Vespa shot in and then went up and down the aisles at a height of about ten feet as the Head of Special Projects looked for Hebe. She eventually found her at the self-checkout, and again went 'toot, toot' as the miniature scooter came to a halt in front of the screen.

"Quick! Quick! I need you to come back to the flat now, Hebe," Rach said insistently before Hebe had realised she'd arrived. "Mega-urgent! Total zapping's about to happen!"

"What are you talking about, Rach?"

"I need you and Artemis to listen to a couple of recordings. Everything's about to blow! Please, please hurry! We need to get back to the flat!"

"Alright," a puzzled Hebe said. "Let me just pay."

"Okey-dokes, but hurry, hurry!"

"I am," Hebe replied, paying with a £20 note and putting the receipt into her carrier bag with the shopping. As she turned to walk out, she realised she'd forgotten the bottle of prosecco which was still in the basket. She quickly picked it up, put it in her carrier bag and hurried after Rach who was 'toot, tooting' as she flew towards the exit.

As soon as Hebe came out of the supermarket, the alarm set off and she stopped.

"What's that?" Rach demanded, turning her scooter around and hovering in front of Hebe.

"I don't know. Better wait and see."

"But we need to get back! This is really urgent!"

"Look, Rach; please pipe down. This will only take a minute or so."

By then a large, burly security officer had come out of the store.

"I don't know what I've done," Hebe said innocently.

"Let me look in your bag," the security officer said. "Have you got the receipt?"

"It's in the bag."

The security man found the receipt and meticulously started checking off the items in Hebe's bag against it. By now Rach was getting increasingly agitated, telling everyone to hurry up.

"You seem to have taken a bottle of prosecco without paying for it," the burly security officer said in an accusatory tone.

Hebe suddenly realised what had happened. She'd been in such a rush because of Rach that she'd put the prosecco into her bag, having forgotten to scan and pay for it. She explained this to the security man, pointing to Rach as being responsible for her hurrying away; the small Lilliputian providing plenty of supporting evidence as she was becoming increasingly vocal about the delay.

"Naturally, I'll come inside and pay now. It's clearly a silly mistake on my part for which I take full responsibility" Hebe said.

"It's not as easy as that," the security officer said in his most officious tone. "Everyone claims it's a silly mistake, whereas it looks like a clear case of shoplifting to me. We always prosecute shoplifters. We'll have to call the police."

Before a somewhat shocked Hebe had a chance to reply, Rach intervened. "Look, Bonzo!" she shouted. "Does she look like a shoplifter? Just because you're wearing a badge and a uniform, you think you can go around----"

"Rach, you're not helping," Hebe interrupted.

"Yes, I am! We've got to go! This is a matter of life and death we're dealing with, and thicko Bonzo here….."

The discussion went on like this and a small crowd gathered round to watch. By now the Duty Manager had come out and was trying to take control. He heard Hebe's explanation, but unfortunately heard a lot more from Rach, whom no one could keep quiet since she was desperate for Hebe to get back to the flat.

"Look, her name is Lady Hebe Olympiakos!" Rach shouted. "She's not a shoplifter! You must see that, Big Ears!" This last statement was directed to the Duty Manager who had rather large ears that stuck out at right angles.

"Lots of titled people are crooks," the security officer commented unhelpfully.

"Shut up, Bonzo!" Rach shouted at him.

One of the crowd also called out "Shut up, Bonzo!" and was soon joined by a few others, with general laughter all round.

The Duty Manager was trying to decide how to bring this scene to an end since it wasn't doing the supermarket's reputation any good. At that moment one of the staff members in the self-checkout area came out and told the Duty Manager that she'd seen some of what had happened. This supported Hebe's explanation about being distracted by the Vespa scooter's arrival, which caused her to leave in a hurry with the result she forgot to pay for the prosecco. She also said that Hebe came in every day to the store and was always courteous and trustworthy, often donating items to the Food Bank basket. The Duty Manager himself recalled having seen Hebe on a number of occasions in the store and he'd also seen her make the occasional donation.

"I think the best thing to do, Lady Hebe, is if you were to come in, give me your address and telephone number and also pay for the bottle of prosecco. It's unlikely we'll take matters any further."

"Thank you," Hebe replied. "Will I be allowed to come back to the store tomorrow?"

"Certainly," the Store Manager said.

"That's put you in your place, Bonzo!" Rach said, looking at the security officer.

The Duty Manager looked at the small Lilliputian. "But you; you're banned from the store from now onwards!" he told her emphatically.

Rach pulled out her tongue and then blew a raspberry. "Up yours, Big Ears!" she shouted as she zoomed off on her Vespa, before adding: "See you at the flat, Hebe. But hurry!"

Hebe went into the store and settled up with the Duty Manager, thanking the self-checkout lady for her assistance. She apologised for her error, apologised even more for Rach's behaviour and then walked speedily back to Alderney Street. When she arrived, she found Artemis and Rach sitting in the living room, with the Head of

Special Projects eagerly waiting to turn on her miniature recorder.

"Listen to what our surveillance teams have picked up," an excited Rach said as soon as Hebe walked in. "They're going to try and zap us!"

She pressed the start button before Hebe even had a chance to sit down.

> "*I do not like zis, Marshal.*"
>
> "*You have said zat before. It does not matter, Ambassador. It will ze happen.*"
>
> "*But it is ze very high risk.*"
>
> "*Life is all about ze risk.*"
>
> "*But ze diplomatic implications; zey are enormous.*"
>
> "*Only if we are found out. We will not be. Ze planning is 'tip top' as ze English say.*"
>
> "*You can never be ze certain.*"
>
> "*I am ze certain! I have come to London to personally make ze organisation. I, Marshal of Blefuscu, who has commanded in many of ze military campaigns. Zis one is 'a piece of cake' to use anozer of ze English sayings. It is ze foolproof. It cannot go ze wrong.*"
>
> "*So please to take me zrough ze plan again, Marshal.*"
>
> "*Very well, Ambassador…. Zis Friday night at one twenty-zree in ze morning---*"
>
> "*So, zat is ze Saturday morning.*"
>
> "*Yes, you are ze correct. Ze Friday night becomes ze Saturday morning.*"
>
> "*Good. I make ze understand. But why is ze time precisely ze one twenty-zree?*"
>
> "*Zat is a military matter. It is not necessary for you to make ze understand.*"
>
> "*Very well. Please make ze continue.*"
>
> "*At one twenty-zree, my commandos, who have been making ze wait on ze bank near West Island, make ze brief transport to ze West Island. We have already ze small group of four men who have made ze secret infiltration of ze West Island.*"

"*And how do you make ze transport to ze West Island?*"

"*We make ze go on ze back of ze swans.*"

"*Ze swans. So why do zey make ze help for us?*"

"*Zey are enemies of ze pelicans. Ze pelicans are ze friends of ze enemy swine from Lilliput, so zey are on ze side of ze Blefuscu.*"

"*Ah; my enemy's enemy is my ze friend.*"

"*I do not make ze understand.*"

"*It does not make ze matter. Purely anozer English phrase. What happens ze next, Marshal?*"

"*At one forty-two, my commandos make ze set off across ze lake. We make ze go from ze west to ze east where is ze Duck Island.*"

"*Ze home to ze Lilliput embassy.*"

"*Ze home to ze enemy swine.*"

"*And you make ze cross of ze lake on ze back of ze swan friends?*"

"*Zat is ze correct.*"

"*Another question about ze swans. What are we giving zem for zer help?*"

"*Nozing. As I have made ze say, zey are doing it because we make ze attack on zeir enemies.*"

"*Umm. I zink ze swans are ze security risk. Zey might make ze admit of our involvement after ze attack.*"

"*We will make ze deny.*"

"*You mean make ze lie?*"

"*Yes, Ambassador; you will do it. You are ze diplomat. We all know ze diplomats spend zeir time making ze lie.*"

"*I make ze disagree wiz you on zat, Marshal, but let us not make ze discuss now. Instead, please make ze carry on as you cross ze lake.*"

"*I will continue. At one fifty- nine, our commandos will make ze arrive at Duck Island. Zey will zen make ze disembark, approach ze enemy swine's embassy and zen make ze Big Boom.*"

"*Ze Big Boom. What is ze Big Boom?*"

"*Zat is anozer military matter. You do not have to make ze know.*"

"*Will zer be any loss of ze life?*"

"Who knows? Wiz ze Big Boom, anyzing could make ze happen."

"I do not like it."

"It does not matter. Zat is ze plan and it will ze happen."

There was a sighing sound.

"Zen what?"

"Zen our commandos make ze return trip. Zey do not make ze stop at West Island. Instead, zey disembark at ze bank, where zey are met by ze human friends and zey return here."

"Ze human friends presumably being ze zree brozers?"

"Yes, zat is ze correct."

"And where will you be during zis attack, Marshal?"

"I will be zer on ze lake behind our gallant commandos. I will be doing ze watch and ze oversee."

"And what if somezing goes ze wrong? What if some of our gallant commandos are ze caught? Zey will be in ze interrogation. Ze role of Blefuscu will be ze known."

"I have ze told you, Ambassador, ze planning is 'tip top'. Nozing will go wrong. Also, our gallant commandos will be in ze disguise. Zey will not be in ze uniform. We are not zat stupid!"

"But some will be recognized. Ze colonel is ze Blefuscu's Military Attache here in ze embassy."

"Zen he will make ze big lie. He will say he decided to take ze action alone, wiz no help from ze embassy."

"Wiz an army of ze Blefuscu soldats who just so happen to be in ze London. How will zat be made to be explained?"

"Yes. Zey will all say zey has come to London as ze tourists and while here zey decided to make ze Big Boom at ze enemy swine's embassy. Zat is what zey will all say. If asked, we will all make ze same explain - you at ze embassy, ze army and ze government."

"Zen you must zink ze Lilliput and British auzorities are ze stupid."

"I do."

"Bah! You speak ze nonsense, Marshal!"

"I hear your opinion, Ambassador, but as I have made ze say, your opinion does not make ze matter. Zis attack has been signed off by ze President and ze State Council. It will ze happen."

"Zat is ze one zing I agree wiz you on. It will ze happen. Why ze government does not just let ze art stealing from Ze Gallery continue wizout getting us involved in zis risky attack, is beyond me. We make ze money from ze art stealing."

"We will do boz. Zis attack will be ze serious big blow to ze enemy swine."

"Well, are you prepared for ze Lilliput reaction? While we will make ze deny, zey will know we are behind ze attack. Zis could lead to ze big war."

"Of course. We are ze ready. It is time we beat ze enemy swine in ze war! Time we conquered zeir land and made it ze colony of ze Blefuscu!"

"And how do you zink ze British will react to zis terrorist act on zeir land?"

"Ze enemy swine embassy is not on ze British land."

"Technically, no, but to get to it, we must make ze cross on ze lake which is British."

"Bah! Ze British are ze fools. Zey voted for ze Brexit. If zey want to declare war on Blefuscu, we are ze ready. We will smash zem!"

"Zen, Marshal, you are ze biggest fool------"

At this stage, Rach stopped the recording.

"Everything else afterwards just became a shouting match between the Ambassador and the Marshal," she said, talking at a thousand knots an hour. "Fergus and the Ambassador want to see you both mega-urgently. We've only got two days to stop getting zapped! But you'd better hear the second recording before we go. This one involves Panos."

Rach pressed the start button again, before either Hebe or Artemis had a chance to reply.

"So, what do you want to discuss first, Marshal?"

"Ze sale of ze Gauguin. Please to give ze explain. We have only ze small money in ze bank."

"There's much more to come. You should have received one and a half million dollars already."

"Is zat ze sum, Colonel?"

"Yes, Marshal. It arrives in ze bank yesterday."

"So, where is ze rest, Mr Pantaloonos?"

"I thought I explained it in my text."

"We could not ze understand."

"Very well; I'll go through it again. We have an agreed sale of the Gauguin and Constable paintings-----"

"Why ze two together?"

"Because the only way of negotiating the full price for the Gauguin was to include the Constable as well. It's not very valuable and was always going to be difficult to get much for it, so I took the opportunity with this client who quite liked it."

"Could we not have got ze more by selling ze two separately?"

"Not in my view unless we were prepared to wait many months or possibly even a year."

"And who is zis buyer?"

"As you know, Marshal, I never disclose such information. Let's just say he's a gentleman from Latin America."

"I will come back to zat ze later. Let us first return to ze money. You were to give ze explanation about ze rest."

"Yes. The agreed price for the Gauguin and the Constable is forty-five million dollars; the balance will be paid in thirty days when we complete."

"So, where are ze two paintings at ze minute?"

"Here; in my possession."

"We can see zem?"

"Yes. Now?"

"Later. Please carry on about ze money. How does ze forty-five million dollars only become ze one and a half million in ze Blefuscu bank?"

"Very simple. We've been paid ten percent of forty-five million which is four point five million. You take a one-third share, being one point five million dollars which I've paid you."

"Is zat right, Colonel? You are good at ze sums."

"Yes, Marshal. Zat seems to be ze correct."

"Zat is good. So, Mr Pantaloonos, what if ze buyer does not make ze pay of ze rest in zirty days?"

"We keep the deposit and have the right to sell the two paintings to someone else."

"Is it ze better if he pays?"

"Yes, much. A bird in the hand is worth two in the bush."

"I do not ze understand."

"It doesn't matter. It's an English saying."

"Ah, anozer English saying. I have been making zese sayings myself in ze recent days."

"There are a lot around. What's next, Marshal?"

"I wish to raise ze difficult question wiz you. A question which has been put to me by ze Blefuscu State Council."

"Which is?"

"How can we be certain ze forty-five million dollars from your buyer is not ze more and you keep ze extra?"

"That is a question I've sometimes been asked before. All I can say is if I got a reputation for taking backhanders, then no one would deal with me. It simply wouldn't be worth my while. Have you any evidence of me being involved in any dishonest activity, Marshal?"

"No. I cannot ze say I have. What about you, Colonel?"

"Well....er...."

"Come on, Colonel. Say what ze know. What is ze evidence of Mr Pantaloonos being dishonest?"

"Well...."

"Speak! Zat is an order."

"Yes, sir. I was going to say zat he does make ze steal of ze paintings. Zat is not ze honest activity."

"Ah! Zat is a good point! What do you say to zat, Mr Pantaloonos?"

"Don't be ridiculous, Marshal! Come on, let's move on."

"Umm.... Before we do, I wish to make ze know Blefuscu does not take kindly to ze people who do ze dishonest zings to us. We eliminate zese people. We understand you no longer have ze powers of ze protection you had long ago. Is zat right?"

"What's your next point, Marshal? We've exhausted this matter."

"Very well. We wish to make ze see of all ze paintings you have in your possession. Zere should be five wiz ze two who are sold. Also, ze update on ze selling effort is necessary."

"Certainly. I'll go and bring them out."

There are a few minutes of silence except for sundry noises of items being placed on chairs.

"The two on the left are the Gauguin and the Constable that are sold. Then we've got the Canaletto, the Turner and the Van Dyke."

"So, how is ze selling making ze progress?"

"Quite well. I have two interested parties in the Canaletto; one I think will make an offer next week. He's also looking at the Van Dyke together with three others. I've currently got one person whom I'm meeting next week on the Turner."

"And ze prices?"

"I'm not changing my ranges from the ones I gave you earlier. I'm hopeful on the Van Dyke; we might do a bit better."

"Zat is good. And Mr Pantaloonos, zese buyers, zey are from where?"

"All from the Far East except for an American."

"You already know zem?"

"I've had dealings with all but one. She was introduced to me by a long-standing contact, who has dealt with her a lot over the years."

"Perhaps we can have ze update again after we have made secure ze Rembrandt? Zat is ze last matter to ze discuss. You have spoken to ze Director yet?"

"I have. He would have preferred to do it this Friday evening, but I explained you are otherwise engaged. However, the next Friday is fine."

"Good, so zat is agreed. We make ze same time and ze same other arrangements, do we?"

"Yes; your men will be picked up at the usual meeting point at one in the morning. It's the same storeroom as last time; again, the canvas will be in the corner to the left of the door."

"*Are you ze happy wiz zose arrangements, Colonel?*"

"*I am, Marshal. But we did ze discuss possibly doing ze job on a day not ze Friday night.*"

"*Zat is right. Mr Pantaloonos, can you please to give ze explain why we always do zese jobs on ze Friday?*"

"*That's the day the Director always works late at the Gallery. Virtually no one else is around in the evening, so he's able to go into the storeroom without being noticed.*"

"*Zat makes ze sense.*"

"*Have you anything else, gentlemen?*"

"*Colonel?*"

"*No, Marshal.*"

"*Zen we are ze finished, Mr Pantaloonos. We will ze go.*"

After they'd all listened to the second recording, Rach soon raced back to the embassy, with the two goddesses agreeing to follow her shortly afterwards.

As they walked through Pimlico towards the park, Artemis said: "Did you hear that bit about the Nutter having lost his powers?"

"Yea; I think you might have been right all along."

"And did you also notice how the Nutter spoke perfectly normally? None of those one-word instructions he barks at us."

"That's probably because he just views us as a pair of useless cleaners."

"Probably…..You know, we'll have to tell Betty about the planned theft from the Gallery as soon as possible."

"I'll get a copy of the recording from Rach and play it to her. But that can wait until the weekend. You and I are going to be involved in protecting the embassy for the next couple of days."

"What do you think we should do?"

"Let's listen to Fergus and the Ambassador first. From what Rach said, Fergus is trying to get the entire regiment flown over by Friday."

"Wouldn't it be simpler if we just handle it ourselves?" Artemis asked. "Isn't this one of those occasions when we can become goddesses again?"

"Yea, I think you might be right, Arty. Blowing up embassies isn't exactly something normal people get involved in every day."

"I'm glad to hear that." Then after a pause Artemis added: "But it's exciting, isn't it?"

"Yea, I suppose so," Hebe murmured as the two of them turned into Birdcage Walk.

20
The Battle for Duck Island

The Blefuscu commandos had gathered on West Island ready to fulfil their mission. The Marshal had just finished giving them a pep talk, where he had emphasised they would become heroes of Blefuscu for their actions that night.

"Are zere any questions?" he asked.

No one said anything, so the Marshal picked on one of his commandos at random. "Come, Soldat. Ask me a question."

The poor commando struggled to think of anything, but a more extrovert colleague of his decided to pipe up: "Marshal, could you please make ze explain how we can become ze heroes of ze Blefuscu if we, ze army, ze government, ze everybody denies our involvement in zis glorious mission?"

The Marshal gave a little cough. "Soldat," he said. "How long have you been in ze army?"

"Six years, Marshal."

"Zat is very ze good. You will go far, Soldat. Well done." The Marshal looked around and picked on another commando, deciding he would now ask a question to keep the discussion flowing: "You are ze brave man, aren't you, Soldat?" he said

"Yes, sir."

"Good. You are prepared to make ze die for your country?"

The commando looked at the Marshal confused.

"Aren't you?" the Marshal asked again. "Please to give ze answer, Soldat."

"Well…er…I do not understand ze question, Marshal."

"What do you not ze understand?"

"Zese words about dying. I zought ze mission was ze foolproof. None of us would have ze harm. I zought you said so earlier, Marshal."

"Ah! You are ze clever fellow. You too will go far, Soldat. Well done."

"Zank you, sir."

The Marshal now looked at his watch. "It is getting close to ze one twenty-zree. Time to set off to deliver ze Big Boom to ze enemy swine. Trust me, all will be ze well. I am here to make ze lead of you, ze gallant heroes of ze Blefuscu. Let us make ze go."

No one moved as they all looked at the Marshal.

"Why do you not make ze go?" he asked puzzled, then looking around at random he said to another commando: "You, Soldat. What are you ze waiting for?"

"You, Marshal," he replied.

"Me! Why?"

"Because you said you will make ze lead. We are waiting for you to make ze go first."

"Soldat," a puzzled Marshal replied. "Do you not ze know zat ze marshals of Blefuscu always make ze lead from ze back!"

"From ze back?"

"Yes, from ze back. Did you not know zat?"

"No, Marshal."

"Zen, learn zese matters and you too will go far."

"Yes, Marshal."

"Good. Now everyone make ze go. I am right behind you, making ze lead from ze back."

The commandos moved the short distance to the water's edge where six swans were waiting for them. The adjutant and three soldiers got on the back of Slasher and set off. They were followed by Spike, Spanka, Scorcher and Smog, each one also carrying four gallant heroes from Blefuscu, together with a number of bags full of bombs, hand grenades and whatever else was needed to make a Big Boom. Finally, the Marshal got on the back of Sir Sigmund by himself and set off as he led from the back.

It was almost a full moon which meant the commandos had reasonably good visibility of their surroundings as the swans glided smoothly along the lake. No one said a word as they passed under the Blue Bridge and headed towards the south side of Duck Island from where they planned their assault.

As this small armada was making progress, exciting things were beginning to unfold on West Island where four Blefuscu commandos still remained, together with a couple of swans. None of them knew precisely what their role was, other than to be 'back-up', so they just rested on the ground expecting to have a quiet time until their comrades returned. They were therefore surprised to hear a paddling noise from the lake and even more surprised when a large black dog with three heads emerged. All these heads had the same face which bore a remarkable resemblance to the Goddess Iris.

The dog raced along the ground towards the commandos. It snarled and growled as it moved at speed, its three mouths spitting out saliva and showing a large number of very sharp teeth. The commandos tried to get up and run, but the dog was on them before they could get away. They were by now all terrified and started to scream.

"Give us a Mars bar or I'll bite yer bums!" they heard, but it made no difference because the dog decided not to bite their bums; instead, it proceeded to kick them all into the water.

"Help!" screamed one of the commandos. "I cannot make ze swim! Help!"

The two swans were nearby in the lake and, considering themselves pretty tough, didn't run away, but instead tried to help the commandos. However, the three-headed dog launched itself from the bank and landed on top of one of the swans. It gave the white bird a number of painful bites and used its powerful front paws to thump the swan in all sorts of sensitive places. Eventually, it's victim was so battered and bruised the black dog left it floating on the lake.

The other swan by now had decided he wasn't quite tough enough to take on a manic three-headed dog and had started swimming away. Unfortunately, it was now the next target for the Iris-Cerberus look-alike who, despite being a four-footed canine, could out-swim any of the St James's Park swans. The dog soon caught up with the fleeing swan, jumped on its back and meted out the same treatment as it had given to its companion. Having left the second swan equally battered and bruised, the dog swam back to the Blefuscu commandos, who were still flailing around in the water. Three sets of jaws each took hold of a commando at the same time and then proceeded to toss them back onto the island. They were soon joined by their final companion as they lay moaning and groaning on the ground. At this stage the three-headed dog turned round and began to swim towards Duck Island.

The next minute a miniature boat arrived at West Island, having travelled along the length of the lake near the north bank. It had a silent motor, specially designed by Rach's Special Projects team. A number of Argyll and Southern Highlanders disembarked, went over to the four Blefuscu commandos, tied their hands behind their backs while at the same time taping their mouths. They were put into the boat which set off on its return journey, again along the north side of the lake.

There had been a fair amount of shouting and screaming by the commandos as well as honking and whistling from the two swans as they were all beaten up by the black dog. However, none of this was heard by the armada as it approached Duck Island. This was in part because they were some distance away, but more importantly because after they went under the Blue Bridge, there was a loud chant from the north side of the lake, led by the pelicans:

"Oggy Oggy Oggy!
Oi Oi Oi!

Oggy Oggy Oggy!
Oi Oi Oi!

Oggy!
Oi!

Oggy!
Oi!

Oggy Oggy Oggy!
Oi Oi Oi!"

"What is zat?" the Marshal whispered anxiously to Sir Sigmund.

"I suspect that is the sound of drunken young Englishmen who've been in the pub all evening," the swan answered.

"But what is zis *'Oggy'* word? What does it ze mean?"

Before Sir Sigmund had a chance to reply, a large beak appeared in front of him, hovering a few feet in the air.

"Ey up!" the beak said before Sir Sigmund was taken hold of by a pair of firm claws and lifted high into the air. A second later the swan was being flown over the park with the Marshal holding on for dear life.

Sir Sigmund honked a great deal and the Marshal shouted for assistance, but the swans and commandos ahead of them didn't hear because the *'Oggy'* song was in full flow. If any of them had looked up at the sky, they might have seen a giant eagle, which was undoubtedly the largest eagle the world had ever known, with a twenty-five-foot wingspan. They might also have seen that the eagle's face was very similar to the Goddess Artemis's. However, no one did look up, so no one saw this remarkable sight.

Sir Sigmund was so petrified his jaws soon shut tight, which stopped him from honking any more. The Marshal was equally terrified and devoted all his energies to holding onto whatever he could find on the swan's back to stop himself from falling to the ground.

The eagle soon left the park and flew down the Mall, going over Admiralty Arch before crossing Trafalgar Square where it passed Nelson's column. From there, the journey continued down the Strand and Fleet Street to Ludgate Hill, which it climbed. Reaching the top it easily cleared St Paul's Cathedral and was now in the City proper, London's financial district.

The eagle didn't know London well but had yesterday undertaken a recce of its planned route. It had decided to keep following the major thoroughfares which would eventually lead it to its destination, even if that was not the most direct way. So, after St Paul's the airborne trio sped along over Cheapside, Poultry and then passed the Bank of England on the left-hand side. From there, it was a direct journey down Cornhill and Leadenhall Street, the City's insurance centre, before coming to Aldgate. They were soon out of the financial district as they flew along the Whitechapel Road which led into Mile End. The eagle began to slow down and dropped some height, as it looked for the tube station. When it came into sight, the bird turned left and then flew along Grove Road, over the railway line and towards a mass of greenery.

This was Victoria Park, the largest park in the East End. Like St James's, it has a lake with an abundance of wildlife although perhaps not quite as varied as its West End cousin. There are certainly no pelicans living in Victoria Park, but it does have a Chinese pagoda. The eagle made for this structure which is beside the lake. Just before reaching it, the bird dropped in height until it was about four feet above the water. Its claws opened and Sir Sigmund, together with the Marshal who was still holding onto the swan's back, were dropped into the lake. There was a splash with Sir Sigmund now able to give a loud honk again as he fell unceremoniously onto his belly. The Marshal unfortunately fell off his back, but the eagle put out a claw and lifted him onto the swan once more.

Both Sir Sigmund and the Marshal started speaking at once, but they quickly shut up when the eagle's large beak appeared about three feet in front of them.

"Ta ta for now," the beak said, and then the eagle's right eye gave a wink, before flapping its wings and setting off on the return journey to St James's.

Meanwhile back on the lake, the adjutant and his three commandos were rapidly approaching the south-west corner of Duck Island. The commandos had already taken out a number of hand grenades while the adjutant was readying a bomb to create a Big Boom when Slasher became aware of something in the water approaching him at speed. Suddenly he jerked and let out a honk as he realised he was looking at a giant swan, which was at least five times bigger than him with a neck ten feet high. Interestingly, this swan had the Goddess Hebe's face, although Slasher would not have been aware of that. He didn't have time to let out another honk because the giant swan's head swiped his own, knocking him on his side. He managed to right himself only to find that his adversary didn't just have webbed feet, but also forearms with bright red boxing gloves which started bashing his head and thumping his body. After a short while the boxing gloves went under his belly and then threw him backwards into the air. When Slasher landed back in the water and his head resurfaced, he found he was due another good beating and bashing until he was left in an even worse condition than his two comrades who'd been attacked by the three-headed dog near West Island.

Slasher's four Blefuscu commandos had fallen into the water shortly after the altercation with the giant swan had begun. Fortunately, they could all swim, but they did a lot of shouting for help. All their bombs and grenades had also fallen into the lake, so they were now useless, but this didn't seem to matter. Getting to dry land was their key objective now. Creating a Big Boom at the Lilliput Embassy was no longer high on the agenda.

The other four swans and their commandos behind Slasher were soon aware that matters weren't going to plan.

They tried to move away from the giant swan and turned back towards West Island. However, they didn't get very far because the giant swan hadn't taken long to deal with Slasher and began chasing after them. It soon caught up with the two in the rear and gave them both the same treatment it had given Slasher. The other two, who were in the lead for a brief while, thought they'd got away, until one of them was hit very hard by a three-headed dog swimming directly at it with the force of a torpedo. As the swan tried to right itself while it's four commandos were flailing around in the water, the three-headed dog jumped high into the air. It landed on the back of the final swan, again knocking its commandos into the water before starting to rough up the bird.

While the giant swan and the three-headed dog were having fun beating up Slasher, Spike, Spanka, Scorcher and Smog, the pelicans had stopped chanting *"Oggy, Oggy, Oggy"* from the lakeside. They got into the water and started looking for the commandos who were splashing around. When they found them, they gently picked the small men up in their beaks and carried them to Duck Island. They were joined by more miniature boats manned by members of the Argyll and Sutherland Highlanders as well as the Lilliput Embassy's security staff. Rach was also hovering overhead on her scooter, shining a powerful torchlight on the lake and calling out whenever she found one of the flailing commandos.

On Duck Island there was a reception party consisting of more Highlanders and security men who shepherded all the wet visitors from Blefuscu into a large hut.

"Where is ze Marshal?" the colonel whispered to the capitaine as they stood in a corner.

"I do not ze know. He has made ze big disappear."

Just at that moment, their attention turned to Acting Captain MacGobo who had walked in to address them: "You 'orrible, miserable pieces of Blefuscu mouse droppings," he started off in his booming voice. "Let me tell you what is going to 'appen now.....You is all wet through and we has generously got a change of clothes for you all. After that, we has got a cup of tea for everyone as well. Suitably dry and refreshed, we then needs to have a little chat with each one of you to understand what mischief you was planning. Any questions?"

No one said anything, so after being instructed to follow a large grizzly Highlander out of the door to the main embassy building, Fergus stood to one side and watched the commandos file out. When the colonel began to pass him, he pulled him to one side.

"Nice to see you again, Colonel," he said.

"I'm sorry, I don't know who you are," was the bland response. "And I don't know why you're calling me Colonel."

MacGobo smiled. "Oh, that's how you is going to play it, is it?" he said. "Very well. By the way, I suppose you is looking for the Marshal?"

The colonel couldn't help but give a start.

"I thought that would interest you. Let's just say he's flown away."

"What do you mean?"

"Just what I has said. He has flown away.... I'll see you later." And the acting captain walked away, leaving the colonel thoroughly perplexed.

•

The Blefuscu Ambassador was sitting at his desk. He was anxious; it was after 6am and none of the commandos had returned, nor had there been any sort of communication. His First Secretary was based next door monitoring the news – he'd just come in to confirm there was nothing about anything happening at St James's Park when the telephone suddenly rang.

"It is ze Lilliput Ambassador," the operator said.

The Blefuscu Ambassador's stomach turned. "Put him zrough," he croaked, and then a few seconds later he forced himself to adopt a more confident tone. "Ah, Ambassador! Zis is ze pleasant surprise."

"I rather suspect not."

"What do you ze mean?"

"Ambassador LeClonk, do you know why twenty-four men from Blefuscu have just had to be rescued from the lake near my embassy?"

The Blefuscu Ambassador shivered. He did know; he also now knew the Marshal's foolproof plan hadn't worked, but he didn't know why. Finally, he knew something else - he was going to have to spend the next few days denying everything; in other words, he would be lying.

"I do not ze understand what you are ze saying, Ambassador," he replied.

"I thought you'd say that. Let me give you some details, which might help to jog your memory."

"Certainly, I wish to ze listen, but I give you ze assure, zere is no memory to be jogged."

"Then I'll spell out the facts for you in precise detail. In the early hours of this morning, members of the Blefuscu armed forces, in disguise, congregated on West Island. This is at the far end of the lake from the Lilliput Embassy. They set off on the backs of a number of swans towards Duck Island, which is where my embassy is based. As they approached, they were intercepted by some other wildlife in the park. I don't know the precise details of what happened, but the result was that all your armed forces ended up in the water. There was naturally a big commotion with lots of cries for help – I suspect a number of your soldiers couldn't swim. Anyway, you'll be pleased to know that my security team, together with a number of the park's pelicans that were nearby, managed to rescue all your men. They were brought into the embassy, given a hot drink and also a change of clothes. Naturally, they were questioned about what they were doing and a rather confusing set of answers were given….. Does any of this ring any bells in your head, Ambassador LeClonk?"

There was a silence for a number of seconds while the Blefuscu Ambassador was frantically taking his blood pressure tablets. His chest had begun to tighten, and it was getting worse the more he listened to what he was being told.

"Ambassador LeClonk are you still there?" the Lilliputian Ambassador eventually asked, tired of waiting for a response.

"Yes, yes. My apologies, Ambassador. You were ze saying?"

"I've said as much as I'm prepared to at this stage. Do you know anything about this and, whether you do or don't, what's your response please?"

"Let me ze say immediately, I am stunned at what ze words you have spoken. Totally stunned!"

"What you mean is you're stunned that the plot to blow up my embassy failed."

"To blow up ze embassy of ze Lilliput, I do not ze understand."

"Oh, come on, Ambassador. A bunch of Blefuscu commandos – because that's what they are – approach Duck Island with bombs, hand grenades, guns, the whole lot. What do you think they were planning to do?"

"But how can you be sure zese men were from ze Blefuscu, Ambassador? Perhaps zey were ze Lilliput terrorists?"

"For a start, they all have Blefuscu accents, not Lilliput accents."

"Maybe zey attended ze Blefuscu universities when ze matters were more friendly between our two countries."

"And maybe they didn't!"

"But you cannot be ze sure."

"Well, another piece of evidence is that all the clothes they're wearing have 'Made in Blefuscu' labels. If that doesn't convince you, perhaps you can explain why one of the men we've rescued happens to be the Colonel, who is your Military Attache. I've met him before."

"It is ze impossible!" was all Ambassador LeClonk could think of saying, and then messed up his denial by asking: "Has he admitted zat to you?"

"No, he claimed to be the twin brother of the Colonel."

"Ah, so he is not!"

"Well, if you believe him, which I don't. Anyway, it can easily be resolved by asking your real Colonel to pop round in the next half hour, so we can see the two together. I'll organise a cab to pick him up in ten minutes time, shall I?"

"I am not ze sure zat I know where ze Colonel is at ze present," was the defensive reply.

"Come on, Ambassador. No more messing around. We both know he's here in my embassy; we've just fished him out of the lake."

"Well, I cannot believe any of zis. If it is ze Colonel he must have been making ze act by himself, alone."

"With twenty-three other members of the Blefuscu armed forces?"

"How do you know zey are ze armed forces of my country? You did say zey were in disguise."

"We took photos of each one and matched them up to our security records of your military personnel."

"You have ze records of our military people?" asked an alarmed Blefuscu Ambassador.

"Of course; just as I'm sure you have records of ours."

"But how so ze quickly? You only have ze few hours."

"We're fast workers."

"Zis is extraordinary! I cannot believe zis. Are you saying zese people you claim are from ze Blefuscu have made ze admit zey are in our army."

"No, I'm not."

"Ah! So, zey deny it," was the relieved reply. "Zat must mean zey are not. You seem to have made ze false accusations, Ambassador."

"If you really want to know, they all said they had a twin brother in the Blefuscu army."

"Zere you are. Zat is ze explanation."

"Come on! All twenty-four having twins in the army. Do you seriously believe that?"

"Of course! If zat is what zey say, it must be ze true."

"Well, Ambassador LeClonk, if that's the case, how come they were all wearing socks which had 'Blefuscu Army Property' labels?"

"Perhaps zey make ze borrow from zeir brozers?"

"And perhaps they didn't because they don't have any twin brothers! Perhaps they just happen to be Blefuscu commandos carrying out a terrorist assault on the Lilliput Embassy."

"Zat Ambassador, is ze very serious charge!"

"Well, it's what this entire conversation is all about."

"But you have no ze concrete proof."

"I think everything I've told you is pretty conclusive. Add to that the fact that two of the men we've apprehended have admitted the whole matter and have applied for asylum in Lilliput."

Ambassador LeClonk swallowed hard. Every time he tried to refute an allegation a new one was put to him. All he could think of saying was: "Zey must have been subject to ze torture to say ze zings which you wish zem to say."

"Rubbish, Ambassador!" the Lilliput Ambassador shouted. "Absolute rubbish! Look, I've told you what the situation is and naturally my government is fully aware. Let's not dance around the mulberry bush anymore-----"

"I do not understand ze 'dance around ze mulberry bush'. What is zat?"

"An English expression. Let me carry on.... What you and I need to decide is what we're to do with all these Blefuscu commandos, or if you prefer, citizens which we have in our possession? Do you want them handed over to the British authorities to face terrorism charges or do you want them put in a taxi and sent to your embassy!"

"You mean you will let zem go?" an astonished Ambassador LeClonk asked.

"Certainly. We Lilliputians know you tried to blow up our embassy and you know we know. Our two governments will sort it out. There's no need to bring the British authorities into it."

"Ambassador, you know zat we strongly deny ze absurd allegations you have ze made. However, as zese people might be ze citizens of Blefuscu, it will be ze best if you give zem to us, zen we can find out what really did ze happen."

"Right, that's what we'll do. They'll be at your embassy within the hour, except for the two who've claimed asylum. That's all, nice talking to you, Ambassador."

"One final zing. You have ze names of zese men?"

"We've both the names they gave us and their army names."

"Could you please give to me zeir army names."

"I'll send a list. However, if you're interested in the senior personnel, we have the Colonel who is your Military Attache, a capitaine and an adjutant."

"Zree. No more?"

"No."

"You are ze sure?"

"Absolutely."

"Zank you," was the pensive reply as the Ambassador wondered what had happened to the Marshal but didn't dare ask.

The two ambassadors quickly finished their telephone call; Ambassador LeClonk aware that for the last five minutes his First Secretary was in the doorway waiting to give him a message.

"What is it, First Secretary?" he asked.

"Ze Blefuscu President and ze Foreign Minister are waiting on ze ozer line, Ambassador. I told zem you were speaking to ze Lilliput Ambassador and zey said not to make ze interruption. But zey need to speak very urgently. Apparently, ze entire Lilliputian Navy is off ze Blefuscu coast and is making ze block of all ze ports.

Ambassador LeClonk sighed. "Please to put zem zrough," he said as he contemplated his next posting, which he suspected was likely to be North Korea or possibly even the Moon!

21
Romantic Interlude

Hebe was being driven to the Victoria & Albert Museum in Octavian's taxi. She was on her way to a private reception where two members of the Royal Family, who were friends of hers, had specifically asked that she be invited. Artemis had also been included in the invitation but declined because she wasn't ready yet to mix with the upper echelons of British society. She also didn't have any elegant cocktail dresses to wear, unlike her sister who had brought a number in anticipation of such invites.

"Wot time does you think you'll be leaving?" Octavian asked as he was navigating round Hyde Park Corner.

"Probably ten at the latest," Hebe replied. "Is that too late?"

"Cor blimey, no! I'll be having me supper with Bet, won't I. You'll give us a call a few minutes beforehand, will you, luv?"

"Yes. A good fifteen minutes before I'm ready. I'll meet you outside at the front."

"Right you are."

Octavian drove along in silence. Hebe was aware he was a bit on edge and sensed he wanted to ask her something. She thought she knew what it was about, so decided to help him.

"Iris is arriving early Friday morning," Hebe said.

"Oh really!" Octavian replied, surprised. "She's not made no contact, if you know wot I mean. Don't she want me to pick her up?"

"She does and she's asked me to arrange it with you. It's early though."

"No matter. Anything for Lady Iris."

"Half-seven in the morning at the Hyde Park stables."

"No problem. I'll be there."

"You're sure?"

"Course, I'm sure."

"You've got a busy day though on Friday, Betty tells me."

"I can cope, me. Got lots of energy for an old 'un, you know. Also, I'll be resting at Bet's when I'm not working, won't I?"

"Fine."

There was another silence for a while until Octavian gave a slight cough.

"Yea, well, as I said, anything for Lady Iris. She's a real top, top nobess."

"She is," Hebe agreed.

"Very classy lady, I say."

"Indeed."

"Very popular too, I would imagine like."

"Very."

"Specially with the gentlemen, I bet."

"Definitely."

"Does she….. um…. 'ave one particular gentleman she knows specially well, if you get wot I is meaning."

"Yes," replied Hebe.

"Oh!" Octavian responded, slightly disappointed. "Well, I ….er …..assume he's a real fine feller, I'm sure."

"He goes by the name of Fearless Frupert."

"Fearless Frupert, eh. Well, yea, he must be quite a man wot with having a name like Fearless."

"He is indeed." There was a silence between the two of them until Hebe added: "He's six years old."

"Six!" exclaimed Octavian, momentarily breaking suddenly. "Wot, is he her son then?"

"No. You know Iris and I live together. He's just a young boy we've sort of informally adopted."

"I got you. So, not her son then?"

"No."

"Got it." The two carried on in silence until Octavian said: "Yea well, a real classy lady is Lady Iris. You know, if I can say this confidential like to you, Lady Hebe - if I were a real and actual younger man and different in all sorts of other ways, if you know what I mean, I'd be keen to get to know Lady Iris sort of better, I would."

"Oh, I don't think the age gap's what you suspect it is," Hebe replied, unsure herself how many thousands or millions of years ago Iris had been born. She decided it wouldn't be helpful to enlighten Octavian on the matter.

"Me, I thinks it probably is, you know."

"Well, assume it's not for a minute. What are all these other sorts of differences you think matter?"

"Cor blimey, where does I begin? It's obvious, in't it?"

"No! Be more specific."

"Well, er like, Lady Iris is posh, whereas I'm wot people call dead common. Big difference there."

"I don't think Iris is as posh as you make out, Octavian. Also, I don't think you're dead common."

"Well, I don't know," Octavian mused in reply. "Anyways, she's having a title like, being an official Lady."

"Titles don't count for anything these days. What else?"

"Headucation. Lady Iris is real well headucated, whereas I left school when I were twelve, didn't I?"

"I don't think Iris has passed many exams, you know. Carry on with all these differences you imagine exist."

"She… um… is always dead smart like, whereas I'm a scruffy bugger."

"You weren't scruffy when you went to Hampton Court. I thought you were very well dressed. Anyone, would have been proud to be in your company."

"That were Bet wot fixed me up like that. It weren't me, you know?"

"It doesn't matter. You showed you can look smart if you want to, Octavian. The only reason you're not all the time is because you drive a taxi. There's no need to be well dressed to be a cabbie. You just need to be a good careful driver."

"Yea, well, that brings up another point. I'm only a cabbie - I don't actually know what Lady Iris's job is, but I bet it's something real important like."

"Iris does all sorts of things, but I'll tell you something, Octavian, she wouldn't know how to drive a taxi."

"It's no great shakes. Anyone can do it."

"Iris can't."

"I bet she could if she wanted to," Octavian grumbled.

"Don't you believe it. Look, what other differences are you thinking of?"

"Well, I don't know," Octavian replied, shaking his head. "Everything, you know. I just don't have wot Lady Iris would want."

"You mean like a big red nose?"

"No, I ain't got a big red nose," he agreed.

"Or big ears which stick out at right angles?"

"No, ain't got them neither?"

"Or two orange horns coming out of the top of your head?"

"No, I ….. You taking the mickey, are you?"

"Yes," Hebe replied emphatically. "I think you're seeing a load of negatives, Octavian, whereas you should be looking at all the positives you've got."

"I ain't got no positives," he replied wearily.

"Yes, you have. For a start you're a very kind man. You're courteous and helpful. You work hard for your living. You're interesting; you're from a good family. Just look at Betty being a friend of those titled people in the Gardens. These are all things which women find attractive."

"I don't know," Octavian replied, shaking his head.

"Look, Octavian, if you'd like to invite Iris out on a date, just ask her. The worst that can happen is she'll make an excuse why she can't make it. But you never know, she might say 'yes'."

"I'd just…. You know, be a bit nervous like asking her…. You couldn't------"

"No, I couldn't!" Hebe abruptly interrupted him.

"But I thought if you-----"

"No, Octavian! If you want to take Iris out, you invite her. I'm not going to do it for you."

"Well, I don't know….. Where am I going to take her?"

"Where do you live?"

"Whitechapel."

"Are there any nice restaurants in Whitechapel."

"Got loads of curry houses."

"Then take her for a curry."

"No. Anyway, I don't like curry, do I? Disagrees with me digestive system."

"Aren't there any decent pubs which serve food?"

"Yea, suppose so. They all serve loads of different types of pies."

"What about fish and chips?"

"Yea, they all do fish 'n chips."

"Good. Take Iris to one of your local pubs. She likes fish and chips."

After reflecting for a short while, Octavian mumbled: "I'll have to think about it, won't I?" He then said nothing more on the matter for the rest of the journey.

•

Hades was sitting by himself in the throne room, feeling slightly unsettled as well as a bit nervous. He was wondering what he'd let himself in for. His wife, Persephone was certain that Cerberus and Billie were developing romantic feelings for each other and had decided that they needed some advice. Hades thought this was clearly a job for Aphrodite, the Goddess of Love, but Persephone felt the Underworld should have a first stab at helping the two dogs. She'd already had a confidential chat with Billie which had only got a shy response and a lot of blushing from the little dog, but it was enough for Persephone to think she was on the right track. It was now her husband's turn to provide the masculine guidance to Cerberus on how to move matters forward.

Hades had needed a considerable amount of briefing in the last few days on how to play the role of relationship counsellor. It wasn't something the King of the Underworld had ever done beforehand – he'd always viewed his job as dishing out punishments to the dead when they first arrived, whereas now he was being asked to establish 'happy families' in his realm. Nevertheless, he'd been unable to resist Persephone in this matter. She'd brought along Aggy and Gigliola to provide him with 'useful advice' on how he should give 'useful advice' to Cerberus! Gigliola had been the most talkative of the three, telling Hades he should speak like an Englishman, using phrases like 'man-to-man', and 'good chap'. He wasn't quite sure about this because the English weren't renowned romantics, but both Persephone and Aggy seemed to agree with Gigliola, so those were his orders. He was also aware the three females were much exercised on how many heads a Cerberus – Billie child might have, if they ever got married. Because there were severe practical difficulties in achieving such an outcome, it was agreed to leave it to Hades to decide if he wanted to pursue this matter.

As he was contemplating these weighty issues, the god suddenly became aware that Cerberus had come into the throne room and was sitting on the floor a few feet in front of him.

"Ah, Cerberus," he said looking up. "Take a seat."

"Woof. I am sitting," was the reply.

"Yes. Very good."

"I got a message you wanted to see me."

"I do," Hades agreed.

"Woof. Why?"

"Why? A very good question," said Hades, struggling with how to get the conversation started, before deciding to take some of Gigliola's advice. "I thought it was about time you and I had a man-to-man chat, if you know what I mean."

The eyes in Cerberus's three heads all blinked at the same time. "Woof; woof," he replied before continuing: "But how can we have a man-to-man chat, Hades, since you're a god and I'm a dog? Neither of us are men."

"Well, we're more like men than women," was the somewhat defensive reply.

"Woof!"

"Yes."

There was a long silence before Cerberus asked: "What exactly are you trying to say?"

Hades decided it was time to adopt a different approach. "You seem to have a lot of friends," he commented.

"Woof. Yes."

"As well as Vesta, Ming, Aggy and many others, you've now got Billie, I understand."

"Woof! Woof!" Cerberus replied and then growled angrily at Hades. "This isn't about you sending Billie away, is it?"

"No! No! Not at all. Whatever gave you that idea?"

Cerberus continued to growl at Hades before replying: "Then why did you raise Billie's name?"

"Oh, I was just going through a number of your friends. She's a new addition, so I thought I'd mention her, that's all."

"You're sure?"

"Yes. Quite sure. I don't really understand why you're behaving so aggressively at the mention of Billie's name."

"Woof! It's no secret, Hades, that you wanted to send her back when she first came to the Underworld. I want you to know I will be really unhappy if you do that. Really, really unhappy! Woof! Woof! Woof!" And Cerberus continued to stare aggressively at Hades.

The god realised this conversation was not exactly going to plan, so he decided to try yet another approach.

"How are you finding your new kennel?" he asked, changing the subject.

"I don't like the word kennel. I prefer palace or house, but home is the best description."

"Yes, well, whatever. It's much bigger than your previous place."

"Yes," Cerberus agreed, still not sure what Hades was driving at.

"Big enough for two, wouldn't you say?"

"Woof!"

"Have you ever thought of sharing it?" Hades asked, deciding to get to the point.

"Woof! Woof!" Cerberus barked, now beginning to feel alarmed at the prospect of some undesirable lodger being foisted on him. "What do you mean?" he demanded, followed by a growl.

"Nothing to get alarmed about, old chap," Hades replied, aware of Cerberus's reaction and deciding to use a bit more English, as advised by Gigliola. "I'm only thinking it must get a bit lonely in such a large place."

"I've got Billie living in the annex next door."

"That's the point!" Hades exclaimed, now sensing an opening. "But that's next door, not in your home."

"Well, she can walk through the doorway between the two properties whenever she wants to."

"But you can't go through the doorway to her, can you?"

"That's because it's not large enough."

"Aha!"

"Aha what? I don't understand what you're trying to say, Hades," Cerberus responded, now totally perplexed.

Hades thought he was making progress, so he decided to go for the jugular. "Come on, Cerberus, have you never thought of settling down with one girl? Sharing your home just as Persephone and I do?"

"No."

"But why not? You now have an ideal opportunity."

Cerberus just shrugged.

"Come on, old chap," Hades continued, deciding that this English term was working. "There must be one of your many girlfriends who ranks above all the others; a special one as far as you're concerned. Grab hold of her before anyone else does and make her yours."

"You mean as you did with Lady Persephone?"

"Precisely!" Hades beamed.

"Woof! Woof! I don't think that's a very good idea."

"Why not?"

"For a start, no one approves of how you made Persephone your wife."

"What!" Hades exclaimed, banging his hands down on the sides of his throne before standing up and shouting angrily: "Who dares question my actions? I'll have those people heated over hot irons for years! Who are they? Give me their names!"

"Woof! Woof!" Cerberus barked back, now standing up to face Hades. "For a start, Lady Persephone!" he shouted back.

"Lady Persephone!" exclaimed Hades, still standing.

"Yes. Have you forgotten you kidnapped her against her will? You upset all sorts of people, especially her mother, Lady Demeter and Lord Zeus, her father."

"Yes, well, that was all a long time ago," Hades mumbled, somewhat deflated by the accusation, which caused him to sit down again.

"Maybe so, but you're suggesting I should do the same."

"Umm," Hades responded reflectively, feeling a bit caught out by Cerberus's accusation. "Well, perhaps not quite in so many words."

Cerberus blinked. "You mean I should use shorter sentences to describe kidnapping people?"

"Shorter sentences! What are you on about?"

"I'm just trying to understand what you're saying, Hades. You said I should go about this matter using not so many words. That means my sentences should be shorter, doesn't it?"

Hades looked up at the ceiling for inspiration before again focusing on his Head of Internal Security. "Do you know what I'm trying to say to you, Cerberus?" he asked with a touch of despair in his voice.

"Bits of it."

"Which bits?"

"Woof! Well, I understand the part about you advising me to kidnap my number one girlfriend against her will and taking her off to live in my kennel, as you call it. I don't understand why, but that's what you're telling me to do. I also don't get why she'd want to live with me in a wooden hut, however large and modern, when she currently sleeps in a nice cosy bed in the Girls' Dormitory."

"Girls' Dormitory!" repeated Hades. "What are you talking about? She lives next door in the annex."

"Woof! That's where Billie lives. Vesta lives in the Girls' Dormitory."

"Vesta!" Hades exclaimed. "Who's talking about Vesta?"

"You are. You're talking about one of my girlfriends who ranks above the others. That's Vesta."

"But I'm taking about Billie!"

"Billie! Billie's not a girl. She's a lady dog!" Cerberus retorted.

Hades sighed. "You do understand what a girlfriend is, don't you?"

"Yes, a friend who is a girl."

"No! No! You don't get it. I'm talking about the difference between a girlfriend and a friend who is a girl. There is a difference, you know."

Cerberus blinked, totally confused. "Well, is a girlfriend a code word for a friend who's really a boy but maybe looks like a girl?"

"No! No! No! Go and talk to Aggy about the difference. She'll explain it," Hades said, feeling he wasn't getting through to Cerberus and deciding to enlist support from the Head Chef. He also couldn't understand what this reference to a 'boy' was about.

"So, is that what you wanted to talk to me about?"

"What?"

"The difference between a girlfriend and a friend who is a girl."

"No. I mean yes."

"That's not very clear, Hades," Cerberus responded. "Could you please try and explain."

The god took a big deep breath. "Billie; that's what I want to talk about."

Cerberus growled. "Woof! What about Billie?" he asked with a touch of aggression in his voice.

Hades' mind suddenly went blank and the only way he could clear it was to blurt something – anything - out of his mouth.

"Have you ever thought, if you and Billie had children, how many heads they would have?" Hades' mouth said, at which point his mind sprung back to life as he wondered why he'd blurted out that question.

"Woof! Woof! Woof! No, I haven't!"

"Well, don't you think you ought to?" Hades responded, deciding he might as well bluster on about the subject of heads since he'd raised it.

"Can you give me some hint of what the answer might be?"

"Just think of what one plus three gives you."

"Four."

"No! No! No! You're looking at one, two or three; definitely not four!"

"Are you sure?"

"Of course; four would be a ridiculous number. It will either be one, two or three. Go and talk through the whole matter with Billie. That's the best approach."

"You mean what one plus three adds up to?"

"Well, the whole issue of how many heads any children, if you have them, might have. It's an important matter for the two of you. In fact, I'd advise you to consult Gigliola as well."

"Woof; I will," Cerberus replied, totally bemused about what this whole discussion was about. He had by now decided that there was something seriously wrong with Hades and it would be useless to ask any more questions, so he just sat there it silence.

"So," Hades said after a lengthy silence between the two of them. "I hope that's helped somewhat, Cerberus. Please spend some time thinking about what I've said and take things forward as advised."

"I will."

"Good."

"May I go now?"

"Yes, of course." As Cerberus got up and started walking out of the throne room, Hades called out after him: "Good to have a man-to-man chat every so often, old chap, wouldn't you say?"

"Woof. Yes," was the only reply he got as Cerberus quickened his pace, eager to escape back to normality.

When he was alone, Hades sat on his throne reflecting on how the discussion had gone. Deep down, there was a little voice in his head telling him it had been a complete disaster. However, he tried to silence that voice by telling himself he'd achieved a number of positives. After all, the difference between a girlfriend and a friend who is a girl was now something he'd got Cerberus to focus on. Also, the issue of how many heads he and Billie's children might have, seemed to be particularly important now. It would definitely be a lively subject for the two dogs to consider. Hades thought it was rather neat how he'd also suggested the involvement of Aggy and Gigliola in taking matters forward. He'd report all of this back to Persephone and suggest she should also be prepared to participate in some of these discussions. So, overall, probably quite a creditable effort on his part, although he would still encourage his wife to invite Aphrodite to the Underworld to provide proper professional advice on the whole affair.

Cerberus had very different feelings as he walked out of the palace. For a start, it was perfectly clear that Hades had gone STARK RAVING BONKERS. He didn't spend too long thinking about all the crazy things Hades had suggested he should do, like talk to Billie about why one plus three doesn't equal four. Instead, Cerberus was concerned with what would happen to the Underworld now Hades had gone mad. Of course, he'd have to be locked away somewhere under the best medical care, but who would run the place from now onwards? He supposed the obvious person was Persephone since she was Hades' wife and a goddess, but she wasn't really forceful enough. It was a tough job running the Underworld – a lot of tricky people were there, and Cerberus wasn't sure if she could keep them under control. Also, she spent a lot of her time on Olympus with her mother and she'd be reluctant to give that up. Vesta would be a good candidate, but she was a bit young, not quite fourteen years old. She had a lot of friends like Sisyphus, Attila, Genghis, Aggy and himself who would help her, but she'd once told him she wouldn't be interested in the job when he'd sounded her out in case Hades ever retired. No, it would probably have to be an experienced Department Head. Satan, who ran the Torturing Department, would do everything possible to take over, but Cerberus disliked him intensely – anyone but Satan! Then there was Mason Bonko, the Head Builder, or even Aggy. Mason was competent, but Cerberus wasn't keen on him because he was as tricky as anyone in the Underworld. Also, food standards might fall if Aggy took on other responsibilities - however competent Gigliola, Vesta, Ming and the other kitchen staff were.

The more Cerberus thought about matters, the more he became convinced he was the only one who could take over the running of the Underworld once Hades was confined to his sanatorium. Yes, it would be a tough job, but he was up to it. He'd make sure he had a strong back-up team, including Vesta, Sisyphus, Billie and others, but he'd have to shoulder the responsibility of being 'The Boss'. He'd also reach out more to the other gods. Hades never attended Council

Meetings on Olympus, but Cerberus would make sure he fully participated in their discussions. He was aware that there was a certain amount of dissent with Zeus at times and perhaps he could provide some advice in that area. In fact, he might have to take over from him as well if he found Olympus had too many problems – a change of leadership could be precisely what was required. Then there was Poseidon's realm. Well, he wouldn't think too much about that at present. Best to spend the next couple of years running the Underworld and Olympus before addressing the Seas and the Oceans.

A lot for Cerberus to think about as he went off to the Kitchens in search of a Mars bar.

22
An Overseas Trip

Meanwhile, in the land of the living, where three-headed dogs don't spend their time planning to become Masters of the Universe, HalfPint rang Panos's doorbell. Shortly afterwards, the door was opened.

"Enter!" barked Panos, pointing at HalfPint who was properly attired with her mask, goggles, hairnet and the like. The two went through their normal routine involving the disinfectant spray as well as further instructions including "Move!" and "Stop!" When it came to Bow's turn, she closed the front door once she was in the flat, rested the ironing board against the wall and then things changed from all the other times the two cleaners had been to the flat. Instead of letting herself be disinfected, Bow walked a pace towards Panos and thumped him in the solar plexus. As he doubled up in pain and shock, Bow ripped the mask off his face. The next thing that happened was he suddenly received a wet cloth in his face which HalfPint held firmly in place until he crumpled to the floor, knocked out by a powerful anesthetic.

"Right," said the smaller cleaner putting away the wet cloth in a sealed bag she'd carried into the flat. "No more Bow and HalfPint. We're back to Artemis and Hebe."

"Agreed," her sister replied as they both pulled off their masks, goggles and all the other protective clothing they'd been forced to wear. "Let's get to work."

The two goddesses lifted Panos up and carried him to one of the sofas in the living room.

"I'll watch him," Hebe said, pulling up a small chair so she could sit next to him. "The slightest sign of him waking and he'll get another whiff of Goodnight Nurse."

"Is that its name?"

"It's my name. Describes what it does."

Artemis nodded. "I'll go and open his secret room then," she said as she turned round and went into the corridor.

Outside the locked reception room door, which none of the cleaners had ever been allowed to enter, Artemis pulled something out of her jacket inside pocket.

"Come on Fergus," she said looking at Sergeant MacGobo whom she was holding in her right hand. "Time to get to work."

"Private! You 'orrible piece of cow dung! How many times is I to tell you, I is called Sergeant or Sir. Not that ridiculous name I is given as a so-called diplomat."

"Shut it, Fergus; you're not in your regiment today. You've been seconded to us for a special mission, specifically approved by your Empress. For 24 hours, you're Fergus not Sergeant MacGobo - understand! It's payback time for us helping you out when you were under attack on Duck Island."

"I does acknowledge your past help, and being a military man, will fulfil my mission today. However, I is uneasy working for two of my privates, I is. It is a reversal of roles I is not used to."

"But you're not working for us," Artemis replied. "We're like you, all working as a team on a special mission."

"Then who is I actually working for, Private?"

"Betty Bungalow. She's the mastermind behind all of this."

"Betty Bungalow. I does not think that is a Highlander name, does you?"

"No, it's not. She's a Pimlicoer."

"A Pimlicoer. I has never heard of a Pimlicoer. Does they have a regiment?"

"They do; and Betty Bungalow is head of it."

"A colonel?"

"A full general."

"A general!" Fergus exclaimed. "That is very unusual for a regiment to have a general in charge. That does not sound right."

This conversation about the Pimlico Regiment was cut short by Hebe shouting out from the living room: "Get a move on, you two! We've got a lot to do!"

Fergus looked at the door he and Artemis were standing by. "I'll deal with the three padlocks first," he said. "But I is not sure about the code lock. I is more of a mechanical man, I is."

"You said that when we showed you the photo of the door earlier. See what you can do, Fergus. If you can't crack the code, we've got another way of dealing with it."

"You is meaning you will use your goddess powers?"

"No. While in London, we're trying to do everything as if we were humans and not goddesses."

"You was not doing that the other night when we was under attack from the Blefuscu bastards."

"That was a necessary exception."

"You is probably right. Can you lift me higher, so I can start on the top padlock."

It took Fergus about fifteen minutes to open the three padlocks. He then spent a similar amount of time working away at the code lock, keeping his ear against the metal for the slightest sound to indicate he had pushed the right number. However, as he expected, he couldn't make any progress.

"I think we has got to go to Plan B on this one," the Lilliputian eventually said.

"Okay. I need to get the jemmy from Hebe's bucket. Do you want me to put you on the floor here, so you can watch, or do you want to go and sit with Hebe?"

"I will watch you, Private," Fergus said, determined to keep emphasizing Artemis's rank, despite today being a non-Highlander Day.

Artemis went into the living room, took the jemmy out and returned to the locked door. She forced it into the crack in the door near the code lock, then leveraged it with all her strength. Artemis was naturally very powerful even without her goddess powers due to her athleticism. Within a few short minutes, she'd broken the lock and pushed the door open. Switching on the light she entered the room.

"We has found what we expected," Fergus's voice called from her side; the Lilliputian having followed her into the room.

"Are they there?" Hebe shouted; aware Artemis had gone into the room.

"Yes," her sister replied.

"Come and baby sit Panos, so I can have a look."

"No need. I'll bring them all into the living room. It will be interesting seeing Panos's reaction when we let him wake up."

"Okay."

"What does you want me to do, Private?" Fergus asked from the floor.

Artemis picked him up. "Come and sit with Hebe," she said carrying him into the living room and putting him down on one of the chairs.

Artemis then returned to the previously locked room and carried out five paintings, all on boards but not yet framed. She placed them on various chairs opposite Panos's sofa.

"Do you recognize them?" she asked Hebe.

"I'm not an art expert, but I'm sure that's the Turner," she replied, pointing to the one on the left; "and next to it is the Gauguin and then the Canaletto. Let me get up and look closer at the other two." After a few minutes examining the signatures she said, pointing to each of the others: "Yea, the van Dyke and the Constable."

"They're all the ones we're expecting, aren't they?"

"Yea."

"So, do we wake Panos up now?"

"I think he'll wake up naturally. Let's get the paintings into the van. I don't think we need to show Panos we've got them. Also, probably best if Fergus isn't here when we interrogate him."

"Why's that, Private?" the Lilliputian demanded.

"God's business, Fergus," Hebe replied.

Sergeant MacGobo took a deep breath but decided not to argue the point.

Hebe continued to watch Panos while Artemis went down in the lift, opened the door to the car park and brought Mopp up to the flat. The two of them took the five paintings down to the blue van as well as Fergus.

"Can't we throw a bucket of water over him?" Artemis suggested once she'd returned.

"I don't think it will work, but I'm pretty sure he'll be coming round in a few minutes. Then might be a good time for the water treatment."

"I'll go and get it ready."

Hebe turned out to be right. Soon Panos was showing signs of consciousness, which were accelerated by Artemis throwing a large bucket of water over his head.

"What! ... What's going on?" he asked confused, before a large towel was thrust in his face as he was dried off. When Hebe pulled it away, Panos began flailing around and shouting, so the two goddesses each took hold of one of his arms and held him back on the sofa.

"Hello, Pan," Hebe said, thrusting her face about a foot away from their former client. "This is your old friend, Hebe, here."

"What the----"

"And this is your other old friend, Artemis," the taller goddess interrupted putting her head next to her sister's so they could both stare at the long-lost god."

"I don't know what the hell you're talking about!" was the shouted response. "Who the devil are you?"

"You used to know us as HalfPint and Bow," Hebe replied, standing back. "But we're really your old pals from Olympus."

"Have you gone barmy?" Pan screeched. "Get out of my flat! Get out!" He tried to get up, but Artemis pushed him back hard on the sofa.

"Don't move. Sit and listen," the Goddess of the Hunt said, standing over Pan. "You do the talking, Hebe."

Artemis looked so intimidating that Pan suddenly clammed up as his eyes moved from one goddess to the other.

"Hello Pan," Hebe again said, this time smiling as she pulled up a chair so she could sit close to him. "I'd do as Artemis suggested, if I were you – just sit and listen, then you can respond. Let me first….."

At this point, Pan made another attempt to suddenly get up; he also started hollering as loud as possible, calling out for help and shouting the word 'murder' very loudly. Hebe and Artemis pushed him back again as well as putting the towel over his face to keep him quiet.

"You hold him down, Arty. I'll go and get some restraints," Hebe said as she raced off to the kitchen before returning with tape which she used to cover his mouth. She also brought a small rope and the two of them tied Pan's arms behind his back and then pushed him back on the sofa.

"Now shut up and listen!" Artemis shouted, pulling out a small knife and pointing it threateningly at Pan.

Hebe sat down again on the chair and repeated her smile before continuing: "I'll start again, Pan… Let me tell you what we know and then afterwards we'll let you speak so you can fill in any gaps. We've also got various options for you, but we'll come to those at the end."

Pan grunted but didn't try to get up and escape.

"First of all, we know full well that Panos Pantaloonos is really the god Pan." There was a vigorous shake of the head which Hebe ignored. "Don't argue the point - just accept we know who you really are. Okay, you're meant to be dead, but there were always some of us gods on Olympus who didn't believe it since Daddy Zeus never gave a proper explanation. Anyway, you're clearly alive and kicking, currently sitting here with your two favourite goddesses in a luxury flat in Knightsbridge." Pan again shook his head but to no avail. "The other thing we also know, Pan, is that you've lost your previous divine powers. You're no stronger than a mortal man." There was no reaction to this statement, merely a look by Pan which was a mixture of defiance and fear.

"Just to ram home the point, Pan," Artemis intervened. "Hebe and I have still got our powers, so don't try any funny business."

Again, there was no reaction, so Hebe carried on. "Next, we're aware of all the criminal activity you've been up to in London. Specifically, the theft of valuable paintings from The Gallery...." At this stage Pan once more started shaking his head. "Don't deny it, Pan. You and Cesare Shiftyopolous, The Gallery's Director, have been in cahoots for a long time. We've already located the five missing paintings in your locked room – the Gauguin, the Canaletto and the like..." At this stage, Pan's face took on a look of incredulity. ".... Also, we're aware you've been working with the naughty little people from Blefuscu as well as using the three brothers from The Estate in Pimlico."

By now, Pan just sank back in the sofa, shocked at what Hebe and Artemis had found out.

"You're no doubt aware of the unsuccessful attack by your little friends on the Lilliput embassy in St James's Park?" At this stage Hebe decided to be a bit naughty herself by making up the following: "We're very aware you were the mastermind behind it; the person who ordered the attack. Everyone's pointed the finger at you."

At this stage, Panos suddenly came back to life. He kept trying to talk, shaking his head wildly as he tried to deny it.

"Your friend the Marshal still hasn't been found, has he?" Hebe continued, resulting in Pan looking questioningly at her. "We know where he is. Artemis got to know him very well last Friday night; the two of them had a good chat about matters, especially you."

Pan continued to shake his head, but Hebe decided not to say any more. She just sat quietly with Artemis as the two of them watched Pan come to terms with what he'd learned. Eventually, he stopped shaking his head and looked enquiringly at his captors for an indication of what was going to happen next.

"If we take off the tape so we can all have a nice friendly chat, will you promise not to scream and shout?" Hebe finally asked.

After a few seconds consideration, Pan nodded his head.

"Remember, Pan," Artemis said threateningly. "This sharp knife's still in my hand." She then got up and ripped the tape from Pan's mouth, causing him to squeal.

"So, what do you think of everything we've told you?" Hebe asked once Pan was more settled.

"Whoever you are, you're in fairy land!" he responded defiantly.

"Okay," Hebe replied. "Well, we'll just have to accept you're a normal human being called Panos Pantaloonos, who's also an art thief. So, we'd better call the police in the next few minutes and hand you and the stolen paintings over to them. Little use considering the other options we were going to give you which would have allowed you to go free."

There was dead silence as Pan looked at the two goddesses, trying to work out how to respond. He eventually decided to give in.

"Alright, how did you find out who I was?" he reluctantly inquired in a dejected tone.

"Oh, a lot's happened to us gods and goddesses since you disappeared from our midst two thousand years ago. Artemis and I are senior partners in the Mount Olympus Detective Agency. We're the real 'Top Banana' in crime detection - we beat Sherlock, Poirot, Maigret and all the others hands down," Hebe responded flippantly.

"You're not going to tell me then?"

Hebe shook her head. "We'd have to reveal trade secrets, and you don't actually need to know. What counts is we've found you and your associates out."

"So, what happens now?"

"Before we get onto that," Artemis interrupted, "I'd like to ask a couple of questions."

"What?"

"Firstly, why aren't you dead? What happened between you and Zeus?"

Pan sighed. "I can't tell you that. If Zeus ever heard I'd spoken about it, he made it clear I'd be subject to the most awful punishments imaginable----"

"You mean you'd be sent to Tartarus?" Hebe interrupted.

"Worse! But what I can tell you is I did something terrible, and Zeus went totally ballistic. He couldn't actually kill another god except by taking me to the one place in the universe where gods can die, and he was going to do that. However, I managed to persuade him to let me live but to take away all my god's powers - it meant I would have to survive by my own efforts, which I've done ever since. As far as all the other gods were concerned, we agreed I'd be pronounced dead, but Zeus wouldn't give any details."

"Do you know where Zeus was going to take you so you could die?"

"Apparently there's some island in the Pacific or Indian Ocean, but I don't know its name. However, I'd heard the matter a long time beforehand, so I believed Zeus."

"It's true," Hebe muttered. "It's Lilliput."

Artemis nodded before moving onto her next question: "The second thing I'd like to know, Pan, is what's happened to your horns and goat's legs?"

"Zeus ripped off my horns, causing more pain than anyone can imagine for a time. Then, as part of the deal, he took me secretly to the Underworld where Hades put me onto the torture rack and ripped my legs off; then he replaced them with a pair of human legs. I can only imagine there's someone in the Underworld who's going around with my old goat legs."

"So, Hades also knows about you being alive?" Hebe asked. "What about Poseidon or any of the other gods?"

"No, only Hades. He had to know because Zeus needed him to replace my legs."

"But why do you limp?" Artemis asked.

"Because the two legs I've been given don't come from the same person. One's two inches shorter than the other."

A confused Artemis looked at her sister.

"Yea, that used to happen. Since Vesta's been in the Underworld, they've got a system to stop that from happening anymore."

"Who's Vesta?" Pan asked.

"Someone sensible," Hebe replied before looking at Artemis and asking if she'd any more questions. On receiving a shake of the head, she asked a final one herself: "What I don't understand is how you've been able to survive for the last two thousand years with only human powers?"

"Through doing what I've been doing in London. I've been a crook, taking advantage of every opportunity which came my way. When you're desperate, you'll do anything. To be honest, Zeus did leave me one power – it's all very vague but it's the natural ability to survive. Without it, I don't know what I'd have done in various situations."

"You can still remember the little people as well. You don't forget them after a few seconds," Hebe said.

"Yes," Pan agreed. "I'm not sure why; I suspect Zeus just didn't think about it."

The three sat in silence for a while reflecting on their discussion. In due course, Pan again asked: "What happens now?"

"There are three options," Hebe replied. "The first one we've already mentioned - we just hand you over to the Metropolitan Police. The second one is Arty and I do nothing except return the five stolen paintings to The Gallery. Oh, and we'll also tell Zeus what you've been up to. I don't think he'll like you being an art thief, so he'll probably initiate all those terrible punishments you're not keen on----"

"He will!" Artemis interrupted emphatically. "And since we're his daughters, we'll really make sure he does. I'd be happy to volunteer to help dish out some of those punishments, especially the really painful ones."

Pan squirmed. "What's the third option?" he croaked.

Hebe again smiled. "That's your escape route, Pan, but it depends on your cooperation."

"Go on."

Hebe got up, went into the kitchen and returned with various papers, which she waived around as she spoke. "Here's a first-class ticket to Buenos Aires on today's 4-30pm flight from Heathrow. You can use your own passport which I saw some days ago in one of your bedroom drawers. You don't need a visa to get into the country. Also, here's an envelope with $20,000 in hundred-dollar notes to get you started. You'll no doubt want to change your identity and take up a new occupation when you're in South America, but that's up to you. All you need do now is pack a suitcase – we'll help you – and then there's a taxi we've arranged to take you to Heathrow."

"Is that all?" Pan asked.

"No. There's a condition you've got to fulfil."

"What?"

"There's going to be another theft from The Gallery this evening involving your little friends from Blefuscu, isn't there?" Pan nodded his head. "We want it to go ahead because we've got a surprise for everyone involved. If you tell Cesare, the little people or anyone that we know, that will mess up our arrangements. Artemis and I will be so upset, we'll tell Zeus who'll be at least as unhappy as we are. We all know you won't be able to hide away forever. We'll track you down eventually and then it will be punishment time."

"And what about you telling Zeus sometime in the future, even if I keep my mouth shut today."

"We promise not to."

"How can I trust you."

"You've got no alternative."

The three of them then spent the next fifteen minutes trying to convince each other they would all keep their word. This involved giving oaths which no god was permitted to break. Eventually they ran out of oaths to give, and Pan stood up.

"I've got no choice," he said. "I'll go and pack."

"I'll pop in a bit later and help," Hebe said.

While Pan was in his bedroom getting packed for his overseas trip, Artemis went down to the car park to tell Mopp they'd be about an hour before they were ready to leave. Hebe, meanwhile, was on the phone organising the taxi to take Pan to Heathrow.

"How are you getting on?" the small goddess asked after she'd finished her call.

"I'm in a real muddle," Pan moaned. "I'm in such a state of shock, I----"

"Don't worry. I've come to help. I've created a list of what you'll need. I'll read it out and you just put the things in your case as I say them."

"Alright," was the grunted reply.

Hebe pulled out her list and started reading from it: "Number one. Underpants."

"Oh yes, I'd forgotten them," Pan said going over to one of his wardrobes and pulling out a load of boxer shorts."

"Number two. Socks."

After half an hour, Pan and Hebe had packed a large case with enough clothes for a couple of weeks. They'd also filled up a smaller shoulder bag which included monies, passport, tickets, spectacles and much more.

"Let's go," Hebe said when she'd ticked off all the items on her list. "Arty will carry the bags because of your legs and stick. As far as the flat's concerned, just leave it abandoned. We know you're renting it and eventually the owner will reclaim it somehow."

Pan grunted.

The three of them went down in the lift, walked through Reception and emerged onto the street where a black taxi was waiting for them with the letters OCTAVIAN STEGOSAURAS written on its side. Octavian got out of the driver's seat and was introduced to Mr Panos Pantaloonos.

"Nice to meet you, guv," he said. "I hopes you don't mind, but me niece and a lady friend of 'ers will be joining us on the journey. You'll all fit in together, nice and cosy like, if you know what I mean?"

All Panos did was shrug since all the fight had now gone out of him. He realised his best bet for surviving was just to go along with whatever had been arranged. He got into the back of the cab without saying anything to Hebe and Artemis. There was someone sitting on the far seat who turned to him once he sat down.

"Hello, Mr Pantaloonos," Betty said. "I'm Octavian's niece. It's very kind of you to let me accompany you to Heathrow. Perhaps I can help you with the luggage at the airport?"

Again, Pan or Panos just shrugged, but as he did so, he was aware of someone else jumping into the taxi, closing the door, and sitting on the other side of him.

"Hello, Pan," this new arrival said. "Remember me?"

Pan looked round and this time he didn't shrug, but instead let out a mighty shriek of "Ahhh!" as the taxi set off for the airport.

"What was that?" Artemis asked as she and Hebe stood waiting for Mopp to pick them up in her blue van.

"I think Pan's just met Iris again," her sister replied.

23
The Long Walk Home

The colonel and the capitaine were having a quiet conversation in the back of Terry's white van. It was Friday night and they, together with a number of soldiers, were being taken from the Blefuscu Embassy in Hyde Park to the Gallery. This was a journey they'd undertaken on a number of occasions, and the team was well practiced in the mechanics of the mission they would soon be undertaking.

"I am glad we have zis task zis evening," the colonel whispered, making sure no one but the capitaine heard. "Ze last week has been ze very unsettling since ze disaster on ze lake."

"I agree wiz you. Ze men need ze action. Zey are all still in ze big shock. I keep having ze nightmares about ze huge swan wiz ze boxing gloves."

"I too have ze nightmares. I was on ze swan zat got attacked by ze zree-headed black monster."

"Ze dog."

"I zink ze word monster is ze better word."

There was a brief silence before the capitaine asked: "Colonel, is zere any news of ze Marshal?"

"No. I was ze talking to ze Ambassador zis afternoon. He speaks many times a day to ze government back home. Zere is nozing."

"You know what ze men zink?"

"I have ze good idea."

"May I say it?"

"Of course, Capitaine. You and I are ze comrades."

"Zank you. Zey zink ze Marshal is ze traitor. Zey zink he betrayed ze whole plan to ze Lilliput for ze mega-bucks. Zey zink he is now in ze Lilliput, in ze big house wiz lots of ze beautiful girls. Zat is what zey zink."

"Umm. In confidence, Capitaine, zere are some people very high up in the government who do zink ze same zing. Zere is one except and zat is zat he in ze Souz of ze France."

"Zat is also possible, but zey only have ze big girls zere."

"Zat would not worry ze Marshal."

"You may be ze right. You know, Colonel zat ze one person who does not make ze agree ze Marshal is a traitor is ze adjutant."

"Yes, I know. What about you, my comrade?"

"I do not know but I zink maybe."

"I too zink maybe. What I do zink not maybe, but definitely, ze Lilliputians knew of our plans."

"Zat is what we all zink, even ze adjutant."

"It must be ze case. Ze Ambassador, he tells me zat tomorrow a small team from ze Blefuscu Secret Service is making ze arrive to make ze big investigation."

"Does he tell you what is ze happening at home?"

"Yes. He says ze Lilliput navy is still blocking all ze Blefuscu ports. Zey will not make ze move until our government makes ze admit zey were responsible for ze planned attack last week."

"How will zat ever be resolved, Colonel? Ze government will never make ze admit."

"I do not know. Zat is all ze high level diplomacy. You and I, we are ze soldats, not ze diplomats."

"Yes, I would not make ze good diplomat. I prefer make ze action."

"I am like you. I also hear we are in ze big trouble wiz ze British. Zey know about ze failed attack and have big fury wiz Blefuscu."

"Better to be ze man of action," the capitaine said with a shrug.

The colonel nodded and then, aware the van was coming to a halt, said: "I zink we are zere. Let us get ready to make ze move."

The white van stopped down a narrow street at the side of The Gallery. Terry got out and opened the back door.

"You alright in there?" he whispered.

"Yes, zank you, Mr Terrence," the colonel replied in a soft voice. "We are all ready to ze go."

Terry pulled out a long plank from the back and rested it from the open door to the ground. As soon as he'd done so, the little people hurried down, all carrying small bags.

"We will be back in ze two hours," the colonel said.

"See you then," Terry replied.

The Blefuscu team ran a few yards along the road until they came to iron railings; they passed through these easily because of their size and then disappeared from sight into The Gallery's grounds.

Terry never knew how the little people broke into The Gallery, but he didn't really care. They got in and got the stuff which was all that mattered. Getting the stuff and transporting them around meant that he and his brothers got paid. It was good money too.

He replaced the plank into the back, closed the rear door and then got into the driving seat. He drove away, turning left after about a hundred yards before stopping again. He turned the lights off, rested his seat back, put a cassette on and started surfing the web on his mobile. He also set the alarm on his watch to alert him when an hour and forty minutes had passed. That would give him plenty of time to return to the side of The Gallery to wait for the little people.

There was little traffic around at that time of night. However, a small blue vehicle soon turned into the same street as Terry. It switched off its lights as soon as it entered the street and then came to a halt. No one got out; whoever was inside just sat there in silence.

A short while later a taxi drew up next to The Gallery. A couple of good-time girls got out and started walking along the street, giggling and gently pushing each other as they tried to dance in the street. They gave every impression of having been clubbing for the last few hours, as well as having consumed a considerable amount of alcohol.

One of the girls was a tall brunette and the other was a small blonde. They were both dressed similarly, wearing short leather skirts, black stockings, high heels, T shirts with illustrations of goths on them, and tight leather jackets which were too small to fasten. Their faces were heavily made up, their eyelashes blackened with extensions, and both wore the same crimson lipstick.

The two girls passed The Gallery and turned into the same street as Terry's van. They behaved as if they didn't really know what they were doing or where they were going, spending as much time on the road as on the pavement. They went past the blue vehicle and then the white van. Both girls were on the road at that moment, when the small blonde stopped and called out to her friend:

"Hold on! I need a bloody fag." She rummaged around in her bag before taking out a small packet from which she took a cigarette. "Do ye want one, Cat?"

"Nah!" was the reply.

The small blonde continued to look in her bag, "Can't find a bleedin light, can I? Ye got one?"

The tall brunette looked in her bag but without any success. "Nah!" she ended up saying again. "Must 'ave left it at the club."

"What am I gonna do? I need a bleedin light, don't I? What am I f.... well gonna do?"

"What about asking him?" her companion replied, pointing at Terry who was sitting in his van.

"Oh yea," the small blonde said and walked over to the vehicle. "He looks interestin; maybe 'ave some fun an all."

Terry had been watching the two girls during this entire performance, trying to work out which one he fancied the most. They both came over to his side window and gave him a smile, the small blonde one also including a sexy gesture with her hands, before knocking on the window. Terry promptly opened it, looking expectantly at the two of them.

"'ello Handsome," said the blonde. "What's a nice boy like you doin alone on a night like this? Specially when you've got a couple of naughty girls nearby wondering what to do with themselves."

The tall brunette now came up and started playing with her tongue.

"Who you got 'ere, Deb?" she asked.

"Got us a nice big plaything, haven't I?"

"Nice. You up for it, Big Boy?"

Terry hadn't said anything so far as he was trying to work out how to take advantage of this situation. Yes, he was certainly up for it with what he viewed as 'gorgeous crumpet', but he was aware he had a job to do a little later. All he could think of saying was:

"Yea, but where?"

"You got a place nearby?" the brunette asked.

Terry shook his head.

"What you got in the back of your van?" the small blonde asked.

"Nothing. It's pretty empty."

"What you think, Cat?"

"Yea; why not?" she replied. "But what about your fag, Deb?"

"Oh, shut it. That can come later. You got a lighter, Handsome?"

"Yea."

"Then bring it with you. We can all 'ave a ciggy after a bit of fun."

"Why not?" Terry replied, realising his dilemma of how to spend some time with the two girls, and still being able to do his job afterwards, was now resolved. Using the van was clearly the answer.

"Well, get off your backside then, and open the back," the tall brunette called out as she started walking along the side of the vehicle. "You've got a couple of nymphos 'ere." She then stopped and looked at her smaller companion. "Are we doin it for money, Deb?"

"Nah; not this time, Cat. He looks a nice boy, and he's got a lighter. Come on," and she beckoned to Terry to get out of his van.

"I've only got an hour," he said as he closed the driver's door after him. "Got an important job to do then."

"That's okay," the small blonde replied. "If you can't satisfy two sexy girls in an hour, you got a big medical problem, I'd say."

The two girls stood by the back door while Terry opened it with a key.

"See you've got an old-fashioned key, not one of them gadget things to open the doors."

"Yea. Van's a bit old but it does its job."

"'Ave you locked the front? Not left the engine key thing in the van, 'ave you? Don't want someone nickin the van and drivin off while we're all 'avin a 'ump in the back, do we?"

"No. All the keys are together," Terry replied, raising his hand and shaking the keys around before putting them in his pocket.

"I'll get in first," the brunette said, taking the lead.

She hopped into the back, followed by the small blonde and then Terry, who closed the door after him.

"Right girls, where do we begin?"

"Here!" the brunette said in a perfectly normal voice and punched him in the solar plexus. While he was groaning, her friend opened her bag, quickly pulled out a cloth which she soaked in anesthetic from a bottle and thrust it in Terry's face. Both she and her friend pushed him back against the floor, Hebe making sure she held the cloth in place until he became unconscious. They also held their faces away, so they didn't inhale any of the anesthetic.

"Okay, Arty," Hebe said. "Can you open the back door. I don't want to touch anything until I've got this stuff off my hands."

Artemis did so, then got out of the van and waved towards the blue vehicle, which was still parked at the end of the street. A minute later, it drove up and Mopp, together with

Scampi, a small, short-haired brunette, got out. Mopp soon brought out a bucket of water with detergent from the back of her van so Hebe could wash her hands. They also had various ropes, handcuffs and tapes. During this time, Fergus sat quietly in the van – his only role was to remind the humans about the little people.

The four of them worked silently as they tied up Terry's inert body which they left in the back of the van. They located his mobile on the front seat, which Mopp took, planning to dispose of it somewhere. Scampi was then handed the white van's keys and got into the driver's seat. Barely speaking, they said their farewells after which Scampi started the ignition and set off to a remote industrial area in East London where she would leave the van with a bound-up Terry in the back. The assumption was that he'd eventually be found and released after all the rest of the night's activities had come to an end. Mopp followed the white van, so she could bring Scampi back to Central London afterwards.

Meanwhile, Hebe and Artemis, still dressed like goodtime girls, but no longer pretending to be drunk, walked down the street to The Gallery. They saw the taxi which was still waiting there, got in and were taken back to their flat in Alderney Street. The taxi then returned to The Gallery, parking in precisely the same spot as the white van when it had dropped off the team of little people from Blefuscu.

•

"Zat is ze Rembrandt. It is magnificent," the colonel whispered from the opening to the air vent where he was standing. He was looking down at the floor where the capitaine, the adjutant and several soldiers were standing on the edges of the canvas so he could see the painting from above. "It is ze self-portrait. It will be worz many millions of ze dollars. Well done. Bring it up and we will make ze go."

The team went through their normal routine of rolling up the canvas, which was then pulled up to the air vent, before they all climbed the rope ladders. The grille was properly fixed back in place and the Blefuscu soldiers made their way through the pipework before eventually coming out of the building. They ran over to the iron railings and then suddenly stopped behind the capitaine who had abruptly come to a halt.

"What is it?" the colonel asked in a whispered voice.

"I do not see ze white van. I see ze taxi and a lady who stands zere by."

"Strange," replied the colonel. "I zink I will go and make ze discreet investigation. You make ze stay here."

"Yes, Colonel."

The commanding officer carefully went through the railings and edged along the Gallery wall towards the taxi. A lady in her early 70's, dressed in a skirt and blouse with a scarf over her head was watching him.

"Hello," she said in a quiet voice as she moved over to the colonel. Now that he'd been seen, he was busy trying to decide whether to run back through the railings or to continue standing there. "No need to panic. I'm Betty, Terry's aunt."

The colonel neither moved nor said anything.

"Are you the colonel?"

He nodded.

"Have you got the Rembrandt?"

The colonel didn't answer but was now beginning to think that this lady knew quite a lot about what was going on. That meant she could well be Terry's aunt, but she might also be an undercover police officer. He would have to be careful.

"I can see you're suspicious," the lady called Betty said, reading his thoughts. "I'll give you a quick explanation, but we must get going soon."

The colonel nodded.

"A big problem's arisen, but don't worry, we don't think you're involved. Terry's eldest brother, Des, has just been arrested by the police on something totally unconnected with what you're doing for Mr Pantaloonos. Rory, his middle brother's scared stiff; he called Terry on his mobile and they decided to get out of London for a few days. It's meant dropping everything, so they've both scarpered, if I can put it like that." Betty stopped at that point, before asking: "Are you with me so far?"

She received another nod of the head.

"Good. Then I'll continue. The one thing Terry did do before leaving was to phone me and ask me to help. I'm with another one of his aunts in the cab, which is also driven by a relative of ours. We all live on The Estate, and we know that the three boys are up to things we might not get involved in ourselves. But they're family, and that counts, doesn't it? Can't always claim to have been perfectly behaved ourselves. Anyway, there's another factor, which is that I've known Panos – that's Mr Pantaloonos to you – for years. Done all sorts of work for him and it was me that introduced my nephews to him in the first place." Again, Betty stopped. "All making sense so far?"

"Yes," the colonel spoke for the first time.

"Fine. So, Terry phoned me up and I agreed to help. Checked with Panos on the phone first though and he filled me in on the Rembrandt. He suggested we don't follow the normal route to his Knightsbridge flat and then the Blefuscu Embassy. Instead, he wants us to take a long detour and change vehicles at some point which we've arranged. It's just in case the police get a sniff of what you, he and the three boys are up to. We don't quite know what they've got on Des and how they got it, although we're pretty sure it's nothing to do with this business. However, Panos wants to be extra careful. So, that's it. You okay with everything I've told you?"

The colonel continued to stand by The Gallery wall, trying to work out what to do. It all sounded entirely credible; indeed, he had always thought the three brothers were not the brightest sparks in the room, so it wasn't really surprising they'd get found out for something. Also, this lady Betty clearly knew a lot about what they were all up to – the plan for this evening, the Rembrandt, Mr Pantaloonos, Blefuscu. She could really only know all this from the sources she had mentioned. However, the colonel wanted to be entirely sure.

"Please, Mrs Betty, will you give me ze five minutes?"

Before waiting for a response, he hurried back along The Gallery wall and went through the railings. He didn't speak to the capitaine, the adjutant and any of his men. Instead, he moved away from them, pulled out his mobile and tried to call Panos. His phone was switched off, so the colonel couldn't make contact. In fact, he thought this was a further indication that Betty was 'bona fides' - Panos had probably turned his phone off as a precaution after hearing from Terry and Betty, whereas in reality he was on a flight to Buenos Aires at that moment. He didn't want to phone any of the brothers because if they were in trouble with the police, the last thing he wanted to do was to leave a trail on their call logs that could lead back to him and the embassy. However, he remembered he'd phoned Terry earlier that day, so he decided he might as well try and contact him. Again, no response. Another phone turned off.

At that point, the colonel decided he should trust Betty. He quickly briefed his men on the change of arrangements and after a short while they trooped through the railings behind him. Betty saw them coming, went over to the taxi and pulled out a plank for them to walk up to the passenger seat area. This was a different plank to the one in Terry's van, but Octavian knew it would be needed. Only a week ago, he'd carried the same soldiers from the Lilliput Embassy to the Blefuscu Embassy in Hyde Park. However, he didn't want them to recognize him, so the words Octavian Stegosaurus on the side doors had been painted out that afternoon and replaced with an advertisement for a popular West End show. Octavian himself had had his beard cut off, his hair cut very short and was wearing a trilby hat as a disguise – all in the call of duty!

Mopp's blue van had returned and was parked some way ahead of the taxi; it now set off ahead of Octavian. Meanwhile in the cab, the Blefuscu team settled down on the floor. They were introduced to Iris, whom Betty said was the three brothers' other aunt. The two aunts had provided a large tray on which were tiny pieces of chocolate, two large beakers of beer and plenty of thimbles for the soldiers to use as glasses. Betty and Iris kept filling up the thimbles and soon the Blefuscu team was becoming more relaxed as the two elderly ladies told amusing stories (entirely made up!) about the three brothers when they were younger. Even the colonel was pretty sure it was 'mission accomplished'. At some point in the journey, the Rembrandt canvas which had been lying on the floor with the soldiers, was picked up by Betty and put on the back seat. This was so it wouldn't get damaged because a certain amount of beer had already been spilled on the floor. No one seemed concerned – these two elderly aunts were viewed as a pair of harmless souls who'd provided much needed refreshment to the little people.

The blue van made its way through North London, going along Finchley Road for some time before moving onto the Hendon Way and then the M1 Motorway. It was about a mile ahead of Octavian's taxi; the two vehicles having practiced the same route a number of times in recent days.

There was little traffic at that time of night, but both the van and the taxi strictly adhered to the speed limit. There was no use taking the risk of getting pulled over by the police, especially with an original Rembrandt painting and a contingent of the Blefuscu armed forces in the cab. Only once, as they were driving along, did the colonel enquire about the route they were taking and the time being taken, but Betty managed to put his mind at ease by offering him another thimble full of beer and telling him they would soon be tracking back to Central London in a separate vehicle.

Just before the turnoff for Luton, the blue van came to a halt on the hard shoulder. Mopp remained in the driving seat, but Scampi got out and opened the rear doors. She looked back along the motorway, waiting for Octavian's taxi. Within a couple of minutes it arrived, drawing up about ten yards behind the van.

"Right," said Betty to the Blefuscu team. "We're all going to transfer to the van in front and then head back to London."

At that instant, Scampi opened the passenger door and pulled out the plank so everyone could get out. Betty was first, carrying the Rembrandt, while Scampi and Iris hurried the little people out of the cab, the goddess staying inside. When everyone else was out and Scampi had taken the plank away, Iris closed the door and Octavian drove away, briefly rejoining the motorway before turning off at the next junction. The cab went over the bridge then came back onto the M1 in a southerly direction as they returned towards the capital.

Scampi ran with the plank to the van where she rested it against the bumper by the open doors. Betty, still holding the Rembrandt, climbed into the back first. Scampi was beckoning the Blefuscu team to hurry up, but before they had started to walk up the plank, she jumped into the back herself. She kicked the plank away just as Betty banged on the far wall and shouted: "Mopp - Go!" The engine had been running all this time and the van immediately sped away, following Octavian off the motorway at the junction before going onto the bridge. Since the back doors were still open, it came to a halt on the bridge. Betty and Scampi got out, closed the doors after them, and joined Mopp in the front. They then set off again towards London.

The Blefuscu team watched both the taxi and the blue van pass on the other side of the road. The colonel couldn't say anything as he just stood there in stunned silence. One of the soldiers asked a comrade how far it was back to London.

"It is ze zirty miles. I have seen ze notice just before we make ze stop."

"Zat will be a long walk home," was the muttered reply before he decided to sit down on the ground. The others joined him, including the capitaine and the adjutant; some sat in protest, some were just tired. Everyone looked at the colonel, waiting to be told what to do next. No one was prepared to start the long walk home.

24
Breakfast at The Gardens

Emily was sitting at the kitchen table eating her breakfast. Her grandmother was opposite her drinking a cup of coffee.

"It's just not fair," Emily moaned.

"What?"

"Having to get up at half past six for breakfast and then having to stay in my room. It's Saturday morning. Why can't I have a lie in?"

"You were given a choice yesterday evening. You could either get up very early or not emerge until after ten. You chose the first, Poppet. It was your decision.

"But why couldn't I have breakfast at a normal time like eight?"

"We went through that yesterday. Grandpa's got a very important person coming at that time for breakfast and he doesn't want anyone else around for a couple of hours."

"Well, that's a load of twat."

"Emily; don't use such rude words!" Lady F said sternly.

"But it is. I reckon something dodgy's going on."

"What do you mean?"

"It's just not true that Grandpa doesn't want anyone around. There are loads of people here."

"Where? "

"In the flat now. Betty's in and out of the kitchen and I've seen Karate Chops and Muscles."

"Who?"

"Kim and Jess. They're in the dining room at the moment with Betty. Then we've currently got the dinosaur in the back room sleeping."

"Who's the dinosaur?"

"You know, Mr Steg….something or other. He drives a taxi."

"Oh, you mean Octavian. He's here because he's going to drive Grandpa's guest to the airport."

"But why's he sleeping?"

"Because he's been up much of the night. He's getting some rest….. Anyway, young lady, how did you know?"

"I've been keeping my eyes and ears open. I knew something was going on yesterday afternoon. You were always shooing me back to my room when people kept coming and going. That other girl Mopp and some friends of hers were putting stuff in the dining room. Ever since, I've been banned from going in there. Then during the night, I heard the bell ring and some voices in the hall; I'm sure some other people arrived. Grandpa's up to something really dodgy - and you're helping him."

"Nonsense!" Lady F replied, while inwardly agreeing that it was an unusual Saturday morning in The Gardens.

Emily finished her scrambled eggs before chirping out: "Have you and Grandpa stolen the Crown Jewels?"

"Don't be ridiculous! Of course not."

"That's a pity because if you had, I was going to ask if I could try them on? Do you think my head would be big enough for them? I'm only ten."

"Your head is so big, Emily, I'm sure it would. Still, since we haven't stolen the Crown Jewels, you won't be able to try them on."

"Then why can't I go into the Dining Room and see what's in there?"

Before Lady F had a chance to reply, the intercom went.

"I'll go," Cedric called, coming out of the living room. "That will be Pauline."

"Who's that?" Emily asked her grandmother. "Is that Grandpa's important guest?"

"One of them."

"So, there's going to be more than one. You didn't say that earlier."

Felicity sighed. "Come on, keep eating up," was all she replied.

"I am. Tell me, Grandma, when will the dinosaur wake up?"

"I don't know. Why?"

"I always like talking to him. He's been teaching me to speak cockney."

"What do you mean?"

"Things like 'trouble and strife'. That's what you and Mummy are to Grandpa and Daddy."

"It's a typical man's phrase."

"I still like it though. The one which is my favourite is 'Brahms and Liszt'. Do you know what that one means?" Grandma nodded. "It's the same as Oliver Twist."

"Yes."

"Do you ever get Brahms and Liszt, Grandma?"

"No!" was the poker-faced reply.

"Do you remember that time when Grandpa and Daddy did?"

"Yes!" Grandma replied sternly.

"That was really funny," Emily continued. "It was that Sunday when they went to the pub at eleven and each drank four pints of beer before coming back for lunch. I think they then got through two full bottles of wine and started telling naughty stories. You and Mummy were so angry with them, you ended up sending them to lie down and have a sleep. When they woke up, I was told to stay in my room while you both told them off. You shouted so loudly I could hear lots of what you were saying. I thought it was really funny. You do remember, don't you?"

"I've already answered that question, Emily. Hurry up and finish your breakfast now."

•

Cedric and Dame Pauline spent their time going backwards and forwards between the living room and dining room as they talked. The two rooms were connected by double doors, which were open for the time being. Dame Pauline was introduced to Karate Chops and Muscles who, despite wearing aprons, looked more like a pair of bouncers. Betty also came in as she double-checked the dining table was properly laid for breakfast.

"Do you think he's going to come?" Dame Pauline asked, as she looked at her watch which was now 8-05am. "He's already five minutes late."

"Yes," Cedric said. "I phoned him late yesterday evening and told him that one of the missing paintings had been located and was going to be returned to us in the next few days. He quizzed me intensively about which one, but I wouldn't let on. I said we'd go through it this morning and that you would join us. Normally he fobs me off, but the fact I'd said one had been located will ensure he comes. He'll want to know what's going on."

"He might have already done a runner."

"I don't----" Cedric cut himself off because the intercom rang. "Right," he called out to everyone. "Action stations! Everyone in position! Make sure all the doors into the dining room are closed!"

Cedric marched into the hallway, lifted up the intercom receiver and let The Gallery's Director into the block. He waited for the lift to reach the top floor before opening the front door.

"Ah, Cesare," he said amicably. "So good of you to come at such short notice. We've got a hearty English breakfast prepared. Pauline's already arrived, and Felicity will join us. Come into the living room."

"Thank you, Sir Cedric. Naturally, I had to come. I'm perplexed at what you said on the phone about some missing painting."

"I'm sure we'll be able to clear matters up," Cedric said in his most friendly voice as he steered Cesare into the living room where Felicity had already joined Dame Pauline. "But come and say hello to the girls first before we go in for breakfast."

After a couple of minutes of small talk, Cedric suggested they should go into the dining room for breakfast. He put his right arm over Cesare's shoulder, moved over to the double doors, opened one, and ushered him in with Dame Pauline and Felicity right behind. Once in the room, Cesare came to an abrupt halt as he looked around.

"Quite a sight, isn't it?" Cedric said, still in his friendly tone. "But sit down first and I'll tell you all about it."

There are times in life when people face the unexpected and how they respond could influence the rest of their lives. On such occasions there is often the choice of 'fleeing' or staying and 'fighting'. Cesare was now in such a situation. There was a lot of what he saw that suggested he should just say nothing but walk out of the room and then disappear. On the other hand, he knew full well that he could bluff himself out of most situations and what he needed to do was sit and listen – find out what 'the other side' knew and then concoct some story to explain it all away.

Cesare chose to stay. He let himself be propelled by Cedric to a chair, Dame Pauline and Felicity sitting either side of him with Cedric opposite. On the dining room table were various dishes full of bacon, sausages, mushrooms, eggs of different varieties, hash browns and much more. There were also coffee and tea pots, as well as milk, toast and marmalade; in fact, everything needed for a full English breakfast. Cedric merely observed these matters, his focus mainly being directed towards six paintings which were all resting on sideboards and chairs around the room.

"Let me introduce you to the team," Cedric said, still at his most affable. "The head honcho is our housekeeper, Betty who will spend the next few minutes filling up our plates with lots of good things to eat as well as serving coffee or tea. Then we have her two assistants, colloquially called Karate Chops and Muscles, who are here to provide Betty with whatever assistance is needed."

At this point, Cesare looked at Betty who had begun to go around the table offering people coffee. He then turned his attention to Karate Chops who was standing in front of the door leading to the hallway, before looking round to see Muscles who was similarly positioned against the doors to the living room, which had now been closed. Both these rather tough looking women in their early 30's stood impassively with their arms folded.

"Last, but not least, is our excellent small friend, Rach," Cedric continued, directing Cesare's attention to the Lilliputian who was sitting on her scooter parked on a side table in front of the Rembrandt. Rach herself was wearing goggles and her helmet, all ready to fly off at a second's notice. She didn't say anything; she just sat there watching Cesare. She knew full well that one of her roles was to just be there – her presence triggered everyone to remember the little people from Lilliput and Blefuscu.

"Rach is from Lilliput, not Blefuscu," were the next words Cesare heard. "You probably know there's a history of animosity between the two nations. Anyway, Rach is Head of Special Projects at the Lilliput Science Institute; she's also an expert in cybersecurity, so she knows all about computer hacking......" Cedric paused before adding: "Not just to prevent it, but also to do it. She's probably one of the best hackers in the world. ..... Oh, I should also add, her grandmother is Lilliput's Empress."

Cesare didn't react in any way. He just sat and listened, sipping a glass of orange juice that Betty had poured out for him.

"As you can see, we have six original paintings dotted around the room," Cedric observed, now in a more serious business-like tone. "Five were retrieved yesterday from a Mr Panos Pantaloonos, a resident of a rather expensive flat in Knightsbridge. All of these five happen to be the property of The Gallery - apparently, they went missing some time ago. We're absolutely certain about this because Rach's team has carried out extensive research to identify that The Gallery was the last purchaser of these works; there are also a number of references in the media to individual paintings being exhibited over the years."

"What you've got are probably all fakes!" sneered Cesare, unable to keep quiet any longer. "This whole performance of yours, Sir Cedric is a joke, an elaborate charade."

"That's a matter of opinion, but you might like to read these two reports on the authenticity of the Gauguin and the Turner. These were prepared by renowned experts who examined them overnight in this very room. I believe you know them both." Cedric handed over various sheets of paper which Cesare took a cursory look at before putting them down. "While we haven't yet been able to obtain similar opinions on three of the others, the last painting is a Rembrandt which is right in front of you. We have no doubt that it's real and belongs to The Gallery because it was intercepted last night as it was in the process of being stolen. It was actually taken into our possession just after it passed through the railings on the west side of the building."

Cedric stopped and stared at Cesare who merely sat there poker faced, deciding not to make any further comments at this stage.

"Let me now tell you what we know about how all these thefts were carried out and you can perhaps correct us, if we've got anything wrong."

Again, Cesare didn't respond. He needed to listen, to find out what the Chairman and his team knew.

"There are three major players, Cesare. You, members of the Blefuscu military and Panos Pantaloonos. In simple terms, you source the product, being specific works of art, placing them in an agreed location in The Gallery. The people from Blefuscu break into the building and remove these paintings. They then take them to friend Panos who sells them on a confidential basis to his worldwide contacts, who are quite prepared to buy them despite being stolen. No doubt they're able to purchase them at a good discount, given the goods are 'tainted' for want of a better word. The proceeds are split three ways between you, Panos and the little people." Cedric paused before saying: "Does any of this ring a bell?"

"This is all total nonsense," Cesare replied calmly. "I've never heard of this person Panos Whatever; nor of this place called Blefuscu."

"Well, that's very interesting," Cedric replied. "What I suggest we all do is listen to this recording between friend Panos and various members of the Blefuscu military."

At this point Cedric looked at Rach, who tapped away at a gadget she'd brought with her. Suddenly, everyone was listening to the recording which she'd first played to Hebe and Artemis in their Alderney Street flat."

"You'll have noted you were referred to on a number of occasions," Cedric said at the end, looking hard at Cesare.

"People can say what they like," was the firm reply. "I've never heard of them. This Panos person is just using the reference to The Director to impress these people. Anyway, how do you know he's talking about The Gallery? It could be some other institution."

"So, you don't know Panos Pantaloonos then?"

"I've made that very clear," Cesare sneered.

"Well, that's very interesting," Cedric replied. "Because Felicity will now hand you a photograph of you and Panos talking on a bench in St James's Park."

Cesare merely glanced at the photo which Lady F put next to his coffee cup.

"And Pauline will now show you a log of Panos's telephone calls over the last month. Your mobile number is highlighted in bright yellow. As you can see, you and he spoke or tried to speak on twenty-eight occasions in that time."

Dame Pauline handed Cesare various sheets of paper, which again he spent little time looking at, merely placing them on top of the St James's Park photograph.

"Then, to cap it all, Cesare," Sir Cedric continued. "Here's a log of all your calls in that same month, up until two hours ago." He stood up and walked round the table, putting the log down on top of the other documents before taking his seat again. "Have a close look at the last twelve hours. He's not tried to phone you, but you've tried to phone him every hour. Each time he's been unavailable. Isn't that right?"

Cesare sat poker faced, saying nothing. He didn't even bother to look at the log of his calls.

"Again, I'm going to ask if you want to respond, or do I carry on?"

"What next?" were the only words spoken.

"Well, before I get onto what's next, I thought you might be interested to know that you've not been able to make contact with your friend Panos because he's fled to Buenos Aires, his role here having been rumbled. He's probably dumped his mobile if he's got any sense."

Hearing this, Cesare couldn't resist raising his eyebrows and pursing his lips, but otherwise he didn't react.

"What's next then is the issue of money," Cedric now said. "So far, we've identified two Swiss bank accounts that you hold. Again, we have copies, going back five years. These show that you've received credits over that time of in excess of thirty-eight million dollars. They tend to come in chunky amounts at intervals of a few months, no doubt once individual paintings are sold. Interestingly, they're all from a bank in Panama, where Mr Panos Pantaloonos happens to have an account. Research a little further and all these credits come from his private account at the Panama bank. Curious, isn't it?"

Cedric stopped talking. No one else in the room spoke or moved except for Betty who went around the room refilling everyone's cups with coffee.

After he felt the silence had gone on long enough, Cedric again asked Cesare if he wanted to respond.

"You know none of this will stack up in a court of law," The Gallery's Director said. "Most of your evidence has been obtained illegally and won't be admitted."

"I don't know that at all," Cedric replied confidently. "You're not aware of what other evidence we've got, such as witness statements from people involved. However, I will grant you that it may not be a total 'slam dunk'. Which means that the obvious route forward is to hand the whole matter over to the police and let them carry out a thorough investigation. Don't you agree that would be best?"

Cesare didn't answer.

Once more everyone sat in silence for a while until Cedric said: "So, that's one option, Cesare. Involve the police, perhaps even the Serious Fraud Office, the authorities generally. But there might be another option. Do you want to hear it?"

Cesare shrugged, which Cedric took as a yes.

"The second option involves keeping matters under the radar. They'll probably get out in due course, but by then they could be easier to handle. Interested?"

Again, Cesare shrugged.

"I'll carry on then. The first part of the plan is that you resign with immediate effect. Pauline, please show Cesare the resignation letter we've drafted."

Dame Pauline handed over the letter which this time Cesare read in detail.

"As you can see, it's very short, merely saying that you're leaving for personal reasons." Cedric continued. "It doesn't involve you waving any rights under your contract, nor are we in any way relinquishing our rights as your employer. Secondly, you disappear today, which should be easy since you don't have a family. Here are two air tickets for this afternoon – one to Beirut, the other to Buenos Aires where your friend Panos went. You choose which ticket to take before you leave the flat. From a logistical point of view, you need to go home to your place in St John's Wood to get your passport and pack your bags. There's nothing else to do, and we'll give you forty-five minutes maximum in your flat before you set off for the airport.... All clear so far?"

Once more a shrug.

"There's a taxi waiting for you downstairs to take you home and then onto Heathrow. Karate Chops and Muscles will be with you all the time, including in your flat. The taxi also has a suitcase containing $20,000 to get you started in your new location. We recognize you've got many millions of dollars in your Swiss bank accounts, but it might take you some time to access those monies in your new location. Personally, I feel sick at giving you anything, but I'm prepared to do it to get shot of you."

Cedric stopped and took a sip of his coffee.

"Finally, Cesare, about the monies you've realised from stealing from The Gallery; I doubt there's any chance of retrieving them. However, be forewarned that if we find a way of getting them back without creating a massive hullabaloo in public, we'll do so." Cedric paused, had another sip of coffee, and then said: "That's me finished. Now it's decision time. What's it to be – police or do a runner? If a runner – Beirut or Buenos Aires?"

Cesare said nothing. Instead, he pulled out a pen and signed the resignation letter. He then stood up and walked round the table to Cedric who had the two airline tickets in front of him. Cesare picked up the one for Beirut and strode out of the dining room and into the hall. Karate Chops and Muscles immediately followed him; all three going out of the flat together, then down the lift and out of the building before getting into Octavian's black cab. He was already waiting in the driver's seat with Iris sitting in the back to accompany the others.

The taxi set off, followed by Mopp in her blue van with Hebe and Artemis sitting next to her. They were followed by Rach on her scooter who'd flown out of a window which Lady F had opened for her. This convoy accompanied Cesare to St John's Wood and then Heathrow, determined that he should leave the country that afternoon.

After they'd all left, Cedric, Felicity and Pauline retreated to the living room and closed all the doors. They needed to discuss the many things they had to do during the rest of the day. The security of the paintings was clearly the most important, followed by calling an emergency meeting of The Gallery's trustees.

Betty was in the kitchen and Chloe, who had just arrived to help Betty tidy up, was in the dining room by herself. She was busy clearing the table when she heard footsteps at the open door. She looked up and saw Emily who had crept out of her room to see what was going on.

"Emily!" Chloe exclaimed, sure she shouldn't be there.

Emily ignored her at first as she looked around the room, focusing on all the original paintings which were still resting on the sideboard and chairs. She then looked at Emily and said in a loud voice:

"I knew Grandpa was up to something really dodgy. He's a tea leaf!"

Note: For the uninitiated in Cockney Rhyming Slang, a 'tea leaf' represents a word beginning with a T and ending with an F; it also has the letters E, H and I in the middle. I'll let you work it out!

Epilogue

After their involvement in preventing a terrorist attack and breaking up a sophisticated international crime syndicate, Hebe and Artemis felt they needed a 'more normal existence'. They decided this would be best achieved by moving away from Pimlico and renting a flat in Whitechapel. Betty was fine about their decision since their only client, Panos, had now left, and she had no more cleaning work to give them. They did, however, agree to keep in touch and see each other once a week.

Whitechapel was where Octavian lived in an old property with a yard where there was a shelter for Bunnykins. The two goddesses lived nearby so they often called in to see the pair. Whitechapel was also where the immense Royal London Hospital was located, being the first hospital established in the East End of London. Hebe and Artemis soon got jobs as hospital porters at The Royal London, where they worked tirelessly for three months. Artemis was keen to start applying her goddess skills to heal some of the patients, but Hebe was very much against it. After all, the whole purpose of living in London was to behave as humans. The two eventually agreed that Artemis could apply her strength from being a member of the deity, to working very long hours, often eighteen at a stretch. The result was that she consistently worked over 100 hours a week to the astonishment of all the doctors, nurses and fellow porters.

Hebe and Artemis, in their time off, started frequenting the curry houses in Brick Lane. When they eventually decided it was time to leave London and return to Olympus, a number of doctors at the hospital arranged to take over their favourite curry restaurant for the evening. This was to host a farewell dinner for the two tireless workers, Artemis in particular. So many people wanted to come that everyone was squashed in for this send-off - most were from the hospital, but also Betty and her team from Pimlico were included. Octavian was there and Iris just happened to be paying a visit to London at that time, so she was naturally included. To no one's surprise, she and the cabbie were seated side by side, engrossed in conversation together the whole evening.

The six stolen works of art were returned to The Gallery and placed under secure lock and key. Sir Cedric and Dame Pauline told the trustees the bare bones of what had happened and swore them all to absolute secrecy. They didn't believe leaks could be avoided, so were pleasantly surprised that the press didn't pick anything up about the scandal for at least six months. Even then, it was very general with vague references to Cesare having departed in questionable circumstances. Cedric himself set about replacing the trustees, many of whom were now keen to leave, given their lack of proper oversight over the years. He also found a very competent new Director, well respected in the fine arts world, who subsequently employed a new management team, which spent its first few months introducing a proper control environment.

The thorny issue of how to remunerate Betty and her team for recovering the stolen paintings was eventually resolved. Technically, their 10% commission would have normally amounted to many millions of pounds. However, Lady F refused to take her share, and both Bow and HalfPint, being the goddesses Hebe and Artemis, agreed they didn't need the money. Betty spoke to the other girls, and they all decided they couldn't cope with such a large windfall, instead opting for £100,000 each which would provide a good deposit if they ever went into the property market. The same amount was allocated to Octavian who claimed not to need the money, so Betty invested it on his behalf. Sir Cedric decided he would fund these amounts out of his personal investments since it would be too difficult to justify these payments to the new Board of Trustees and the Charity Commission without proper documentation – something which Betty refused to provide. However, he never had to dip into his own personal finances thanks to Rach.

After Cesare had been despatched to Beirut, the small Lilliputian spent the rest of the weekend retrieving much of the value of The Gallery's paintings which had already been sold. She hacked into Cesare's, Panos's and various Blefuscu government bank accounts, taking $30 million from each. This gave a total of $90 million, of which she decided that the Lilliput Special Projects Unit should be paid a commission of 10%. Since her Maths wasn't very good that day, her calculation came out as $10 million. This left $80 million, allowing Betty's team to be paid directly, with the balance going to The Gallery over five years as a series of charitable donations from a range of different sources. This was all worked out between Rach and Lady F to avoid any questions being asked if the whole amount was paid in one go. Sir Cedric was told about these arrangements with firm instructions not to ask too many questions.

Before Hebe and Artemis returned to Olympus, Rach's project at Imperial came to an end and she went home to Lilliput. She was soon followed by Fergus who, having gained experience of the diplomatic corps, was keen to get back into day-to-day military life. He immediately dropped the name of Fergus and ceased being an Acting Captain, which he never really enjoyed. While expecting to return as Sergeant MacGobo, he was informed that his new title was to be Regimental Sergeant Major MacGobo, a position which had not been filled for more than twenty years. Indeed, he found out in time that one of the reasons for sending him to London was in anticipation of this new responsibility.

As Regimental Sergeant Major, one of his first duties was to participate in an award ceremony attended by the Empress, the Cabinet and the entire regiment. This was to give medals for gallantry to three corporals, all recently promoted, for their role in The Battle for Duck Island. Corporals MacHebe, MacArtemis and MacIris (yes, the Goddess Iris was recruited into the Highlanders shortly before the night of the battle) arrived by chariot from Olympus to receive their awards. There was naturally a reception afterwards which went on late into the night. As expected, the following morning the three corporals all resigned from the regiment, with RSM MacGobo reminding them that at times of emergency they could be forcibly called up.

The Marshal never made it back to the Blefuscu embassy or indeed his own country. He was found walking down the Mile End Road by a couple of female research students from Queen Mary College, as he tried to escape from the East End. They decided to keep him as a pet and took him home to their nearby flat which they shared. Despite the Marshal's strong protests, he was given the name of Snotty and placed in a cage with Barty, their budgie, where he's lived ever since.

Panos remains in Buenos Aires under an assumed name. He continues to walk with a stick because of his legs and always wears a face mask whenever he goes out, which means he's noticeable in a crowd because no one else does. He's been joined by Cesare, who has also taken a new name. The two of them meet daily in cafes either in or just off the Plaza de Mayo where they plot and scheme new ventures, which never come to fruition. Occasionally, one of Hebe, Artemis or Iris will visit the Argentinian capital to keep an eye on their activities, always letting Panos know when they're there so he's aware he remains under supervision from the gods on Olympus.

Cerberus, as Head of Internal Security in the Underworld, has decided to also appoint himself as the Underworld's Sheriff. He's had a Medallion created with the word SHERIFF written on it with a chain for wearing around his neck. Since he's got three necks, Vesta regularly moves this medallion from one neck to another to stop any jealousy between his three heads. Billie has been appointed Deputy Sheriff and she also wears a medallion, which does not need moving because she only has one neck.

At Hades' and Persephone's request, Aphrodite, the Goddess of Love, did visit the Underworld to speak to Cerberus and Billie. She explained to them that there were many ways for people to express their feelings for each other, and that experience showed it was best to let them work it out for themselves. They've taken this advice, and they seem to muddle along perfectly well together without any assistance from anyone else.

Finally, we come to Emily. A family conference consisting of Grandpa, Grandma and her parents eventually convinced her that Sir Cedric was not a tea leaf. After an initial half hour of getting nowhere, Lady F decided to tell her the whole truth without consulting the other adults in the room. As usual, Lady F's judgement turned out to be right. Emily felt she was being treated as an adult and believed everything she was told. She felt particularly proud of Grandpa and Grandma for what they'd done. There was naturally a concern that she'd whisper the secret to her friends, but to everyone's surprise, except for Lady F's, she kept totally quiet about it.

Emily's role in recovering The Gallery's stolen paintings was clear to everyone. After all, it was her photograph of Panos and Cesare in St James's Park which had provided the crucial link between the two. Lady Felicity's friend, who had written the letter about her two sisters coming to London, had heard all about the events of recent weeks and months. She arranged to come to the capital herself because she was keen to meet Emily. So, during her granddaughter's next school holiday, Lady F organised a special lunch at Emily's favourite restaurant which was Zizzi in Victoria. The two of them arrived early, and while Emily was looking at the menu busily deciding if she wanted pasta or a pizza, her grandmother wandered off to speak to the General Manager and some of the other staff whom she knew well since she was also a fan of Zizzi.

For some reason Emily looked up just at the moment a tall, beautiful lady with long auburn hair, walked into the restaurant. She wore a light blue gown, had golden sandals and carried a silver spear which she held vertically. She seemed to glide through the restaurant, smiling at various customers who looked up momentarily, before continuing with their lunch -

without realising it, many of them tilted their heads to her by way of a small bow. She soon arrived at Emily's table and looked at the young lady in front of her.

"Hello," she said, giving a smile. "Are you Emily? I'm-----"

But Emily didn't hear any more. At that instant the plans for her entire life changed. Until then, she'd always assumed that after having been a spacewoman for a few years travelling around the Solar System, she'd return to earth and would become similar to her mother and then, as she got much older, she'd turn out just like Grandma. Now, everything was going to be different. Why? Because she was going to become like this beautiful lady in front of her – Emily was going to be a GREEK GODDESS!

Printed in Great Britain
by Amazon